ROTTER

NATION

By Scott M. Baker

A Schattenseite Book

ISBN-10: 0-9963121-0-2
ISBN-13: 978-0-9963121-0-3

Rotter Nation
by Scott M. Baker.

Cover art by Zach McCain
Formatting by Kody Boye

To my mother and father, for nurturing the
Monster Kid within me, and for encouraging me
to follow my dreams and reach for the stars.

BOOK ONE

CHAPTER ONE

Mike Robson stood behind the barricade of Jersey barriers. To his rear lay the southern ramp to Tukey Bridge. Ahead of him, Portland was silent and surprisingly deserted of rotters. That only increased his apprehension of having sent out Dravko and Tibor to scout the area. He reasoned that being vampires they had the best chance of surveying the city and making it back on their own. They had been gone for over three hours and should have returned long ago, unless something had happened to them. He stared into the night, wondering what lay in the darkness.

"Where are they?"

"Don't worry. They'll be back soon." Natalie Bazargan reached out and slid her hand into his, giving it a reassuring squeeze.

Robson appreciated the gesture. He couldn't help but notice that, as she spoke, Natalie scanned the area to check on her Angels, making sure the twelve girls were in place and prepared to defend against an attack.

Not that he could blame her. Everyone who had survived the expedition to Site R to retrieve the vaccine to the Zombie Virus was unusually jittery, which was to be expected after watching so many of their group get killed in the underground complex. And that didn't include the three they had lost on the way to Pennsylvania. Because of this, he had chosen an alternate route home that went due north through the countryside before swinging east in central New Hampshire, bypassing the rotter-infested cities they had driven through on the first leg of their journey, not to mention the rape gang they had encountered outside of Barnston. The return trip added more than a hundred miles and two days to their travel time, although it did have the advantage of avoiding major population centers. At least it had until the group reached Portland, where they found that Route 95, the primary highway running parallel to the Maine coast, was impassible due to a multi-vehicle collision that blocked all the southbound lanes and created a "gawk factor" traffic jam heading north. Backtracking to the Maine Turnpike, the group cut across to coastal Route 1 and again headed south until they reached the city limits where a roadblock across the Tukey Bridge barred their path into the city. The presence of the abandoned barrier didn't bother Robson as much as there being no signs of a struggle or of rotters. Because his gut feeling told him something wasn't right, he had sent out Dravko and Tibor to investigate.

Right about now, Robson regretted being so damn overcautious.

"We should have tried to maneuver around that accident on 95," he said, more to himself than anyone else.

"It wouldn't have worked," Natalie reassured him. "The Hummers would have been able to navigate the median, but the school bus and Ryder would never have made it."

Robson glanced at his watch for the hundredth time. "I shouldn't have sent them out on their own. We should have made a dash for it."

"That worked so well for us in Glens Falls and Montoursville." Natalie sighed and squeezed his hand tighter. "I didn't mean that the way it sounded."

"It's true." Robson had lost too many people retrieving this damn vaccine, and had compensated by becoming cautious. Maybe too cautious. Being overly hesitant could just as easily get them killed.

"There!" Natalie let go of Robson's hand and pointed toward movement in the darkness. Robson raised his Atchisson AA-12 assault shotgun, an automatic version of a shotgun that held twenty rounds in a drum magazine. Off to the left and right, Ari and Emily raised their M-16A2 semi-automatic rifles into firing position. Farther out, several of the Angels had heard Natalie's exclamation and moved closer to provide fire support.

Dravko and Tibor emerged from the shadows.

Emily lowered her weapon. "Honey, call out to us next time before you get your fool head shot off."

"You would have missed, little girl," replied Tibor in his East European accent. His grin took the edge off of the insult.

"What took you so long?" asked Robson, the relief evident in his voice.

Dravko sat on the top of the Jersey barrier and swung his legs over. "Whoever planned out the defense of this city knew what they were doing. They almost succeeded in keeping it rotter free."

"So Portland is infected?" Robson's shoulders drooped.

"Yes, but it won't affect us." Dravko reached under his jacket and pulled out a tourist map of downtown Portland. He stepped over and spread it out across the hood of the Humvee. The downtown area sat on a peninsula bordered to the north by Back Cove and to the south by an inlet. Route 1 ran west of the downtown area, cutting off the peninsula from the rest of the mainland. Dravko pointed to the interchange south of the bridge spanning the inlet. "There's a huge roadblock set up here and nothing's getting by. We saw at least thirty or forty cars parked in front of it, probably people trying to avoid the traffic jam on 95. Between the barricades and the vehicles, there's no way we're getting through that."

"Then we're screwed."

"Far from it." Dravko ran his finger along the eastern coast of the peninsula to where a smaller bridge, the Casco Bay Bridge, crossed over onto the mainland. "This is Route 77 into South Portland. There's a small roadblock on the far end, a pair of police cars blocking the bridge, and a couple of dozen rotters beyond that. The police cars are parked nose-to-nose, so we should be able to shove them aside with the Ryder. Once we're clear of the bridge, we can cut through the suburbs and pick up the main road a few miles to the south."

"What about rotter activity in the downtown area?" Natalie asked.

"Minimal. Like I said, whoever mapped out the defenses for this city did a great job. Trucks and Jersey barriers are lined up all along Route 1, so nothing made it in from outside the city. Chain links fences have been erected along the main road

3

downtown, trapping the living dead in the residential and dock areas. There's a dozen rotters at most in the street between here and the bridge."

Robson studied the map. It looked easy enough. Less than three miles stood between their current location and the bridge that crossed over into South Portland, with only a handful of rotters in between. It should be easy. However, many times before he had thought that and lost lives in the process.

He looked at the Angels, who formed a perimeter around the vehicles. They had lived through a nightmare at Site R, battling several hundred rotters in the confines of the facility's access tunnel, and the experience had destroyed their confidence. Before that incident, they would have formed a tight perimeter circling the group, guns ready and aimed against any potential danger. Now the girls milled around, a few of them with their weapons slung over their shoulder. The best word to describe them was ragtag. All cohesion and discipline had been destroyed in that access tunnel. They hadn't run into any of the living dead on the trip back, so no one knew how badly their fighting cohesion had suffered. He would find out soon enough, and he needed them at their best if they hoped to make it through this.

Robson glanced to the east. The first hint of sunlight tinted the horizon. "Do you think your girls are up to it?"

"They have to be." Natalie kept her eyes focused on the map. "I'll round them up."

"Let me." Robson stepped away from the Humvee and called out loud enough for the others to hear, and hopefully not loud enough to attract any rotters. "I know you've been through a lot the past few weeks, and we're almost home. Portland isn't overrun, so it's a clear shot to the bridge south of us. Once we reach it, all we have to do is move two squad cars and push through a few rotters, then it's clear until we get back to the fort. All I need is for you girls to stay sharp for a little while longer. Are you with me?"

Twelve faces stared blankly at him. *Damn*, thought Robson. *Not the best pep talk I've ever given.*

Natalie pushed past him. "You heard him. Pull your shit together and get your asses in gear. I'll be goddamned if I'm going to lose anyone else."

The Angels perked up, if only slightly. Breaking formation, they sauntered onto the school bus. Natalie turned to Robson and grinned. "Out here they're not girls, they're soldiers, and sometimes they need a kick in the panties to motivate them."

"Let's hope we keep them motivated for the next thirty minutes." Robson leaned forward and kissed Natalie. "Be careful."

She reached behind his neck and held him in place, her lips hovering close to his. "Please don't do anything foolish."

"I won't." This time they kissed longer and more passionately.

Ari cleared her throat. She stood by the passenger door to the second Humvee, smiling. "Are you two done?"

"Yes." Natalie slid her hand across Robson's face, cupping his cheek. She turned away and climbed into the driver's seat of the Humvee.

Robson stepped over to the Ryder, which headed up the convoy. Dravko stuck his head through the driver's window. "Are we ready?"

"You lead the way since you got the layout of Portland."

Dravko gave a thumbs up. A second later, the Ryder's engine kicked over. With a grinding of gears, the truck lurched forward and headed into downtown Portland.

Robson climbed into the passenger seat of the first Humvee. Jennifer sat beside him. He noticed she had drawn the Magnum she had confiscated in the bunker and clutched it between her hands. He chuckled. "Are you expecting trouble?"

"Always." With her thumb, she drew back the hammer and sat with the revolver between her legs.

Shifting into drive, Robson set out after the Ryder. The second Humvee fell in behind, with Doreen bringing up the rear in the school bus.

The convoy drove for nearly a mile through a residential neighborhood. A chain link fence had been erected on either side of the road, segregating the homes. In the glow from the headlights, Robson could see movement in the shadows as they raced pass. Ahead of them, the living dead pressed against the fence, decomposed fingers reaching through the links and decayed teeth chewing at the metal in a desperate attempt to get at the commotion along the road. Thank God for that fence, otherwise the convoy would have been swarmed.

The road skirted a cemetery and made several dog legs before straightening out again. For a moment, Robson had no idea where they were until the convoy entered onto Thames Street, which bordered the waterfront. Off to his left, he could see dozens of boats and pleasure craft still moored to the docks, which surprised him. He figured that the owners would have sailed them to safety long ago. Then he noticed the hordes of rotters shambling around the vessels, and the realization struck him. The outbreak had overrun Portland before anyone could escape. The security fences, rather than keeping out the living dead, had instead trapped them inside the city like animals at the zoo.

Only a few rotters wandered the street, which made the dash through Portland easy. The sound of the approaching vehicles attracted them. Not enough bunched together to pose a threat, and the convoy maneuvered around them with ease. A rotter in National Guard cammies staggered out in front of the Humvee. Robson swerved around it. It swung out an arm as they passed, smearing the side windows with bits of decayed flesh and gore. Robson couldn't bring himself to stare at the smudge.

Dravko steered right, exiting through a gap in the fence onto a road that branched off from Thames Street. The fence continued along both curbs until the road started to elevate. Robson realized they had entered the ramp leading to the Casco Bay Bridge into South Portland. They were almost home free. He pulled into the opposite lane for a better view and saw nothing ahead of them. As they crested the top of the bridge, their headlights reflected off the two police cars parked bumper-to-bumper blocking the exit. Robson counted twenty to thirty rotters milling about on the opposite side of the roadblock. At the sound of the approaching vehicles, they moved toward the noise, massing around the police cars.

The Ryder slowed. Robson eased his foot off of the gas pedal, still following closely behind.

"What are you doing?" asked Tibor.

"Trust me." Dravko drained off the Ryder's speed and inched up to the police cars. He didn't want to crash through the roadblock and risk damaging the truck. Instead, he hoped to shove the cars out of the way. On the opposite side of the barricade, the living dead grew frantic, clawing at the vehicles. Dravko wrapped his hand around the gear shift. Once he pushed aside the two cars, the rotters would swarm them, and he wanted to get out of there fast.

Bumping up against the fenders of the police cars, Dravko eased forward. Instead of the two vehicles being shoved aside, the Ryder pushed them along in tandem in front of it. The rotters opposite stumbled back and toppled over, becoming stuck under the vehicles and making it more difficult to push them. Others flowed around the ends of the barricade and lumbered toward the truck. Dravko didn't notice them, his attention focused on the cars.

"Fuck!"

"What?" asked Tibor.

"Someone chained them together by the bumpers. We're not going to bust through." Dravko stopped and shifted into reverse. The incessantly loud beep cut through the silence, and would attract every rotter for at least a mile. He checked the side mirror, and swore under his breath when he saw Robson's Humvee only a few feet behind him.

"Damn it. Back up."

Dravko jumped when a female rotter in a soiled nurse's uniform slammed its hands against the door and tried to crawl up to the driver's window.

* * *

"What the hell is going on up there?" Robson asked.

"It probably has something to do with them." Jennifer pointed to the rotters approaching the Humvee along either side of the Ryder.

Robson tried to back up, but Natalie and Doreen had stopped right behind him, blocking his path. Opening the door, he started to climb out to warn the others when a rotter ten feet away in a State Police uniform quickened its pace toward him, its arms outstretched. Robson jumped back in and slammed the door shut. The decayed hands grasped the upper rim, preventing him from closing it all the way. A second rotter in the tattered remnants of a Portland Police uniform stumbled up alongside the first, and both tried to pry open the door. Robson wrapped his hands around the handle and leaned back. He knew he wouldn't be able to hold it closed for long.

* * *

Natalie watched the rotters coalesce around Robson's Humvee. She knew that if too many of them swarmed the vehicle, he would not be able to get away. Grabbing her M-16A2 in her right hand, she reached out with the left to open the driver's door.

Ari leaned over the massive center console and clutched her wrist. "Where are you going?"

"To help Mike."

"There's nothing you can do for him."

"I can—"

Ari yanked her back into the seat. "You need to be behind that steering wheel in case we have to move in a hurry."

"You're right." Natalie sighed. *Please don't let me lose Mike so close to home.*

* * *

Emily made her way to the front of the school bus when she heard Doreen mumble, "Dear God."

"What's the matter?"

Doreen pointed to the lead vehicles, her hand shaking.

"There's only a dozen, honey. We can take them down easily enough."

Josephine moved up behind her. "Not without risking hitting our own people. Those things are all over the lead Humvee."

"Then we move in close so we're sure not to miss."

Josephine stepped back and shook her head. "I d-don't know if I can."

"Damn it! You just want to leave them there to be overrun?"

Emily's heart sank when no one rose from their seats to help her.

A third, naked rotter joined the other two by the driver's side of the lead Humvee. Two more shambled forward on the left, both in blood-stained State Police uniforms, and a naked female with its right arm torn off above the elbow on the right. Jennifer knew that if she didn't act now, they ran the risk of being trapped.

Pushing open her door, she stepped out onto the bridge and raised the Magnum. The rotter closest to her, the naked female, moaned and stretched out its arm. Jennifer aimed and fired. The .357 round tore off half its head, leaving only the lower jaw dangling from a fragment of skull. It dropped to its knees, swaying a few seconds before falling forward. Swinging to the left, Jennifer fired off three more rounds, each shot taking down the living dead crowding around Robson's door. She used the last shots on the two State Police rotters near the front fender.

Jennifer swung open the chamber and let the empty shell casings fall to the pavement. Reaching into her jacket pocket, she withdrew six more bullets and began reloading, alternating her gaze between the Magnum and the Ryder to see if any more rotters approached.

* * *

Dravko heard the sound of gunfire behind him, snapping his attention away from the living dead nurse banging against his door. In his rearview mirror, he saw six rotters around the Humvee go down one by one. Only then did he realize how untenable their situation had become.

"Screw this." Dravko shifted back into second gear. "If those assholes won't back up, then we'll have to go forward."

Dravko pushed his foot down on the accelerator. The Ryder lurched into gear, shoving the chained police cars in front of it. Metal ground against metal. The tires on the police cars popped and their windows exploded. The rotters behind the vehicles were either shoved along or knocked to the ground where they got caught up in the undercarriages. Dravko cringed when he felt the truck's tires bounce over the mangled bodies, afraid of getting a flat. After moving clear of the bridge, he spun the wheel right, maneuvering the police cars to the side of the road. Dravko shifted into reverse, but when he backed up the Ryder dragged the two police cars along with it.

"Fuck! They're hooked on the front bumper."

Tibor leaned out his window. They had pushed past the rotters, most of which converged on the vehicles still on the bridge. A few followed the Ryder, but they were still a dozen yards away. Opening his door, Tibor slid out and rushed around to the front of the truck.

* * *

"Get in here!" Robson yelled to Jennifer.

Flipping shut the reloaded chamber, she surveyed the situation. The Ryder had driven off, shoving the cars in front of it and leaving behind a trail of metallic and human debris. Most of the living dead that had been trying to get into the truck now turned their attention to the lead Humvee, eight in total. There was no way she would win this one with a Magnum. Sliding back into the passenger seat, she closed the door behind her.

Robson followed the Ryder.

* * *

Thank you, thought Natalie as she fell in behind Robson's Humvee.

* * *

Once Doreen saw the other vehicles moving, she pushed her foot down on the gas pedal. The bus lurched forward, knocking Emily and Josephine off balance. The women reached out and found something to hold on to.

* * *

Tibor stood by the Ryder's fender and immediately saw the problem. The truck's right bumper had shattered one of the car windows and the end had become hooked around the frame.

Grabbing the rear end of the police car, the vampire lifted and twisted, hoping to break it free.

Robson drove past and slowed. "What's the matter?"

Tibor didn't look up. "We're lodged on one of the police cars."

"Leave it. You and Dravko get on the bus."

"We need the truck to survive during the daytime. Besides, this will only take a minute."

As much as Robson hated to admit it, the truck was worth the risk, especially with the sun about to rise. He noticed ten rotters stumbling across the bridge. They could handle this.

"I'll be back." Robson drove one hundred feet beyond the Ryder and stopped, leaving the engine running. He grabbed his AA-12 and climbed out of the vehicle. Jennifer slid out the passenger side.

"Where are you going?" he asked.

"To help you."

"Stay here and guard the Hummer. I'll have a couple of the Angels back you up. Fire a warning shot if any of them get close."

"Copy that."

Natalie and Ari stood by the open doors of their Humvee as Robson approached. Natalie started to ask a question, but he cut her off. "We need to cover Tibor."

Both women nodded. Ari fell in behind him. Natalie circled around to the front door of the school bus, where Emily and Josephine waited. "You two are with me. The rest of you, set up a perimeter."

Robson approached the Ryder on its passenger side. The first rotter lumbered around its rear, heading for Tibor. It wore an orange road construction crew safety vest, with the yellow stripes covered over with dried blood and gore. It snarled at Robson. He raised his AA-12 and fired, and its head disintegrated into a mist of blood and gore. Ari, Josephine, Emily, and Natalie moved up on his left, taking out the next four rotters that approached. Slowly and methodically, the five humans moved forward, bringing down any of the living dead that came near them.

The sounds of scraping metal came from the Ryder's driver's side. Circling around the rear of the truck, Robson saw three rotters trying to claw their way into the cab. He raised the AA-12 and aimed.

"Hey!" he yelled.

As one, the three turned toward him and shambled toward their prey. When they closed to within five feet, Robson squeezed the trigger and swept the barrel from left to right, decapitating all three rotters.

At that moment, Tibor broke the two police cars free from the Ryder and shouldered them across the road onto the sidewalk. He raced back to the truck, waving. "Let's go!"

Robson barely heard the vampire, his attention focused instead on the convoy. None of the other Angels had gotten off the bus. Jennifer defended the entire perimeter by herself. If any rotters had attacked from the surrounding neighborhoods, Robson and the others would have been outflanked before any of them knew they were in danger. Hell, if this had been Glens Falls or Montoursville, they would be among the living dead by now.

Tibor stood on the Ryder's running board, staring at the humans. "What are you waiting for?"

Natalie sighed. "I'll round up my team so we can get moving."

"You don't have a team anymore." Robson shook his head and walked back to his Humvee.

Two minutes later, the convoy raced through South Portland on its way back to camp.

CHAPTER TWO

"Camp" referred to Fort McClary, an early-eighteenth century fort that occupied twenty-five acres along the Maine coast outside of Kittery where the Piscataqua River navigated around a series of small islands before emptying into the Atlantic. When the Zombie Virus broke out, it had been a tourist attraction. Paul Martin, the commander of the camp, had seen the advantages to setting up a compound in a fort surrounded by ten-foot-high granite walls enclosed by trees on three sides and a cliff overlooking the ocean on the fourth. Over the course of several months, Paul and the other survivors had raided local construction sites, outlet malls, and farms until they had stockpiled enough supplies to create an austere yet self-sustaining community to ride out the apocalypse. They had survived just fine until Dr. Compton, the creator of the Zombie Virus, had shown up at camp stating he had a vaccine for the virus in an underground facility in southern Pennsylvania, and convinced them to drive five hundred miles and retrieve it. That promise turned out to be a lot easier made than filled, and had proven extremely costly. Despite everything, they had acquired the vaccine and, in a few minutes, would be home. At which point, Robson planned to crash in the steel container that served as his quarters and sleep for a week.

Robson glanced in his side mirror. The school bus followed right behind him, and Natalie brought up the rear. Emily now drove the Ryder, with Josephine riding shotgun. A few miles outside of South Portland, the convoy had stopped long enough for Dravko and Tibor to crawl into the back of the truck, the trailer of which had been covered in sheet metal and fitted with blackout curtains so the vampires could travel in sunlight. It had

13

been designed to house four vampires; they were returning with half that number, a loss that devastated the clan.

Hell, even he had lost more people than he had anticipated.

Traveling down Route 1 South, Robson could see ahead of them a swarm of rotters still lingering around the Kittery Outlet Mall, attracted to the location by the frequent raids they had made there in search of supplies. They would not have to run the gauntlet today, thank God. He took a left onto Harley Road, which wound its way to the coast. After a few minutes, he glanced at his watch. 8:09. With any luck, they'd be back in time for breakf—

"That can't be good," said Jennifer.

Robson followed her gaze. Black smoke billowed into the early morning sky.

Jennifer glanced over at him. "Isn't that where the camp is?"

Robson nodded.

As the convoy exited Harley Road onto Route 103, Robson's worst fears were confirmed. Down the road to the right was the entrance to Fort McClary. The front gate sat wide open, which would be unacceptable under normal circumstances. Black smoke mushroomed over the tree line.

Natalie's frantic voice came over the hand-held push-to-talk radio. "Mike, what the hell is going on? Is that smoke from the compound? What happened?"

Robson removed his radio from the dashboard and clicked the talk button. "Calm down. We don't know anything yet. Natalie, you and Ari follow me into the compound, and be ready for anything. The rest of you, stay here. If you see any rotters or humans, get away and come back in an hour. Is that clear?"

"Roger that," Doreen answered from the bus.

"Ditto," replied Emily. "And be careful, honey."

Robson cruised down Route 103, pausing a few feet from the camp. He studied the entrance and the surrounding trees, looking for any sign of movement, but saw nothing. Accelerating slightly, he turned into the driveway and coasted down into the parking area.

"Oh, dear God," said Jennifer.

The parking area was empty except for a Subaru Outback and six bodies that lay scattered across the ground. The metal container by the fort's main entrance, the one that the vampires used as an emergency dark room, had been destroyed, its doors ripped off and holes punched through the surface. The rebar-reinforced main entrance to the fort had also been torn from its mountings, exposing the passageway through the wall into the compound.

Robson reached into the backseat and removed his AA-12. Getting out of his Humvee, he approached the closest body. Jennifer followed, scanning the area for movement. The body lay face down, its back covered in blood. Robson examined it for bite marks. There were none. Even so, he nudged the body with his foot. When it didn't move, he knelt down, placed one hand under its shoulder, and rolled it over. It was Hodges, the head of their motor pool staff. He had five bullet wounds in his chest.

Robson heard a gasp behind him. Ari stood with her hand over her mouth. "Are you going to be okay?"

She nodded. "I always assumed we might be overrun. I just never expected we'd be attacked by other humans."

"They're not human," spat Natalie. "They're animals. They came in here and took what they wanted."

"What do you mean?" asked Jennifer.

"There's only one SUV left. Someone took the other vehicles."

Robson suddenly got that uneasy feeling cops get when something about a situation doesn't add up. "Why did they leave one good SUV behind?"

Natalie's eyebrows rose at the implication. "Because some of them may still be here."

The four spread out and cautiously approached the tunnel leading into the compound. Robson and Natalie went first, their weapons trained on the far end, while Ari and Jennifer brought up the rear. At the opposite end of the tunnel, Robson waved for the others to halt and peered around the corner.

Very little remained of the compound. A few bodies dotted the grass, obvious victims of the ambush. The two-story, nineteenth-century blockhouse that dominated the center of the compound and served as the dining quarters had been torched. Only the stone foundation remained, with black smoke pouring from the debris where internal fires still raged. Off to the right, the wooden fence surrounding the barnyard had been knocked down. From this distance, Robson saw several large mounds resting in the dirt, and assumed they were the camp's livestock. Though he could not see them from this vantage point, he guessed that the metal containers on the other side of the hill that served as their living quarters had also been trashed. This had been a methodical raid intended to scavenge what they needed and scorch anything left behind.

Robson leaned back into the tunnel. "Looks like everything is gone."

"Shit," mumbled Ari.

"So what do we do now?" asked Natalie.

"I want to clear the grounds and make sure no one is here. Then we can go through whatever wasn't destroyed." Robson turned to Jennifer. "You stay here and guard the entrance. Don't let anyone in. If we start taking fire, cover our escape."

"Gotcha."

"You two girls are with me. Stay a hundred feet apart, and be ready for anything."

Once they acknowledged, Robson dashed out from the tunnel toward the base of the hill in the center of the compound, half expecting to hear the crack of a weapon and feel the burning pain of a bullet enter his body. Moving toward a stone wall at the base of the hill, he ran up beside it and crouched, giving himself some cover. Natalie and Ari joined him a moment later.

"Ari, you have my back. Natalie, you keep your eyes on the hill. I'm going to check out the containers."

Natalie's eyes widened. "Don't you want me to come with you?"

"No. If you hear gunshots, coming charging in like the cavalry."

Staying hunched over to conceal himself, he moved along the wall until he reached the seacoast side of the compound. As expected, the row of steel containers that served as their living quarters had also been vandalized. Furniture and personal belongings lay spread across the ground, doors had been twisted off their hinges, and bullet holes had been shot through the sides and tops. He approached the first container from the left, out of line of sight of the opening. He assumed nothing could be salvaged because whoever had been here had made this place uninhabitable, but at least he could check it out.

A tall man in a safari vest jumped out in front of Robson and raised a shotgun in his face. "Freeze, assho—"

In one fluid move, Robson sidestepped to his left. With his right hand, he grabbed the barrel of the shotgun and pointed it away from him. His right knee came up fast, catching the man in the groin. When the man bent over in agony, Robson yanked the shotgun out of his fingers and tossed it to one side. He aimed his AA-12 at the man's head, who knelt on the ground sobbing.

"Jesus, Chuck." Robson moved the AA-12 to one side. "I almost killed you."

"Sorry," Charles DeWitt gasped through his tears. "We thought you were one of them."

"Who's 'we' and who's 'them'?"

"Mike, it's us," said Roberta Giovanni, emerging from the container, her hands held up so Robson could see she posed no threat. Jean Allard and Aaron Frakes stepped out behind her. The four were members of the camp.

Robson pointed his weapon down. "Is anyone else with you?"

"No."

"Where are the others?"

"On the other side of the blockhouse," said Roberta.

"Show me."

"Okay. But..." Roberta cast a nervous glance at the other men.

"I understand," said Robson. "I still need to see it."

* * *

The eight of them stood by the western façade of the charred remains of the blockhouse. Robson clenched his fists tight, trying to calm the storm of emotions raging inside of him: sadness, depression, revulsion, fury, and a lust for revenge. In the nine months since the outbreak of the zombie virus and the complete destruction of civilization, he thought he had seen every horror imaginable. He had grown accustomed to widespread devastation from the rotters. The betrayal at Site R had taken him by surprise, though in hindsight he should have been less trusting of Compton and Thompson, and his misguided trust had cost them some good people. This was man at his cruelest.

In front of them sat a tangled mass of corpses, all members of the camp. They had been lined up against the wall and gunned down. A few bodies stood out from the pile, those who had tried to escape or had charged their attackers. Most formed a death pile at the foot of the structure. Gunshot wounds riddled each body, and blood soaked the ground beneath them. Hundreds of spent shell casings littered the area. He had seen photographs similar to this, only now it involved people he knew. People he had lived with and cared for. People who had survived the end of the world, only to wind up massacred in the relative safety of their haven by people with even less humanity than the rotters.

Thousands of flies swarmed around the corpses and maggots crawled through the open wounds, feeding off of the remains. Robson wanted to fire his AA-12 into the insects, although he knew that would be futile. He would only desecrate his friends. He might kill a few flies, but the rest would come back and resume their feeding, like the hordes of living dead. Instead, he vented his anger on the survivors.

Robson whipped around, startling Natalie and Jennifer, both of whom stood beside him. Tears rolled down Ari's cheeks. He ignored the women and focused on DeWitt, his voice shaking with rage. "What happened?"

DeWitt glanced over his shoulder for support, receiving none. Allard and Frakes stepped back and averted their gazes. Only Roberta stood her ground.

"Well?"

DeWitt took a deep breath to steady his nerves. "It began when an SUV drove past the compound heading toward Portsmouth. The driver didn't see us and kept on going. Hodges noticed it, and Paul sent us out to follow. He told us to keep our distance and only make contact if we thought they were friendly. We searched for almost three hours. When we couldn't find them, we came back here. That's when we found that the camp had been taken over by about twenty guys. They had busted through the front gate, shot Hodges and the motor pool crew, and stormed the compound. We hid the Outback in the woods not far from here and made our way back. By the time we made it here and scaled the walls, they had rounded up everyone in camp and lined them up in front of the blockhouse. This young kid was telling the others that he had told them monsters were here and ranting about the death of his friends. Paul tried to calm the kid down when the leader of the gang... at least I think he was the leader... smashed Paul across the face with the butt of his rifle. A few of our people went after them and... and ...."

"And that's when they shot everyone," Roberta finished for him. "They gunned down our people in cold blood. Then they ransacked the compound. They took most of our supplies, our personal belongings, the small livestock, and all the vehicles. Whatever they couldn't take they destroyed. They took a sadistic pleasure in it."

Of course they did, thought Robson. *They wanted revenge.*

"I can't believe they killed everyone," Ari sniffed.

"Not everyone," said DeWitt. "They took Windows with them."

"And you let them?" yelled Robson.

"What could we do? There were only four of—"

Robson punched DeWitt in the jaw, knocking him onto his ass. DeWitt massaged his bruised jaw. "Why'd you do that?"

"Because you're a fucking coward."

"Screw you."

When Robson went after DeWitt, Natalie raced forward and grabbed his arm, holding him in place. He spun around to face her, his eyes blazing in anger. The young woman refused to back down. Robson yanked his arm free, but did not go after DeWitt.

"You had automatic weapons, the element of surprise, and cover. You could have stopped them."

"Maybe *you* could have," snapped Roberta. "*We* aren't soldiers. This wouldn't have happened if you or the Angels had been here. It's not our fault that Paul decided to send you all off with Compton to save the world."

"Paul just never got it," DeWitt remarked as he got to his feet. "Even after those assholes overran the compound, he tried negotiating with them like they could be reasoned with. A lot of good that did."

Robson felt his anger at DeWitt flow away. Roberta was right. They couldn't have done anything to stop this. If they had fought back, at best they would have taken down a few of the gang members, and the end result would have been the same. Everyone would still be dead, including Dewitt's team.

"When did this happen?" asked Natalie.

"Yesterday afternoon. They stayed about four hours, long enough to trash the place, and then left." DeWitt paused, as if trying to recall something. "We overheard one of them say something about wanting to get back before the sun set."

"Did you follow them?" she asked.

DeWitt shook his head. "We couldn't keep track of them without being seen ourselves, so we decided to wait here and hope you'd return."

Natalie shook her head. "So we have no idea who they are or where they went."

"We know exactly who they are," Robson said. "DeWitt, you said there was a kid in the group saying he told them monsters would be here?"

"Yeah. We found Elena's ashes outside her container. We assumed that when they dragged her into the sun, she burst into flames, and that scared them."

"I don't get it," Natalie said.

"This is the same group we ran into outside of Barnston, the ones that Dravko and the others took care of. My guess is the kid went back to their camp, told them what had happened, and they sent out a search party to find us."

"And somehow they just stumbled across the camp?" asked Natalie. "That sounds unlikely."

"Not really," said Ari. "We left a pretty good trail of destruction on our way down to Site R. It wouldn't have been too hard for them to follow it back here. It was pure luck that they found the camp."

"Bad luck." Robson grimaced.

A pause in the conversation ensued as everyone processed what they had heard. DeWitt's eyes widened. "Good God, please don't tell me this is all that's left of you."

"The rest of us are waiting outside," Natalie said. "Should I call them in?"

Robson nodded.

"We can't stay here," protested Ari. "The place is trashed."

20

"We have no other choice. We need to time to regroup, and this place is as good as anything out there."

"What are we going to do next?"

Robson walked away without giving her an answer. He couldn't because he had no idea himself.

CHAPTER THREE

Robson stood on the southern portion of the wall surrounding the compound, the side facing the Atlantic and overlooking a steep cliff that dropped one hundred feet to the water. The light from the moon reflected off the ocean, its image rippling in the waves. This used to be his favorite spot in camp. He could lose himself in the quiet, listening to the sound of the surf breaking against the shore, and reminisce about the vestiges of his old life. Now it brought back memories of his two lives that had been shattered: the one torn apart by rotters nine months ago, and the one violated by humans a few days ago. He could excuse the rotters because they were mindless creatures acting on instinct. What the humans did was malicious and cruel for its own sake.

Reaching into his jacket pocket, he pulled out a pack of Camel cigarettes. Even these brought flashbacks of the incident that led to this tragedy. It had been twelve days ago, and he had all forgotten about it in light of what had happened afterwards. It had taken place on the first morning after leaving camp. The convoy had raced through Dover, the first of many cities they would encounter infested with the living dead, and had stopped for breakfast west of Barnston along the Suncock River. He had been rummaging through a backpack he had stumbled across earlier in the trip when he found an unopened carton of Camels. A few minutes later, four gang members ambushed the convoy. Ambushed was not the right word. They had snuck up on the group because Robson had let his guard down, and that mistake almost cost everyone their lives. The gang had roughed up Sarah, and were about to shoot the men and bring the women back to their camp as sex slaves when Natalie had the foresight to sucker them into checking out the back of the Ryder where Dravko and his team slept. The vampires took care of two of the team members, and the Angels overpowered the third. In his opinion, each of them deserved their violent fates. The fourth member, a teenager with long blond hair tucked behind his ears and held in place with a Yankees baseball cap, panicked and ran. Robson had wanted to hunt him down and kill him, but Colonel Thompson had advised otherwise; he wanted to follow the kid back to his camp so they knew what they were dealing with. Thankfully, Robson had listened to the colonel because the convoy would have stumbled across a rape gang held up in a self-storage facility a few miles ahead of them, and thus they avoided a confrontation. As it turned out, the teenager must have warned the others and, while Robson and his party proceeded south toward Site R, the gang set out searching for them, eventually coming across Fort McClary.

Removing a cigarette from the pack, Robson placed it between his lips. He struck a match and covered it with his hand, struggling to keep the flame going despite the breeze blowing in from the ocean. Eventually the tobacco ignited and the tip glowed red. Robson inhaled, sucking the smoke into his lungs. He relished the feeling. Sure, he knew smoking was dangerous for his health, although not as dangerous as fighting rotters every day of his life. Besides, it gave him a sense of self-punishment for failing to defend the camp. If they had come straight back from Site R along the route they had originally traveled rather than using the safer one that took them through upstate New Hampshire before cutting over to Maine, adding two days to their trip, then they would have been here when the gang attacked. The camp wouldn't have been overrun and everyone massacred. He could have changed....

Robson exhaled. The cloud of smoke dissipated in the breeze. *Stop blaming yourself*, he chastised himself. Every step of the way, he had made the decision that, at the time, seemed best under the circumstances. Sure, maybe if he had gone with his instinct and killed the teenager, none of this would have occurred; that didn't mean he could blame himself for what happened to the camp. How could he be expected to know that this gang would be fanatical enough to track them all the way back to the fort?

Taking another drag on the cigarette, he recalled the past twelve days. It felt like an eternity since Doctor Compton arrived at camp claiming he had a vaccine for the virus at Site R, an underground military facility outside of Gettysburg, Pennsylvania. Paul had placed such importance on acquiring the vaccine and turning the tide of the apocalypse that he had stripped the camp of its protection in order to send both his recon team and the Angels on the mission. Thank God he had. Most of them had forgotten the horrors of those first few weeks of the outbreak and had grown accustomed to the splendid isolation of camp. None of them had been prepared for what they found out in the world: rape gangs, rotter-infested cities, a devastated country, and literally tens of thousands of the living dead. In hindsight, it was a miracle they made it to the facility; however, they lost a lot of good people along the way. Whitehouse. Sultanic. Rashid. Mad Dog.

Yet nothing they had faced on the drive compared to what awaited them once they made their way inside the underground facility. While Compton had been telling the truth about the vaccine for the Zombie Virus, he had never intended on sharing it with the vampires, and in fact had planned on infecting them with the virus and putting them down. When Robson and the others refused to murder their friends, Compton decided to sneak away on his own. To cover his escape, he released four hundred zombies onto the compound as well as a dozen swarmers inside the facility. The group had managed to stop Compton and Colonel Thompson and fight back the rotter horde at the cost of four of their number: Daytona, Tatyana, Caylee, and Leila. He didn't count O'Bannon, who had betrayed them to side with Compton and never made it out of the facility alive.

Almost as bad as the human losses was the shattering of the Angels' fighting ability. Originally, they had been established as the camp's zombie fighting unit, fourteen women self-trained as marksmen. While they had accompanied Robson's recon team on every mission and kept them safe, nothing had prepared them for facing down those four hundred rotters inside the cramped confines of the underground facility's access tunnel.

The Angels had fought until they exhausted their ammunition, and then finished the task in hand-to-hand combat, losing Leila in the process. The confrontation had left them shell-shocked and stripped of their bravado. It was mostly because of their shattered confidence that he had decided to bypass their original route to Site R and take the one straight north that avoided major population centers. Given the Angels' inability last night to even man a defense perimeter against a minimal number of rotters, he knew he had made the correct decision.

Paul had usually made the strategic decisions, and had done well by the camp, leaving Robson to make all tactical decisions when on missions. With Paul dead, that left him in command. Truth be known, Robson would rather face a horde of rotters armed with a baseball bat. Now he had to face a dilemma he wished he could avoid.

After retrieving the vaccine, Compton planned on transporting it to Northern Command Headquarters in Omaha, Nebraska where the president of the United States had set up his government-in-exile. The doctor had prepared numerous doses of the vaccine, including enough to inoculate every member of the group, as well as several copies of his notes to ensure it could be reproduced. With Compton and Thompson dead, Robson had no way of contacting the government-in-exile to come and collect the vaccine, which meant he had to find a way to take it to them, which promised to be next to impossible.

He also had to deal with the kidnapping of Windows. They had experienced these assholes firsthand, and Robson had a pretty good idea what the poor woman would be going through. He refused to leave her behind. At the very least, he had to attempt to get her out, although considering the compound's fortifications and the limited forces he had available, he would be taking on another near impossible task. Though with this one, at least he would have the pleasure of bringing payback to the guys who ruined his life.

Robson tapped the cigarette, letting the burnt ash tumble to the stones. He had run through various scenarios all day, and kept coming back to the only one that made sense. It was far from perfect, but then neither were the circumstances his group faced. If he didn't get the vaccine and notes to Omaha, all these deaths would be in vain. And if he didn't go after Windows, he had forfeited his last link to humanity. He knew what he had to do. Now he needed to convince the others.

He went to take a last puff on the cigarette and paused. For some reason, it had lost its appeal. He flicked it toward the shore, watching as the wind carried it off to the left where it exploded in a shower of sparks on the rocks below. Reaching into his pocket, he pulled out the pack of Camels, crumpled it in his hands, and whipped them over the side.

Turning back to the compound, Robson went looking for the others.

CHAPTER FOUR

Dravko knelt by the opening to Elena's container. The door had been pried apart with crowbars so that it hung at an awkward angle on its hinges. A pile of gray ash sat in front of the threshold, the remnants of Elena, the mistress of their coven. Unlike the other containers in camp, this had not been ransacked and burned. Dravko assumed that once the gang had dragged her into the sunlight and she ignited, no one had the nerve to go anywhere near the container after that. It provided her resting place with some reverence, unlike the killing field for the humans.

Tibor stood behind him, his arms folded across his chest. Dravko could sense the fury emanating from him. They both had known something had happened that morning when, after arriving back at camp, no one opened the back of the Ryder and let them scurry into the more comfortable emergency dark room outside the main gate. Robson came to them after sundown and related what happened, how the camp had been destroyed by the gang they had run into outside of Barnston, and how Elena had been one of the victims. Robson appeared to be genuinely remorseful over the vampires' loss, an emotion he doubted the human would have had before they traveled through a living dead hell to Site R. Dravko had appreciated the feelings. Tibor had not.

"Goodbye, Elena." Reaching out, Dravko placed his right hand onto the ashes and glided his fingers through the pile. "I'm sorry we let you down."

"We *did* let her down," said Tibor. "By not killing the humans when we had the chance."

Dravko glared at him, aghast. "You mean the one who got away outside of Barnston?"

"No, I mean Robson and the others."

Dravko rose to his feet. "How can you say that?"

"Deep down you know I'm right, but you've been devoted to Elena for so long you've lost sight of that. From the very beginning, none of us wanted to join up with the humans, not even you. Elena insisted, saying the only way for us to survive the outbreak was to have humans around to protect us during the day. We went along with it out of respect for her. And where has it gotten us?"

Dravko didn't want to discuss this, not now. Elena had been murdered, along with everyone else in the camp, and he refused to debate the wisdom of her decisions. He attempted to walk away. Tibor raced ahead and cut him off.

"Every loss we've incurred has been because of humans."

"That's not true," protested Dravko halfheartedly.

"You know it is. O'Bannon infected Tatyana with the Zombie Virus. And we lost Sultanic in Saratoga Springs because of them."

"Sultanic became infected trying to save Whitehouse from rotters," argued Dravko. "How many times did Robson and the others put their lives on the line for us?"

"Really? Do you see any corpses of humans who tried to defend Elena?"

Dravko averted his gaze. "No."

"When the gang murdered Paul, several of the humans attacked them and were gunned down. No one tried to stop them from killing Elena."

"We don't know what happened here, so we can't say for certain," said Dravko, trying to talk down Tibor. "You know the humans would never willingly harm us."

"Really?" Tibor sneered. "What about Vladimir?"

Dravko had forgotten Vladimir. The incident had occurred shortly after the coven had joined with the camp. Despite Elena and Paul agreeing to have their groups cooperate, hatred still existed between the two species and came to a head one night when Vladimir and two humans went after each other. To ensure discipline, Paul had sentenced the two humans to serve as blood cows for the rest of the coven for a month, giving up a pint a week to feed the vampires. In turn, Elena had banished Vladimir from camp, condemning him to almost certain death out among the rotters. Although the mistress made the decision to exile Vladimir without being asked to by Paul, it was not lost on the rest of the coven that not a single human had argued against such a harsh sentence.

"And consider this," added Tibor. "We risked our lives and lost half our clan to retrieve a vaccine that isn't even effective on us. You know Robson is going to ask us to help him get that vaccine to their government-in-exile. What do you think our reward will be for that? Do you think the humans in Omaha will welcome us with open arms? Do you think they'll accept us like Robson has? Or will we meet the same fate as Elena?"

Dravko found himself at a loss for words. Everything Tibor said made sense. Because of his efforts to coexist with the humans, he had never seen it that way before. If Sultanic and Tatyana had thought the same way, neither of them had expressed it to him. Dravko realized that by remaining loyal to Elena and her wishes, he had inadvertently betrayed the rest of the coven. He and Tibor were the only two vampires left. With the destruction of the camp, that left them in a precarious situation. They couldn't stay with Robson's team if they hoped to survive, yet their life expectancy if they set out on their own would be measured in weeks.

"I know Elena and I have put the coven in a tough spot," said Dravko. "There's nothing we can do about that now."

"Yes, there is." Tibor smiled, his expression malicious. "We can rebuild the coven."

"What are you talking about?"

"There are less than twenty humans left. The Angels are useless as a fighting force. The only ones we really have to worry about are Robson and Natalie, and we could easily take them down. By this time tomorrow night, we could rebuild the coven to its original size."

Dravko took a step back, fearful of where this conversation was going. "What if you're wrong and they fight back?"

"I'd rather die on my feet than live on my knees as pets of the humans."

"You're serious about this?"

"I am. Without this camp, what are Robson and the others going to do? They'll try to find a new place to live until they're eaten by rotters. They have a much better chance of surviving as vampires." Tibor paused and laughed, as if he had thought of something humorous. "Come to think of it, it's probably more humane to turn them."

"I won't even consider it. It's barbaric."

"Barbaric?" Tibor stared at him. "That's how we survived for centuries. By turning humans and growing the covens. Now that we're almost extinct, I'd think you'd want to rebuild our numbers. What changed?"

"Everything changed when we released the Zombie Virus on mankind." Dravko got directly into Tibor's face, his human features morphing into the furrowed brow and fanged mouth of a vampire. "We brought this on ourselves. And you're right, we do need to increase our numbers and start new covens. Not with Robson's people. He's played straight with us, and has protected us when others in the group would have left us overnight in the middle of a rotter-infested city."

"Okay," Tibor acquiesced. "If not them, who?"

Dravko did not have an answer to that. He didn't need one. He headed the coven now, even if it only consisted of him and Tibor. Tibor would obey. "I will let you know when the time is right. Until then, you are to do nothing to harm Robson or the others. Is that understood?"

"Is that a threat?"

"No," snarled Dravko. "Threats are idle."

Tibor stepped back and bowed his head, acknowledging his acceptance of Dravko as the dominant vampire. Dravko morphed back into his human form, ending the confrontation. Inwardly, he sighed with relief because he doubted he could win a physical confrontation with Tibor.

Tibor started to walk away and paused. "Just remember one thing. If it looks like the end for us, I will make certain that you are not the last vampire to survive."

CHAPTER FIVE

The group had built a large fire near the main entrance of the camp, as far away from the pile of bodies as possible in order to avoid the stench as well as the continuous drone from the flies that swarmed over the corpses. Tomorrow morning they would hold a memorial service and cremate the remains. Half the group huddled around the fire, as much for warmth as for protection from the horrors that inhabited the night. The other half stood watch on the perimeter wall. No one had seen Dravko or Tibor since they had been told about what had happened. Of those gathered around the flames, most had fallen asleep from exhaustion. Only Robson, Natalie, and DeWitt remained awake. The three sat in a small circle away from the others so as not to wake them.

"Are you sure we'll be safe tonight?" asked DeWitt.

Robson nodded. "There are no rotters in the area. And I doubt that the gang will come back since they already trashed the place. Even if they do, the Angels will spot them in enough time for us to defend ourselves."

"We can't live like this forever," added Natalie. "How are we going to repair the camp?"

"We're not."

The other two stared at him.

Natalie spoke first. "Are you serious?"

"You remember how long it took us to set up camp the first time, and then we had twice as many people as we do now. And we no longer have the blockhouse. We don't have the resources to start over here. Besides, whoever did this now knows we're here, and I don't like that idea of them coming back for a visit."

"Okay," said Natalie. "So what are we going to do?"

"*You're* not going to do anything." Robson hesitated, knowing his next statement would not go over well. "I'm sending the Angels to Omaha with the vaccine."

"You can't!" Natalie yelled so loud that some of the Angels stirred.

Robson shook his head. "We lost a lot of good people retrieving the vaccine. You have to get it to the government-in-exile."

"I want to stay with y... I mean, the group needs to stick together," Natalie said.

Reaching out, he slid his hand over Natalie's and squeezed. "I don't want to be separated either. But the Angels have lost their edge. They couldn't even form a perimeter defense last night. I can't rely on them to deal with rotters."

Natalie averted her gaze. "I let you down."

"No, you didn't. Considering what the Angels have gone through, I can't blame them for cracking. It's only natural. I need a team in top form for what we have to do next."

"Which is?" she asked.

"We're going to rescue Windows."

"Now you're the one who's cracked," said DeWitt. "How many gang members are there?"

"About thirty."

"Thirty?" DeWitt shook his head in frustration. "So the five of us are going to take on a gang of thirty by ourselves?"

"There'll be eight of us. We have Jennifer, Dravko, and Tibor."

"That's not the fucking point. You yourself said me and the others are useless. Yet you want us to go into combat with you to save Windows?"

"I never said you were useless." Lowering his voice, Robson tried to calm down DeWitt. "I said you were untrained. We can work around that."

"Don't bullshit me. It took the Angels months to become as good as they are now. You don't have the time to train us."

"We can work around that too."

"No, you fucking can't," spat DeWitt. "We don't have what it takes to be like you and Natalie. It's why none of us joined your teams. If you take us into battle, we're as good as dead."

34

"So what do you suggest?"

"That we go with the Angels to Omaha and get as far away from here as possible," DeWitt said.

"What about Windows?"

"We leave her. I know that sounds cruel, but how bad can it be for her?"

Natalie motioned toward the Angels asleep around the campfire. "Maybe you should ask Amy, Josephine, and Sarah."

Naming the Angels who had been victims of rape gangs before finding their way to the camp had the desired effect. DeWitt nodded. "You're the boss. We'll do what you tell us to." Without waiting for a reply, he stood and wandered off into the darkness.

Robson waited until DeWitt was out of earshot before nodding at Natalie. "Thanks for mentioning the girls. That put things into perspective for him."

"No problem," Natalie said. "At the risk of sounding defeatist, how do you expect us to get to Omaha? Even if my girls were in top form, that's halfway across the country, way too far for us to drive."

Robson grinned. "Who said anything about driving?"

CHAPTER SIX

Windows sat in the corner of the storage unit, resting her head and back against the walls. It was the only way she could get comfortable because the room contained no furnishings other than a small wooden table. She couldn't sleep, though. Her captors had shoved her into this unit after arriving back at the storage facility last night, and no one had bothered with her since. Though Windows had no idea what to expect, based on what had happened at camp, she anticipated the worst.

The events of the past twenty-four hours had happened so fast, she barely remembered how things went down. Those images she could recall had been burned into her mind. The attack took place with such ferocity the camp had little time to respond. Within minutes, the gang murdered the motor pool crew, ripped open the main gate, and stormed the compound. The situation deteriorated rapidly after that. The gang had rounded up everyone in front of the blockhouse, with Paul trying to talk to their leader to calm the situation. Then this crazy kid ran up ranting about there being vampires in camp just like he had said. She assumed that somehow the gang had run across Robson's team, with bad results. When a gruff, burly member of the group dragged her away from the others, Windows thought she would be raped. She almost would have preferred that to watching everyone else in camp being gunned down and her home ransacked and torched.

Arriving at the storage facility the gang used as their compound did nothing to boost her confidence, especially when she saw their defense system. They had erected a chain-link fence topped with barbed wire thirty feet away from, and running parallel to, the facility's stone wall. At forty-foot intervals between the fence and the wall, men and women had been chained to stakes hammered into the ground with nothing more than blankets to protect them against the elements. At first, Windows worried that this would be her fate, then thought better about it. If the gang wanted to bolster the perimeter defense, they would have taken more people than just her. She feared they had different plans for her.

Windows considered herself attractive, having a slim body and a cute face like any twenty-two-year-old girl. She also had a shy, nerdy side to her, and as such cut her blonde hair in a short bob and wore librarian-style glasses. When it came to looks, she could not compete with any of the other women in camp, especially the Angels. That would not help her here, though. From what she saw of this bunch, none of them seemed fussy.

The clanking of metal as someone unlocked the door caught Windows' attention. Every muscle in her body tensed. At first, she thought of making a break for it when the door opened, quickly ruling it out. She would get only a few feet before her captors caught her, and then she'd have to face their anger. She decided to play the next few minutes by ear. Windows stood and brushed down her clothes, not wanting them to find her in a submissive position.

When the door rolled up it revealed two men standing there. The shorter of the two, the one raising the door, wore a leather bombardier jacket and carried a hunting rifle strapped over his shoulder. The other was the burly guy who had pulled her out of line back at camp. She finally got a good look at him. He stood just over six feet, about thirty pounds overweight, and sported a bushy blond beard and long hair, like a caricature of a hillbilly. He wore jeans and a flannel shirt that had seen better days. The hillbilly carried a blue plastic tray of food. Windows inhaled. She could smell the aroma of hot food, and it made her mouth water.

The hillbilly entered the unit and crossed over to the table, placing the tray down on it. His companion closed the door again, remaining outside.

"Hi. My name is Duane. My friends all call me Meat."

"Hello."

"Ya must be hungry." He smiled. It looked friendly enough. "I brought ya dinner."

She approached cautiously. "What is it?"

"Bacon and eggs. We took it from ya camp, so the least we can do is share it with ya."

Windows moved closer to the table. Taking the metal fork, she scooped some of the eggs and sniffed them.

"Jesus Christ, girl. I ain't tryin' to poison ya. If we was gonna kill ya we wouldn't have brought ya back here."

Windows placed the eggs in her mouth and nearly moaned. She hadn't eaten in God knew how long, and these tasted pretty good. She chewed quickly and swallowed. "Thank you."

"Oh, ya gonna thank me good."

From behind her, Windows could hear the sound of a zipper being undone. She spun around as Meat dropped his jeans, and her eyes went wide. Now she understood his nickname. A cock at least ten inches long and three inches thick stuck out from his underpants.

"Why don't ya give me some head for bringin' ya dinner?"

"Fuck you!" she yelled.

"Fine by me as long as I get off."

Windows turned to run and banged into the wooden table. Before she could move, Meat came up behind her. His left hand grabbed her by the back of the neck and pushed her forward, bending her over the table until her face pressed against the surface. His right hand grabbed the back of her jeans and started to yank them down. She could feel his erection pressing against her. Instead of struggling to break free, she fought back the panic threatening to overwhelm her. She felt around the table until her fingers brushed against the plastic tray and, finding the metal fork, she clutched it in her right hand and swung back as hard as she could.

"Fuck!" Meat released his grip and moved away.

Windows spun around. She had plunged the fork into his crotch. Blood poured over the prongs and down his leg, and his erection had started to go limp. Meat grabbed the fork and yanked it out.

"Ya fuckin' cu—"

Windows drove the edge of the tray into his face with such force that the plastic shattered. One shard sliced across his cheek and forehead, barely missing his eye and opening a five-inch laceration that began dripping blood. Meat covered his face with both hands and turned to run, but tripped over the jeans drooped around his ankles and fell forward, hitting the ground hard. Windows rushed forward and began jabbing the sharp end of the broken plastic tray into his back. He writhed around on the floor to ward off the blows.

The door to the unit slid open and three men entered. The captor in the leather bomber jacket rushed over to Windows and used his hunting rifle to push her off of Meat and into the corner. The second man, who wore a camouflage jacket and carried a double barrel shotgun, knelt beside Meat and helped him up. Windows still held the bloody shard of plastic in her hand and brandished it like a knife, ready to defend herself, her eyes darting between each of the four men. The guy in the leather jacket aimed his rifle at her.

"Enough."

The command came from the third person to enter the room, who seemed more civilized than the others. He stood at nearly six feet tall, with a clean-shaven face and neatly-cut blond hair. Both his clothes and his mannerism bespoke of a level of sophistication she had not seen within this group. He wore black jeans and a black cotton shirt, both of which, while worn, were clean and pressed. Placing his hand on the barrel of the hunting rifle, he pointed its aim toward the floor and focused his attention on Windows.

"Drop the tray."

Windows clutched it tighter and moved it closer to her chest.

"Miss, I could easily have my men beat the shit out of you and take it from you. I'd rather do this without anyone else getting hurt. Now, please, drop the tray."

Knowing one way or the other they would disarm her, she tossed the plastic shard onto the wooden table and waited for the inevitable.

The man in black gestured to his two companions and nodded to Meat. "Take him to the infirmary and have Jane patch his wounds. Make sure he doesn't leave there until I've been by to talk to him."

"Yes, sir." The two men lifted Meat by the shoulders and dragged him to the exit, leaving a trail of blood behind.

The man in black offered his hand to Windows. "I'm Andrew Price, leader of this group."

She ignored the gesture. "You're the leader of a gang of murderers and rapists."

Price lowered his hand. "You mean what my men did to your compound?"

"That, yes. And what almost just happened to me."

"It's not easy keeping these guys under control, especially in a world where there are no longer any rules."

"What the fuck is this place?" Windows demanded. "What are you planning on doing with me?"

Price stepped over to the door and banged his knuckles against it three times. Someone on the other side raised it, and he turned back to Windows. "I'll have one of the girls bring you something else to eat and a sleeping bag. Get a good night's sleep."

"Why?"

"Because tomorrow you're going with us on a deader hunt. I'll explain everything to you then." Price exited the unit and motioned to one of his men, who closed the door.

Windows watched him leave, not quite sure what had happened or what to expect tomorrow.

CHAPTER SEVEN

The four-vehicle convoy departed the storage facility and headed north along Route 28. Windows noted the vehicles were the same ones that had raided her camp a few days previous: a white Jeep Liberty Sport, a military-style Humvee, a black Hummer H3, and a green Jeep Wrangler with the top removed. Price drove the Wrangler and led the way, with Windows riding shotgun. Four men traveled in the military-style Humvee. Each of the other vehicles carried two heavily-armed men.

She still felt apprehensive about her situation, though not as much as she did last night. So far, Price had kept his word. No one had tried to hurt her after she whaled the shit out of Meat. The only visitor had been a woman who brought Windows dinner. She assumed the woman to be about thirty, although her hollow expression and sallow skin made her appear much older. Windows had tried to talk to the woman who refused to answer, constantly shifting her gaze to the open door as if afraid someone would hear her if she spoke. The woman stayed long enough to drop off the tray and rushed out. She had been the last visitor until Price and his men came to get her.

At least the weather made her feel more optimistic. It was a beautiful autumn morning, with a warm sun and an almost cloudless sky. The surrounding countryside contained only woods and wildlife. It had been months since she had left the confines of Fort McClary. She found it refreshing to see the outside world, even if deep down she knew rotters infested it. This would have been a pleasant ride if she hadn't been a prisoner.

"Where are we going?" she asked.

"There." Price pointed to a white wooden fence along the right side of the road a hundred feet ahead of them. He stopped the Wrangler near a gate, and the other vehicles pulled in behind him. A tall man climbed out of the Humvee and approached the Jeep. Windows saw him in the side mirror. He stood over six feet tall, with a lean yet muscular body. He had close-cropped dark hair and a well-groomed beard and mustache. Though physically attractive, something about his sneer, the glare in his blue eyes, and his demeanor gave him a menacing aura. He approached the Wrangler from her side, and Windows felt a shiver race down her spine.

Price turned in his seat to face the man. "This is Greg Carter. He's our resident sniper."

Carter lifted his hand to the rim of his baseball cap with the NRA logo on it and tugged. "Pleasure to meet you."

His smile left an emptiness in the pit of Windows' stomach.

"You're going to be helping him out today," said Price.

"How?"

Price ignored the question and directed his comments at Carter. "Are you all set?"

"Give me five minutes to set up," said Carter.

"What's that?" she asked.

Carter raised the weapon. "It's a Macmillan TAC-50 .50 caliber long range sniper rifle. Best little weap—"

"Radio me when you're ready," Price interrupted him.

Carter smiled and walked off. The other three men from the Humvee joined him. They made their way down to the trees bordering the right-hand side of the field and disappeared into the woods.

Price tapped Windows on the shoulder to get her attention and, when she looked, pointed to the field. "See out there?"

Windows followed his line of sight. She noticed eight rotters shambling around at the far end of the field. "Yeah."

"Your friends are responsible for that."

"My friends?"

"The ones who came through here about two weeks ago and murdered my men. Their convoy must have gone through the area like a bat out of hell. Drew the attention of every deader around. Even after your friends were long gone, these things continued to follow them. Every day for the past week we've had to comb the area and clean up their mess before these things make it to our place."

"Oh." Windows did not know what else to say.

"I spent a lot of time setting up our compound, making sure we had plenty of supplies, and making it secure. It took three months and half a dozen of my men to clean the deaders out of the surrounding area. Now we have to start from scratch thanks to your friends."

"Is that why you destroyed my camp?"

"I admit, my men overreacted when they did that," said Price with a tone of sincerity. "They were taking revenge for what had happened to our own people."

"Why did you let me live?"

"You can thank Meat for that. He made sure the others kept you safe." Price chuckled. "You almost found out why last night."

Windows involuntarily crossed her arms across her chest.

The radio attached to the Wrangler's dashboard crackled and Carter's voice came over the speaker. "We're in place."

Price picked up the microphone. "Thanks. Good hunting."

He shifted the Wrangler into drive and pulled into the field, pushing open the wooden gate. The Liberty Sport followed. Price drove toward the far end of the field. The living dead heard the two vehicles approaching and turned. Spotting the Jeep, they began to lumber forward. Price stopped in the center of the field, and the Liberty Sport pulled up on the driver's side.

Windows stared at the rotters. Though still a few hundred feet away, they were getting too close for comfort. She glanced over at Price. "You said you needed me to help Carter. How?"

"Like it or not, you're now a member of my compound. And everyone who lives on my compound provides some service for the common good, whether you work in the compound or are part of the hunting group."

"Or become a sex slave for your men?"

"I'm not going to lie. There are women on the compound who do that." Price grinned. "You made it clear last night that wasn't how you wanted to contribute."

"Then what do you need me to do?"

"You're going to serve as bait."

Price grabbed Windows by the back of the head and slammed her face into the dashboard. A bolt of pain shot through her when her nose shattered, and she felt blood pouring down across her lips. Something slapped hard across her left wrist. When she raised her head, she saw one end of a pair of handcuffs on her wrist, and Price attaching the other end to the Wrangler's steering wheel.

"What are you doing?" Windows gagged, blood flowing down her throat.

Price grabbed his M&P15-22LR semi-automatic rifle as he climbed out of the Wrangler, and then opened the rear door of the Liberty Sport. "I'm giving you a chance to be useful. The deaders will be attracted by the blood and will swarm you. That'll give Carter a clear shot to take them down. So you better be nice to him."

"What do you mean?"

Price laughed as he climbed into the SUV. "You are fucking clueless."

When the Liberty Sport drove off, Windows jerked on the handcuffs, with no effect. She tried sliding the other end over her wrist with no success. Price had attached it too tight. Glancing at the ignition, she hoped to find the keys, but Price had taken them. She was trapped out here with a swarm of rotters approaching.

Carter's voice came over the radio. "I hear you did a number on Meat last night."

Windows grabbed the microphone and pressed the talk button. "The prick tried to rape."

"He just wanted to be friendly."

"My ass."

"That's what I said. He wanted to be friendly with your ass."

A moan caught Windows' attention. A rotter in a tattered and soiled business suit neared her from the right. As it drew closer and smelled the blood, it became more agitated, rushing toward her in a stumbling gait. When it got to within ten feet, a loud crack emanated from the woods, followed by the squish of a bullet entering its skull. Its head exploded, showering the front of the Wrangler in congealed blood and pieces of skull and brain.

"You know, Meat is a good friend of mine," Carter resumed. "You should be nicer to him."

"You need to choose your friends better."

"Is it really smart to piss off the guy who's saving your life?"

Another moan, this time to the left. A rotter in a paramedic uniform, its left arm missing below the elbow, shambled toward the Wrangler. Carter waited until it neared the front fender before taking it down with a head shot. As it dropped, Windows saw another one directly behind it, a little girl in a Sleeping Beauty nightgown. A shot from Carter tore its head clean off, the force of the bullet tossing the tiny body to the left.

"You didn't answer my question," said Carter. "Is it really smart to piss off the guy who's saving your life?"

"You can't be serious?"

"I am. It doesn't matter to me whether you make it through this or not." Another shot from the woods caught the head of a naked female rotter. "You should be nicer to me."

"Fuck you!"

Carter chuckled. "That's what I had in mind."

A rotter in a priest's uniform approached the front of the Wrangler. It slammed its hands on the hood and snarled. A second later, its head exploded, creating a cloud of congealed blood and splatter. The body fell forward onto the hood, rested for a moment, and then slid off to the ground.

"Did I just take down a priest?' asked Carter.

"What?" Windows had pissed herself.

"I asked if I just took down a priest."

"What does it matter?"

"I want to know."

"I don't...." Windows' fear threatened to overwhelm her. "Yes, you did."

"Good. I hate those motherfuckers. Got molested by one of them when I was an altar boy."

A rotter in a nurse's scrubs dragging its twisted left leg drew closer, coming around the passenger side of the Wrangler. Windows waited for Carter to take it down. It got to within five feet before its head exploded. A stream of gore sprayed across the inside of the windshield, some of it catching Windows in the face. She frantically wiped it off with her hand.

"So how are you going to do it?" Carter asked.

"Do what?"

"Be nice to me. You mentioned fucking me."

"I'd rather die."

"Have it your way."

The radio went silent. Three rotters remained. The closest, wearing a wedding dress no longer white from dirt and gore, had approached to within twenty feet. Close behind shambled a rotter in a sheriff's uniform and another dressed only in slacks and a tattered shirt. She waited for Carter to take them out, but nothing happened. She began tugging again at the handcuffs, even though she knew she couldn't break free. When she looked up, the bride was within ten feet and came around to her side of the Wrangler, with the sheriff following. Tattered shirt rotter circled around on the driver's side. And still the gunshot never came. Her fear was turning into panic.

Raising the microphone to her lips, she yelled, "Carter, are you there?"

No answer.

The rotters were now less than three feet away, and Windows couldn't go anywhere. She used her right leg to lash out at the bride, kicking it in the chest and face. The sheriff moved to the bride's right and leaned over. Windows retched when the stench of decayed flesh and rotting meat vomited from its mouth. She clutched its shirt in her right hand and locked her elbow, holding the living dead in place. To her left, tattered shirt rotter came up alongside the Wrangler and reached for her. Windows batted at it with her left hand.

"You want some help?" Carter asked over the radio.

Windows stopped swiping at tattered shirt rotter long enough to grab the microphone and bring it to her mouth. "Yes!"

With her hand gone, tattered shirt rotter leaned in close. Still holding the microphone, she punched it several times in its decayed face.

"I thought you said you'd rather die than fuck me," Carter snickered. "Have you changed your mind?"

Windows stopped her attack on the rotter and screamed into the microphone. "I'll fuck you! I'll suck you! I'll let you do whatever you want to me! Just get them off me!"

"I'm holding you to it, baby."

A second later, a .50 caliber bullet slammed into tattered shirt's skull. Its head vaporized, showering the inside of the Wrangler. Windows screamed, drowning out the moans and snarls of the other two rotters. She didn't hear the gunshot that ripped open the sheriff's skull, but she did feel its corpse drop down on top of her, and the congealed blood that oozed from its neck onto her chest. She didn't realize that Carter had decapitated the bride until her leg pushed the headless body back onto the ground. It ended as quickly as it had started. The only sound came from her whimpering. Windows was vaguely aware of being covered in gore, and of sitting in her own urine.

A minute later, the Liberty Sport approached and parked across from her. Price climbed out and strolled up. Through her tears, she saw he sported a condescending smile. He came over to her, grabbed the sheriff, and pulled it off of her. "Are you okay?" he asked.

Windows shook her head. Snot flew from her nose.

"Did any of them bite you? Did you get any of their blood in your mouth?"

"No." She snorted and gagged on her own phlegm.

"Good." Removing keys from his pocket, he leaned across Windows, unlocked the end attached to the steering wheel, and then unlatched them from her wrist. Wiping off the gore with a handkerchief, he slid the handcuffs into his pocket and let the handkerchief drop to the dirt. Placing his hand on her left cheek, he lifted her head until their eyes met. "Are you ready to go back?"

Windows' eyes closed tight and tears flowed at the prospect of being safe.

Price suddenly gripped her mouth tight and slammed her back against the head rest. When she opened her eyes, he leaned into her, his face menacing and mere inches from her own.

"Now listen to me, you little cunt. You do as you're Goddamned told from now on, or next time I won't let Carter save you. Do you fucking understand me?"

Windows was too scared to answer.

Price slapped her across the cheek hard enough to make her teeth clatter. "Do you?"

Her eyes closed and the tears flowed even heavier. She croaked, "Yes."

"Good. Because tonight we're going to have a victory party, and you're the entertainment."

Clutching Windows by the hair, Price dragged her out of the Wrangler and shoved her into the back of the Liberty Sport.

CHAPTER EIGHT

"I feel like I'm in a war movie," said Josephine as she paddled the four-man inflatable boat across the inlet from South Portland to the downtown area.

Sarah chuckled. "You're a real G.I., Josephine."

Emily leaned forward. "Honey, I'd gladly do this rather than fight rotters."

"If you two don't keep quiet you'll be fighting a whole city of rotters," whispered Ari.

The four Angels stopped talking as they made their way toward the row of marinas in the downtown area. Ari glanced over her shoulder. Clouds obscured the moon, and she could not see the others waiting for them along the banks of South Portland. She knew the rest of the Angels waited with two inflatable boats, all of which had been requisitioned, along with the night vision goggles that each woman wore, after a supply run to the Deerskin Trading Post. Once Ari's team found a working vessel large enough to carry them all, she would radio back to shore, and Natalie would bring the rest of the girls over while Robson provided cover. Once at sea, the Angels would then sail to Omaha. A simple plan, if not insane. Insanity had worked well for them so far, so why mess with a good thing?

When they drew closer to the first marina, Ari pulled the night vision goggles over her eyes and switched them on. She scanned the various boats, hoping to find a yacht or other large craft that could hold all thirteen women and endure the trip. She had several to choose from, and concentrated on those closest to the end of the wharves where there were fewer rotters. The first wharf contained tourist shops and restaurants, with only small pleasure craft tied to its moorings. In the green light of the goggles, she could see hundreds of living dead swarming along its length. Ari raised her forefinger in front of her lips and pointed toward the wharf. The other Angels nodded and silently paddled past.

Not as many rotters were on the next wharf, although there were still way too many for her liking. A fifty-foot yacht sat docked at the end, making the risk worth it. Ari maneuvered the inflatable boat along the port beam, which faced into the bay. She scanned the length of the yacht for any signs of movement and saw nothing, and then the wharf beyond. None of the living dead were aware of their presence, which suited her just fine. They should be able to sneak aboard.

A pair of rotters appeared on the back deck and raced over to the guard rail, snarling at the women. Ari jumped back and nearly shoved Emily out of the boat. Josephine had the presence of mind to use her oar to push the inflatable boat away from the fifty-footer and back out into the inlet. The rotters leaned over the railing, grasping for the Angels as they paddled away. The commotion attracted the attention of those scattered along the wharf, and soon dozens of the living dead shambled toward them. Within minutes, the rotters on the two surrounding wharves had also become agitated, letting out a collective ungodly wail that shattered the silence and followed the Angels back out into the darkness of the inlet.

"I guess that's the end of that," said Josephine. "Should we head back?"

"Not yet," replied Ari.

"Honey, you're not serious about going back there?"

"Not there." Ari pointed ahead of them. "There."

The other Angels looked in the direction Ari referred to. Wharves extended into the inlet all along the coast. About a quarter of a mile to the east, one large wharf jutted out farther than the others. It belonged to the Casco Bay Ferry Terminal. Two smaller piers extended from the main wharf. The car ferry was moored to the first. Tied up to the second was a seventy-five-foot yacht. In the green light of the goggles, the Angels saw only a handful of rotters on the wharf.

"Well I'll be damned," said Sarah.

"You will be if those things catch you," added Josephine.

"Can the chatter," ordered Ari. "And start rowing."

They paddled across the inlet and let the moaning of the living dead recede behind them. Ari scanned the ferry terminal, praying they wouldn't stumble across a horde of the living dead wandering around out of sight. The closer they got, the better their prospects appeared. She counted only five rotters. Even more importantly, the yacht appeared operable. They needed to sneak on board without being detected, make sure the engines worked and the gas tanks were filled, get it started, and slip away before the hordes of the living dead set upon them. No sweat.

Coasting up to its starboard beam, Emily and Sarah used their hands to prevent the inflatable boat from bumping too loudly into the larger vessel's hull, and then hand walked the inflatable boat down to the stern. Stopping before the end of the hull, Ari peered around the corner. The nearest rotter was more than a hundred feet away and walking away from them. The Angels gently paddled around to the stern. Ari turned to the others and spoke in a hushed voice.

"Josephine, once we're on board, move the boat out of sight and wait for us. Warn us via radio if you're spotted. Emily will check out the yacht to see if it's sea worthy. Sarah and I will cover her. Any questions?"

The three women shook their heads.

"Let's go."

Ari withdrew her machete from its sheath and stepped onto the boarding platform built into the yacht's transom, and then climbed the three steps onto the main deck. Emily followed. Brandishing her hunting knife, Sarah brought up the rear. When the others were safely aboard, Josephine paddled around to hide alongside the starboard beam.

While Sarah climbed the ladder to the flying bridge, Ari peered through the hatch into the main cabin.

"It looks clear," whispered Ari.

"No rotters up here," Sarah reported as she descended the ladder.

"Are the keys in the ignition?" asked Emily.

Sarah climbed back up. "Dammit, no. What do we do now?"

"Don't give up hope, honey. There's a lot of places they could be." Emily made her way into the main cabin. "First, we need to see if this thing has any gas in it."

Emily opened the floor hatch leading down to the engine room, ushered the other two down the stairs and followed, closing the hatch behind her. "Take off your night vision goggles."

When both women complied, Emily switched on the light, illuminating the engine room in the soft glow of fluorescent lights. Emily made her way down the stairs and over to the twin engines.

"We know the batteries still work. That's a good sign."

"Can we do anything?" Ari asked.

Emily pointed to the work station behind and to their right. "Look around there for a spare set of keys."

Emily stepped over to the gas tank and checked the gauge. "It's full. With the batteries working, we should be able to start her up with no problem."

"How do you know so much about yachts?" Ari asked.

"Honey, it's all part of my sordid past." Emily chuckled. "As a grad student I dated a frat boy whose dad came from old money. One summer, we borrowed his family yacht and toured the East Coast. He taught me a lot about running a yacht, as well as other things."

"Got them." Sarah lifted the keys above her head.

"I want to check on the food supplies," said Ari. "And we have to make sure there are no rotters on board. Last thing I want are any surprises out at sea."

Emily took the keys from Sarah and led the way back upstairs. Before opening the door, she switched off the lights. The women donned their night vision goggles. Moving down the yacht, they checked on the kitchen, pantry, and each stateroom. Whenever they reached a closed door, they would knock three times and wait. If no sounds came from the other side, Ari would open the door and Sarah and Emily would step in, ready to dispatch anything that greeted them. They found each stateroom empty. The two near the bow contained boxes of canned goods, bottled water, and other supplies.

54

Ari opened the closest unmarked box and found medical equipment as well as over the counter medicine. "Someone was getting ready to ride out the apocalypse on the high seas."

Sarah reached in and pulled out a bottle of Motrin. "Thank God for us they never got a chance to shove off."

"I wonder what happened to the owner," Ari wondered aloud.

"He's probably roaming the wharf," said Emily. "If you ladies are ready, we can get this show on the road."

Ari nodded. "Let's get into position. I'll call Robson."

The three girls headed back to Josephine. None of them realized that the owner was still on board and had been immobile in the main stateroom's bathroom, the one room they had failed to search. Now alert to the presence of humans, it made its way out into the stateroom, down the hall, and followed the sound of the food at the back of the yacht.

* * *

Robson leaned against the school bus' fender. He stared across the inlet, although he knew that between the distance and the darkness he would not be able to see Ari's party. That made him nervous. So far he had heard no commotion from Portland or received any calls for help, so he kept telling himself that no news was good news.

This time DeWitt's team provided the perimeter defense because the Angels were down on shore with their inflatable boats ready to move out once they got the signal from Ari.

"Mike, are you there?" Ari's voice could barely be heard over the radio.

"I'm here."

"We found a yacht that we think is ready to travel. Now we need our diversion."

"Where are you?"

"We're at the end of the ferry terminal."

"One diversion coming right up." Robson dropped the radio back into his jacket pocket. He stepped down to the shore line, each of the Angels watching him expectantly. "Ladies, it's show time. You know what to do."

As the other Angels pushed their inflatable boats into the water, Natalie walked up to Robson and put her arms around him. The feel of her body against his was comforting, yet bittersweet. He had no idea how long it would be before he held her again, or if either of them would survive. Wrapping both arms around her shoulders, he hugged her tightly, savoring the last seconds they had together.

He couldn't think of anything to say other than, "Be careful."

"I will. Make sure you take care of yourself." Natalie broke the hug, placed her hands on Robson's cheeks, and kissed him. "I love you, and I don't want anything to happen to you."

"I love you, too." Robson hugged her back. "See you soon."

"I hope so." Natalie ran down to the shore and climbed into the last inflatable boat. As the Angels paddled away and the pair of craft disappeared into the night, Robson walked back to the vehicles. He nodded to Dravko. "Are you ready?"

The vampire shrugged. "As ready as I'll ever be."

"Let's go."

DeWitt stepped up Robson. "Are you sure you don't want us to go with you?"

"I want you guys to follow us only as far as the bridge and wait there. This should be easy. Be ready to come get us if we get into trouble."

"Like that never happens," said Dravko, sliding into one of the Humvees.

Climbing into the school bus, Robson sat in the driver's seat, started the engine, and shifted into drive. Dravko moved the Humvee in behind him. The other vehicles followed, keeping their distance. The convoy moved through the deserted back streets of South Portland until they came upon the exit ramp for Route 77, which led to the Casco Bay Bridge. The other vehicles stopped on top of the span while Robson and Dravko continued across into Portland.

Robson raced into the downtown area, pressing on the horn, blaring in a single, continuous wail. From behind the chain link fences paralleling the road, thousands of gray, dead eyes turned in the direction of the noise. The living dead flowed toward the fences, pushing against them until the surfaces bulged like waves gliding across the ocean surface. More and more rotters joined the throng, shoving against the fence until Robson feared it might collapse. While that would provide the perfect diversion for the Angels, it would suck for him and Dravko.

He continued down Commerce Street until he reached the intersection with Franklin. The entrance to the Casco Bay Ferry Terminal sat off to his right. There were fewer rotters here than farther down, so the pressure on the fence would be less. He stopped and shifted into park. Dravko passed by and pulled the Humvee into a three-point turn. While the vampire reversed direction so they could get away, Robson pressed the horn, attracting the attention of those living dead around the terminal. Slowly, they made their way toward Commerce Street, leaving the terminal behind them.

* * *

From the flying bridge, Ari heard the commotion coming from Commerce Street and knew Robson was drawing the rotters away.

"Emily, that's our cue."

Emily slid the key into the ignition and twisted it to the right, then pressed the start button. From below decks, the twin engines turned over but would not catch. Emily tried three times without success.

"What do we do now?" asked Sarah.

"We find another boat," answered Ari, forcing down her panic. "And fast."

"With the rotters all stirred up? No fucking way."

Emily switched the key to the off position. "Come on, honey," she coaxed. "Don't let me down."

Turning the key back to the on position, Emily pressed the start button again. The twin engines turned over, this time catching and roaring to life.

Ari whooped and patted Emily on the back. "You did it!"

"Of course I did, honey." Emily smiled. "Now cut us loose."

Ari and Sarah ran down to the main deck, rushing past Josephine who had brought the inflatable boat around to the transom landing and had climbed on board. The two women made their way to the fore and aft dock lines anchoring the port side of the yacht to the wharf. Using their machete and hunting knife, respectively, they cut the lines. When both women yelled up to Emily that they were clear, she pushed the throttles forward. The water behind the yacht churned as the twin propellers began spinning and the yacht moved away from the pier. Once two hundred feet into the bay, Emily throttled back to neutral. She removed her night vision goggles and told the others to do the same.

"What are you doing?" asked Ari.

"Making sure the others find us." Flipping another switch, the exterior lights on the yacht came on, the glare slicing through the dark.

* * *

"Over there," said Doreen. Not that anyone needed her to point it out. The yacht was the only thing lit up in the entire Portland area. The Angels paddled in its direction.

* * *

Dravko leaned out the window of his Humvee and waved until he attracted Robson's attention. Robson rolled down the school bus window.

"What's wrong?"

"Don't you think we should get out of here?" The vampire pointed toward the fence opposite the school bus where a horde of rotters yanked against the links. "That fence is not going to hold much longer."

"Give it a few more minutes. We need to make sure the girls get away."

"You're the boss. But if that fence collapses, we're the ones who aren't going to be making it out of here."

* * *

The first of the inflatable boats reached the yacht. Sarah stood by, waiting to help the Angels on board. Doreen grabbed the mooring cleat and held the boat in place against the transom's boarding platform. Tiara jumped off first, spun around, and reached out to assist Bethany, who struggled with the broken arm she had received on the journey down to Site R. Tiara had helped Bethany onto the platform when the women heard a moan from behind them. They turned to see the rotter that had been lurking in the stateroom exit the hatch to the main cabin and lumber toward them. It fell off the deck onto the boarding platform. Tiara dodged out of the way. Bethany, being off balance, could not move fast enough, and the rotter landed on top of her, clutching her leather jacket by the collar. The two toppled backward into the inflatable boat, bounced off the surface, and landed in the bay.

Bethany had the presence of mind to take a deep breath before they hit, not that it would be of much help. The dead mass weighed her down, and the pair sank into the bay. With only one hand free, she could not break away. The rotter lunged for her neck, its movement slowed by the water. Bethany slapped at its mouth. Rather than her neck, it bit her on the right side of her face. She felt its teeth slice through the skin and scrape against her gums. Bethany grabbed the rotter by the hair and held its head in place so it could not tear away a chunk of flesh. The pain overwhelmed her. For a moment, her senses went numb. She didn't even realize that she had gasped, sucking sea water into her lungs.

Sarah saw a cloud of blood turning the water crimson, so she dived into the bay after her friend. As she swam after the two, she withdrew her hunting knife. When Sarah reached the pair, she grabbed the rotter by the back of its shirt and plunged the knife into the base of its skull, twisting the blade and severing its spinal column. The rotter went limp and released its grip on Bethany, who continued to descend into the darkness. Sarah pushed away the rotter, grabbed Bethany by the jacket, and swam for the surface. She couldn't see where Bethany had been bitten, but judging by the amount of blood, she assumed it was bad.

Sarah breached the surface and gasped for breath. Tiara and Doreen knelt on the boarding platform waiting for her. They reached out, took Bethany under the arms, and dragged her onto the main deck. While Sarah climbed onto the boarding platform, the second inflatable boat came into view.

"What's all the commotion?" asked Natalie.

Sarah took a deep breath. "A rotter bit Bethany."

"Oh, God. How is she?"

"We don't know yet." Sarah scrambled up onto the main deck.

Bethany lay prone, blood flowing from the bite wound and pooling around her head. Tiara had her head on Bethany's chest. "She's not breathing."

"Give her CPR," ordered Natalie.

Tiara hesitated. "She's infected."

"No she's not." Natalie knelt on the opposite side of Bethany. "We've all taken the vaccine. Remember?"

Bending over, she administered CPR, alternating between breathing into Bethany's mouth and compressing her chest. On the fifth attempt, Bethany sat up and hacked, spewing sea water from her lungs. She drew in several deep gasps, desperately sucking in air, and each time coughed up more water. The choking stopped and Bethany lay back on the deck, trying to calm her nerves. She reached up to touch her face, but Natalie grabbed her wrist and stopped her.

Bethany's eyes went wide. "How bad is it?"

"Pretty bad. But you'll live."

It didn't help that when the rest of the Angels climbed onto the main deck, Katie saw Bethany and gasped. Natalie slid off her leather jacket and pulled her t-shirt over her head. Folding the shirt several times, Natalie placed one surface against Bethany's ravaged cheek and pressed. Bethany winced from the pain. Placing her other hand on the opposite cheek, Natalie held her friend's head in place.

Ari's head appeared over the railing of the flying bridge. "Is everyone on board?"

"Yes!" Doreen yelled.

"Good. I'll tell Em.... Jesus, what happened?"

"A rotter attacked Bethany," said Natalie. "We need to do something for her. Now."

"Okay. I'll get some medical supplies." Ari yelled something the other girls couldn't hear. A second later, the engines came to life and the yacht sailed forward. Ari made her way down to the main deck and headed inside. She waved for the others to follow. "Come on. We'll put her in one of the cabins and take a look at her wound."

Natalie and Tiara picked up Bethany and carried her inside. Sandy, who held the briefcase with the vials of vaccine, entered behind them. The others milled around for a few seconds, uncertain what to do, before finally following their friends.

* * *

DeWitt's voice crackled over Robson's radio. "I think the Angels are safe."

"Can you see them?" Robson asked.

"No, but the yacht is on the move and it's heading out to sea."

"Roger that. We'll be there in a few." Opening the door to the school bus, Robson jumped out and rushed over to the Humvee. Upon seeing him, the rotters along both fences broke into a frenzy, moaning and snarling as they tried to reach him through the links.

Dravko motioned to the bus. "Are you leaving it here?"

"Without the Angels we don't need it anymore. Right now it's more of a burden than anything else." Robson opened the door and slid into the passenger seat. "Let's get out of here before these things break through."

"No argument here." Dravko pushed his foot down on the accelerator.

A minute later, they left Portland behind them and raced over the Casco Bay Bridge. The rest of the group waited at the top of the span. When Robson and Dravko joined them, they stared over the rail and out into the bay.

"What's up?" Robson asked.

DeWitt pointed to the horizon. "That set of lights is the Angels' yacht. It looks like they made it out okay."

Although glad the Angels were safe, it devastated Robson to see them go. He had never intended to fall in love with anyone after the apocalypse, but it had happened between him and Natalie. Just as he began to harbor a vague hope of maybe rebuilding his life, he had to send the woman he loved on a suicide mission to get Compton's vaccine for the Zombie Virus to the government-in-exile in Omaha. He knew the Angels had a slim chance of succeeding. Even worse, he knew the chances of his ever seeing Natalie again bordered on non-existent. Things like personal happiness were no longer luxuries anyone could hope for in this terrifying new world.

Robson watched the lights of the yacht recede into the night. He closed his eyes and mentally said goodbye to Natalie, hoping somehow she would sense him.

Turning from the bay, Robson faced the others. "Okay, let's go."

"Where are we going?" asked DeWitt.

"To get Windows from that rape gang."

CHAPTER NINE

Windows lay curled in a fetal position in the corner of the storage container, as much to ward off the damp and cold as to hide her shame.

Last night, Price threw the victory party he had promised, and she had fulfilled her role as the "entertainment". It had started as soon as they got back to camp. Price and the rest of the hunting party brought her to one of the larger storage units that contained only a large, sturdy table. He forced her to strip and then raped her on top of the table while two others held her down. When Price finished, he let the rest of the party have their turn. One by one, other gang members filtered in to get in line. Windows mentally distanced herself from the assault, losing track of how many men violated her. She vaguely recalled two and sometimes three men taking her at once. Of course, she remembered her last assailant, Meat. He had gotten his revenge by sexually brutalizing her so badly she passed out. When she came to later, her attackers had left her alone on top of the table in the same condition as when they had finished, naked and covered in semen and blood. Gathering her clothes, she had dressed and crossed over to the corner, hoping to catch some sleep.

Of course, that never happened. Every time Windows began to doze off, the images of her gang rape replayed in her mind.

Dealing with the self-recrimination proved worse than constantly reliving the nightmare. Rationally, she knew she could have done nothing to prevent last night, but her subconscious argued otherwise. Maybe she shouldn't have willingly undressed for them. Maybe she should have fought back, not that it would have prevented what had happened. In fact, it more than likely would have made her situation worse. She would still have been raped, and probably have been beaten senseless as well. At least she would have some dignity in knowing that she had fought back and didn't willingly submit. This internal argument had gone on all night. Every time Windows convinced herself that she had done the right thing by not resisting, or determined that in the future she would fight back, self-doubt set in and the internal argument began all over again.

Windows had been curled up for God knew how long when she heard voices outside the unit, followed by the clanking of the sliding metal door being raised. She bolted upright and pushed herself into the corner, trying to put as much distance as possible between herself and the intruder. Her heart pounded, her skin flushed, her stomach went nauseous. The door slid open and a woman stepped into the unit. Windows recognized her as the same woman who had brought her dinner and the sleeping bag on her first night. Windows finally had a chance to get a close look at her. At one time, she probably would have been considered attractive, but not now. Her five-and-a-half-foot frame was gaunt, and she walked with her shoulders hunched forward. She wore shabby, filthy clothes. Scraggly red hair flowed over her shoulders, and appeared as though it had not been washed in weeks. Several strands covered her face. When the woman ran a hand through them and pushed the hair behind her ear, Windows saw that the woman's beauty had been beaten out of her. Hollow eyes stared vacantly from sockets blackened by lack of sleep, remnants of bruises darkened her cheeks, and a scar ran across her upper and lower lips. She carried a tray with a plate of food, a bowl of water, and a towel and facecloth.

A young girl about eight years old followed behind the woman. She had long brunette hair pulled into a ponytail that hung past her shoulders. The girl wore overalls, a sweatshirt, and sneakers that had seen better days. Like the older woman, she was dirty and haggard, although the girl looked more scared than abused. She held clothes in her arms.

The two stepped over to the table without saying a word. The older woman placed the tray on top, and then took the clothes from the young girl and set them alongside it. Only when the guard outside slid shut the metal door did the woman speak.

"I'm Debra Caslow. This is my daughter, Cindy."

The young girl raised her hand and waved.

Debra regarded Windows and sighed under her breath, "Fucking animals."

"Mom, it's not nice to swear."

"You're right, dear." Debra ran her hand across Cindy's hair. The barest hint of a smile crossed her lips. She turned back to Windows. "Let's get you cleaned up."

Windows sat there, not sure what to do. Debra went over to the bowl of water and immersed the facecloth in it, soaking it for several seconds before wringing it out and returning to Windows.

"You have to keep going. Trust me, I know. Every woman here has spent time in the Clubhouse."

"Is that what you call it?"

"No. The men call it the Clubhouse. *We* call it the Rape Room. You get used to it after a while. Every day in this hellhole is a struggle to maintain even a shred of self-respect." Debra motioned with her head. "Come on."

Windows stood up and walked over to the table. Debra began cleaning her face as if she was a child. Windows made no effort to do it herself, desperate for any gesture of kindness. Cindy passed behind her mother and stood by the opposite end of the table, playing with the towel.

"What's your name?" asked Debra with the nonchalance of a hair stylist chatting with a customer.

"Windows."

"Is that your last name?"

"That's what they call me."

"You mean the people back at the fort?"

Windows nodded, fighting back tears.

"I'm sorry about that." Debra let the conversation lapse. When done cleaning Windows' face, Cindy handed her the towel.

"Who are these people?" Windows asked as she dried herself.

Debra glanced over her shoulder to make certain no one could hear. "Most of them are criminals who broke out of a nearby federal penitentiary during the first weeks of the outbreak. They set up camp here and have been preying on anyone unfortunate enough to wander past, or anyone they come across on raiding missions. Most of the men are killed outright, unless they have a skill that can be put to use. Or if they fight back, in which case they're brought back here and put on the Line. All the women are raped. The lucky ones are murdered afterwards. The unfortunate ones are brought back here to be sex slaves. When the men grow tired of them, they join the others on the Line."

"What's 'the Line'?"

"That's what they call the defense perimeter. Anyone who pisses off Price gets sent outside where they're chained to the ground outside the wall surrounding this place. It's his sick idea of an early warning system. If any of the deaders get close to the compound, they stop to feed off of someone on the Line first. The screaming warns the guards."

"Has it happened before?"

"Only once since I've been here. Others said it happened a lot in the early days. You can hear the screaming all over the compound. It's terrible." Debra took the towel. "Take off your clothes."

Windows wrapped her arms across her chest and squeezed tight. "Why?"

"I have clean clothing for you. You don't want to wear those. Trust me, I know. They're soiled with *them*." Debra spoke the last word with bitterness.

Windows slid off her shoes.

"The Line is the reason most of us put up with what we do," Debra continued. "It's worse than being dead. At least death is quick. Out there, you slowly die of starvation, or you become a meal for a deader."

"Don't they feed those on the Line?"

"It's a punishment detail. Everyone gets a cup of soup and water a day, plus a blanket to cover up at night. No one has lasted more than a few weeks. That's why most of the people in here do as they're told. It's better than the alternative."

"Is it?" Windows sneered as she slid off her jeans. Semen that had leaked from her vagina stained the crotch. Windows fought back the urge to vomit. "How often do you have to give yourself to them?"

Debra avoided her gaze. "Every night."

"I'd rather take my chances out there with the rotters and the elements than submit to them." She flung the soiled jeans at Debra.

The woman grabbed them in mid-air. For a moment she glared at Windows, then her expression softened into one of self-contempt. "So would I, but I have other considerations."

Windows realized she meant Cindy and regretted her accusation. "I'm sorry."

"So am I. I'm sorry for what I've done to keep her safe." Debra knelt in front of Windows and began wiping down her pubis, trying to clean off the encrusted remnants of the assault. "It's not as bad as you might think if you learn how to play the system. There's a lot of girls around here who haven't figured it out, and they get gang raped every night. Not me, though."

"So, what's the system?"

"Figure out which ones want a girlfriend and be nice to them."

"You mean fuck them?'

"Yes, but also treat them well. Compliment them, do special things for them, make them feel special. If you become their girlfriend, they'll be protective and won't let the others have their way with you." Debra stood up and handed Windows the towel. While Windows dried herself, Debra rinsed out the face cloth. "I have that relationship with Meat. That's what he makes all the women here call him."

Cindy glanced up. "He makes me call him Daddy."

Debra's face expressed the humiliation for both of them. "He won't share me with others, and he keeps Cindy safe as long as I do what he wants. I'll do anything to protect her."

"I'm sure you have." Windows meant it as a gesture of sympathy, not a condemnation.

"You have no idea." Debra smiled, but the anguish in her eyes and the quivering around the mouth said it all. "Meat likes you. It's why he wouldn't let you be killed back at your camp."

"I thought you were his girlfriend?"

"*I'm* expected to be monogamous, not him." Debra held up the facecloth. "Take off your shirt."

Windows unbuttoned it and let it slide to the floor. "I don't understand. Why are you telling me this? Do you figure if he's fucking me, then you get a break?"

"Stop being a cunt." Debra threw the facecloth at Windows. It slapped across her chest. "I'm trying to help you. If you prefer to be gang banged every night, then that's your choice."

Visions of last night flashed through Windows' mind. She would do anything not to have to repeat that. "Sorry. It's just that... you know."

"I do." Debra motioned for Windows to clean herself. "And yes, I have an ulterior motive for arranging this."

"What's that?"

Debra glanced over at Cindy. Her face beamed, the first positive emotion Windows had seen from her. "I'm terrified for her safety if something happens to me. If I help you out, if I arrange it so you're Meat's girlfriend, you have to promise to take care of Cindy if something should happen to me."

Windows nodded halfheartedly. "I promise."

"No," snapped Debra. "I mean this. You have to swear on your life that you'll protect her."

Cindy gazed up at the two women for just a moment before glancing back down at the table. Windows' heart ached for the girl. Her world had been turned upside down in the past year, first by the rotter outbreak, and then by winding up in this place. All she could look forward to was growing up to be molested. It probably would have been better if she hadn't survived the first few days. She had, however, and fate had dealt her the shittiest hand in the deck. Nothing Windows could do about that now. She could at least try and prevent the situation from getting worse, although deep down she knew she had about as much of a chance of that as stopping the rotter apocalypse by herself. Still, she had to try.

"I promise that if you help me, I'll help you protect your daughter."

"Thank you." Debra rushed forward and threw her arms around Windows, hugging her tightly despite the awkwardness of Windows being naked. "Cindy, honey, bring the jumpsuit."

Cindy did as her mother asked. When she approached, Debra kneeled down to her daughter's level. "Miss Windows is going to be our friend and she's going to help keep you safe."

"Thank you." Cindy's expression remained unenthusiastic, though her eyes expressed gratitude.

Debra took the jumpsuit and handed it to Windows. "This is the only thing we have that will fit you. It used to belong to a female Air Force major who the raiding party stumbled across."

"What happened to her?"

"After a week inside the compound, Price put her on the Line. By then she was so far gone she lasted only a few days. Now get dressed and eat. Afterwards, I'll take you to see the doctor for a regimen of morning after pills, and then you'll move into Meat's quarters with us."

Windows tried to conceal the fear that began to well up inside of her.

CHAPTER TEN

Price slowed the black Hummer H3 as he approached the facility and turned left off of Suncock Valley Road. He felt the tension in himself and his three passengers replaced by a sense of security at having safely arrived home. One of his men on guard duty raced out to the perimeter fence and pulled aside the gate, letting in the vehicle. As Price passed through, he glanced off to his left at those staked to their positions along the Line. The ones within eyeshot averted their gazes or bowed their heads. Price smirked. Nothing like fear to keep his followers under control.

Another guard pushed open the security gate leading into the facility. Price drove into the compound, made a U-turn, and parked in front of the storage facility's main office, which also served as his headquarters. The others climbed out and headed back to their units. Price gave a final check of the gas and oil gauges before shutting off the engine. As he slid out of the Hummer, he noticed Carter standing a few feet away. Holding the keys in his right hand, Price raised them over his shoulder and pressed the lock button. The lights on the Hummer flashed and the alarm beeped twice.

Carter chuckled. "Why do you always do that?"

"Do what?"

"Lock the Hummer. It's not like anyone's going to steal it."

Price shrugged and headed for his quarters. "We're surrounded by criminals. Better safe than sorry."

Carter fell in beside his boss. "Any luck?"

"Not a thing. We found plenty of evidence of them going through the area on their way down to Pennsylvania, but nothing indicating they've come back this way."

"Considering what's out there, I doubt they made it that far. I wouldn't worry about it."

"I have to worry about it," Price said. "It's how I've kept us safe all these months."

"I understand."

"Besides, I wouldn't count them out yet," said Price, now more conciliatory since he had made his point. "They have vampires with them, which gives them an edge against the deaders. You saw what they did to Ike and his team. I don't want to think about what will happen if those things get lose in here."

"Do you think that's a possibility?"

"We can't rule it out. If they make it back to their camp and find it wiped out, they'll probably figure out we were involved and try to get revenge. Fuck, I know I would."

"Do you want me to send a scouting party back to their camp and watch out for them?"

"No," said Price. "It's too risky. Chances are if the survivors don't kill our people, the deaders will. We can't afford to send enough men to keep the scouting party safe."

"I could put skirmishers around the perimeter and set up roadblocks."

Price stared off to the west to where a hill overlooked the storage facility. He studied the high ground for a few seconds and shook his head. For the first time since taking over this compound, he felt nervous about their safety. "If there are vampires in their group, they'll take out anyone you post outside the compound before we can be warned."

"Well, we have that cherry picker we found here when we took over the place. I could put it at one end of the compound and post guards on it."

"You mean a makeshift watchtower?"

Carter nodded. "We have those night vision goggles we took off that National Guard unit we ambushed a few months ago. It would give us an edge."

"Do it." Price opened the door to his office and stepped inside, waving for Carter to follow him. "However, we have a bigger problem than this raiding party and its vampire pets. We have an internal threat."

"What do you mean?"

"Close the door." Price leaned his M&P15-22LR against the wall. He dropped into his chair, pulled out a drawer, and propped his feet on it. When Carter sat opposite him, Price continued. "Half of this compound poses a threat to us."

"I haven't heard any dissatisfaction from the men."

"Not them. They're loyal. I'm talking about those on the Line and the whores we're keeping here."

Carter looked confused. "You don't think they'll rise up against us?"

"Not on their own. They're too beaten down. And I doubt most of those on the Line would have the energy. But if that renegade patrol comes after us, I don't rule out the possibility that some of these people might take up arms against us. We'd then be facing a threat from inside as well as out, and we could find ourselves outnumbered. If that happens, we'll need to even the odds."

"What are you suggesting?"

"It's more of an order than a suggestion." Price pointed a finger at Carter. "I want you to develop a contingency plan to murder everyone on the Line and all the whores in the compound if we come under attack."

CHAPTER ELEVEN

The medication seemed to be working. After they had set sail from Portland, Bethany had moaned for several hours before finally drifting off to sleep. Natalie stroked her hair. Bethany's wound was worse than they had first thought. The rotter had not only bitten deeply into her cheek, it had scraped away parts of her gum, exposing the teeth.

Natalie had volunteered to sit with Bethany for a while longer when most of the other Angels left to find a place to bunk down, leaving Emily topside to teach Ari and Josephine how to operate the yacht. Natalie had told the others she wanted to sit with Bethany in case Bethany woke up and needed anything. In truth, the situation scared her and she wanted to hide her fear from the others. Acquiring the vaccine to the Zombie Virus meant the outbreak entered a different phase. Prior to this, even the smallest bite meant a death sentence for the victim, leaving the only questions as when and how to put them down. With the Angels now immunized, even several bites would no longer condemn them to turn into a rotter. However, that brought with it a host of other, vastly more complicated issues. In Bethany's case, how were they to treat a massive wound without the necessary medical facilities, especially large-scale trauma that would leave a disfiguring scar when it healed?

If it healed.

A knock sounded on the door. "Come in," she said softly.

Josephine stuck her head inside. "Sorry to bother you. We need you topside."

"Is everything okay?" she asked nervously.

"Yes, but you need to see this."

Natalie followed Josephine out of the room and up to the bridge. Once she was topside, she saw Logan International Airport, which she recognized by the twin supports of the air traffic control tower, a mile to their rear. The two women climbed the ladder to the flying bridge. Ari manned the helm, and every few seconds she glanced to the left in the same direction as Emily. Natalie made her way to the port beam and stood beside Emily.

"What do you see?"

"The ninth circle of Hell, honey."

Natalie followed their gaze and gasped.

Boston stretched out in front of them. She had made enough trips to the city to be familiar with the skyline, and felt a mixture of shock and despair over how significantly the outbreak had changed it. Two miles in the distance in the Back Bay area, the most iconic landmark, the sixty-story John Hancock Tower, was literally a shell of its former self. The sun had risen over an hour ago, bathing the city in warm light; however, the reflection on the Hancock's all-glass façade appeared disjointed because half the panels were missing, giving the impression of a partially-finished jigsaw puzzle. Its neighboring structure, the fifty-two-story Prudential Tower, no longer existed. Only wisps of white smoke marked the location where the building once stood, more than likely from fires still burning underneath the debris. Glancing toward the bow, she saw the remains of the Tobin Bridge, which connected Boston to the North Shore. The eight-hundred-foot-long, double-deck center span was gone, leaving only the on ramps and the twisted steel girders of the cantilever trusses mounted atop the cement supports.

The devastation of the skyline couldn't compare to the carnage that existed along the waterfront. The Boston Harbor Hotel had been gutted by fire, with streaks of black extending from shattered windows along the seafront façade. Less than one hundred feet from Rowes' Wharf, the top deck of a Boston Harbor cruise ship stuck out of the water at a slight angle, surrounded for hundreds of feet on either side by a virtual forest of masts and antennas from sunken sailboats and pleasure crafts. A few boats still remained tied to the pier. Natalie could see that every wharf and harbor-front street swarmed with thousands of the living dead. She didn't even want to think about the nightmare that had befallen those who had rushed to the harbor seeking safety.

As they cruised past, the horde of rotters spotted the vessel. Like a wave, the living dead pressed forward, dozens being shoved off the wharves to splash into the harbor. Even from this distance, their moans sounded deafening. Natalie felt fear start in the pit of her stomach and spread along her spine.

"How the fuck did we get here?" she barked at Ari. "Did you get lost?"

"N-No. I...."

"Don't blame her, honey. Since it wasn't that far inland from our route, I thought maybe we could find a place to refuel."

Natalie looked again at the waterfront. Even more of the rotters dropped into the harbor.

What if those fucking things can swim?

"Head back to the coast," Natalie ordered. "It's too dangerous here."

"Aye, aye, Captain," said Emily, trying to lighten the mood. She stepped up to the wheel and tapped Ari on the shoulder. "I'll take over for a while."

"Thanks."

Emily turned the yacht into a tight U-turn that brought it close to the waterfront. The horde burst into a full frenzy. The yacht maneuvered close enough to shore that she not only could smell the stench of thousands of decayed bodies, but could start to make out individual rotters in the crowd. Only when the vessel had passed Castle Island and returned safely to the outer harbor did she take her eyes off shore.

Ari stood beside her, her head bowed like a chastised child. Natalie placed an arm around her shoulder. "I didn't mean to snap at you."

Ari smiled. "Don't worry about it."

"That's my fault," said Emily.

"You're right that we need to find fuel," Natalie replied. "We just need to be more careful about where."

"There should be a lot of more isolated places where we can refuel. I just hope others didn't have the same idea."

Natalie gave a final glance toward Boston. "If what we saw back there is any indication of what we'll find up and down the coast, I doubt we'll see many survivors out here."

CHAPTER TWELVE

Robson's team had been traveling the better part of a day searching for a new, secure location to serve as their base. After making certain the Angels had gotten safely on their way, Robson led the convoy back to Kittery and then retraced the original route they had taken to get to Site R. The journey led them along the east bank of the Piscataqua River, where they eventually crossed over into New Hampshire through rotter-infested Dover. Once clear of the city, they made their way west, stopping only once before dawn to allow Dravko and Tibor to switch to the back of the Ryder before continuing. Thirty minutes after sunrise, the convoy entered Barnston.

Robson stopped on the western outskirts of town and picked up the microphone to his radio. "Heads up, people. We're not far from the spot where the rape gang ambushed us."

"I hope you're not planning on setting up camp here," DeWitt responded.

"I want to put a few more miles between us and them. I'm just getting my bearings. Hang tight, and keep your eyes open."

Robson looked over at Jennifer, who had the map spread across her knees. "What do you got?"

"Up ahead to the left is Parade Road, which is where we were camped when those assholes attacked. Just beyond that is Suncock Valley Road. I suggest we take that north and see what we can find."

"Sounds good to me." Robson continued on until he reached Suncock Valley Road and turned right. Trees lined both sides of the road, casting the area in shadows. Robson drove cautiously, half expecting to run into a roadblock set up by the rape gang. Every few seconds, his eyes glanced to the rearview mirror to make sure no one followed them. He remembered the first time they came through this territory, how peaceful and serene he found it, and how he would like to have settled down here one day if this outbreak could ever be brought under control. This time, every nerve remained on edge because he knew too well that a danger lurked in these woods greater than any rotter they could encounter.

"We should be coming to the residential community of Locke Lake any minute," said Jennifer, her concentration still focused on the map.

"You mean the former residential community," replied Robson.

"I don't under...." Jennifer's voice trailed off when she saw what he referred to.

The remnants of the town sat off to their right. Every home they could see had been ransacked, with furniture and clothing spread across the front lawns. The windows on each home had been smashed and the doors torn from their hinges. A few had been torched. Even the vehicles had suffered the same fate, with every one of them having been stripped of tires and, judging by the open gas caps, siphoned of fuel before being set ablaze. Most disturbing of all, bodies lay strewn throughout the area. At first, Robson thought they were rotters, until he drove past a group lying near the road. Though the corpses had decayed, they wore clothes in relatively good condition, something not found on the living dead. None of them seemed to have experienced head trauma. It dawned on him that these were the local citizens gunned down and left to rot.

Jennifer took a deep breath and shuddered. "None of them are women or children. That's a good sign."

"No it isn't. It means the residents of this town are probably manning the gang's outer perimeter."

The convoy approached a crossroads. The sign on the left spur read North Road. Robson pointed to it. "Where does that take us?"

"Hang on a minute." Jennifer consulted the map. "There's a small town named Gilmanton about three miles down."

"It's good enough for me. At least it's away from here." Slowing the Humvee, he veered left onto North Road and accelerated, making sure the others followed.

The road appeared as if it had not been traveled for several months. After less than ten minutes of driving, the convoy entered the outskirts of Gilmanton. The town consisted of fewer than twenty buildings, with a single street bisecting the main thoroughfare. A general store and post office sat off to the left, with private residences on the right. Two hundred feet farther down, the spire of the local church stood above the tree line. The area looked serene and untouched. None of the buildings were ransacked, like in Locke Lake. The only indication that the area had undergone a living dead apocalypse came from half a dozen rotter corpses littering the center of town, each felled with a clean shot to the head. For Robson, the place seemed as good as any, so he pulled into the parking lot of the general store.

He stepped out of the Humvee, and DeWitt joined him. "Is this where we're setting up camp?"

"This town is as good a place as any. It doesn't appear that anyone has bothered with it, rotters aren't a concern, and it's far enough off the beaten path that we shouldn't have to worry about the rape gang finding us. Just in case I'm wrong...." Robson stepped into the street and pointed to the building they had passed on the way in, the one that read Gilmanton Iron Works Construction, "there's a couple of garage bays in that building. We can park the Humvees in there to keep them out of sight."

"What about the Ryder?"

"Pull it around back. If anyone drives by, I doubt they'll even notice it."

"We'll take care of it, and we'll make sure the building is clear of rotters."

"Good. Jennifer and I will check out the general store. Call on the radio if you need back up."

"Gotcha."

After DeWitt walked away and called the others together, Robson motioned for Jennifer to join him and headed for the general store. He stepped up onto the front porch and peered through the window, scanning the aisles. He couldn't detect any movement.

"See anything?" Jennifer asked.

"Nope." He rapped on the glass several times, but still saw no signs movement.

"That's good."

"Remember what happened last time we went into a convenience store we thought was free of rotters."

"I'd rather forget that, thanks." Jennifer withdrew her .357 Magnum and grabbed the door handle. "Ladies first?"

"Be my guest," replied Robson, clutching his AA-12.

Jennifer opened the door and leaned in. "Is anyone in here?"

Silence. Jennifer stepped inside, her Magnum raised and ready to fire, and moved along the front of the store, peering down each aisle as she passed it. Robson followed to her right. When they reached the wall, he moved down the aisle to the back of the store, checking for danger. The store was empty.

Lowering the shotgun, he yelled out, "Clear!"

"Are we going to check out the back room?"

"Not yet. I want back up before we do."

Robson walked down the second aisle. All the shelves had been emptied, but not from looting because no debris lay scattered across the floor. The only items not taken, such as household goods, remained neatly stacked.

"Did you find anything?" called Jennifer from one aisle over.

"Just toilet bowl and glass cleaner."

"Nothing here, either."

"Whoever cleaned out this place did a thorough job."

Jennifer met him at the end of the aisle. "Are we making Gilmanton our new camp?"

"Just until we figure out a way to get Windows back. Then we'll find someplace more secure." He motioned toward the front door. "Come on. Let's help DeWitt and the others check out the construction company and get settled in."

CHAPTER THIRTEEN

The hand slid up Windows' back and cupped her shoulder, squeezing gently. Her eyes popped open as she jolted out of her sleep. A cold shiver shot down her spine and her skin crawled under the touch. She felt her vagina clench. She'd already had sex with Meat twice tonight. The first time, she had woken up to find her pants down around her knees with him on top of her. Then, a few hours later, he had roused her and demanded a blow job. Christ knew what he wanted now. Swallowing hard to force down the bile rising in her throat, she rolled over to face the latest indignity.

Debra knelt beside her. "How are you doing?"

"How do you think I'm doing?" Windows sat up and pulled the end of the sleeping bag across her chest, holding it tight against her. "He raped me twice last night. And Jesus Christ, doesn't he ever bathe? He smelled so bad it gagged me."

"Hygiene is not a priority around here." Debra stood up. "Besides, last night was better than the alternative."

Windows' face flushed. "That's easy for you to say. I'm the one who took over being his play toy while you got a break."

"Not for long. Meat will soon get bored and want to do us both at once." Debra wrapped an arm around her daughter, hugging her close. Her tone became hard and angry. "I went through the same thing you did my first night here, only Cindy was made to watch the entire time. So don't lecture me about how bad *you* have it."

"Sorry."

"Forget about it." Debra rubbed her daughter's head, and then looked over at Windows. "Come on. We all have chores to do around here. I got you assigned to work the kitchen detail with us. It's the best job available."

"Why's that?" Windows rolled on to her knees and began folding the sleeping bag.

"It's not that difficult. You have to prepare three meals a day, which is challenging considering how limited the food supplies are. More importantly, there are four of us in the kitchen most of the time. You'll make the fifth."

"Safety in numbers?"

Debra nodded.

"And we can sneak food," said Windows trying to lighten the mood.

"Trust me, you won't want to sneak any of what we serve here."

Five minutes later, the three girls reached the "kitchen", an empty storage unit facing the northern wall of the compound. Outside the open sliding door, a large pot hung by a chain from a tripod, with embers from a dead fire piled up underneath. One woman, a blonde in worn and dirty jeans, swept the ashes into a dustpan while a brunette with short-cropped, badly-cut hair poured water into the pot and cleaned it. Along one wall inside the unit sat a fifty-five-gallon drum filled with dirty water. A teenage girl stood in front of it, taking a soiled dish, pushing it beneath the surface, and wiping it clean with her hand. When she pulled out the dish, she flicked off the excess water and used a towel almost as dirty as the water to dry it.

Debra stepped into the middle of the women. "Girls, this is Windows. She'll be joining us on kitchen detail."

The brunette glanced up. "So, this is Meat's new whore?"

Windows bristled, but Debra interceded. "We all do what we have to in order to survive."

The brunette huffed and went back to cleaning.

Debra turned her back on the woman and spoke to Windows, gesturing behind her to the brunette. "The pleasant one here is Tracey. That's Karen." She pointed to the blonde sweeping the ashes, and then to the teenager cleaning the dishes. "And that's Lisa. Follow me."

The two stepped inside the container unit. Against the rear wall sat a stockpile of boxes of rations. Windows read the labels.

Almost everything came in cans, from luncheon meats, tuna fish, beans, and chili up to a variety of fruits and vegetables. A few cartons contained packages of jerky.

"This is all you have for rations?" asked Windows.

"It's all we have left. We went through the perishables within the first week, and all of the frozen foods shortly after. Every time the raiding parties go out foraging, they bring back as many canned goods as they can find. The past two months they've come back empty. Everything within a forty mile radius has either been cleaned out by us or someone else, or it's in one of the big towns where there are too many deaders to get it. At the rate we're going, we'll be out of food in a month."

"Then what happens?"

Debra shrugged and looked away. She picked up a metal plate that held a pile of baked beans and two strips of beef jerky, and handed it to Windows. "Since we're done here, you get to feed our special guest."

"Special guest?"

"The creepy man," whispered Cindy.

"He's not creepy," Debra gently admonished. "He's just old."

"I don't understand," said Windows.

Debra motioned for Windows to follow. They walked down to the end of the compound to the last unit in the far corner. The words KEEP OUT were written on the door in red paint. A padlock kept the sliding door secured to the frame. Debra bent down, removed a set of keys from her pocket, and opened it. Sliding the lock out of the ground mounting, she placed it to one side and lifted up the door halfway. When Windows didn't move, she motioned inside. "Go ahead."

Windows bent down and ducked under, and Debra closed the door behind her.

This unit was even more Spartan than her own living quarters, which said a lot. The "furniture" consisted of a dirty sleeping bag crumpled up in one corner and a bucket in the opposite. The only light came from a battery-operated lantern placed in the center of the floor, its beam so dull that it barely lit the corners. A heavy stench of urine and shit permeated the room. She assumed the odor came from the bucket, which must have served as a toilet.

A raspy voice came out of nowhere. "Hello."

Windows spun around, searching for the person associated with the voice. Fear threatened to overwhelm her, and she fought back the urge to scream. Instead, she prepared to fight, fueling it with her rage, rage that came from Debra having set her up. Windows would deal with her if she got out of here alive. Right now, her eyes darted around the unit, but she couldn't see into the corners because of the dark.

"I didn't mean to startle you."

Something stirred inside the sleeping bag. One of the flaps fell to the side, revealing a haggard old man sitting underneath. She had not noticed him at first because his clothes appeared as threadbare and filthy as the sleeping bag. Long, white, unwashed hair hung in clumps off his head and draped across his shoulder, with several loose strands sticking against his scraggly beard. His features were drawn and gaunt. She could hardly see his eyes between the dark circles under them and the lack of light, but they mirrored a broken and defeated soul. The fingers on both his hands twisted in unnatural positions and curled in against the palms at awkward angles. Placing his deformed hands on the ground, he struggled to sit upright, and then leaned back into the corner. When he did, the odor of feces became so overwhelming Windows gagged.

"Sorry about the smell." The old man raised his gnarled hands. "Hygiene is not easy for someone in my condition."

Windows hesitated. Nothing in his manner was threatening, so she cautiously approached. "I have your dinner."

"Is it that time already?"

He pulled the loose flap of the sleeping bag back across his lap to mask the stench and held out his hands. Windows tried to hand him the plate, but he could not hold it because of his fingers. The plate started to slide, threatening to spill the food across his lap. Windows caught it at the last minute and tilted it so the contents moved back to the center. Moving closer to the old man, she knelt beside him and scooped up a forkful of beans.

"You don't have to do this," he croaked, his tone neither defiant nor proud, but one of a man long used to being mistreated.

"I know."

Windows moved the fork closer, and the old man leaned forward and opened his mouth. He chewed furiously and swallowed, and opened his mouth for more. Windows obliged. The poor old man was starving, a sensation she remembered well from her first few weeks on the road right after the outbreak. It dawned on her that no one had ever fed him before. Oh sure, Debra and the others had brought him his food. With his deformed hands he couldn't eat, which explained his appearance and his soiled clothes. She couldn't imagine what hell he must have gone through these past several months.

Windows noticed a single tear sliding down his cheek, leaving a grimy path through the dirt.

CHAPTER FOURTEEN

DeWitt stood in the center of the doorway. "We need you outside."

Robson set down his end of the desk that he and Jennifer were moving out of a windowless office to convert into living quarters for Dravko and Tibor. "Is there a problem?"

"Not yet. We have company."

Robson reached for his AA-12. "Rotters or gang members?"

"Neither." DeWitt stepped aside and held open the door. "Come see for yourself."

Robson and Jennifer followed DeWitt outside into the parking lot. A single figure approached the compound from the same direction they had driven in earlier that day. Robson assessed him as approximately thirty years of age, with an average height and build. He wore a hunter's camouflage jacket and matching pants, plus a black baseball cap with the Boston Police logo emblazoned across the front. A sniper rifle hung over his left shoulder. The visitor walked down the center of the road so everyone could see him, approaching at a slow pace so as not to pose a threat. By his demeanor and actions, Robson pegged him as a cop. That meant he probably represented no immediate danger. If he did, then his skill level would outmatch everyone except Robson.

Out of the corner of his eye, Robson noticed Jennifer place a hand on her holstered Magnum and move off to the right to provide cover fire if necessary. When the others saw this, they also spread out, forming a phalanx around the visitor. The visitor paused. He spread his arms to the sides with the palms out, showing that he held no weapons.

"I'm not here to start trouble," said the visitor. The "r" in start sounded more like an "h," signifying a Boston accent.

"Good," said Robson. "Because that's the last thing we need. Put your weapon on the ground and slowly approach."

"Sorry, I'm not going to disarm myself."

"Then I guess we'll just have to shoot you."

"I doubt that."

Man, this guy has balls, thought Robson. "And why won't I?"

"You're a fellow cop, so I assume you won't shoot me without good reason."

"Stay where you are and don't move." Robson approached the visitor, watching for any sudden movement. The visitor looked relaxed.

When Robson got to within ten feet of the visitor, the latter said, "If you're planning on frisking me, I have a Colt .45 strapped in a shoulder holster and a hunting knife lodged against my back."

"Show me."

The visitor slowly reached for the flaps of his jacket. Robson heard the others raise their weapons. Without taking his eyes off the visitor, Robson waved his hand in a downward motion, ordering his people to stand down. The visitor clasped the flaps of his jacket and opened the ends, and then turned in a circle. Sure enough, he wore a Colt .45 strapped into a shoulder holster and had a hunting knife lodged against his back.

When the visitor faced forward again, he let the flaps of his jacket drop and again extended his hands with the palms open. "Are we okay?"

"For now." Robson stepped forward and extended his hand. "I'm Mike Robson, the leader of this group."

"Neal Simmons. Consider me the local welcoming committee."

"I assume there are more of you?"

Simmons nodded.

"And I assume at least one of them has a sniper rifle trained on my head ready to take me out if we moved against you?"

"I knew a fellow cop would have figured that out. No offense."

Robson chuckled. "I would have done the same thing. How did you know I was a cop?"

"We've been watching you all day. You give orders like someone used to commanding authority. The clincher was when you approached me like I was an armed suspect."

Impressive, thought Robson. "What can I do for you?"

"We wanted to invite you to have dinner." He pronounced it "dinnah."

"Are you serious?" Robson must have said it louder than he meant to because he heard the others raise their weapons again. He shouted, "Put those things away!"

"Thanks," said Simmons.

"Don't mind them. We've been on the road so long we're all a bit jumpy."

"Well, the invitation to dinner is still on. It's been awhile since we've talked to anyone, and we would love to know what's going on out there."

"I don't know. There's still—"

Simmons cut him off. "I can offer you a hot meal and a cold beer."

"What time do you want us there?"

* * *

Simmons wasn't kidding about a hot meal. Robson could not remember the last time he ate this good. Dinner consisted of vegetables and venison, real venison cooked over an open fire rather than dried jerky. And cold beer. Honest to goodness, cold beer. He hadn't had one of those since before the apocalypse. By the end of his second bottle, he felt his thinking getting fuzzy, the effect of not having a drink for so long. But damn, did it taste good. After everything they had gone through the past few weeks, this return to normalcy, even if only brief and surreal, was refreshing.

Robson focused his attention on the others. The survivors of Fort McClary sat around the dining room table of the church rectory, eight in total. Two weeks ago, before that fateful mission to Site R, they had numbered more than fifty. Now his numbers were half that, and most of his people had been sent off on a yacht to Omaha. He tried not to dwell on it.

"You have a sweet deal going on here," said Robson as he speared carrots onto the end of his fork. "We haven't seen anything like this before."

Simmons nodded his thanks. "We lucked into this."

"We" referred to Isaac Wayans, Simmons' partner. He stood over six feet tall and weighed at least two hundred and fifty pounds, all of it muscle. Wayans wore his Boston Police BDUs. He hardly said a word during dinner, eating his meal with a sullen expression that furrowed his bald pate.

When his buddy refused to respond, Simmons patted him on the shoulder. "This town is so small, we're the only ones who care about it. The general store is the most significant spot, and the locals emptied that out before they left."

"So the locals just abandoned this town?"

"Not a soul in sight when we arrived, although as best as I can tell there were only a few people living here to begin with. That's why we set up camp around the church. The steeple gives us a good vantage point to survey the surrounding area. Over time, we commandeered a few solar-powered generators to keep the meat we hunt frozen."

"And keep the beer cold," said DeWitt, holding up his bottle.

Simmons smiled. "We live here in the pastor's house, and keep a get-away vehicle hidden off the road half a mile to the north. So far, no one has noticed us."

Jennifer sat forward and leaned her arms on the table. "How did you wind up here?"

"When we left Boston," started Simmons, "we headed north—"

"I mean, what's your story? What made you guys abandon the city to take up residence in a pastor's house in the middle of nowhere."

Simmons went silent and averted his eyes from his guests. Wayans glanced over at his buddy and then the others. He spoke in a low, deep tone tinged with an anger and disgust that seemed menacing.

"Lady, we left the world behind when it went to friggin' hell."

CHAPTER FIFTEEN

Everyone stared at Wayans. He took a deep breath, held it for ten seconds, and exhaled. Although his anger dissipated, the disgust still remained.

"Simmons and I made up the Boston Police sniper team and were on duty when those friggin' things... what did you call them, rotters? ... started coming back from the dead. The mayor was friggin' useless. The first day of the outbreak, when they brought the first bite victims into Mass General, he went on television and ranted about the gun culture and violent video games causing people to attack each other. It took him two days to figure out this wasn't a bunch of friggin' druggies strung out on bath salts, but a real pandemic. By then the outbreak had spread all over the city. Downtown became a killing zone, and in places like Southie and Roxbury, people took matters into their own hands. They couldn't hold it back. By the end of the third day, everyone not already dead was making an exodus out of the city.

"For some friggin' reason, the mayor took it upon himself to contain the outbreak. There were already reports of infections as far north as Beverly and as far south as Fall River. He closed down the Callahan and Sumner Tunnels and set up roadblocks on the roads out of the city, checking everyone for bite marks before letting them pass. One was set up in the center of the Tobin Bridge. We were assigned to the Chelsea end, and set ourselves up in one of them three families alongside the bridge. We had orders to shoot anyone who jumped the roadblock and tried to escape. Only one attempt occurred, some guy with a wife and three kids. Can't say I blame him. I wouldn't want to be trapped in a city being overrun by the dead just because some friggin' politician is looking out for his political future. But orders are orders. So we blew out the tires and immobilized his car, and then held him at gunpoint until the cops came for him and brought him back to the roadblock. After that, no one made a run for it. Talk about a friggin' crappy assignment. It beat manning the roadblocks though. We were in constant radio contact with the guys on the bridge, and every time they called in you could hear screaming, arguing, crying. A friggin' madhouse.

"About two hours into our shift, all hell broke loose. Not sure exactly what happened. As far as I can tell someone must have either turned at the roadblock, or the dead finally reached them. Whatever happened, everyone broke and ran, a couple of thousand people swarming across the bridge hoping to get to safety. We didn't know what to do and then... then...." Wayans paused, fighting back his emotions. "Someone blew up the friggin' bridge. The charges were rigged to detach the two center spans. They collapsed onto each other and pancaked into the Mystic River. I don't know what bothered me more; listening to the cries of help of all those dropped into the river, or the terrified screams of those still trapped on the southern span of the bridge being overrun by the dead."

Jennifer placed a hand over her mouth. "Oh, my God."

"God had nothing to do with it, lady."

"The mayor ordered the bridge destroyed with all those people on it?" asked Robson.

Wayans shrugged. "The mayor, or someone who took his orders too seriously. It doesn't friggin' matter. Thousands died on that bridge. Plus we heard explosions throughout the city. Not sure where they came from. From what I could tell from the smoke, they also detonated the Sumner and Callahan Tunnels as well as the underground expressway. Few people made it out of Boston alive."

"What'd you do?" asked Jennifer.

"Nothing we could do. We got the friggin' hell out of there as fast as possible. We made it as far as Revere before the highway became impassable. We took the back roads until we found a Harley shop, confiscated a few bikes, and headed north."

"And that's when you found this place," said Robson.

"Yeah. Friggin' paradise."

Wayans went silent, so Simmons took up the conversation. "It actually took us a few weeks to find this place. By that time, I had a bad case of the flu, so we crashed here for a week until I got better. Once we realized how secure it was, we decided to stay permanently. We've been here almost seven months."

"No one else ever came by?" asked DeWitt.

"They did, but we never reached out to them. Most were either trouble or stupid, and we didn't want to be holding their hand." Simmons slapped a hand against Wayans' arm. "Remember that moron who came by here a few weeks ago?"

Wayans chuckled. "The jerk was driving a Toyota Corolla, not the best vehicle for surviving the zombie apocalypse. He left his wife and kid sitting in the car while he walks into the general store like everything was normal. Don't know how that friggin' guy lasted so long."

"What made you want to reach out to us?" asked Robson.

"*We* didn't," Wayans sneered.

Simmons cast his friend a disapproving glance. "I saw you when you rolled into town, and you looked like you knew what you were doing. I figured you were safe. Besides, we've been cut off for so long, I hoped to get some news about the outside world and find out your story."

Robson spent the next hour relating the details of Fort McClary and how their lives fell apart with the arrival of Dr. Compton, his claim to have a vaccine for the Zombie Virus, the disastrous journey down to Site R, and what they found upon returning to the fort. He concluded with their recent escapade in Portland.

When he finished, Wayans stared at him. He pointed to Dravko and Tibor. "You mean those two are friggin' vampires?"

Tibor leaned forward and smiled, baring his fangs.

Wayans shook his head. "Friggin' unbelievable."

"You don't seem surprised," Robson said to Simmons.

"Are you serious? If you told me a year ago I'd be hiding out in a church avoiding the zombie apocalypse, I would have locked you up. The existence of vampires seems blasé now." Simmons glanced over at Dravko. "No offense."

The vampire nodded. "None taken."

"What now?" Simmons asked.

"We're just going to rest up here a few days and scope out the rape gang's hideout, and then we'll get Windows back and be gone."

"Is that the gang who took over the old storage facility down off of 28?"

Robson nodded.

"Do you need help?" asked Simmons.

"You don't have to do this," answered Robson.

"Yeah, man." Wayans looked confused. "Why do you want to get involved?"

"Because I'm tired of just sitting around here," said Simmons. "This is the same gang that destroyed Locke Lake five months ago, and we did nothing."

"We *couldn't* help them. There are only the two of us. You friggin' want to blow this deal to get involved in a fight that's not ours?"

"Yes. We used to *protect* people. If these guys have the balls to take on the rape gang to save one of their own, I want to help them."

"Why?" Wayans nearly spat the word.

"Because I'd rather die on my feet than live on my knees."

Wayans huffed and crossed his arms across his massive chest.

"That is," Simmons directed to Robson, "if you want our help?"

Robson smiled. "Hell, yes."

CHAPTER SIXTEEN

Natalie checked her watch for the tenth time that hour. It read six minutes before eight AM.

Good. Only a few minutes left until shift change.

She glanced over at the others. Tiara was napping on one of the seats. Sandy sat in front of the radar, her head drooping until any sudden motion woke her up. Sandy had been doing this every few minutes for the past hour. Normally, Natalie would chastise her for falling asleep at her post, especially since a dense fog had rolled in a few hours earlier, cutting visibility to less than a hundred feet. She would probably be dozing off herself if she wasn't so wound up. Not that she had a reason to be. Other than flotsam near some of the larger port cities and the occasional stray small boat, they had not run into anything significant since Boston. As far as she could tell, they were the only ones around for hundreds of miles.

Having three people on duty to run the yacht during each eight-hour shift might have been superfluous; however, it kept the Angels occupied, which she considered important right now. They had spent the entire previous day cruising down the coast, every city or town they came across ravaged and swarming with rotters. Nowhere did they see any signs of survivors. By late afternoon, the Angels had become morose, so Natalie ordered Josephine to take the yacht twenty miles off shore where they couldn't witness the endless destruction and devastation. She then set up the three-team shifts so they wouldn't just sit around growing more depressed. With luck, it would keep up their spirits for the rest of the trip.

If her own emotions served as an example, it would fail miserably.

Natalie sighed. She had not been this miserable since the first weeks of the outbreak. She missed Robson. Ever since his team had picked her up outside of York Beach in southern Maine and brought her back to Fort McClary, the two of them had been together. She had even fallen in love with him, and they had consummated their relationship at Site R. At that time, everything had seemed so promising. They had become lovers, had defeated Compton's plan to kill them all, and had brought samples of the Zombie Vaccine to Fort McClary to forward it to the government-in-exile in Omaha. That's when everything fell apart. Now she sat on a yacht heading for Omaha while Robson went on a suicide mission to save Windows from the rape gang.

God, she missed him. It went beyond a physical attraction, though that was a major part of it. She missed the little things. The way he'd smile at her from across the compound. The way he laughed. The way he used to make hand contact with her, which appeared innocent enough even though it harbored deeper feelings. He had been a major part of her life for these past seven months, one of those constants in her day-to-day existence, and one of the few things that gave her focus. Now he was gone. Not dead, although he might as well be. Even if he and the others survived the raid on the compound, the chances of the two of them ever seeing each other again were minimal.

The sound of approaching footsteps jarred Natalie out of her self-pity. Emily, Ari, and Bethany ascended the ladder to the flying bridge.

"Morning, honey." Emily slid up beside Natalie. "Anything exciting happen last night?"

"Thank God, no."

"You didn't run into any zombie sharks?"

"No!" Natalie had never considered the possibility that the Zombie Virus could species jump, and didn't want to start thinking about that now.

"Just teasing." Emily gave her a hug around the shoulders. "What's our location?"

"My best guess is we're somewhere off the Outer Banks of North Carolina. I can't tell for certain." Natalie pointed to the state-of-the-art GPS chart plotter. "The GPS is acting funny."

"That's not surprising. GPS satellites require ground control station updates to maintain coverage. Without that guidance, readings become inaccurate and many areas will suffer from low confidence. We're making good time." Emily examined the navigation charts. "How's Doug running?"

Natalie furrowed her eyebrows. "Who's Doug?"

"That's what I call our yacht."

"Why Doug?"

"I named it after an old boyfriend who treated me like shit in college. Like him, I'm going to use it to my advantage, run it into the ground, and then leave it when I'm done." Emily flashed a conspiratorial smile. "Never screw over Southern women."

Natalie chuckled. It had been a long time since she found humor in anything. She gave Emily a mock salute. "The bridge is yours, Captain."

Emily slid behind the wheel. "Aye, matey." The pirate accent mixed with a Southern drawl didn't sound right.

Ari replaced Sandy at the radar. Ari checked the screen when she called out, "We have a contact at bearing 338."

"Shit, I missed that?" asked Sandy.

"It just appeared. It's five miles out."

"Is it a lighthouse?" Natalie asked.

"It's too far from shore to be a lighthouse. And it's too big." Emily studied the charts. "There's nothing listed in this area as a navigational hazard. It has to be a ship."

"It's pretty big," said Ari.

"What's its course and speed?"

Ari watched the radar for several seconds. "It's not moving."

"A derelict?" asked Tiara.

"Possibly," said Emily. "Or they could just be coasting. Where else can they go? I'll set a course so we steer clear of it."

"No," countered Natalie. "Let's check it out."

"Do you think that's a good idea?" asked Ari.

"They may have fuel we can use. I'd rather get it out here than have to try and go ashore for it."

"Suppose they're not friendly?" asked Emily.

Natalie thought about that for a minute. "Sandy, go downstairs and wake the Angels. Take Tiara and Bethany with you. I want all of you locked and loaded in five minutes. Stay below deck. It this ship turns out to be trouble, I want to have the element of surprise. If it's friendly, then you can stow the weapons and come on up."

Sandy nodded and led the others down below.

Natalie turned back to Emily. "How long until we reach it?"

"Just a few minutes. I sure hope you know what you're doing."

"So do I."

The fog surrounded the yacht like a cocoon. Natalie had appreciated it because it offered them a sense of security, however superficial. Now it worked against them, preventing them from knowing what was ahead. With each passing minute, she became more uncertain about her decision. Every time Ari called out the distance from the mysterious vessel, Natalie wanted to order Emily to change heading. Yet she knew she couldn't. Avoiding the unknown was not an option, especially if they might be able to refuel without having to go ashore. When Sandy came up to let her know the Angels were ready she felt a little more secure.

"We're a mile out." Ari lifted her head from the radar and visually searched for the vessel. Emily reduced speed to zero knots, allowing the yacht to coast.

A few seconds later, a shadow appeared in the fog, becoming a virtual wall of steel that loomed out of the murk stretching out for hundreds of feet. As they drew closer, an outline began to form in the mist. Natalie recognized it as a cruise ship. Multiple decks stacked one on top of the other towered above them, the top decks obscured by fog. Even the gloom could not conceal the dried blood that flowed through the drain holes and stained the hull red. The yacht drew closer, and Emily steered to starboard to parallel the vessel.

A sudden shift in the wind to the north confirmed her worst fears. As the breeze flowed across the cruise ship and past the yacht, it brought with it the stench of decay. A second later, the collective moaning of hundreds of living dead broke the silence. Looking up, the women saw a mass of rotters lining the deck and leaning over the rail, arms flailing at the only food they had seen in months. Some lost their balance and tumbled over the side, others were shoved off by the mass of living dead forming behind them. The yacht coasted by, the swarm following along the deck, moving en masse.

"This is as bad as Site R," Ari mumbled.

The words rang loud to Natalie. The battle with the four hundred rotters in the access tunnel leading to the underground facility had destroyed the Angels' spirit and fractured their unity as a fighting force.

A gasp from behind her caught Natalie's attention. She spun around to see the rest of the Angels on deck, staring up at the mass of living dead swarming along the rail. Josephine's mouth hung agape. Those shoved off deck splashed into the water and sank beneath the surface.

"Get us out of here," she said.

Emily pushed the throttles forward. The yacht picked up speed, racing along the cruise ship's beam. With the increased noise and movement, the horde went into a frenzy. They chased after the yacht, pushing along the rail and spreading out across the fantail. Between their mass and momentum, the horde couldn't stop when they reached the stern and began dropping from the ship like lemmings off a cliff. A virtual rain of living dead flowed from the fantail into the ocean, disappearing beneath the surface. Within a few seconds, the fog engulfed the cruise ship, although the wail of the hungry rotters and their splashing into the ocean followed the yacht for almost a minute before fading away.

The Angels went back below deck, their fragile cohesion damaged even further. Josephine sat down on the deck and cried. Natalie didn't blame her. Hell, she wanted to do the same thing, and probably would have if she didn't have to maintain this stoicism of command façade.

Emily clasped her shoulder. "Honey, go below and get some sleep."

"Who can sleep after that?"

"You have to. You're what's holding those girls together. If you fall apart, we might as well just scuttle this thing at sea and get it over with."

Emily was right. The rest of the Angels had always looked to her for guidance, even more so now after Site R. She hated the idea of having so much responsibility, but couldn't shirk it. Once they reached Omaha and passed along the vaccine, she planned on disbanding the Angels and going her own way, which meant heading back to Maine to find Robson.

"I'm heading below," said Natalie. "You're in charge."

"I'll call you if we run into anything else."

"Thanks."

Natalie did not even want to contemplate what other horrors waited for them out here.

CHAPTER SEVENTEEN

Last night had been a good night for Windows. Meat had gone out for several hours and returned horny and drunk. He had almost been gentle with her, foregoing rough sex and his usual litany of derogatory remarks. Thankfully, he finished after a few minutes and passed out, which allowed her to get a good sleep for a change. As an added bonus, Meat was still asleep when she got up this morning, so she snuck out to do her breakfast detail without having to perform a morning quickie.

It didn't dawn on Windows until she reached the kitchen that she had not seen Debra or Cindy all night, and neither of them was there to help prepare breakfast. A sense of panic began to set in.

Tracey saw her and frowned. "It's about time you showed up. The three of us have been doing all the work while you and Debra whore for Meat."

"I haven't seen Debra or Cindy since yesterday," snapped Windows.

Karen and Lisa glanced at each other with an expression of concern.

"What's wrong?" Windows asked. The women averted their eyes. Windows grabbed Tracey by the arm and yanked to get her attention. "Tell me."

Tracey shrugged her arm away. "You don't fucking get it. You're the new flavor of the month for Meat, so Debra is out on her ass."

"What does that mean?"

"That means the bitch and her little brat are fair game now. They're either in the Rape Room or on the Line."

Windows rushed out of the kitchen, ignoring Tracey's protests about having to cook breakfast on her own. She found Cindy crouched in front of the Rape Room, clutching her knees tightly against her chest.

Windows sat down beside her and wrapped an arm around her. Cindy leaned in close, but would not meet her gaze.

"Hey, kid. Are you okay?"

Cindy nodded.

Windows did not want to know the answer to the next question. She took a deep breath and asked. "Did anyone touch you or hurt you?"

This time Cindy shook her head. Windows exhaled with relief.

The little girl looked up. Tears filled her eyes. "They hurt Mommy."

"Who hurt your mother?"

"They all did."

Cindy leaned her head into Windows. She felt the girl's tears soaking her shirt. Windows held her tight and let her cry. After a few minutes, she asked, "Where is your mother now?"

Cindy pointed to the Rape Room. "She's in there. They took her in last night. Mommy told me to stay out here and wait for her, and not to go in no matter what."

"You're a good girl." Windows hugged Cindy and kissed the top of her head. "Let me go check on your mother. Stay here and don't move, and scream like hell if anyone bothers you."

"I will."

Windows stood up and stepped over to the door. Grabbing the handle, she raised it just enough to crouch and duck under, and then lowered it behind her. The moment she saw the interior, the memories of her second night on the compound rushed back to her, numbing her senses. She fought back the urge vomit. She had to check on Debra.

She found Debra curled up naked in a fetal position on the floor under the wooden table, her back to the door. The torn remnants of her pants and blouse covered her bruised body, providing scant protection against the cold. At first, Windows feared the worst until she saw Debra's chest rising and falling with each breath. Inwardly, she breathed a sigh of relief until she moved around to her front. Debra had been roughed up pretty bad. She had discolored bruises across her thighs and cheeks as well as a split lip. Her right eye was swollen shut from where someone had punched her. Small streams of blood trickled from her anus and vagina. Windows didn't even want to imagine what had gone on in here last night.

Bending over, Windows placed her hand on the woman's shoulder and gently shook her. "Debra, are you okay?"

Debra's eyes shot open, growing wide in terror. A sharp, fearful cry escaped from her mouth. She punched and kicked at Windows, so stricken with panic that most of the blows glanced off. After a few seconds, Debra rolled over facing the opposite wall and scurried on her hands and knees for the far corner. She crouched there, her back to Windows, whimpering.

"It's okay. It's me, Windows. I'm not going to hurt you."

Debra turned her head and, seeing her friend, calmed down. Windows came closer and crouched three feet away, just out of striking distance. "Are you all right?"

"Do I look all right?" Debra screamed.

"What happened?"

"They... they...."

"Who are 'they'?"

A few moments passed while the woman sobbed. She then took a deep breath and began. "Meat brought me here last night. I thought maybe, after spending so much time with you, he wanted some alone time with me. When we got here they.... Fifteen guys were waiting for me. They were all drinking and having a good time, and Meat made me have sex with all of them."

"I'm sorry."

Debra shook her head. "That wasn't the bad part. By the time I had finished and gotten dressed, they were all rowdy. They wanted a second go around. When I refused, they beat me up, tore my clothes off, and took me two and three at a time. Meat stood in the corner, laughing and egging them on. The more they humiliated me, the louder he laughed."

"Where was Cindy during all this?"

"Outside the door." Debra panicked and sat upright. "Oh, my God. Where is Cindy?"

"She's fine." Windows wrapped and arm around Debra. "I found her sitting outside. No one harmed her."

Debra leaned into Windows and sobbed. "This is my fault. I hooked you up with Meat hoping to get a break, and instead he picked you over me. This is going to happen to me every night now!" she wailed.

Windows hugged Debra close and let her cry. She remained silent. Partly because she didn't know what to say, and partly because she knew this could just as easily be her.

CHAPTER EIGHTEEN

Robson, DeWitt, Simmons, and Wayans lay prone on top of the hill overlooking the storage facility, concealed behind a row of bushes. Robson realized he had spied on the rape gang from this same hill just two weeks earlier. Each of them examined the facility through a pair of binoculars, except for Wayans, who used the scope on his sniper rifle, ready to defend the group if necessary. The afternoon sun sat high in the sky, allowing them to get a good view. DeWitt divided his attention between the binoculars and a notepad, jotting down every detail of the compound.

"Jesus Christ," whispered Simmons. "What the fuck are those people doing tied down outside the compound?"

"We think it's their version of an early warning system," Robson replied. "While the rotters are feeding on them, it gives the compound time to man their defenses."

"But who are those people?"

Wayans huffed. "Probably survivors from Locke Lake and other towns they raided."

"Have you ever been here before?" asked Robson.

Simmons shrugged. "About five months ago, right after we first noticed these guys cruising the area. We tracked them back here to see what trouble we faced. At that time, they were turning the facility into a fortified compound and hadn't set up an outer perimeter yet."

"It's disgusting," said DeWitt.

"It's friggin' ingenious," said Wayans.

Robson lowered the binoculars. "What do you mean?"

"Those people tied up out there are gonna make a fuss no matter who shows up, including us. Our chances of sneaking in to get your friend just dropped by more than half."

Robson hadn't thought about that. If just one of those people started screaming, mistaking them for rotters, the entire compound would be alerted. A tough job just got damn near impossible.

"We got activity," said Simmons.

A black Hummer H3 sped down the main road and slowed as it approached the compound. The vehicle bounced off the road and into the driveway, dislodging a backpack from the rear that fell onto the pavement. The driver came to a stop in front of the gate and sounded the horn. After more than a minute, the main gate to the facility opened a few feet and two figures emerged. One stopped in the center of the security zone while the other rushed to the chain link fence, unsecured the lock, and slid the gate aside. While the Hummer pulled in and stopped by the first figure, the one who opened the gate stepped past the Hummer and walked outside to get the backpack.

* * *

Price climbed out of the driver's seat and frowned as Carter approached. "What took you so long to open the gate?"

Carter stopped ten feet from his boss. "You're back earlier than expected. I wanted to be sure everything was okay before I let anyone in. Those vampires are still out there."

"And you think they're a threat in the middle of the fucking day?"

"No, but the assholes who took down Ike and the others are."

Price held up his hands in mock surrender. "Sorry. I'm pissed. We've been out there for weeks searching for these people, and all we've done is waste half our gas reserves."

"Maybe we should stand down."

Price shook his head. "I don't want to get caught with our pants down like we did last time."

"Last time was different. No one expected to run into a truck full of blood suckers. Besides, if they were coming after us, they probably would have done so by now."

Price turned from his deputy and stared out across the road. Of course, Carter was right. This band of mercenaries had only been passing through when Ike's team had come across them. Sure, they would want revenge for what he did to their compound, assuming these guys even made it back from Pennsylvania, which under the circumstances....

A flock of birds took flight from the tree line around the compound, their wings flapping furiously as they made a sudden turn and headed for the safety of the nearby woods. Seconds later, a herd of deer bolted down the road. Price knew what caused the mass panic.

"Runners!"

Jimmy had picked up the backpack when he heard Price yell. He stared at Price, confused, and then glanced over his shoulder as five runners broke through the tree line, chasing after the deer. On seeing Jimmy, they veered off the road and rushed the gate. Jimmy dropped the backpack and broke into a run.

Those inside the Hummer had already climbed out of the vehicle and dashed toward the compound gate. Carter made the first steps in that direction, pausing to check on Price.

"Come on!" Carter yelled.

Jimmy slowed down and tried to close the gate. It cost him his life. He had slid it halfway shut when the first runner reached him. Jimmy turned to escape, but from a standstill could not get up enough speed, and made it only a few feet before the runner tackled him to the ground. The second runner fell on him. Jimmy howled in agony as they tore open his abdomen and feasted on his intestines.

The other three pushed their way through the half-open gate, their attention fixed on Price.

"Price, move your ass!" yelled Carter, who had retreated to the main gate. The guards were already sliding it shut. "Now!"

The last yell brought Price back to reality. He didn't have time to get his M&P15-22LR from the Hummer, so he sprinted for the gate. Around him, everyone tethered to stakes in the security zone screamed or begged for help. With luck, the runners would ignore him and go after the easy prey.

* * *

Windows and the rest of the kitchen staff were preparing lunch when all hell broke loose inside the compound. Those gang members milling around waiting to be served dropped their plates and dashed off, their voices joining the fray. Windows could feel the panic spreading through the compound.

Debra clutched Cindy against her chest.

"What's up?" Windows asked.

"We're under attack."

Windows' hopes soared. Maybe the others had come to rescue her. "From who?"

"Not from who. From deaders."

Windows dashed out of the kitchen, leaving the other women cowering, and ran off after the men to see if she could be of help.

* * *

Price raced as fast as he could, and still the gate seemed too far away. Terrified shrieks came from behind him. Turning his head, he saw two of the runners break away and head into the security zone, each singling out one of the people tethered to stakes. The closest, a woman, yanked so hard against her restraints that blood spurted from her wrist. The other, an older man, screamed and drew his tattered blanket over his head. Both runners ripped into them. The fifth followed behind Price and closed in fast. Christ, if only he hadn't left his weapon in the Hummer.

The gate stood partially open, with just enough space for him to slide by. Only a few feet to go. He could hear the footsteps of the runner closing in. Price increased his speed. The gate opened a little wider, allowing Price through. Just as he passed, Carter stepped into the opening, a Model 986 9mm revolver clutched in his hand. He raised the weapon and fired five rounds into the runner's face, vaporizing its head. The decapitated body crumpled to the ground inches from the gate. Stepping inside, Carter closed it shut and ordered the others to secure it.

Price leaned against a nearby motorcycle, trying to catch his breath. "Thanks."

"No problem. Are you okay?"

"A little winded." Taking a deep breath, Price pointed to the gate. "But we need to take care of those things."

"I'm on it." Carter snapped his fingers to get the attention of the closest gang member. "Get my rifle."

* * *

Windows reached the main gate as two of the gang members secured the lock. Carter issued orders while Price leaned against a motorcycle and bent over, panting. With luck, the son of a bitch had been bitten and would die soon. Ignoring them, she made her way to the gate. She hoped to see something, but the gate was closed too securely, leaving less than an inch of space. She placed her eye against the opening and peered out, moving her head from side to side to get a better view until a hand grabbed her shoulder and yanked her away.

Carter glared at her. "What the fuck are you doing here?"

"I wanted to see what was going on. Maybe I can help."

Carter lifted her up by her arm, forcing Windows to stand on her toes. "Maybe you'd like to be bait again and draw those things into the open?"

The memory of that afternoon cowed her. She averted her gaze and shook her head. Carter shoved her aside with such force she nearly fell over. "Then get back to the kitchen with the other cunts."

Someone ran up with a rifle and a satchel of ammunition and handed it to Carter. He swung them over his shoulders and made his way toward where a cherry picker sat against the outer wall. Windows took advantage of the momentary distraction and snuck away, chastising herself. This wasn't Fort McClary. She'd be dead in no time if she kept on trying to be part of the team. She headed back to the kitchen to check on Debra and Cindy.

* * *

"There she is!" DeWitt nearly yelled.

"Who?" Robson asked, his attention focused on the rotter attack.

"Windows. Approaching the main gate."

Robson swung his binoculars to see inside the compound. Sure enough, Windows was amongst the throng of people racing around the main gate. She didn't appear to be in the best shape. Then he saw the tall asshole who had been issuing orders grab her by the arms and rough her up. No wonder she looked like she did. Robson studied the asshole's face. If he had the chance, he would make sure the fucker got some karmic payback. Robson kept his eyes on Windows until she skulked out of the area and disappeared from sight. They needed to get her out as soon as possible.

"Shit," Simmons spat.

"What's wrong?" asked Robson.

"Things for us just went from sucks to sucks big time." Simmons pointed.

Robson followed his finger, and from \the other side of the compound, a cherry picker basket lifted above the opposite side of the wall. In it stood the asshole, a Macmillan TAC-50 sniper rifle clutched in his hands.

* * *

Carter scanned the outside perimeter and gauged the situation. Two of the runners had devoured Jimmy, and had his intestines spread out on the pavement around him. The third was still chewing on the woman. Attracted by the panicked screams from the nearby people, the fourth had stopped feeding on the older man and moved on to the next person, a middle-aged woman who pleaded with it for mercy.

Like that would work, you stupid fucking cunt.

Shouldering the Macmillan TAC-50, Carter aimed at Jimmy and peered through the scope. The kid's arms still twitched. Poor bastard. Carter didn't have a clear shot at Jimmy's head, so he centered the crosshairs on the back skull of the nearest runner that was bent over Jimmy's abdomen and shoving intestines into its mouth. Carter took a deep breath and held it, wrapped his finger around the trigger, and squeezed in one fluid motion. The recoil from the rifle pushed against his shoulder. Through the scope, he saw the runner's head explode in a cloud of blood and gore. It fell forward across Jimmy, covering the gaping wound and startling the other runner. A second later, that one's head jerked back when a bullet entered its forehead above the bridge of its nose, blowing the entire rear skull against the chain link fence. Carter now had a clear shot at Jimmy. Chambering a third round, he lined up on the kid's head, steadied himself, and took off Jimmy's head with a single shot.

Swinging the rifle to his right, Carter aimed at the first of the other two runners feeding on the woman. It sat hunched forward, dipping its gore-laden hands into her chest. Carter noticed it chewing on something solid, either her heart or liver. He set the crosshairs above its right ear and fired. The concussion from the shot spun the runner around one hundred eighty degrees and propelled it to the other side of the body.

The last runner had ripped the left arm off of its victim and sat on its haunches, chewing the flesh like a dog on a bone. The middle-aged woman tried crawling away on the stump, getting only so far because of her restraints. Carter finished off the runner with a single shot directly between the eyes, giving a mental fist pump when its head exploded.

Carter then centered the scope on the middle-aged woman. It dawned on him that he didn't know a damn thing about the people on the Line. He didn't know their names, where they came from, or even how long they had been out there. In fact, until now he had not even given these people much thought. Not that it mattered. They meant nothing to him. However, they had served their purpose, providing decoys long enough for the others to make it to safety. Price wouldn't be alive if it not for them. He owed them something for the service, something humane.

Carter's next three shots put each of the victims out of their misery.

* * *

Simmons waited until the cherry picker began its descent before placing the binoculars down on the dirt in front of him. He gestured toward the gunman. "That guy is a first-class sniper."

"So are you and Wayans," Robson said.

"He's probably military, which puts him in a league way above us." Simmons rolled to one side to face Robson. "Sorry, man. There's no way to get your friend out."

"Oh, yes there is."

"Weren't you watching? Between those people chained up in the perimeter and that sniper, our chances of taking this place by surprise are damn slim, at best."

"Yes, I saw. And you're right." Robson smiled. "Who says I'm planning on taking this place by surprise?"

Simmons stared at him incredulously, and then a huge grin split his lips. "I've only known you for a day, but I believe you're crazy enough to pull this off."

CHAPTER NINETEEN

A mile outside of Barnston, Robson pulled his Humvee into the parking lot of a Home Depot. Jennifer and Roberta waited by a well-ransacked Kentucky Fried Chicken. They were to provide back-up available in case anything went wrong while scouting the security storage facility while Allard and Frakes stayed behind in Gilmanton to protect the Ryder housing Dravko and Tibor. Seeing the Humvee approaching, the women stepped through the empty frame of the shattered glass door, each scanning to their right or left to make certain no rotters were nearby. Robson made his way to the rear of the restaurant, pulled up alongside the other Humvee, and shut down the engine. Once certain that nothing had noticed them, Jennifer and Roberta joined the rest of the group.

"What did you find out?" asked Jennifer when Robson stepped out of the vehicle.

"Well, we saw Windows. She's alive, although she's pretty roughed up. And they've set up a cherry picker as a sniper tower inside the compound."

"Shit," cursed Jennifer. "Then we won't be able to get her out?"

"I have a plan."

"What is it?"

"He won't say," said Simmons as he joined the conversation. "Which concerns me."

"Don't be," Jennifer said defensively, moving a few inches closer to Robson. "We would never have made it to Site R and back without him. If he has a plan, it'll work."

"Sorry, ma'am."

Jennifer patted Robson on the forearm. "I'm going to use the restroom before we go."

Robson nodded, and Jennifer walked off.

"No offense, man," Simmons said to Robson.

"None taken."

"Your girlfriend is pretty protective of you."

"Jennifer?" Robson watched her walk away, and then turned back to Simmons. "We're not dating."

"Really?"

"Yeah." He didn't bother explaining his relationship with Natalie.

"You could be. She has the hots for you."

Robson again studied Jennifer, thought about it for a moment, and shook his head. "No way."

"Trust me, she's sweet on you."

"I hate to interrupt you girls while you're talking about who likes who," Wayans said, walking up to them, "but we have someone keeping an eye on us at Home Depot."

"Human or rotter?" Robson asked.

"Human. When I got out of the Hummer, I noticed something move behind the glass doors. I've been keeping an eye on the building without being obvious, and someone is definitely there."

"Do you think it's a gang member?" asked Simmons.

"Could be, though I doubt it. So far I've only seen the one person, and he's not very friggin' good at concealing himself."

"I don't want to take any chances," said Robson. "If he is one of the gang members, I don't want him tipping off the others. Simmons and I will take a Hummer, circle around in back of Home Depot, and check it out. Wayans, stay here and watch the others. See if you can set up a firing position to cover us, and stay out of sight."

Wayans nodded. "If I see this guy again, do you want me to take him down?"

"Not unless he's about to shoot first or make a break for it. I'd like to take him alive."

"Isn't that risky?" Simmons asked.

"If he is a gang member, maybe we can interrogate him and get some insights into the compound before we attack it."

"Makes sense." Simmons headed for their Humvee. "Come on. I'll drive."

* * *

Less than five minutes later, Robson and Simmons pulled up behind Home Depot. Robson stepped out, combing the area for intruders, his AA-12 in firing position.

Simmons keyed his radio. "Isaac, any change in the situation?"

"Not a thing," responded Wayans. "He's prone by the exit, watching us through the glass."

"Where are you?"

"I'm at the end of the restaurant farthest away from Home Depot. I have a clear shot at our friend. He can't see me."

"Is he armed?"

"Not with anything I can see."

"So if we get close to him, we can surprise him."

"Roger that."

Simmons motioned to Robson. "You hear that?"

Robson nodded. "Tell Wayans to let us know if our friend moves."

Simmons relayed the message. Robson checked the back door to the building. As he assumed, it was locked. He moved down to the loading dock and grasped the handle to the sliding doors, but they were locked, too. "Shit."

"What's wrong?" Simmons asked.

"All the doors are bolted from the inside. We have no way of getting in without making so much noise we'll tip off whoever is out front."

"We could circle around." Simmons moved to the edge of the building and peered around the corner. "Isaac says the guy is inside the building. If we stick close to the walls, we could be on top of him before he knew we were there."

"Let's do it."

The two men moved along the right side of the building staying as close to the wall as possible. Every few seconds, Simmons checked behind him to make sure they weren't about to be ambushed. When they reached the end, Robson peered around the corner. The exit doors were fifty feet down. From this vantage point, they could not see the intruder, which meant he could not see them.

Robson grabbed his microphone and whispered. "Isaac, we're about to move toward the doors. I'm going to stop ten feet away. When I wave, fire one round through the glass over the guy's head."

"Roger that."

Both men made their way along the front of the building, their backs pressed against the wall. Robson held his AA-12 beside him, and Simmons had his Colt .45 drawn and ready. When ten feet from the exit door, Robson waved.

A shot rang out. The glass door shattered, and a muffled curse came from inside the building. Robson charged, with Simmons right behind. The two centered themselves in the doorway, their weapons aimed. A middle-aged man in jeans and a gray sweatshirt lay on the floor, shaking his head and brushing off shards of glass. When he saw the two men standing in front of him, he gasped and tried to get to his feet.

Robson stepped toward him. "Move and you're a dead man."

The man's gaze darted between Robson and Simmons. He raised his arms, his hands shaking as he lifted them above his head. "Come on, guys. Don't hurt me. Please!"

Simmons leaned closer to Robson. "I don't think this guy is with the rape gang."

CHAPTER TWENTY

The entire group sat around the rectory's dining room table, all eyes focused on their guest from Home Depot who sat at the far end. "Guest" was the best word to describe him, because this guy posed no danger. He possessed no survival skills. When they confiscated his Smith and Wesson .38 Special and his Heckler and Koch 223 semi-automatic rifle, he had the safety locked on the former and had not chambered a round in the latter. He had barricaded all but one entrance into the store, and had set up his safe room in a corner office with no other way out, trapping himself inside Home Depot. He didn't even have a bug-out bag in case he had to make a run for it. Robson figured this guy presented more of a danger to himself than to them or the rotters.

Robson knew nothing about him. He was middle-aged and of average height and looks. His demeanor reeked of cowardice, from the constantly hunched shoulders, the inability to make eye contact, and his avoidance of confrontation. They had not talked to him on the way back to Gilmanton, and the presence of Wayans seated beside him in the Humvee kept their guest silent and sullen. After sunset, when Dravko and Tibor joined them, he freaked out. He perked up only after they offered him something hot to eat. Their guest wolfed down his food as if he had not eaten in weeks, yet he still hadn't spoken. Robson pitied the guy. If he had been out here this long, he had definitely seen some heavy shit. Unlike the rest of them, he was not prepared psychologically to process what he had experienced.

Robson leaned forward and rested his elbows on the table. "I know you're hungry, friend. But can you slow down long enough to tell us your name?"

Their guest stopped eating, his cheeks still stuffed with food. His eyes darted back and forth between the various people seated at the table.

Robson sighed. "If we were going to hurt you, do you think we'd feed you first?"

"You might if you were fattening me up for *them*." Their guest focused his gaze on the vampires.

Dravko rolled his eyes. Tibor sneered, showing fangs.

When no one responded, their guest put down his knife and fork and swallowed. "I'm Tom Caslow. From Salt Lake City."

"How did you make it all the way to the East Coast?" asked Simmons.

"My family and I were vacationing in New England when the outbreak hit. You know, the Freedom Trail and stuff like that. We were in Salem when we first heard about the virus. In the Witch Museum, of all places. We spent the next two days in the hotel room watching the news, hoping it would all blow over. It didn't. So we headed to Logan to catch a flight out. By then the city had been quarantined. We had no idea what to do. Thank God we ran into Nick, a retired cop, who took us with him to Nahant. That's where he lived. Have you ever been there? It's an island off the coast of Massachusetts connected to the mainland by a causeway. Nick said he and some of his friends had closed the causeway and isolated the island, and would ride out the outbreak from there. He seemed trustworthy, so we followed him. It's a good thing we did, or who knows what would have happened?"

"Slow down," said Robson, holding up his hand to cut off Caslow. Had they missed someone? "Who's 'we'?"

"Me, my wife, Debra, and my daughter, Cindy. The three of us had come to New England because we wanted something different and exciting." Tom forced a chuckle. "I guess we got our wish."

"If you were holed up in an isolated community, how did you wind up here?" asked Robson.

"Nahant saved our lives. Nick and the other retired cops maintained order and controlled who would be allowed in to the community. Because the only access was the causeway, they kept out anyone who they thought might be trouble. Too bad it didn't stop the dead."

"They overwhelmed the causeway?" asked Simmons.

Caslow shook his head. "We would have been prepared for that. None of us ever thought that those things could walk underwater, though I guess it makes sense since they don't breathe. One night, about six weeks ago, several thousand came ashore near the southern tip of the island. No one expected it, and the living dead overran Nahant in a few hours. Practically no one made it out. We wouldn't have either if Nick and some of his friends hadn't helped us. They shoved us into a pair of Dodge Rams, crashed their own barricades, and got us off the island. We headed inland, trying to avoid the heavily populated coasts."

"What happened to Nick?" asked Simmons.

"Our group got ambushed a few miles north of Concord. We had stopped to refuel when a swarm of the dead came out of nowhere and overran our vehicles before we could get to them. I grabbed the only car we could find. A Toyota Corolla. Nick and the others tried to fight them off and were swarmed. We barely got away with our lives."

"Where's your family?" asked Jennifer.

For the first time, Caslow didn't ramble. His body trembled. He closed his eyes tight, fighting back tears. Finally, he took a deep breath and continued. "I remembered what Nick had said about being safer where there were fewer people, so we headed west. Everything was fine until we reached this area. We had nothing other than the rifle and the revolver Nick gave me. All the surrounding towns had been stripped clean. We were driving around when we passed this storage facility that looked occupied. I wanted to stop and ask for help until I saw all these people tied to the ground out front."

"The rape gang," said Robson. The others around the table nodded.

"You know them?'

"We've had dealings with them before."

"Then I'm surprised you're still here." Caslow sighed. "I got out of there as fast as I could. Drove for about an hour and pulled off near one of those convenience store-gas station combos. I was inside checking for food when two military

Humvees pulled into the parking lot. They dragged Debra and Cindy out of the car and took them away. When I realized what happened, I followed them back to the storage facility. That happened about a month ago."

"And you just friggin' *left* them there?" Wayans said with such anger that it startled Robson.

"Of course not!" Caslow's eyes darted to the others, begging for approval. "I've spent almost every day for the last month watching that compound and trying to come up with a way to get them out. Have you seen that place?"

"Yes," answered Robson.

"Then you know it's impossible to get in, especially for one guy." Caslow glared at Wayans. "Why would you think I just left my wife and daughter there?"

"Because you did nothing to save them." This time Jennifer spoke, and her words dripped with contempt.

"W-what could I d-do?" Caslow stammered. "I have no clue what I'm doing in a situation like this. I'm not a survivalist. I never even served in the military. I don't even own a gun. I'm an elementary school teacher."

"You're a man," said Jennifer. "You should have defended your family."

"I-If I had tried, the gang would have killed me. Then where would my family be?"

"The same place they are now. But at least they would know their husband and father cared enough to fight for them and not just leave them with a rape gang."

Caslow stared at Jennifer, stunned. At first, Robson thought he was shocked by the harshness of her tone and the accusation against him, until he spoke.

"D-did you say 'rape gang'?"

"Yeah."

"Oh, God." Caslow dropped his head and sobbed.

Robson glanced around the room and noticed that no one showed sympathy toward him. Jennifer stood up and stormed into the kitchen. Wayans glared, shaking his head in disgust. Robson was the only one who had even a shred of empathy toward Caslow. Maybe because he couldn't get Susan out of his mind, how they had been attacked by a horde of swarmers in traffic outside of Newington, and how he had left her when the living dead overtook them because she couldn't run fast enough.

"What do we do with him?" Simmons asked.

"I say we send him on his way first thing in the morning," suggested Frakes.

"Why wait that long?" asked Wayans.

DeWitt cleared his throat. "We should at least wait until sunrise to give him a fighting chance."

"Fuck him," snapped Roberta. "He doesn't deserve one after what he did to his wife and kid."

Caslow raised his head. "I'm right here, you know."

The glare that both Wayans and Roberta shot his way cowed Caslow.

Robson wondered how the others would react if they knew he had once displayed a similar lack of courage. "I vote to keep him around a while longer."

"Are you friggin' nuts?" Wayans blurted out.

Simmons agreed, though he was more reserved. "I agree. This guy's a coward, has no useful skills, and would be nothing but a drain on resources. He's of no use to us."

"Actually, he has something very valuable. Information. If what he says is true, he's been spying on their compound for almost a month—"

"It's true," Caslow said animatedly, trying to curry favor.

Robson flashed him an expression that warned him not to press his luck. "He probably knows things about that compound and how the gang operates that could be of use to us. As long as he cooperates, I think we should keep him around."

"Makes sense," agreed Simmons.

Wayans begrudgingly nodded his approval.

Tibor stood up and stormed out of the dining room, startling everyone at the table. Dravko watched his fellow vampire leave, and then shrugged his shoulders in confusion. He finally said, "We're in."

Everyone else concurred, except for Jennifer, who had returned from the kitchen. She stared out the window into the dark, her back to the others and her arms folded across her chest. After a few seconds of silence, Robson prodded, "Is it unanimous?"

"I won't object as long as I have to have nothing to do with him," Jennifer said, her eyes filled with contempt for Caslow. "To be honest, though, I don't trust the bastard. If I have one bullet left and it's between him and a rotter, I'll shoot him in the leg and leave him behind."

"Deal."

"Thank you all." Caslow sniffed. "I won't let you down."

"You better not." Robson stood, picked up his mug, and headed for the kitchen. He paused by Caslow's chair. "I'm going to get some more coffee. When I come back, you're going tell me everything you know about that compound."

CHAPTER TWENTY-ONE

Dravko found Tibor at the construction company. The vampire had pulled an acetylene torch and some discarded sheets of metal over to one of the Humvees. As Dravko approached, Tibor was welding something to the windshield.

"What are you doing?" he yelled to be heard over the noise.

When he saw his friend, Tibor shut off the torch. "I'm adding metal panels that can be closed during the daytime and block out the sunlight."

"Why? We already have the Ryder for that."

"We needed the Ryder when we had five of us. Now you and I are all that's left, so the Hummer is more than enough."

Dravko sat inside the cab and studied the additions. Tibor had removed the windshield and replaced it with a one-inch plate of metal welded to the frame along all four edges. Two slits were burned out of the surface in front of the driver's and passenger's seats, each two feet wide and one foot tall. Sliding metal hatches had been attached to runners on the interior surface of the plate, large enough to cover the openings, and with the ability to be bolted into place from inside. Once in the Humvee, he and Tibor would be the only ones who could control the sliding hatches.

"This is impressive."

"Thanks." Tibor nodded. "I plan to do the same thing to the side windows, and to add deadbolts to the turret hatch and rear panel."

"What made you think of this?"

"When we ditched the school bus back in Portland, I realized we didn't need the truck anymore. It keeps us confined to the main roads and limits where we can go."

Dravko climbed out of the Humvee. "By us do you mean the group, or you and me?"

"That's up to you." Tibor turned away and picked up the acetylene torch. "You know how I feel about the humans."

"Is that why you stormed out of dinner?"

Tibor spun around to confront his friend, failing to control his anger. "I stormed out because I am fed up with the way Robson disrespects us."

"Robson has always treated us with respect."

"He *accepts* us. He doesn't *respect* us!"

"What's the difference?"

"You really don't see the difference." Tibor's tone softened. "As much as I disagreed in the beginning with this alliance with the humans, it worked because Paul and Elena believed in it and did everything in their power to make it work. Each of them risked alienating their own kind to show the other side that they believed in it. That's what I mean by respect."

Dravko was taken aback. "Robson stood up for us at Site R when Compton wanted to eliminate us."

"Don't get me wrong. Robson is a decent human, and I like him for that. There were many times on the way to Site R that he could have left us for dead. However, this alliance is not going to work unless he starts showing us the same respect that Paul did."

"How can he do that?"

Tibor stared at Dravko, frustration in his eyes, like a professor trying to get one of his students to comprehend a simple thought. "When Robson decided to risk all of our lives to save Windows from the rape gang, did he consult with you or ask if you're willing to go along?"

"No."

"Do you know what his plan is for getting Windows out?"

"No."

"Who did he take with him today to check out the compound? His new friends, Simmons and Wayans. Hell, he's even embraced that asshole Caslow. Maybe he doesn't realize it himself, but Robson is rebuilding the ranks of the humans with our group, replacing those we lost with people we know nothing about. And because he doesn't have the same dedication to our alliance that Paul did, he's more prone to listen to these new humans."

"You're misjudging him."

"Am I?" Tibor wore that infuriatingly smug expression he always did when about to make a point. "For the past two nights, Paul and the others have been over at the rectory dining on fresh meat and vegetables like it's a big party. When was the last time we ate?"

That last question struck Dravko. He had been so preoccupied with everything that had happened since arriving back at Fort McClary he had not realized they had run out of their prepared blood supply two days ago. Sure, he felt hungry, but it had not yet developed into a lust to feed.

"You know I'm right," Tibor continued. "Robson hasn't even thought to ask for volunteers to supply us with blood. What do you think is going to happen when he asks his new friends to ante up a pint? Sure, Caslow would let us feed off of him because he's too much of a coward to refuse. Do you think Simmons and Wayans will roll up a sleeve? And how long do you think it'll be before they start telling Robson that this is his chance to get rid of vampires once and for all?"

"He'd never go for that."

"Did you expect him to marginalize us like he has these past few days?"

Dravko could not respond. Actually, he could, but he did not like the answer.

The lack of a response told Tibor he was correct. "With the death of Elena, you are now the master of the coven. As such, I am sworn to obey and protect you, which I will to the very end. Deep down you know I'm right, and I hope you realize we need to act before the humans turn against us."

"You're not suggesting we turn them?"

"You wouldn't let me even if I did suggest it." Tibor smiled, although Dravko could not be sure if out of humor or irony. "No, we need to set out on our own as soon as possible. The Hummer will give us the chance to break away."

"And then what?"

"Then we find a small band of humans somewhere and rebuild the coven."

CHAPTER TWENTY-TWO

Windows sat beside the haggard old man, her legs crossed, feeding him his dinner. Even though the stench still overpowered the room, she had grown used to it. Other than a few pleasantries when she entered, he had not spoken throughout the meal, although every time she spoon fed him he did acknowledge her kindness with a nod. When they had finished, the old man struck up a conversation.

"I heard a lot of commotion outside today. What happened?"

"Some swarmers stormed the outer perimeter."

"Swarmers?"

"That's what I call them." A strand of long gray hair with remnants of baked beans hung across the old man's face. Windows pulled off the food and pushed the hair back behind his ear. "I think your people call them runners."

"We've been seeing a lot more of them and the deaders the past few weeks. Soon we'll all be trapped in here." The old man paused. "Did anyone get hurt?"

"One of the gang members was killed, along with two or three on the Line."

"I wish more of the gang had been killed." The slightest trace of a smile graced his lips, then disappeared. "I feel bad that those people on the Line had to die so horribly. At least they're better off. They live worse than animals out there."

"You're not living in the best of conditions yourself." Windows said it lightly, trying to change the depressing tone.

"Kid, this is a Best Western compared to what those poor bastards on the Line have to go through. In here I'm protected from the weather and I'm safe. It's because of my *privileged status.*" The old man spoke the last two words with heavy sarcasm.

Windows saw the opportunity and took it. "Privileged status? Who are you to warrant that?"

The old man lowered his head. "I'm nobody important."

"Don't say that. We're all important."

"Not in this place. The only ones who matter are Price and his gang. And even they live or die on his whim. The rest of us are just toys to be used for their amusement. You know that better than I do."

The humiliating memories came back to her and Widows winced.

The old man noticed the grimace. "I'm sorry. I shouldn't have said that."

"That's okay. It's true." She reached out and gave his wrist a gentle, reassuring squeeze. "Will you tell me your name?"

The old man shook his head.

"Don't worry about it." Windows released his wrist and stood to leave. When she approached the sliding door, the old man called to her.

"Kid, will you take some friendly advice from a nobody?"

"Of course."

"You're strong-willed with a good heart. That's a deadly combination around here. Trust me, I know. I've been here from the beginning and seen a lot of people like you wind up on the Line. Or worse."

"You're telling me to change my attitude?"

"Hell, no. I'd hate to see them break you. I'm warning you to be careful who you trust. Most people around here would gladly feed you to the deaders for an extra ration of food or one night of not being raped."

That's for damn sure, Windows thought as she recalled how Debra had arranged for her to be Meat's new play toy so she could get a break. "Does that include you?"

"No. I'm the only person around here who has nothing to gain or lose." Again a slight smile. "You're learning though. And I wouldn't blame you if you stopped treating me kindly."

"You don't have to worry about that." Windows lifted the door and stepped out. Before she closed it, she stuck her head back into the unit. "I'll see you in the morning."

CHAPTER TWENTY-THREE

Natalie sat on the edge of Bethany's bed, stroking the unconscious woman's hair. When her hand brushed across the woman's forehead, she could feel the heat emanating from Bethany's skin. The fever had started late in the afternoon and became progressively worse. Natalie had been sitting with her for several hours, praying it would break. With each passing hour, the fever brought with it the realization that everything they had gone through these past two weeks had been a complete failure. Bethany was turning into a rotter, which meant the vaccine had failed.

A light knock sounded behind her and Natalie saw Ari standing in the doorway.

"How's she doing?" Ari asked.

"She's turning."

Ari's mood brightened. "You mean she's getting better?"

"No. I mean she's turning into a rotter."

"Oh." Natalie could feel the enthusiasm drain out of Ari. The young woman entered the room and crossed over to the bed. "She's not turning into one of them. She's going into septic shock."

"What's that?"

"She has a staph infection that can't be treated because we don't have antibiotics." Ari gestured for Natalie to move so she could sit beside Bethany. Ari slipped on a pair of rubber gloves, reached over, and carefully peeled away the adhesive tape holding the blood-soaked bandage to Bethany's cheek. "That's one thing we never considered with the vaccine. While we're no longer in danger of turning, the threat of infection is now much greater. God only knows what diseases are in a rotter's mouth."

Ari removed the bandage. Yellowish-green pus mixed with the dried blood around the bite marks. The skin was red and inflamed. Ari sighed. "She's going septic We'll survive the initial bite to die a more painful death from a staph infection."

"How painful?"

"The infection has already entered her bloodstream, which is why she's feverish. The blood will spread the infection to her organs, which will eventually fail." Ari poured rubbing alcohol onto a sterile gauze and used it to wipe away the pus and blood around the wound. Even while unconscious, Bethany moaned and moved her head to one side. Ari placed a hand on the opposite side of Bethany's head, pushed it back, and continued to dab. "In the end, she's going to suffer a lot more pain than if she just turned into one of those things."

Natalie hovered over the two women, feeling powerless. "How do you know all this? Were you a nurse?"

"I wanted to be. I couldn't afford nursing school, so I volunteered in a hospital to gain experience while I saved up for classes. Michelle, one of the floor nurses, appreciated my enthusiasm and mentored me. We were on duty together the night of the outbreak. Michelle died when one of the victims turned on the ER table and ripped a chunk out of her throat. I guess this is my way of paying back all she did for me."

"She'd be proud of you." Ari placed fresh gauze over Bethany's wound and taped it into place.

"Is there anything you can do for her?"

"Without antibiotics, no. All we have are over-the-counter pain relievers, so we can't even make her comfortable in her final days. And believe me, she's going to suffer a lot over the next few days." An uncomfortable silence followed while Ari finished taping the gauze to Bethany's face.

"Is there anything we can do to stop her suffering?" asked Natalie.

"Yes." Ari stood up. She dropped the soiled gauze into a plastic bag, removed her rubber gloves, and dropped them into it as well. "You're not going to agree with it."

"How?"

"We can put her down gently."

"You mean kill her?"

"I mean euthanize her. Unfortunately, we have no way of doing it humanely. We don't have morphine or prescription pain killers, so there's no way to put Bethany to sleep."

"So the only way to stop her from suffering is to let her go?"

Ari's lips tightened. "Yes."

Natalie didn't even want to consider the possibility. "There's no way I could do that to Bethany."

"I wouldn't want to have to make the decision, either. Just so long as you realize that one way or another, Bethany is not going to make it. How much she suffers is up to you."

Ari exited the room, pausing just long enough to give Natalie a reassuring pat on the shoulder. Natalie sat back down on the edge of the bed and began stroking Bethany's hair again, struggling with the decision about what would be best for her friend.

CHAPTER TWENTY-FOUR

A soft hand against Windows' shoulder brought her out of her slumber. At first, she didn't realize someone was trying to wake her because of the deep sleep she had been in, the result of not having to satisfy Meat the night before. The nudging continued until Windows stirred and groaned.

"Miss Windows, are you awake?"

"I am now." She rolled over. Cindy knelt beside her. "What's up?"

"Can you help me? Something happened to my mother."

Windows sat up and threw off the folds of the sleeping bag. "What happened?"

"Something bad."

When Windows got up, Cindy took her hand. She led Windows out of the container unit and toward the far end of the compound near the kitchen. The first rays of sunlight streaked across the eastern horizon. Everyone was still inside, either sleeping off their drunken binges from the night before or, in the case of the women, resting up after another night of abuse. Cindy maneuvered through the landscape without concern, either oblivious in her youth to the dangers it posed, or showing an incredible ability to adapt.

They reached the end of the compound. Cindy turned the corner at the end of the row of storage units and pointed ahead of her without saying a word.

Windows let go of Cindy's hand and covered her mouth, stifling a scream.

Debra dangled from one of the light fixtures bolted into the top of the perimeter wall. One end of a rope was anchored to the fixture, the other end forming a noose around Debra's neck. A wooden stool lay overturned by her feet.

Windows' initial shock turned to anger. She knelt down and turned Cindy to face her. "Who did this to your mother?"

"She did it to herself."

The nonchalant manner in which Cindy spoke the words caught Windows off guard. "Why did she commi... do this?"

"She had a fight with Meat last night. Meat told my mother he wanted to break up with her. They argued for a few minutes, and Meat told her to shut up and go back to the Clubhouse or he would see that both of us went on the Line."

Windows fought back the urge to vomit.

"After that, Mom took me to the kitchen. We stayed there for a few minutes while she found some rope. She told me to wait there until either she returned or you showed up for work, gave me a big hug and kiss, and left."

"You didn't listen to her."

Cindy shook her head. "When she didn't come back, I went looking for her and found her like this. I figured it was bad, so I came to get you."

Windows glanced over to the corpse hanging from the light fixture. Flies had already started to swarm around the body. She didn't know if she should be angry at Debra for taking the easy way out, or envious that she had the courage to end this nightmare. Not knowing what to do, she clasped Cindy's hand in her own.

Cindy reached into her pocket with her free hand and withdrew a sheet of paper carelessly folded several times. She handed it to Windows. "Mom wrote this before she left. She asked me to give it to you."

Windows took the piece of paper. "Did you read it?"

"No."

Windows unfolded the letter and began to read:

> By now you've found my body. You probably think I'm a coward. I guess in a way I am, but I'm doing this for Cindy. I've known for some time that Meat was getting bored with me. Usually when one of these assholes gets tired of us, we either

become gang rape fodder or are banished to the Line. I couldn't let that happen to Cindy. When you came along, I saw the chance to provide for her safety. Meat likes you and will take good care of you, in his twisted way. He always protected Cindy from the others when he was with me. I'm hoping he'll do the same for her now that he's with you. Please adopt Cindy as your own and take care of her. Always tell her I love her. And no matter what you think of me, please don't bad mouth me to Cindy. I would say God bless the both of you, but I stopped believing in Him when I got to this place. So instead I'll wish you the best of luck.

Windows could barely read the last few sentences through her tears. She refolded the letter and shoved it into her back pocket.

Cindy squeezed her hand. "It's okay to cry. I used to do it all the time when I first got here."

Windows ran her palms across her face. "Why don't you cry now?"

"Why bother? It doesn't do any good." Cindy paused for a second. "Who's going to take care of me now?"

"I am, if that's okay with you."

Cindy nodded her head and hugged Windows tight. "I'd like that."

Windows wrapped her arms around the girl and gently rocked her, outwardly showing strength. Inside, however, fear gripped her. She knew the degrading things Debra had done to protect Cindy, and wondered if she had enough courage to do the same.

CHAPTER TWENTY-FIVE

The knocking on the cabin door roused Natalie out of her restless sleep. She ran her hand across her face and rubbed her tired eyes. Twisting her neck from one side to the other, she felt the muscles strain. A deep yawn escaped from her mouth, and she opened her eyes to see Sandy standing in the doorway.

"Is it shift change already?" asked Natalie.

"Nope. Emily wants you to come to the bridge."

"Oh, fuck." Natalie shoved herself out of the chair by Bethany's bed. Her arms were so tired she almost fell back into the cushions. "What now?"

"This is something you'll want to see."

Natalie followed Sandy. The sun had risen and sat low on the horizon, nearly blinding her when she came on deck. She stumbled, trying to see through squinted eyes, and banged her shin against a deck chair. By the time she reached the flying bridge, her eyes had adjusted to the light.

Ari stood behind the wheel, with Emily standing to the left holding a pair of binoculars. Natalie moved in between them. "What's up?"

Emily pointed straight ahead. "That."

A massive container ship floated two miles in the distance. "Big deal. It's another derelict. What's so special about it?"

Emily handed her the binoculars. "See for yourself."

Natalie lifted them to her eyes. The container shop had run aground on a sandbar, with approximately one hundred feet of its bow lodged onto the sand. A Coast Guard cutter was tethered to the vessel's starboard beam near the stern. She saw no signs of movement, either living or living dead.

"I don't get it."

"That container vessel didn't get hung up on the sandbar because it was adrift. It had to have been moving at a pretty good speed to run aground like that. And that Coast Guard cutter has fuel lines running from the container ship, which means there's probably fuel aboard one of those two ships."

"Thank God. What's our situation?"

"We're practically riding on fumes, honey."

The fuel situation had been precarious for most of the trip. They had been fortunate in finding a fueling station on an isolated portion of Nantucket that allowed them to fully replenish their tanks. However, after that it became hit or miss. Every station they stumbled upon had been infested with rotters, forcing them to siphon off what little fuel they could scavenge from derelict small boats. Finding the container ship was fortunate. Now, if only their luck held and it still had fuel on board.

Natalie scanned both the container ship and the cutter, panning their decks for anything unusual. Corpses, dried blood smears, debris, evidence of a battle, anything that might provide a clue as to what happened to the men aboard the two ships. Yet everything looked normal, which bothered her. Nothing was normal any more.

"What do you think?" asked Emily.

"We're limited in our options." Natalie lowered the binoculars. "Do you know how you transfer fuel from one ship to another?"

"I do. We're going to have to go below deck to do it."

"Shit." Natalie thought for a moment. "Go get the Angels, and have them bring their weapons. I want to make certain we're ready for anything."

"Sure thing, honey."

Emily rushed off to get the Angels, and Natalie went back to studying the two vessels. A large access hatch sat open on the starboard beam of the container vessel, about fifteen feet above the cutter's main deck. A large hose draped over the bottom of the hatch, dropped down onto the cutter, and wormed its way along the deck before disappearing behind the superstructure. She couldn't see any movement aboard either vessel and, as far as she could tell, both were deserted.

A few minutes later, Emily returned with her M-16A2 slung over her shoulder. "The rest of the girls will be here shortly."

"I don't get it. Why would the Coast Guard just abandon one of its ships?"

Emily shrugged. "Maybe one of the engines broke down. Or the crew transferred to a larger vessel. Who cares as long as it has gas?"

The rest of the Angels came topside just as Ari cut back power and maneuvered the yacht alongside the Coast Guard cutter's access ladder. Emily grabbed one of the dock lines and moored the yacht to the cutter. Ari shut down the engine, and everything went quiet. Natalie listened for the telltale moan of rotters. The only sound came from the water slapping against the side of the yacht.

"Ari, you stay here and be prepared to move out if anything happens. We're going on board."

Emily placed her hand on Natalie's shoulder. "Why don't you stay here within Ari and make sure everything is okay topside? I'll take care of things aboard the cutter."

As much as she wanted to be involved, Natalie knew Emily was right. Emily knew about ships and how they operated, and could handle this. Natalie would only get in the way and slow things down as the Angels looked to her to give orders. Reluctantly, she nodded her approval.

Emily boarded the cutter. One by the one, the Angels followed.

Ari saw the concern on her friend's face and leaned closer. "Don't worry. They'll be fine."

"I know." Deep down she thought, *I hope you're right.*

* * *

When the Angels had gathered on the cutter's main deck just aft of the superstructure, Emily motioned for them to move closer. "Chances are this ship is abandoned, but I don't want to take any chances. Stephanie and Josephine, you're with me. The rest of you stay here and keep your eyes open. If anything happens, start shooting and we'll come running."

The rest of the girls spread out, and Emily led Stephanie and Josephine across to the port side of the superstructure.

"Do you think this is safe?" asked Stephanie. "I mean, just the three of us going below?"

"We don't have to go that far." Emily pointed to the hose. After emerging from the container vessel, it snaked around the cutter's superstructure before disappearing into an open hatch. "If the fuel tanks were below, those hoses would have gone through a hatch on deck. What we want is right behind this bulkhead."

Emily raised her M-16A2 and inched her way along the superstructure, the other two Angels close behind. She paused by the open hatch long enough to take a deep breath to steady her nerves, and then centered herself in the hatchway. She exhaled audibly. Turning to the other women, she gave them a thumbs up and entered. Stephanie and Josephine followed.

Four large fuel tanks filled the space, two on the port side and two starboard, the fuel hose attached to the tank on the far end. Removing a flashlight attached to a wall mount by the hatch, Emily switched it on and walked along the line of fuel tanks to port. She bent over to check out the first fuel gauge.

"Empty."

She moved down to the next one.

"Empty."

She crossed over to the starboard tanks.

"Empty."

"Fuck," mumbled Josephine. "This was a waste of time."

Emily stood in front of the last tank and grinned. "No, it isn't."

"You're serious?" asked Stephanie. "It has fuel?"

"More than enough." Emily made her way back to the women and offered a flirtatious wink. "Ladies, get ready. We're about to be pumped."

* * *

It took less than twenty minutes to make the preparations. Emily followed the fuel line along the deck, finding a segmented break just underneath where the hose exited the open hatch in the container vessel. Unscrewing the connection, she dragged the hose onto the yacht and attached the lose end to their own fuel tank. Leaving Stephanie aboard the yacht with a two-way radio to let her know when they were full, Emily went back aboard the cutter and switched on the generator that powered the pump. It made an unbearably loud noise and disrupted the calm of the ocean. None of the Angels cared. It was worth it to see the pulsing of the hose transferring fuel into their yacht.

Emily and Josephine were standing in front of the pump and fuel tank checking on the process of the transfer when Sarah stuck her head through the open hatch. "I'm going to check out the rest of the ship and see if there's anything worth salvaging."

"Don't press your luck," warned Emily.

"Normally I wouldn't, but they may have some antibiotics and morphine for Bethany."

Emily couldn't argue with that. She pointed to the two remaining wall-mounted flashlights. "Take those with you. And for God's sake, honey, be careful."

"I will." Sarah pulled the flashlights off the wall and exited the space.

* * *

Sarah met up with the rest of the Angels on the port beam of the main deck by the hatch leading into the superstructure. She pointed to Amy and Katie. "You two are with me. We're going below to check on the crew quarters. The rest of you take the main deck."

"What are we looking for?" asked Tiara.

Sarah handed Tiara and Sandy the other two flashlights. "Mainly antibiotics or painkillers for Bethany. If you see anything we can use, take it. And for God's sake, don't take any chances. We'll meet back here in fifteen minutes."

Sarah flicked on the flashlight, removed her hunting knife from its sheath, and stepped inside the superstructure. A set of stairs led up to the pilot house and down to the lower deck. She stood at the top of the stairs and flashed the light below. She heard no sounds and saw no signs of movement, so she descended halfway down, pausing just long enough to direct the beam along the corridor. Nothing. She waved on the others and proceeded ahead, shining the beam on the nearest doors. The one to starboard bore a sign that read Secure Communications. The one to port said Storage.

Sarah stepped toward the latter. "This is what we want."

She knocked three times and received no response from the other side. Grabbing the knob, she said to Amy and Katie. "Ready?"

Both women unslung their M-16A2s and raised them into firing position. Sarah opened the door and jumped back. Nothing emerged from the room. Inching forward, she splayed the light around. She saw boxes of canned goods, toilet paper, spare clothes, and the like. Typical military fare and nothing fancy; however, in this post-apocalyptic world, a virtual treasure.

"What should we do with this?" asked Katie.

"Leave it for now. We can load it aboard the yacht after we've checked out the rest of the ship." Sarah led the way out of the storage room and down the main corridor.

Twelve doors stretched ahead of them, six on either bulkhead. Approaching the first door on the left, the women used the same procedure as with the store room – three knocks, wait, and then enter while being prepared for the worst. The cabin contained two bunks, both neatly made up to regulation standards, and showed no sign of a struggle or hasty departure. Sarah stepped over to the first locker, which was secured with a padlock. The second was not locked. Opening it, she showed the light around. Several pictures of a middle-aged couple with a young girl of around fourteen were taped to the inner door, more than likely the owner's family. Coast Guard uniforms and civilian clothes rested on hangers. A few personal belongings sat on the top shelf, such as a shaving kit, a Kindle, and a cigar box. Pulling the box off the shelf, she opened it. Inside she found letters, a watch, and other trinkets that at one time had obvious significance to the owner. Placing the cigar box back on the shelf, Sarah closed the locker and exited the cabin.

The three women checked the next eleven doors, finding either more cabins or heads. When they finished with the last cabin, Amy asked, "What now?"

"We get the rest of the Angels and bring the supplies to the yacht."

* * *

Sandy and Tiara led the way down the main deck corridor inside the superstructure, with Doreen and Virginia following behind, M-16A2s at the ready. Tiara and Doreen checked the two doors opposite the stairs, knocking and waiting for a response before entering. The rooms turned out to be crews' quarters and a head. Moving farther along the corridor, the bulkhead opened up into the galley.

"This is more like it," said Doreen.

Sandy tapped Virginia on the shoulder. "Stay here and keep your eyes open. We're going to see if there's any food."

Sandy and Tiara entered the galley, with Doreen providing fire support. The twin freezers stood to the rear off to the left. Sandy approached the first one, rapped on the heavy metal door, and, when she got no response, pulled on the handle. When the door opened, the heavy stench of rot and decay poured out into the galley.

"Jesus Christ!" Sandy jumped back, slamming her back against the metal bulkhead. Doreen ran in front of her and aimed the M-16A2 into the freezer. No rotters stumbled out. Sandy inched forward and directed the flashlight inside. The stench came from the meat that had thawed and decayed once power had been cut off. Doreen closed the door.

Virginia rushed up. "Is everything okay?"

"I'm jittery, that's all." Sandy let her heart stop racing. "Let's check out the rest of the deck."

Once back in the corridor, they proceeded to the next door on the right. A plaque attached to the front read Office. Sandy stood in front of it and knocked. As expected, she got no response, so she opened the door and flashed the light around. The room appeared immaculate, almost as if no one had ever used it. A safe mounted in the opposite wall had attached to it a red magnet emblazoned with the word CLOSED in white. Even the desk drawers were shut tight. Sandy played the light around the office until the beam fell across a wall-mounted cabinet with a red cross surrounded by a white circle. She stepped over to it and jiggled the handle. It was locked.

"Give me your weapon," she said to Doreen.

Doreen handed over the M-16A2. Sandy banged the stock against the handle several times until it snapped off and the door popped open. She handed back the weapon and peered inside. It contained medical supplies such as gauze, scissors, suturing kits, and hypodermic needles. Her interest focused on a row of pre-filled syringes on the top shelf. Scanning the labels, she said, "Bingo."

"What did you find?" asked Tiara.

Sandy pulled out the syringes and slipped them in her jacket pocket. "Morphine."

She had removed a handful of needles and was sliding them into her pocket when all hell broke loose.

CHAPTER TWENTY-SIX

Natalie stood on the main deck of the yacht, watching the fuel line pulse as the transfer took place. She checked her watch. They had been pumping gasoline for close to fifteen minutes. She wished the process would go faster because she hated being immobilized. The roar of the pump's engine blasted through the yacht's open engine room hatch and could be heard for miles. At least if anyone tried to approach the yacht, they would see it in plenty of time to respond.

The creaking from the cutter caught her attention because it sounded out of place. Natalie listened carefully. After a few seconds, she heard it again. Only now it sounded more like a moan. She ran to the access ladder leading up to the Coast Guard cutter's main deck and began to climb. Halfway up, a loud thud came from the vessel. Reaching the gunwale, Natalie peered over and scanned the deck. Another noise caught her attention, this time distinctly a rotter. The combined moan of several of the living dead washed over her from above. Looking up, Natalie saw five of them centered in the open hatchway of the container vessel. Even worse, they had spotted her. She realized that they must have been trapped aboard the container vessel, and had been attracted by the roar of the pump. One stumbled toward her, dropping the fifteen feet to the main deck of the cutter with a thud and a crack of bones. Two others dropped out of the hatchway, with more rotters filling the empty space behind them. One crawled around the rear mount for the catamaran, pulling itself along on decayed fingers and dragging a severely distorted leg behind it.

Natalie climbed back down to the yacht and raced over to the engine room hatch. She yelled down to Stephanie. "We've got rotters! We need to stop refueling now!"

"All I need is ten more minutes and we'll be topped off. Can you give me that long?"

Another three rotters tumbled out of the open hatch. "I'll do what I can," Natalie said.

Ari raced to the end of the flying bridge. "We've got fucking rotters pouring out of the container vessel."

"I know. Give me your M-16A2."

"It's down below."

Fuck. "Okay, get ready to haul ass out of here. Once they're done refueling, start the engines."

"Roger that." Ari darted back to the console.

Natalie searched for a weapon, and found a crowbar that had been used to pry open the engine room hatch. Grabbing it from off the deck, she raced to the access ladder and climbed onto the cutter.

By now, three disabled rotters crawled across the deck toward the yacht. Natalie stepped over to the first, raised the crowbar above her head with the straight end pointed down, and drove the metal tip through the back of its skull. She felt the tip scrape against the metal deck. Placing one foot against its shoulder for leverage, she yanked the crowbar free. Chunks of gore stuck to the metal. Whipping it to the side to clean off the excess, she disposed of the next two crawlers in the same fashion.

So many rotters had fallen from the container vessel that they formed a living dead pile on the main deck. The broken bodies of the first to tumble out cushioned the fall of the latter, and these landed intact. They crawled and stumbled along the pile, eventually reaching the main deck and staggering to their feet, where they closed in on Natalie.

* * *

The constant thudding on the main deck attracted Emily's attention. "Josephine, do you hear that?"

"What?"

Another thud. "That?"

"I do now. What is it?"

Emily stepped over to the hatch and pushed it open. A rotter in gore-laden overalls stood ten feet away on the stern. It glanced over and, upon seeing Emily, snarled and lumbered toward her. Two others, one in a tattered Coast Guard uniform and the other naked from the waist up with most of the flesh chewed off if its chest, staggered along behind it.

"Fuck!" Emily slammed the hatch. It would not close all the way because of the fuel line. Clutching the handle, she held the hatch in place. Three pairs of dead hands clasped the outer rim, attempting to pull it open. Emily leaned back, using her weight to hold it shut, and shouted over her shoulder to Josephine.

"I need some help here!"

* * *

Natalie knew she could not take on the rapidly-increasing horde of rotters with a crowbar. Yet if she retreated and allowed those things to get aboard the yacht, they were all screwed. Looking around for a solution, she saw it in the stairs at the rear of the superstructure leading up to the pilothouse. Maybe she could lead the rotters away and give the Angels enough of a chance to finish refueling and get off the cutter. Jumping over the corpse of the rotter whose brain she had just scrambled, Natalie pushed past the closest one and ran halfway up the stairs, and then spun around. The horde crowded around the superstructure, stumbling over each other to get at their meal. One by one, they found their footing and began climbing.

Natalie carefully backed up, making sure to stay several feet ahead of the rotters.

* * *

Even with Josephine's added weight, they couldn't keep the door closed. The rotter in gore-laden overalls widened the opening enough to slip his arm through, and eventually pushed through his upper torso. His teeth snapped shut inches from Emily's face. She leaned back and crouched down, giving herself more leverage.

151

"Go check and see if the other hatch is unlocked," she ordered Josephine.

"You can't hold them by yourself."

"I can hold them for a few seconds. We need to get out of here."

Josephine grabbed her M-16A2, rushed over to the starboard hatch, and spun the handle. It popped open. Josephine stuck out her head, scanned the deck, and called to Emily. "It's clear."

Emily let go of the handle. With nothing lodging him in place, the overalls rotter fell forward onto the deck. The other two pushed their way inside. Emily did not have a chance to reach for her weapon, and instead ran backwards as the two rotters clutched for her. Josephine stepped in front of Emily and fired off two three-round bursts, blasting their heads across the bulkhead. Emily rushed back to grab her M-16A2. The overalls rotter reached out and wrapped its fingers around her ankle, pulling itself toward her. Josephine stepped forward, placed the barrel of her semi-automatic rifle against the back of its head, and fired a single round. A pool of gore exploded out from underneath the rotter's face. Emily kicked away the lifeless hand and the two women raced out the opposite hatch.

Josephine paused. "What about the fuel line?"

"Nothing we can do here, honey. Ari's pumping it from the yacht. We've got to get out of here before we're trapped."

The two Angels made their way aft to the access ladder, passing by the horde of rotters swarming around the stairs to get at Natalie. Both women swung over the gunwale and descended to the yacht.

Five rotters from the horde noticed the two women and moved away, staggering toward the gunwale.

* * *

Sandy had dropped the pre-filled syringes into her pocket when gunfire echoed through the cutter.

"What the fuck is that?" asked Tiara.

"Nothing good." Sandy raced down the corridor toward the stairwell with the other Angels close behind.

* * *

Down below, Sarah, Amy, and Katie also heard the shots. They stared at each other without saying a word. None of them had to. They knew that the situation had just gone to shit. As one, they turned and headed back to the main deck.

* * *

Natalie quickened her pace when the first rotter reached the top of the stairs, making sure to keep plenty of space between them. She maneuvered between the bulkheads until reaching the edge and then back stepped. The rotters continued to follow, arms outstretched and fingers grasping. She led them past the pilothouse toward the forward section of the deck, and glanced over her shoulder for the forward ladder. She suddenly realized the fallacy of her plan. The only way off this deck was the set of stairs crammed with the living dead. She continued to back away. Once she had lured them as far toward the bow as possible, she would jump down to the main deck and rush back to the yacht.

Natalie backed into a metal object jutting up from the deck. She glanced over her shoulder, and her eyes lit up. A tripod extended from the deck, the top portion covered by a tarpaulin. Grabbing one end, she pulled the material up and forward, revealing a .50 caliber machinegun with an ammunition box mounted on one side. She lifted the lid, relieved to find it filled with rounds. Natalie grabbed the machinegun and swung it around toward the approaching rotter horde, pulled back the charging handle, and wrapped her hands around the firing grips.

Dear God, let this motherfucker still work.

Natalie placed her thumbs on the hinged trigger mechanism and squeezed.

A string of .50 caliber rounds eviscerated the first three rotters.

* * *

Ari watched the action from the flying bridge of their yacht, cursing herself for becoming lackadaisical. If she had her M-16A2 on deck with her like she should have, she would have been able to provide fire support for Natalie. Now she could only watch her friend face a rotter horde with nothing but a crowbar. She couldn't go below and get her weapon because that would mean abandoning her post, which would be disastrous when they had to get out of there in a hurry.

She saw Emily and Josephine exit from the fuel storage area and retreat back toward the yacht. Once the two women had climbed over the gunwale, she breathed a sigh of relief. At least they made it out safely. Ari then noticed the five rotters stumbling toward the yacht. The first, wearing a Coast Guard uniform ripped open at the chest, moved so fast it toppled over the gunwale. Ari rushed to the edge of the flying bridge and yelled, "Get out of the way!"

Before either woman could react, the rotter slammed into Emily, knocking her to the deck. It sunk its teeth into her right shoulder, trying to rip through the leather jacket. Josephine grabbed the rotter by its hair and yanked. Its hair came off in a massive clump, tearing off a chunk of skin that clung to the strands like soil on grass roots. She tossed it aside and wrapped her hands around the front of its neck, pulling with all her strength. The Coast Guard rotter released its grip and the two fell backwards, with Josephine slamming into the deck so hard it knocked the wind out of her. Momentarily stunned, Josephine couldn't fight back when the rotter rolled over onto her and crawled toward her neck.

Ari abandoned the flying bridge to help. Rushing down to the main deck, she kicked the rotter in the side of its head. It stared up at her and snarled. Ari kicked it again, this time in the face. Teeth and chunks of skin splattered across the deck as the rotter toppled over onto its back and off of Josephine. Ari grabbed her friend by the collar and dragged her away.

A second rotter with half its right arm missing tripped over the cutter's gunwale and crashed onto the deck. Slowly and awkwardly, it rose to its feet and staggered toward Ari and Josephine. The Coast Guard rotter rolled over onto its stomach and dragged itself toward Emily.

Even over the drone of the fuel pump, Stephanie heard Ari shouting, followed seconds later by the thump of something hitting the deck above her. Grabbing an axe off of the workbench, she made her way topside, exited into the main cabin, and stepped out onto the deck.

The Coast Guard rotter had just reached Emily and clawed at her leather pants, while the one-armed rotter closed in on Josephine and Ari. Brandishing the axe like a baseball bat, Stephanie charged the second one. When she got close enough, she swung. The blade landed on the left side of the rotter's head, cleaving four inches into the skull. A spray of congealed blood and brain matter erupted from the back of its head, and both eyes popped loose from their sockets. It went limp and dropped to the deck, yanking the axe from Stephanie's hand. She didn't have time to dislodge it.

Stepping over to the Coast Guard rotter, she kicked it in the chest with enough force to roll it off of Emily. Grabbing the stunned woman, Stephanie dragged her to the other side of the deck and released her alongside Josephine, then crossed back over to the rotter. Its mouth frantically bit at the air. Stephanie stood beside it. It grabbed at her pants leg, trying to get a grip on the leather. She glared down at the rotter.

"Eat this."

Stephanie raised her boot and slammed it into the rotter's head. Its jaw shattered with a loud crack, although the remnants of its mouth still moved. She stomped on its head repeatedly, each blow more violent, deforming its features and breaking off chunks of skin and bone. Finally, its head exploded across the deck, and the body went limp.

Ari stepped over and touched Stephanie's shoulder. "Are you okay?"

"I am now."

Above them, the other three rotters moaned and leaned over the gunwale.

Stephanie walked over to the one-armed rotter and grabbed the axe handle. The blade wouldn't dislodge. Shoving her foot against its neck, she held the head in place and twisted the handle, cracking the skull. The blade slid free and she handed the axe to Ari.

"Keep an eye on them. I'm going below to disconnect the fuel line so we can get out of here."

* * *

Sandy and the other Angels reached the end of the corridor when they heard something coming up the stairs. Sandy flashed her light down the opening and the other women aimed their weapons.

"Watch it," warned Sarah, her hand across her face to blot out the beam. "It's us."

"Sorry." Sandy moved the flashlight's beam to the side. "Are you okay?"

Sarah nodded. "It sounds like all the action is topside."

As if on cue, the repetitive booming of a machinegun echoed through the ship. The Angels exchanged glances.

Sandy headed for the open port hatchway on the superstructure and stuck out her head. The gunfire was coming from the forward section, although she couldn't see who was shooting. Turning aft, she saw the pile of crippled rotters underneath the open hatch, with a few of the less disabled crawling around the main deck. One spotted her and moved in her direction.

"What's it like?" asked Tiara.

"Not good." Sandy moved back inside. "We've got rotters. I don't know where or how many. We need to make our way back to the yacht."

"What about the supplies we found downstairs?" asked Sarah.

"No time for that now. Make sure you're loaded and locked, and be ready for anything." Sandy stepped back through the hatch, raised her M-16A2, and put a single round through the crawling rotter's head. Waving the others on, she made her way aft.

* * *

Stephanie ran back to the yacht's engine room and checked the fuel gauge. Ninety-seven percent full. That would have to be good enough. Working rapidly, she shut down the pump, disengaged the fuel line, and replaced the cap on the tank. She then made her way topside where she pulled the fuel line from the yacht, dropped it the ocean, and secured the access hatch.

When she reached the main deck, Emily was just regaining consciousness, with Josephine attending to her. The other Angels had dispatched the three rotters by the gunwale, one of which had fallen onto the yacht. With everything under control here, Stephanie made her way into the flying bridge.

"We're all set."

Ari switched on the engines. They roared to life and settled down to a dull thrum.

Stephanie stepped to the end of the flying bridge while the Angels climbed on board. When the last one reached the main deck, she called to them, "Cast off the line so we can get out of here."

"We can't," protested Sandy. "Natalie is still on board the cutter."

* * *

Natalie kept up a continuous barrage against the horde, even though the vibrations from the machinegun rattled every part of her body. The bullets cut through the heads of the living dead like a scythe, blasting them away or ripping them from their bodies. Chunks of body parts flew through the air, generating a cloud of gore. The insects feeding off of the dead flew in every direction, some swarming around Natalie. As the decapitated corpses collapsed to the deck, those to the rear moaned and surged forward, stumbling over the bodies or maneuvering around them. None, however, got to within ten feet of her. A semicircle of living dead formed around the gun mount. When no rotters remained standing, Natalie dropped the angle and swung the machinegun to the right and left, strafing the pile. Bullets thudded into lifeless bodies. She kept up the attack to make certain none of them survived.

The thoughts that flowed through her mind had nothing to do with stopping the rotters, focusing instead on what the zombie apocalypse had taken from her. Her previous life. Her family. Her fiancée. Her innocence. Her home at Fort McClary. And now Mike, the only other man she had ever loved and who she would probably never see again because of that damn vaccine. Everything she had known and loved had been ripped away from her. Twice. In less than a year. By this fucking plague of the living dead and the assholes who took advantage of the outbreak. She hated the latter more than the living dead. The rotters couldn't control themselves and didn't know better. Fuck them. Fuck this. Fuck everything. She should just take her fingers off the fucking trigger and let them overwhelm her and end this fucking nightmare.

The sound of her name being called snapped her back to reality. Only then did she notice that the .50 caliber had jammed, yet she still pressed her thumbs down on the trigger mechanism and swept the gun across the pile of dead. She concentrated on the voice.

"Natalie?" yelled Sandy. "Are you okay?"

"I'm fine," she lied.

"We're ready. You need help?"

"No. I'll be right there."

Stepping away from the gun mount, Natalie waded through the gore spread across the deck. It looked as though the viscera drain of a slaughterhouse had vomited forth its contents. She crossed over to the port side of the pilothouse where there were no corpses, made her way to the stairs, and descended to the main deck. Sandy and Tiara waited by the access ladder. The concern on their faces was evident as she approached.

"Is everything all right?" asked Sandy.

"No. And it won't be ever again." Natalie crawled over the gunwale and boarded the yacht. She saw the three rotter corpses sprawled on the deck.

Jesus Christ, is there anything these fuckers won't ruin?

Ari stepped out of the flying bridge. "We're all set to go."

"Good. Get us as far away from here as possible." Natalie continued below deck without saying another word. By the time

Ari pulled away from the cutter and headed back out to sea, Natalie had crashed in her cabin and fallen sound asleep.

CHAPTER TWENTY-SEVEN

Price sat on the edge of his desk and stared at the map taped to his office wall, the one that followed deader activity since that convoy had passed through the area two weeks ago. It confirmed his fears. When those assholes drove through Barnston, they attracted the attention of half the town's deader population, which followed the convoy west. He already had to send out several hunting parties to clean out the surrounding area. That didn't even take into consideration the pack of runners that had attacked them just the other day. According to his recon patrols, several hundred of these things prowled the woods and back roads between Barnston and the facility. His people didn't have much ammunition left, and this would put a severe drain on their resources. They would probably spend the next month making the area safe again, until some other group of assholes fucked it up.

In hindsight, he wished the raiding party he had sent out to track the convoy hadn't destroyed the compound they found in Maine. From what they told him, it was much nicer and more secure than the one he had here. They could have lived much more comfortably, eliminated the extra mouths to feed by not having to maintain the Line, and been better protected from deaders and rivals. Plus, it would have been the ideal payback to those fuckers for murdering his people and ruining what he had worked so hard to create. Under the circumstances, he didn't blame his guys for what they did. He blamed himself. He had sent the raiding party out under Kingston's command knowing they would go medieval on whoever they came across. If he had put Carter in charge, then saner heads would have prevailed and right now they'd be living in the better compound.

No matter. What was done was done. He had kept them alive this long, and through situations a lot worse than this.

The knocking on the door broke Price's concentration. "What is it?"

One of the sentries stuck his head in. "You wanted to be told when Carter got back. He's pulling through the gates now."

"Thanks."

By the time Price made it outside, Carter had parked the Hummer H3 in front of the office. Three men climbed out and headed back to their quarters. Carter exited from the driver's side and tossed the keys over the hood to his boss. Price caught them, aimed them at the vehicle, and pressed the door lock button. The headlights flashed and the alarm beeped twice.

Carter chuckled.

"What?" asked Price.

"You always set that damn alarm."

"Force of habit." Price hid his frustration and slid the keys into his pocket. "Did you get rid of the body?"

"We took her a mile down the road and threw her into a drainage ditch."

"No proper burial?" Price asked sarcastically.

"The bitch took her own life, so that's good enough for her. Besides, I didn't want to expose my men too long and get attacked by deaders."

"Are there a lot out there?"

"No more than usual. Most of the ones we're finding now are those traveling across the countryside. If we went into the woods to hunt them down, we could clear the area quicker."

Price shook his head. "I considered that, but it's too risky. I don't want any of our guys getting overrun by deaders. We can't afford to lose any more manpower. It's safer if we just sit tight and let them come to us. Which reminds me, we're going to take a chance soon and make a supply run to get more ammunition."

"Shit. We've cleaned out every gun store in a fifty mile radius."

"It's a shame that asshole Kingston didn't loot the compound in Maine before he torched it. I bet they had a good stockpile."

"Excuse me!"

Price and Carter saw one of the camp followers race up to them. Price knew she worked in the kitchen, but couldn't remember her name. "I'm in the middle of a conversa—"

"You need to come quickly."

"Why?"

"There's trouble in the kitchen."

CHAPTER TWENTY-EIGHT

The women had almost finished breakfast detail. Tracey planned the next meal while Lisa and Karen cleaned up, with Lisa washing the utensils in the cooking pot of boiling water while Karen dried them. Cindy sat in the corner amusing herself while Windows prepared a plate for the old man.

A commotion took place by the sliding door. Three latecomers stood at the entrance.

"Breakfast was over two hours ago," Lisa said.

"We're not here for breakfast. We're here for dessert."

The voice sent a chill down Windows' spine. It belonged to Kingston, the asshole who had raided Fort McClary and butchered her friends. Glancing over her shoulder, she saw him standing in the center of the doorway. Behind him and to the left stood Rogen, the most sadistic son of a bitch in the compound. To the right, Earl stood with his hands in the pockets of his jeans, trying to hide the massive bulge between his legs.

"What the hell are you talking about? We don't have desser—"

Kingston slapped Lisa across the face. "Shut up, you stupid cunt." He pointed to the corner where Cindy sat. "I'm talking about her."

Rogen sneered. "Now that her momma's dead, she's fair game."

"Yeah." Earl massaged the erection through his jeans.

Windows glanced at Cindy, who had curled up in the fetal position, shaking in fear.

Kingston grabbed Lisa by the hair and yanked her close so their faces were only inches apart. "You got a problem with that?"

"N-no."

"I didn't think so." Kingston whipped his hand to the side, throwing Lisa against the wall. She yelped. "Everyone out so we can be alone with the girl."

Lisa bolted for the exit, hiding her head in shame. Karen went next, pausing long enough to see if Windows would follow. When Windows refused to move, Karen disappeared around the corner.

Kingston took a step toward Windows. "I said, get the fuck out of here."

"No!" Windows summoned every ounce of courage she could. She knew she would die in the next few minutes, but she would hurt them as much as she could, and maybe take their minds off of Cindy for a few minutes.

Dear God, don't let me suffer too much.

"*What?*" The menacing tone in Kingston's voice made her blood run cold.

"I'm not going to let you hurt Cindy."

Earl stepped forward. "And just what the fuck do you think you can do to stop—"

Windows kicked Earl in his erection, generating so much pain he couldn't even cry out. He dropped to his knees, his hands clutching his crotch and tears streaming down his cheeks. Windows kicked out again. This time the heel of her boot caught him in the bottom half of his face. The crack of shattered bones reverberated off the walls, and bits of broken teeth and blood splattered the floor. Earl fell backwards. His gasp for air made a gurgling sound as blood filled his mouth.

Windows didn't see Kingston throw the punch until it connected with the side of her head. She felt the blow, the bolt of pain shoot through her body, and then everything went fuzzy. She had a vague sense of falling until someone grabbed her by the back of her shirt, lifted her up, and slammed her chest first onto the table. That jarred her back to consciousness. Windows felt one hand wrap around the back of her neck and press her throat into the tabletop, pinning her down. A second grabbed the back of her trousers and started to rip them off.

"Knock it off!" She recognized the voice as Kingston's.

"You gonna let the bitch get away with what she did to Earl?"

"Fuck that. Do you really want to waste a good load on that skank when we have virgin pussy here?" Kingston stepped over to Cindy and reached out for her. She shoved his hand away and scooted into the corner. Kingston grabbed her by the hair and lifted her into a standing position. The little girl screamed, as much from fear as pain, and began to wail. "Clear the table. And make sure she watches this."

Rogen lifted Windows off the table, dragged her to the center of the unit, and forced her to her knees. Grabbing her by the top of her head and her jaw, he forcefully turned her face in the direction of the table. When Windows refused to open her eyes, Rogen yanked on her hair, forcing her to watch. Kingston had Cindy bent over the table like Windows herself had been a few moments before. He dropped his trousers and shorts down around his ankles, grabbed the little girl's pants, and started to pull them down her legs.

Rogen leaned over close to Windows' ear. "Enjoy the show, whore. We're gonna tap us some nice virgin pussy. And because you tried to stop us, later tonight we're gonna gangbang the living fuck out of you."

Windows could not watch the scene because of the tears welling up in her eyes. At first she thought the blur on her left was unshed tears, until she heard Kingston let out a painful huff. She closed her eyes tight, squeezing out the tears, and reopened them. Meat had raced into the room and body checked Kingston, sending him flying into the wall where he sat against the wall, dazed and confused. The force of the blow had also knocked Cindy onto the floor. She seemed all right and scurried under the table for safety. Meat grabbed the cooking pot of boiling water, grunting as the hot metal seared his skin, and emptied the contents onto Kingston. Kingston screamed in agony and thrashed around. Windows smirked as she saw the blisters well up on his face and exposed genitals.

"You fat fucking bastard!" Rogen released Windows and charged at Meat. Meat spun around, swinging the cooking pot in a wide arc that connected with Rogen's head. Windows heard the crunching of bone even over the other sounds in the room. When Rogen collapsed to the floor, his skull had been crushed, with the entire left side of his head caved in.

Meat dropped the cooking pot and flexed his hands, grimacing from the pain. He only concentrated on himself for a second. Crouching down, he reached out to Cindy with a hand raw and covered with blisters.

"Come on, kid."

Cindy backed against the wall, lifted her knees up to her chest, and wrapped her arms tightly around her legs.

Rather than get mad, Meat showed uncharacteristic kindness. "It's okay. No one's gonna hurt ya anymore. I promise."

Cindy looked to Windows, and the woman nodded her approval. The girl got on her hands and knees and emerged from under the table, with Meat coaxing her along. When she reached him, Meat placed a hand on her cheek, then jerked it back and shook it to ease the pain. He smiled, not the sadistic grin Windows had grown used to, but one of actual tenderness.

"Everything'll be okay."

The three of them all turned to the commotion at the entrance. Lisa ran into the room and gasped. Price and Carter followed a few seconds later.

"Okay. What's the trou... Jesus fucking Christ." Price looked around the unit, aghast. "What the fuck happened?"

Meat stood up and wrapped one arm around Cindy's shoulder, careful to make sure the palm of his hand didn't touch anything. "These assholes tried raping mah girl."

"*Your* girl?" The way Price said it sent an ominous chill down Windows' spine.

"Yeah."

"And you did all this to them?"

"No. Just Kingston and Rogen. I don't know who fucked up Earl."

"That would be me." Windows mustered as much defiance as she could and faced Price. "I was defending Cindy."

Price glared at her, his face devoid of emotion. She could tell from the iciness in his stare that he wished her harm. He finally averted his gaze to Meat. "Take these two back to your quarters. Wait there until you hear from me."

"Yes, sir." Meat headed for the door, ushering Windows along. She fell in behind him, grateful to be alive, and even more grateful that Cindy had not been harmed, though she knew the emotional scars would run deep.

What lay in store for her, though, was far from certain.

* * *

Price waited until the others had left and turned his attention to Lisa. "Take Earl to his quarters, and then come back in thirty minutes and clean up this mess."

"Yes, sir." The young woman raced over to Earl and helped him to his feet. The man groaned when he tried to straighten up, winced, and doubled over. Placing his arm over her shoulders, she walked him outside.

While Lisa escorted Earl out, Carter walked over and knelt beside Rogen, placing two fingers on his carotid artery.

"How is he?" Price asked.

"He's dead."

Price motioned to Kingston. "What about him?"

Carter walked over to Kingston and examined him, and then shook his head. "Kingston is pretty bad. He's suffered second and third degree burns. If we had a proper medical facility, we could take care of him."

"Fuck him. There's still daylight. I want you and some of the boys to take them out and dump them with that bitch you got rid of earlier."

"You don't even want to try and save him?"

"The asshole had it coming. We don't have time and resources to spend on him." Price headed for the exit, motioning for Carter to follow. "We have another issue we need to take care of."

"What's that?"

"That woman, Windows. She's been nothing but trouble since she got here."

"Good luck with that. Meat is infatuated with her."

Price spun around and got into Carter's face. "Is Meat in charge here, or am I?"

"You are."

"Remember that." Price continued walking, and his tone softened. "The problem is, Meat is getting soft because of her and that kid. We've lost two good men because of it. We can't afford to lose any more."

"I understand."

"Give it a few days, and then make it look like an accident. I'll leave the details up to you. Just make sure Meat doesn't suspect us."

Carter nodded. "Roger that."

Price shook his head. "We have to get rid of Windows and that brat before they undermine morale around here."

CHAPTER TWENTY-NINE

When Robson finished explaining his plan for breaking Windows out of the storage facility, he leaned back in his chair in the rectory's dining room and placed his thumbs through his belt loops. The expressions of those around the table made him want to grin. Caslow stared at him as if he had rotters sprouting from his forehead. His own people looked far from convinced. Robson noticed DeWitt lean closer to Roberta and ask if he was serious, to which she just shrugged and said, "I think so." As always, Tibor showed his disgust. Robson was disappointed to see Dravko disturbed because he could usually count on him to go along. Wayans huffed and shook his head. When Wayans attempted to gauge his partner's response, his eyes registered surprise that Simmons was actually contemplating this scheme. Simmons sat there, calculating the possibilities. Robson hoped Simmons would approve since he and Wayans were an integral part of the plan. The only one who supported him was Jennifer, who nodded her approval.

"Well?" asked Robson after a few seconds. "What do you think?"

Simmons sat forward and rested his arms on the table. "It has a lot of moving parts, which increases the chances of something going wrong."

"I don't like that either, but it can't be avoided. And most of the moving parts are in the preparatory stages of the plan, so if something goes wrong it can be corrected. Once we make contact with the enemy, the plan becomes much simpler and has a higher chance of success."

Simmons nodded.

"Wait, wait, wait." Wayans held up his hand and stared at

Simmons. "You're not actually buying into this friggin' plan, are you?"

"Why not?"

"Because it's friggin' insane," Wayans said. "No offense, man," he said to Robson.

Robson smiled. "None taken."

Simmons placed a hand on his friend's shoulder. "It's the only chance we have of getting those people out of that facility."

"We don't owe them anything." Wayans nodded to the others at the table. "I'm not meaning to sound like a friggin' jerk, but they're not our concern. Yeah, their situation is bad, but life friggin' sucks. We can't save everyone."

"Think of it as saving ourselves," Simmons responded. "Sooner or later that gang is going to find us. We're going to have to deal with them at some point and, personally, I'd rather do it on our terms when we have the advantage of numbers and the element of surprise."

Wayans sat back in his chair, folded his arms across his chest, and huffed. "I friggin' hate it when you're right."

"So that's it?" complained Caslow. "We're going ahead with this scheme?"

"Do you have a better idea?" asked Robson.

"No, but...." Caslow looked to the others around the table and, seeing their displeasure, became embarrassed. "I mean, isn't there another way other than going into the facility to get them?"

"According to what you told us, the only ones who ever leave the compound are the gang members," Robson said. "If we want the civilians, we have to go in and get them."

"Is it worth the risk?"

"Are you fucking serious?" Jennifer yelled. "Your wife and daughter are locked in there with those rapists. You're willing to abandon them to keep yourself safe?"

"That's not what..." Caslow stumbled for the right words. "I mean, we're putting a lot of us on the line to rescue only three people."

"It's your *family*, you little shit. You should be—"

Robson placed his hand on Jennifer's and squeezed enough to stop her tirade, keeping his gaze fixed on Caslow. "We're not just getting Windows and your family out, but everyone who is being held prisoner there."

DeWitt leaned toward his boss. "That's kind of ambitious, don't you think?"

"We can't leave them there," Robson said matter-of-factly, without sounding accusatory. "Most of them wouldn't last a week on their own. We need to give them time to build up their strength so they can either join us or go on their own."

"How do you plan on feeding them?" asked Simmons.

"I'm guessing there's plenty of food stored away at the facility. We'll use their supplies."

Wayans chuckled. "Good luck getting the gang to agree to that."

"That won't be a problem," said Robson. "We're going to kill all the gang members."

A stunned silence fell over the room.

"You can't do that without due process!" Caslow protested.

"It's not like we'll be executing anyone who hasn't brought it upon themselves. Everyone in that facility who isn't a rapist or murderer is being used as a sex slave or is chained to that perimeter defense line."

"What about your humanity?" Caslow asked.

Wayans snorted derisively. "Where'd you get this guy?"

Jennifer glared at Caslow. "In case you hadn't noticed, legal niceties went out the window with the release of the Zombie Virus."

Robson held up his hand to cut off further arguments. "I'm not passing any judgments a court of law wouldn't impose. There are no more police, no more jails, and no more trials. Justice comes from the end of a gun now. We've made it this far without killing any innocent people or taking something that belonged to someone else, and we've saved quite a few people along the way. *That's* humanity. That gang is only out for themselves. They attacked us when we were by here earlier, and would have murdered us if it wasn't for Dravko's people. Then they found our compound and butchered everyone there, close to thirty people. If we let any of them live, they're going to hunt us down. I'm going to protect my people. If that means I have to kill off a bunch of assholes who are trying to take me down, I'll gladly put a bullet in their heads and not lose any sleep over it. So it's up to you. If you disagree with the way I'm running things, you can pack up your stuff and head out on your own, and we'll save your family for you. Otherwise, shut the fuck up, grow a pair, and get with the program."

Robson had seen men emotionally break down before, usually punks who realized they had finally gone too far and would now spend time in prison. Caslow collapsed like a house of cards in a tornado. One second he stared angrily at Robson, then what little defiance he had left drained away. Caslow took a deep breath and, as he exhaled, his head and shoulders drooped. He sobbed uncontrollably.

No one spoke. One by one, everyone around the table stood and exited the room, most ignoring the shell of a man. Jennifer and Wayans flashed him an expression of disgust before leaving. Robson waited until the others had departed before standing up and crossing around the table to where Caslow sat. He patted the man on the shoulder and gave a reassuring squeeze, and then followed the others outside.

Dravko waited near the door of the rectory. When Robson passed by, he fell into step with the human. "Can we talk?"

"What's up?"

"I wanted to know why you gave me and Tibor the task of protecting the humans outside the facility rather than fighting with the rest of you. Don't you trust us anymore?"

"It has nothing to do with trust. You and Tibor are not immune to the Zombie Virus like we are. If I asked you to fight alongside the rest of us, you run the risk of being infected. I've lost a lot of people the past few weeks. I don't intend to lose any more"

"Is that the real reason?" Dravko asked.

Robson stopped walking abruptly. "How can you even ask that?"

Dravko hesitated, as if not wanting to broach the subject. After a moment of silence, Robson prodded him. "What's wrong?"

"Do you realize Tibor and I haven't eaten in several days?"

Robson hadn't. His mind had been focused on getting the Angels to Omaha and on rescuing Windows from the rape gang. Even worse, he had cultivated the friendship with Simmons and

Wayans, and gone so far as to take that idiot Caslow under his wing, yet had forgotten to provide for his own people. Not his own *people*, technically, but the vampires existing with them. No wonder Dravko and Tibor questioned him.

"Jesus, I completely forgot that we had run out of your blood supply when the gang butchered the livestock. I'm sorry about that, Dravko."

Dravko appreciated the sincerity of Robson's response. "That's okay."

"No," Robson said, "it isn't. I'll round up some donors right away."

The vampire shook his head. "You can't do that."

"Why not?"

"You can't ask Simmons or Wayans to contribute. They're uneasy as it is having us here. And Caslow would shit himself."

"The rest of us can ante up some blood. We've done it before."

"Not before a raid. If you do that, you'll weaken yourselves." Robson tried to protest, but Dravko held up his hands to cut him off. "We can last a long time without feeding. I'm not worried about that. I just wanted to be sure we weren't being marginalized."

"You're not." Robson placed a hand on the vampire's shoulder. "I promise you that."

Dravko reached up and patted Robson's forearm. "Thank you."

"Come on. You can help me get things ready." Robson headed back to the warehouse, with Dravko beside him. "If you want, tomorrow night you can help me get our school bus back."

CHAPTER THIRTY

Each of the Angels came by to say their farewells to Bethany. Some spoke a few words of solace while others offered nothing more than a silent prayer. A few squeezed her hand. All of them shed tears. Natalie sat at the head of the bunk, taking it all in and fighting back her own, trying to remain stoic for the others.

Emily paid her respects last. She walked to the other side of the bunk opposite Natalie and sat on the mattress, clasping Bethany's hand in her own. After a few seconds, she leaned forward and whispered, "Everything will be okay, honey. You're going to a better place. We'll see you soon enough."

She kissed Bethany on the cheek and left. Ari took her place and glanced over at Natalie. "Are you ready?"

Natalie held up three pre-filled syringes, each containing ten milliliters of morphine sulfate. "Thirty milliliters, just like you said. How long will it take?"

"Normally twenty to twenty-five minutes, maybe less considering her condition." Ari reached her hand across the bunk. "I'll do it."

"No. It's my responsibility."

"Have you ever given an injection before?"

"Never."

"Then let me. We have to do it right the first time."

Natalie handed her friend the three syringes. Ari removed the first one from its wrapper and detached the plastic cap covering the needle. She pushed Bethany's head to one side, placed the hypodermic against a vein, and inserted it under the skin until a little blood backwashed into the syringe. Ari slowly depressed the plunger. When she had finished, she withdrew the needle and placed it on the nightstand, and then did the same with the other two syringes. When finished, she placed the plastic caps back on the needles and slid the syringes into her pocket.

"I'll leave you alone. Come get me when it's over." Ari left the cabin, closing the door behind her.

Taking Bethany's hand in her own, Natalie sat with her friend during the last moments. Her mind wandered back over the previous nine months. How they had picked up Bethany walking along the side of Route 95 during one of their supply runs. How many of the girls at camp began training on a cache of World War II German Mausers to stave off boredom. How Bethany, despite being the youngest woman in camp at nineteen, soon became one of their best marksman. How the girls had proved their worth one day when rotters overran the fort and the girls fought them back, a feat for which Robson gave them their name the Angels of Death. Those had been heady days. In a few short weeks her girls had gone from being a band of camp hangers-on to the group's premiere rotter hunting unit. The Angels supported Robson's foraging team on every raid and, because of them, the team had not lost a single person on these missions. The Angels began to believe they were invulnerable.

That all changed when the Angels accompanied Robson's team to Site R to retrieve the vaccine for the Zombie Virus. Natalie never admitted it to the others, but by the second day she realized that the Angels had gotten in well over their heads. Gunning down thirty to forty scattered rotters on raids to isolated locations did not prepare them for what they faced outside their compound, did not prepare them for the realization that society had collapsed and been replaced by a world of the living dead. Sure, they had all gone through the early days of the outbreak, but by the time the world had completely collapsed, most of them had joined the community at Fort McClary and hadn't witnessed the end. The trip down to Site R brought home to the Angels the reality that society as they had known it had been supplanted by a rotter world. By the time the Angels had finished battling those four hundred rotters in the access tunnel leading to the underground facility, their morale had been shattered. Her girls no longer functioned as a cohesive fighting unit. In some respects, they were worse off now than when each of them had arrived at camp, because back then they each possessed an ember of hope she could fan into the flame of self-respect. After Site R, those flames had been extinguished.

Bethany's breathing grew labored as the effects of the morphine began to take hold and impaired her respiratory functions. Natalie pushed the loose strands of hair off of Bethany's face and stroked her forehead. The skin burned with fever. A part of her wanted to get a cloth soaked with cold water and place it over Bethany's forehead, but what could would it do now? Natalie sniffed back her tears, tears for Bethany's suffering as much as her own guilt.

Everything that happened after finding Fort McClary scorched seemed aligned against her. Someone had to get the vaccine to Omaha, otherwise everything they had endured and everyone they had lost to retrieve it would have been for nothing. Because Robson's team had been annihilated at Site R, that left the Angels as the only ones available to make the trip, even though they were in no condition to do a cross-country trek through rotter-infested territory. But what else could she do? Even if she had refused, where would they go now that the camp had been destroyed? Natalie had desperately wanted to ask Robson to lead them, as much to have him with her as to take on the responsibility. However, that would mean abandoning Windows to the rape gang, which she couldn't condone. So she agreed to take on a suicide mission.

Despite the inevitably of the circumstances beyond her control that brought her to this moment, Natalie still blamed herself for Bethany's death.

She would also blame herself for the other Angels who would die before they reached Omaha.

Bethany's chest heaved slightly. Natalie clasped her hand and held tight. The woman tried to suck in air, but her lungs no longer functioned. She kept up the quiet death struggle for nearly a minute. Bethany gasped, and it was over. As her friend crossed over into a better realm, Natalie allowed tears to stream down her cheeks.

BOOK TWO

CHAPTER THIRTY-ONE

The old man glanced up when Windows and Cindy entered his quarters. "I'm glad to see you. I was getting worried."

Windows forced a pleasant attitude. "I'm sorry I missed breakfast."

"That's not what I meant. When you didn't show up, I thought something bad had happened to you."

This time, the smile was genuine. "Thanks. You're the only one around here who cares."

Cindy scurried into the corner and curled into a ball, hiding in the shadows. Windows knelt beside the old man and began feeding him.

After swallowing the second mouthful, he asked, "What happened this morning?"

"Nothing much."

The old man held up a crippled hand and placed it on her forearm, preventing her from continuing. "Please tell me."

Windows sighed. "Three guys tried to assault me and Cindy, but Meat broke it up. He killed one of them and threw boiling water on another."

"What about the third?"

"I kicked him in the nuts."

The old man laughed and spit out his food. Windows used the spoon to scoop the excess off of his chin.

"Sorry." He snorted. "Good girl, though."

"Thanks. It could have been worse. Price showed up and put an end to it."

The old man's humor evaporated. "Don't trust him."

"I don't."

"I'm serious. Price is dangerous. He didn't get to lead this group of murderers by winning a popularity contest."

"I know that."

"I don't think you do." The old man's eyes pleaded for her to listen. "Has anyone told you about Price?"

Windows shook her head.

"Price was an inmate at the state prison down in Concord when the outbreak began. He had a history of violent assault, and had even hospitalized several people. The kid had been in and out of jail several times. One night he came home to find another man in bed with his wife. He threw the guy out a second-story window, paralyzing him, and beat his wife so badly she went into a coma and died three months later. The courts sentenced him to ten years for manslaughter. He had served half that when the dead began to rise. Unfortunately, prison made him even more violent. When the virus reached New England, he orchestrated a riot. Most of the prisoners used the chance to escape, but Price, Carter, Kingston, and several others stayed behind to get revenge on the guards."

"You mean they murdered them?"

"That would have been humane. They beat the guards and warden senseless, then dragged them outside and handcuffed them to the perimeter fence so the dead could get them. After cleaning out the prison armory, they made their way north, causing as much destruction as the outbreak. They kidnapped families and forced the husbands to watch their wives and kids be molested and murdered before being tied up and left for the deaders. Others were killed just for the fun of it. When they ran across people like themselves, they were given the opportunity to join the group under Price's leadership or were gunned down."

"Didn't the police try to stop them?"

"By then all the police had been overwhelmed by the living dead. Price's gang executed the few police or stray military units they came across. They eventually found this place and turned it into an armed camp. Unfortunately, a lot of innocent people also stumbled across it and sought shelter. Price allowed them in and let them think they had found a safe haven, lulling them into a false sense of security until it was too late. He ordered the men shot or put on the Line, and allowed his gang to do whatever they wanted to the women and children. The lucky ones were kept inside to serve as camp followers. The rest joined the others outside."

Windows shivered, recalling her first two days.

The old man nodded. "Then you know what I'm talking about. You experienced the same thing?"

"Pretty much. The day I arrived, Price made sure no one touched me and assured me everything would be fine."

"And on the second day you were gang raped."

"But not before being taken hunting and used as bait to lure rotters."

"How do you get here?"

"They raided the compound where I lived, killed everyone, and torched the place. I survived because Meat took a liking to me."

"Lucky you," the old man said sarcastically. "But that's typical. From what I hear, they've raided up to half a dozen places where people have been holed up, and slaughtered everyone. I doubt there's anyone left alive within a twenty-mile radius."

"I guess it was just bad luck that Price decided to settle down here."

"Luck had nothing to do with it. He came here purposefully."

"Why?"

The old man's eyes locked on her. "No one told you?"

"Told me what?"

"Who I am."

"No."

The old man broke eye contact and averted his gaze. "I'm Price's father."

CHAPTER THIRTY-TWO

Windows could only stare at the old man for several seconds, dumbstruck. "Price is your *son*?"

The old man nodded. "My name is Lee. And I know what you're thinking. What type of asshole am I to raise a son like that?"

"Not at all," she responded much too quickly.

"I don't blame you for thinking that way. In most cases it's true. God knows I wasn't the best father. I never hit him, and I tried to raise him right. His mother loved him, too. If anything, she was overprotective. He was a good kid until he reached high school, and then the fighting and bullying started. We tried to discipline him, but it never worked. The harder we tried, the more violent he became. Some kids are just bad, I guess."

"You don't have to explain yourself to me."

Lee glanced up and mouthed "Thank you."

"So why did Price come back?"

"To check on Judith, his mother. Despite the way he treated her, he really loved her."

"What happened?"

"I killed my wife about a week into the apocalypse. She...." Lee paused, overwhelmed by grief. His face grimaced and tears welled up in his eyes. After a minute, he regained control. "Sorry about that."

"That's okay." Windows held his hand and didn't let go. "You don't have to go on."

"I do." Lee sniffed and wiped snot from his nose. "We had planned on heading north. I had gone to fill up the H3 while Judith went to the grocery store to stock up. When I got back, I found her sitting in the living room crying, with a huge bite mark on her arm. Someone in the store had turned and attacked Judith and several others. I stayed with her and comforted her until the end, and then used a shotgun to put her out of her misery. After that, I stayed just to be with her."

"Is that why your hands are broken? Did Price punish you for killing his mother?"

"No. While I don't think he ever forgave me it, he knew it had to be done, and would have shot her himself to prevent her from becoming one of those things." Lee held up his hands. "He did this because I challenged him. About two weeks after he set up camp here, he came up with the idea of the Line after one raid that netted him a lot of prisoners. He called a meeting to discuss implementing the plan. Afterwards, four of his people got together and decided to stage a coup. I don't know, maybe they thought the idea inhumane. Maybe they thought he had become uncontrollable. Maybe they thought they'd wind up on it someday. For whatever reason, they came up with a plan to kill off Price and Carter, and lead the group themselves. After that, they intended to look for more comfortable accommodations."

"How did you fit in?"

"They asked me if I would be a part of the plot to lend it legitimacy. I said no. I couldn't be involved in killing my own son, no matter what he had become."

"But you never warned him."

Once again, Lee averted his gaze. "No. Although I couldn't pull the trigger, I wanted to see him dead for what he had done to all those innocent people. Instead, I chickened out and made things worse."

"What happened?"

"One of the conspirators, a little prick named Ross, went and told Price what the others planned. He figured by betraying his friends, he would get himself in good with my son. Dumb bastard had no idea who he was dealing with. Price beat the three other conspirators half to death. He then held a public meeting, gave the typical speech about how everything he did was to keep the group safe, and used them as examples of what would happen to the others if they disobeyed. Because Ross considered conspiring against him, Price made him the first person on the Line. Gave him just enough food and water to keep him alive. It took nearly six weeks before Ross died of exposure. When his point had been made, he had Carter drive the other three into Barnston and leave them in the center of town."

"And you?"

"Because I hadn't warned Price about the plot, I had to be punished. Since I was his father, he wouldn't kill me or put me on the Line. He broke my hands so I wouldn't be able to hurt him, and then isolated me in where I couldn't cause trouble." Lee shrugged. "I guess I got off lucky."

Windows stroked the old man's hair. "It's okay now. I'm here to take care of you."

"You may not be for long."

She stopped in mid-stroke. "Why do you say that?"

"Price eliminates anyone who is a threat to him or causes him trouble."

"How am I a threat?"

"You're not. You are trouble, though. He lost two of his men today because of you, and he won't forget that."

Windows lowered her hand. "What am I going to do?"

"There's nothing you can do. If you get a chance to go off the compound, take it and run. At least that way you have a chance of escape."

"What about her?"

Lee glanced over his shoulder at Cindy and sighed. "Be careful and keep your eyes open."

"I will. And thanks."

"Don't thank me. I didn't do anything to help you, only make you nervous."

Windows went back to feeding Lee. By trying to protect her, he had made her more paranoid than before. She knew Price would be trying to find a way to get rid of her, and probably Cindy as well. Rather than sit here complacent until the end, at least now she had a fighting chance. All she had to do was figure a way for her and Cindy to escape.

CHAPTER THIRTY-THREE

The Angels gathered on the stern of the yacht to pay their final respects to Bethany. Emily and Ari stood below them on the transom's boarding platform, with the body of the young woman between them. They had placed Bethany in a funerary pose, wrapped the body in a blanket, and secured it with rope. To weigh the body down, they placed two twenty-pound barbells they had found in one of the closets inside the blanket.

Natalie moved closer to the boarding platform. "Dear Lord, we are about to commit our friend and comrade to the sea. Please take her in your loving arms and watch over her, and give her the peace and comfort she has rightfully earned. In your name we pray. Amen."

Natalie closed her eyes and nodded. Crouching down, Emily and Ari each grabbed one end of the burial shroud and lifted Bethany off the boarding platform. With as much respect and gentleness as possible, they tossed the body over the side and watched it disappear beneath the surface.

While Emily and Ari climbed back up to the main deck, Josephine looked at the others. "Shouldn't we say something?"

"Natalie just did," said Sandy.

"I mean a eulogy of some sort."

"What purpose would it serve?" Tiara asked.

"I don't know," said Josephine. "I just thought we should say something that would make her death have some meaning."

Natalie separated herself from the group and turned to face them. "You want Bethany's death to have meaning? Then use her as an example. Bethany is dead because she couldn't handle the pressure and got sloppy."

The Angels stared at her incredulously.

"We've all become sloppy. Ever since we left Site R, we've barely functioned as a cohesive unit. When we returned via Portland, most of you didn't even get off the bus to set up a perimeter. Bethany got bit because we got careless and let that rotter slip by us. If we don't shape up soon, we're all going to wind up like her."

"To be fair," argued Ari, "we were never trained to handle what happened at Site R."

"I have news for you." Natalie moved closer to the group. Several of them stepped back. *Good,* she thought. *They're afraid of me. Maybe what I have to say will sink in.* "What we encountered at Site R is what this world is really like now. We fooled ourselves into believing we could handle it because we made a few supply runs to isolated stores where rotter activity was minimal. If we couldn't deal with what we ran into in Pennsylvania, what do you think is going to happen on the way to Omaha?"

"Most of this trip is by water." Even Emily seemed intimidated.

"The last part isn't. We're going to have to sail through New Orleans, navigate the Mississippi, and travel cross country to reach our destination. Are you ready for that?" Natalie faced the others. "Are any of you? Shit, we almost got our asses handed to us back at the Coast Guard cutter."

"So what do you recommend?" asked Ari.

"That we put our heads on straight and get back in the game." Natalie pointed toward the main cabin. "Remember, our whole reason for doing this is to take the vaccine to Omaha so the government can mass produce it, and maybe start taking this country back from the living dead. I'm not exaggerating when I say we may well be the last hope of humanity. But we're never going to make it unless we get our shit together. And if we don't make it, then Bethany, Leila, everyone who died at or on the way to Site R, and everyone slaughtered back at camp, will have died for nothing."

Without saying another word, Natalie stormed off and headed back to her cabin, letting her Angels take in what she had just said. In reality, she didn't know where to go from there. A pep talk was a poor substitute for action. She had yet to figure out a way to restore the Angels' shattered morale and make them a cohesive fighting unit again. And she only had a few days to figure it out.

CHAPTER THIRTY-FOUR

Robson stood on the Casco Bay Bridge, staring down the span until it disappeared into the darkness of Portland. Dravko and Tibor stood to his left, Simmons and DeWitt to his right.

"We're clear on this?" asked Robson. "Dravko, Tibor, and I go in and get the school bus. You guys wait here and come after us if we get in trouble."

"It sounds risky," Simmons replied. "Wouldn't it be easier to find another school bus?"

Robson shook his head. "We'd chew up a lot of time and gas trying to locate one. And good luck finding one that runs. We know this one works."

"What about the dead?" asked Simmons.

"They're locked up behind fences and won't be a problem. We'll be in and out in ten minutes." Robson tapped the radio attached to his belt. "If we get into trouble, help is only a phone call away." He gave a final look to the others. "Ready?"

Simmons nodded. "I guess. I'm just glad I'm not the crazy one driving into a dead-infested city. Good luck."

As Simmons and DeWitt joined the rest of the group, Robson and the vampires walked over to their specially-prepared Humvee. Tibor climbed in behind the wheel and Dravko took the passenger seat.

Robson got in back and closed the door. "Let's do this."

Tibor headed into downtown Portland.

They had driven five hundred yards when Robson noticed something wrong. On the northern approach of the bridge, they passed a rotter in a blood-stained jogging suit shambling aimlessly. At first Robson paid no attention. Then they passed a second and third. He leaned forward between the front seats.

"We've got a problem."

Dravko turned his attention over his shoulder. "Why do you say that?"

Robson pointed to the fourth rotter they passed, a woman in a tattered sundress. "The streets were empty last time we came through here."

"Maybe they came across the bridge after we destroyed the barricade."

Tibor pointed ahead of him. "Or maybe they came from downtown."

As they neared the end of the ramp, the headlights shone on hundreds of the living dead milling around Commerce Street.

"What the fuck?" Dravko asked.

Robson shrugged. "The chain link fence must have collapsed."

Upon hearing the approaching vehicle, the living dead turned in the direction of the noise and surged forward.

Tibor slowed the Humvee. "Should we go back?

"No," Robson responded. "There aren't too many."

Tibor glared at him. "One is enough. Remember, we're not immune to them."

"Don't worry. We can make it."

Tibor glanced over at Dravko, who nodded toward downtown. Tibor grunted and pressed his foot down on the accelerator. The Humvee plowed into the first rotter, bursting its midsection and sending the body cartwheeling to one side.

"Careful," Dravko admonished.

"I know what I'm doing." Tibor swerved around another of the living dead, clipping it with the rear fender.

The farther they got into downtown Portland, the heavier the rotters became. With each passing minute, the living dead closed in tighter around the Humvee to the point that Tibor couldn't maneuver around them. Each time he slammed into one of them, it slowed their speed. At this rate, they would be swarmed within a minute. Maybe Robson had miscalculated this one.

Dravko pointed ahead of them. "There it is."

The Humvee's headlights reflected off of the rear of the school bus. Off to its right, one section of the chain link fence had collapsed, probably right after he had used the bus as a decoy to lure the living dead away from the ferry terminal so the Angels could escape. A few dozen rotters mingled around on the other side of the fence. Another score wandered around the vehicle. They turned at the approach of the Humvee and headed toward it.

Robson leaned forward and tapped Tibor on the shoulder. "Drop me off by the door. I can take it from there."

Tibor snarled. Veering to the left, he swung the Humvee around the front of the school bus. Robson cursed to himself when he realized he had left open the folding glass doors. When Tibor stopped, Robson jumped out. Something caught on the door latch. With a yank of his hips, he pulled himself free, slammed shut the Humvee's door, and bounded onto the school bus. Grabbing the door handle bar, he slammed it shut. A quick glance in the side mirrors showed the nearby rotters converging on both vehicles. The folding doors would only hold them for a few seconds. Sliding into the driver's seat, he brushed away the swarm of flies around his head and reached for the ignition key. "Fuck!"

The ignition was already set in the ON position. He remembered he had left the engine running when they dropped off the bus. It had used up all of its gasoline. He had to get back to the Humvee. Robson headed for the door. Three rotters had moved into the space between the two vehicles. Even though their attention focused on the Humvee, they still trapped him inside. He wished he had brought along his AA-12. As Robson reached for his Colt detective .38 special, two things happened he did not expect.

The Humvee pulled away.

The moan of rotters echoed from the interior of the school bus.

* * *

Just as Robson closed the door to the school bus, three rotters emerged from around the vehicle's corners, two from the front and one from the rear. Dravko wanted to get out so he could clear them away, but the first pair was too close. One wore a yellow rubber fishermen's coat and sported a heavy beard caked in gore. It ran its hands across the window, smearing the surface with decayed skin. It snapped its jaws at Dravko. When its mouth hit the glass, several teeth tore loose, ripping out chunks of gum that stuck to the window. The other two rotters closed around the door.

Tibor pressed his foot down on the accelerator. The Humvee shot forward, knocking the three back against the school bus. Once free from the threat, Tibor did not slow down.

Dravko's attention switched between the school bus behind him and to Tibor. "What are you doing? You can't leave Robson behind."

Tibor said nothing and continued down Commerce Street.

* * *

Robson aimed his firearm down the length of the bus. It was too dark to see anything clearly. In the limited light from the Humvee's taillights he could make out three, maybe four, shapes approaching. Aiming as best he could, Robson fired a single round. The sound of a bullet striking bone and the collapse of the shadow told him he had scored a hit. Switching his aim, Robson fired again. The shadow jerked back and kept on coming. Another shot and the shadow dropped to its knees and fell forward. Moving the Colt toward the last shadow, he fired off a fourth round. The shadow swayed to one side and dropped to the floor.

The sound of the folding doors being pried open drew Robson's attention back to the front. The three rotters that had swarmed the Humvee had turned to attack the school bus. The one in a yellow fishermen's coat had pushed against the centerline, opening it enough for the other two to get their hands inside. Only the weight of the first rotter against the glass prevented them from opening it. Sliding the firearm into his belt, Robson grabbed the support bar by the front seats for leverage and slammed his right foot onto the center frame of the folding door. The jamb closed around the fingers of the two rotters. They didn't withdraw them. Robson kicked again. This time a finger broke off. The door opened wider, and one of the rotters tried to shove its head inside. Removing the Colt from his belt and placing it against the rotter's forehead, Robson squeezed the trigger. Within the confines of the school bus, the blast was deafening. The rotter's head exploded and the limp body fell back, releasing its grip. Rushing forward, Robson slammed his weight against the door, shutting it with such force that he severed the fingers of the other rotter, each one plopping to the floor like pieces of dead meat.

With the door now secure, Robson leaned his weight into it and braced his feet against the steps. At best, he had a few minutes before enough rotters swarmed the door that he couldn't hold them back. He would deal with Dravko and Tibor later. Right now he needed to call DeWitt to come get him. Reaching for his belt, he realized his radio was gone. He frantically felt around, hoping maybe it had shifted with all his moving, but couldn't find it. Then he remembered something getting caught on the door of the Humvee. Checking the pavement outside, he saw his radio on the ground.

"Fuck!" Robson slammed his hand against the glass.

* * *

At the rear of the school bus, the third rotter grabbed one of the seat backs and lifted itself up. It had not been shot by Robson. It had stumbled over the corpse in front of it just as he had fired, falling to the floor as the bullet thumped harmlessly into its shoulder. Climbing to its feet, it made its way toward the noise at the front of the bus.

* * *

"Tibor!" Dravko grabbed the vampire's forearm and squeezed tight. "What the fuck are you doing? We can't leave Robson there to die!"

Tibor stopped the Humvee five hundred feet away from the bus. The two glared at each other. Dravko struggled not to morph into his vampire form. At the first sign of aggression from Tibor he would tear out his throat. As the standoff went down inside the vehicle, rotters gathered outside. Dead hands slapped against the metal and scratched the glass, trying to get at the food. Within a minute, most of the living dead in the area had closed around the Humvee. Without taking his eyes off of Dravko, Tibor shifted into reverse and backed the Humvee toward the school bus. He glanced behind him to maneuver the vehicle behind the bus, stopping when within a few feet of the rear bumper. The maneuver left the rotters down the road. En masse, they turned and followed the Humvee.

"There's a chain in the trunk," said Tibor. "Attach it to the school bus and we'll pull it to safety."

Knowing he only had seconds to act, Dravko jumped out and raced around to the rear of the vehicle. As he opened the trunk, he half expected to find it empty and have Tibor drive away. To his surprise, a twenty-foot tow chain with twin hooks on either end lay rolled up. Grabbing one end, he attached it to the tow hitch on the Humvee. Taking the other end, Dravko dropped to the ground, crawled under the bus, and wrapped it around the axle and crankshaft. Once secured, he crawled out. The nearest rotter was less than fifty feet away.

Jumping back into the Humvee, Dravko closed the door. "Let's get out of here."

* * *

Robson heard the moan a split second before he saw the shadow move. He hadn't heard it approach because of the noise outside, and now it stood a few feet away. With not enough time to aim, he raised the Colt close to his chest and fired a single round into the rotter's sternum. The force of the shot caused it to stagger back. Extending his arm and aiming at its head, Robson fired his last round. The skull exploded, showering the far side of the bus in brains and gore. He was safe for the moment.

He was also out of bullets.

Another noise at the rear of the bus caught his attention. He leaned forward to check in back, afraid he would find more rotters. Instead, he saw the Humvee backing up. Just in time, too. Four more rotters had gathered around the door to the bus. They were pushing to get inside, and his back and legs were buckling under the pressure. He saw Dravko jump out and attach both ends of the tow line, then get back in the Humvee. The vehicle drove away. A moment later, the bus jerked when the towline pulled taut. The rotters against the door fell away, and Robson's back slammed against the glass when the pressure let up. He sighed, every muscle in his body protesting the strain of the last few minutes.

The two vehicles crept along Commerce Street and through downtown Portland. Rotters closed around them, though not enough to impede their progress. For twenty tense minutes, Robson stood in the stairwell of the bus, his back against the door to prevent any stray living dead from getting in, anticipating either being swarmed to a standstill, the towline breaking, or Dravko and Tibor abandoning him. Not until they pulled onto the ramp leading to the Cisco Bay Bridge did he breathe a sigh of relief.

Glancing out the windshield, he saw that only a handful of rotters bothered following them, more than enough for DeWitt and Simmons to handle.

Moving over to the driver's seat, Robson sat down to wait out the rest of the journey.

CHAPTER THIRTY-FIVE

They made it back to the warehouse a few hours before dawn. Once out of Portland, the rest of the trip had been easy. They had stopped on the southern approach of the Cisco Bay Bridge to unhook the towline and transfer gas from the other vehicles. The few rotters that had followed had been dispatched by Simmons and Wayans. Once the bus had enough gas, the convoy made its way to Gilmanton.

When they pulled into the parking lot of the construction company, Jennifer ran out of the garage. Caslow followed her out and hovered around the door, embarrassed to join the others. Robson pulled the bus alongside the building and stopped. When he opened the folding door, Jennifer bounded up the steps, slowing when she reached the landing.

"I'm glad you're all right," she said.

"Why wouldn't I be?"

"It took you so long to come back I thought..." She sniffed a few times, and turned toward the rear of the bus. Her eyes widened when she saw the three corpses on the floor. "Jesus, what happened?"

"I'll tell you over breakfast." Robson placed a hand on Jennifer's shoulder and led her off the bus.

She smiled. "Who's going to clean it up?"

Robson nodded toward Caslow. "Maybe it's about time he pitched in."

"It's probably as close he'll ever get to them."

Tibor brushed past them and stormed into the garage. Caslow saw the vampire approach and jumped aside, disappearing around the corner of the building. Robson glanced over his shoulder. Dravko stood by the specialized Humvee, his expression distraught. Robson halted.

"What's wrong?" Jennifer asked.

"I need to talk to Dravko. I'll be inside in a few."

Jennifer headed back to the garage, and Robson walked over to Dravko. The vampire leaned against the Humvee and averted his gaze, which meant they hadn't planned on leaving him in Portland. Well, at least Dravko hadn't. He took a deep breath as he approached.

Fear and worry tinted Dravko's eyes. "I have no idea what happened back there. I think Tibor planned on leaving you."

"Are you certain?"

Dravko shook his head. "That's the thing. I asked him if that was his intention. He never answered, but he did stop and go back for you. I don't know if he planned on leading the rotters away from you so he could go back and attach the towline, or if he planned on abandoning you."

"What would you have done if he did mean to leave me?"

Dravko stiffened his back, not in anger but in determination. "Then either Tibor or I would have died in Portland."

"Thanks for having my back."

"I may not always have it."

"What do you mean?"

"Ever since we got back from Site R, Tibor has been talking about leaving the group and setting out on our own, rebuilding the coven and eventually the vampire nation. He's convinced that if we don't do it now, before you humans use the vaccine to stop the rotters, then our species will be wiped out along with them."

"Do you agree with him?"

Dravko sighed. "As the only remaining vampires, we are an endangered species. However, I've lived among you so long I can't go back to hunting humans for food."

"I take it Tibor doesn't see things the same way."

"No. The only concession he's willing to make is that, after what we've all gone through together, he won't turn any of you. He's adamant about leaving the group and rebuilding the coven with other humans. So far I've been able to keep him under control. Since we're the only two of our kind left, my authority is wearing thin. I'm afraid the first chance he gets, Tibor is going to kill me off and turn on your group."

Robson had not thought about that before. They had grown accustomed to living with the undead these past nine months, and had taken it for granted that under Elena's leadership the vampires had assimilated into human culture. It seemed only natural that, as a species, they would want to avoid extinction. The only way Dravko and Tibor could accomplish that was if Robson gave his blessing for them to go off on their own to prey on humans and rebuild the coven. Robson knew he couldn't allow that, couldn't spend so many lives wiping out one species of creature to turn around and allow another one to thrive, even if he had come to know them personally and respect them. Ironically, because he knew and respected them he couldn't slaughter Dravko and Tibor in cold blood. Based on what Dravko had just told him, he might have to.

While Robson contemplated his next move, Dravko made eye contact. The vampire must have seen the concern in his friend's eyes because he said, "Don't worry. I've already made up my mind to take down Tibor if he becomes an immediate threat to me or any of you."

"Hopefully you won't have to make that decision."

"We both know I will. If not now, sometime down the road."

Robson pitied the dilemma his friend faced. "This must be a horrible decision for you."

"It is, but it's inevitable. My species can't live in this world we created. Maybe it's time we died out." Dravko laughed sullenly. "Ironic, isn't it? We created our own extinction event."

CHAPTER THIRTY-SIX

Natalie woke up slowly, that long process when you emerge from a dream into reality. She was aware of the gentle rocking of the yacht underneath her, and the soft rays of morning light shining through the porthole. For one blissful moment, she imagined herself aboard a cruise ship, waking up beside Robson. As the fog of sleep wore off, it struck her that she was aboard a yacht traveling along a dead coast trying to get a vaccine to a government-in-exile deep inside a rotter-infested country. She wanted to bury her head into the pillow and sob.

The sound of heavy footsteps echoed from the deck above her. Natalie's eyes shot open in anticipation of the inevitable yelling and gunfire. It never happened. The sound continued, now in a pattern. Swinging her legs out of bed, Natalie put on her boots, grabbed her M-16A2, and made her way topside.

To her surprise, she found the Angels lined up in three rows and engaged in jumping jacks, each one stripped down to their panties and t-shirts. Ari faced them, keeping cadence. Once they reached twenty, Ari ordered them to drop. Lying prone with their feet together and their hands flush on the deck and level with their shoulders, they began a series of pushups, again with Ari leading the cadence. This time the Angels performed fifteen reps of double pushups, and then jumped to their feet. Ari told them to take a breather.

Ari glanced over and saw Natalie standing by the hatch and grinned. "About time you woke up."

"How long have I been asleep?" Natalie asked as she crossed the deck.

"Sixteen hours."

"Shit."

"Don't worry. You needed the rest."

Natalie tried to hide her embarrassment about showing such weakness. She turned to the rest of the Angels. "What's going on here?"

"You were right yesterday," replied Ari. "We've become sloppy."

"I'm sorry. I shouldn't have said that."

"You should have because it's true. We let what happened at Site R get the better of us. We have to reverse that."

"With calisthenics?" Natalie joked.

Ari grinned. "It's a start. Besides, we have to make sure we look good in our uniforms when we meet the President."

Natalie laughed. The other Angels took that opportunity to move forward and greet her, letting her know that they harbored no ill feelings about the previous day's dressing down. For the first time in almost two weeks, the women acted like their old selves. It felt good. Although Natalie wouldn't show it, deep down she wanted to cry. Once again her girls had risen to the occasion. For the first time since setting out from Portland, she began to feel like they might just pull this off.

The Angels enjoyed the moment for only a few minutes before Emily called out from the flying bridge. "Sorry to break this up. You'll want to come up here."

Natalie felt her emotions sink. "Coming."

She made her way to the bridge, followed by Ari and the rest of the Angels. Ari grabbed the binoculars when she reached the steering house.

"What's up?" Natalie asked, standing beside Emily.

"We're about to round the southern tip of Florida. I estimate we're twenty-five to thirty miles west of Key Largo." She pointed ahead of them to a land formation that stretched along the horizon. "My guess is those are the Keys."

The yacht sailed closer. The land formation took on a more defined shape into a series of islands ranging in length from several hundred yards to several miles, each connected to the other by an elevated highway spanning the water. When the yacht got to within a mile, the Angels could make out buildings dotting the islands. Thousands of vehicles generated a traffic jam along the elevated highway that extended as far to east and west as they could see.

"What is it?" asked Tiara.

"It's the Overseas Highway," Emily answered. "It runs from Key Largo to Stock Island, a distance of about one hundred miles, and connects the Keys."

Josephine shook her head. "It looks like everyone had the same idea. Make it to the islands where they'd be safe from the outbreak."

"That didn't work out too well," Sandy said sarcastically.

"Where is everyone?"

Ari removed the binoculars from her eyes and pointed straight ahead. "There."

Natalie reached for the binoculars and used them to scan the highway. Her stomach churned. Thousands of rotters stumbled around the stalled traffic and along the parallel bike trail, staggering into vehicles, bumping into each other, and wandering mindlessly. Even from this distance, she could see that the sun had baked these rotters, blistering the skin and drying it out until they resembled mummified skeletons. Their lips had pulled back to reveal jaws and decaying teeth, and the lids had shrunk to reveal sockets in which the eyes had long since shriveled from the intense heat. That explained their movement. They were blind. She almost pitied them.

After a few minutes, a female rotter in a sun-bleached summer dress heard the yacht's engines. Its head shifted up and down and to the sides, trying to determine where the noise came from. Eventually it turned its head in the yacht's direction and moaned. Those rotters closest to it joined in and gazed around. It spread like a wildfire through the horde, making its way along the highway until every rotter within sight thrashed about. Soon the moaning reached the Angels aboard the yacht, the loudest and most ungodly chorus any of them had ever heard. It sent a shiver down Natalie's spine.

Then the feeding frenzy began. One rotter stumbled into another. Maybe it was frustration over not being able to see the food, or fear generated by its blindness, but the first rotter lashed out at the one it stumbled into. It tore at its face, ripping away dried-out chunks of flesh, and lunged. Sinking its teeth into the second rotter's face, it ripped out most of the latter's cheek. Others exhibited the same behavior and attacked those nearby, while others attempted to avoid the conflict, which became difficult as more and more battles broke out along the highway.

"Holy fuck," Ari mumbled.

Natalie lowered the binoculars. Each of her Angels stared at the melee, most with an expression of horror.

She moved closer to Emily. "If we cut the engines, would we be able to coast under the highway?"

"We should. The current isn't strong here. Why?"

"I don't want to draw attention to ourselves."

Emily aimed between the two closest islands, throttled forward to give the ship momentum, and shut down the engines. The only sound now came from the water slapping against the side of the hull and the ungodly moaning. Five tense minutes passed as the yacht coasted along and passed underneath the highway. The sound became more eerie with the noise from thousands of rotters scraping along the cement echoing off the underside of the highway and walking trail. Everyone stared up, half expecting the battle above them to spill over onto the deck. Thankfully, nothing happened and the yacht emerged from the under the highway. Once it had coasted a hundred feet away, Natalie nodded to Emily.

"Let's get out of here."

"With pleasure." Emily started the engines and throttled them forward. The sound excited the rotters, increasing the intensity of the battles. Within a few minutes, the yacht left the horror of the highway behind them.

"I'll steer us back toward shore."

"That'll take too much time," Natalie said. "Do we have enough gas to cut across the Gulf toward Louisiana?"

Emily checked the fuel gauge. "We should."

"Are your navigational skills good enough to get us to New Orleans?"

"I'll get you to within five miles of the Mississippi River."

"How long will it take?"

"If everything goes well, we should reach the coast late tomorrow afternoon."

"Good." Natalie leaned closer so the others couldn't hear.

"The less time we spend out here the better."

"Next stop, Bourbon Street."

"Angels, when did you ladies clean your weapons last?"

The women exchanged glances, embarrassed. Sandy said, "Not since we left Maine."

"Then what are you waiting for?" Natalie barked the order, although the grin on her face betrayed her feelings. The Angels responded with good-natured complaints and sauntered below deck to gather their weapons. Natalie wanted to keep their morale up and build on their newfound cohesion. The drill to check and clean their weapons was much more than that.

Natalie realized that as of this time tomorrow, they would be entering a rotter nation.

CHAPTER THIRTY-SEVEN

Removing his last bottle of Jack Daniels from the desk drawer, Price poured the whiskey into a tumbler, filling it halfway. He had gone through a whole case in their first few months here, and had saved this bottle to celebrate a special occasion. At the time, he had thought it would be to toast the end of the deader outbreak and the rise of a new world order in which strength prevailed over so-called justice. That dream died along with the rest of the world. He still kept the bottle hidden away, hoping that something positive might happen that he could celebrate. It never did. He broke out the bottle this morning because he needed a stiff drink.

Price walked over to his office window and took a swig, staring out into the storage facility. The sight of it burned in his stomach worse than the whiskey. Everyone except himself lived in unheated and unventilated storage units. Their bathrooms consisted of portable toilets and makeshift showers rigged from hoses siphoning water brought in from the Suncock River. Their kitchen was primitive, and their food stocks were running low. Plus they had limited medical supplies and even less in the way of health care expertise. He had already lost more than half a dozen of his men to illness and serious wounds. To put it bluntly, this compound was a shithole. He always knew it and, up until a few days ago, it had not bothered him. For Christ's sake, it was the fucking apocalypse. Nobody expected to be living in luxury. They were lucky to be alive. Now he couldn't stand the sight of the place.

The catalyst for all this was the discovery of the other group's compound along the coast of Maine. He had fooled himself into thinking he had done a good job caring for his men until he heard about their set-up. Adequately-furnished container boxes, a well-stocked mess hall, agriculture and livestock, a medical facility. It had everything he had failed to provide for his people, which pissed him off. Those assholes were no better or smarter than him. They sure as hell weren't stronger judging by the way they allowed his search party to take over their compound without a fight. Yet they had ridden out the deader outbreak a lot better than his group had. Though he would never admit it to any of his people, not even Carter, what really pissed him off was his own failure of leadership. The other group had done well for itself because their leaders focused on the correct priorities, while he had dropped the ball. Sure, his reasons for choosing the storage facility seemed sound at the time. It had been the most secure location they had found in weeks, with concrete buildings closed off by metal doors and surrounded by a brick wall with a security gate, ideal for keeping away deaders and humans. Besides, no one could have foreseen that the outbreak would last this long, so he hadn't seen the need to make the compound more amenable. At some point, he should have realized that the world had permanently gone to shit, and should have concentrated on either fixing up their own compound or finding a better location. Instead, he focused on keeping his men happy rather than protected. So the blame for their current situation rested squarely on him.

Hell, even he had enjoyed those first few days after the outbreak. It got him off getting revenge on the prison guards, especially those three that took turns holding him down while another raped him. They used to taunt him that they would show him how it felt to be an abused bitch. He had handcuffed them to the fence outside the prison and left them to be deader food. If they were lucky, the deaders completely devoured them, although a part of him hoped they did come back to spend forever chained to that fence, starving. Carter had joined him because he had wanted to get back at the guard who had been fucking his wife while he sat in jail. And Kingston... Kingston was just a psycho who enjoyed killing.

He knew he should have put an end to the violence after they left the prison. Now he couldn't remember why he didn't. He didn't necessarily enjoy it. He hadn't been with a woman since the outbreak began, except for Tina. She had given herself to him willingly until a deader bit her, forcing him to shoot her in the head. He rarely killed anyone unless he needed to cull out those who posed a threat to his authority. While in prison, he had read a magazine article about mob mentalities and how groups of people will follow the strongest wills or their basest instincts. When your group consists of murderers and rapists, those instincts are pretty base.

Price took another long sip, letting the whiskey settle in the back of his throat for several seconds before swallowing. It burned going down, causing him to cough. Truth be known, now he was just making up excuses. Price could have reined them in at any time because he had the strongest will in the group. He *should* have reined them in. Instead, he had allowed his people to do a Mickey and Mallory across New Hampshire, and he condoned it just so he could keep the group loyal to him. In that he had succeeded. They stuck by him as long as he provided women to rape and people to kill. By focusing on that, he had placed his group in a precarious situation. Winter would soon be here, and their food supplies would run out long before then, especially with so many camp whores and those on the Line to feed. Even with ample food, he doubted they would survive another winter in this place.

He had royally fucked up the entire situation.

Price drained the tumbler and swallowed hard. His old man would get a kick out of knowing how bad a fuck up his son had become. Thank God he kept him isolated and restricted his contact with others. He should have gotten rid of his father months ago. The bastard let deaders get his mother, and later turned on him, along with the other conspirators. The old man didn't deserve to live, and for the life of him Price couldn't remember why he allowed it. He wanted to take a baseball bat, go into the old man's unit, and bash in his skull.

He decided he would settle for another drink.

Going back to his desk, Price picked up the bottle of Jack Daniels when someone knocked. "Come in," he barked.

Carter stepped inside. He held a map in his hand. "Sorry to bother you. One of the scouting parties you sent out yesterday came across something you might be interested in."

"Let me see." Price placed the bottle and tumbler back in the drawer.

Stepping over to the desk, Carter spread out a map of the local area. He traced his finger along the surface. "One of our teams was scouting twenty-five miles northwest of here when they found a gated community...." He paused until he found the site. "Here. A few miles east of Andover."

"So? We've run into a lot of gated communities. Right now we're in no position for another fight."

"That's the thing." Carter smiled. "This is an unfinished community. The gates were still closed and locked, so our guys broke in and checked it out. About three quarters of the houses have been built, and none of them were occupied. A brick wall surrounds the entire community. And there's more than enough construction supplies left behind for us to fortify it."

"What are you suggesting?"

Carter leaned forward and spoke softly. "That we get the hell out of here. Set ourselves up in a place where we can be comfortable for a change. We could steal furniture from that community we trashed just east of here. Make a few runs into Andover to stockpile food. Hell, we can even start growing our own like those assholes in Maine."

Price walked past Carter and stared out the window again. This was his chance to redeem himself. He could finally get his men some decent living quarters, and give them a chance to survive the upcoming winter. It would also give him a chance to clean house and put things in order. He could dispose of those who had become a burden and then concentrate on rebuilding their lives.

"What do you think?" Carter asked.

"I think it's a great idea."

Carter gave a fist pump.

Stepping back over to his desk, Price slid into the chair. "How long would it take to prepare for the move?"

"We don't have much to move. Two, maybe three days."

"Then we'll leave in three days."

"Roger that." Carter hesitated. "What about those on the Line?"

"Leave them. We won't need them where we're going."

"Do you want me to untie them after we're gone?"

Price shrugged. "Either way. Your choice."

"What about the women?"

"Bring them with us. We can't expect the boys to behave all the time."

"What about that bitch Meat has hooked up with, and the little girl?"

"Bring them along. Just make sure they go missing on the way to Andover."

"Understood." Carter turned and walked out.

Price waited until Carter had left, and then withdrew the bottle of Jack Daniels and the tumbler from his drawer. He poured himself another two inches of whiskey and swigged. Now he celebrated the change in their luck.

CHAPTER THIRTY-EIGHT

Another string of expletives came from the school bus, which made Robson chuckle. It had been like this for the past hour. Being the most entertainment he had in months, he sat down on the plastic chair in front of the garage and nursed along his morning cup of coffee.

Jennifer exited a few minutes later. Upon seeing him, her eyes lit up. "Good morning."

He raised his mug as a greeting. "Morning."

"How'd you sleep?"

"Pretty good. Everything is falling into place."

From inside the bus, Caslow yelled, "Son of a bitch!"

Jennifer stared at the bus and back to Robson, confusion in her eyes.

"That's Caslow. I woke him up this morning and told him he had to clean up the school bus before we modify it."

"What did he do with the bodies?"

"I drove him up the road a few miles and had him throw them in a drainage ditch. Now he's cleaning up the gore." Robson chuckled again. "He's thrown up twice already."

"Good."

"You really hate that guy."

"Do you blame me? The coward let a rape gang kidnap his wife and daughter because he was too afraid to stand up for them. I hope he chokes on his own puke."

"Don't be too hard on him."

"*Please* tell me you don't feel sorry for that little prick?"

"Not at all. What he did was a disgrace. As a cop, I ran into a lot of guys like him, guys who, at a critical moment, panicked and allowed a loved one to get hurt because of their inaction.

219

Every one of them regretted that decision. Caslow knows what he did, and what is happening to his wife and daughter, and it's eating him up inside. He's going to have to deal with the guilt and shame for the rest of his life, which is worse than anything you can do to him." Robson didn't add that he knew the feeling well. A mental image of his fiancée Susan flashed through his mind.

"Sorry."

"Don't be. He's a useless piece of shit. He knows that, he doesn't need us reminding him of it."

Caslow emerged from the school bus carrying a pail full of gore. He stumbled down the steps and dropped to his hands and knees, nearly spilling the contents, and vomited again. This time he had nothing left to spew, so he dry heaved onto the pavement. Jennifer glared at him. Robson noted that her expression still showed contempt, although not as intense as previously. He stood up and tenderly rubbed her shoulder, eliciting a smile. She reached up, patted his hand, and went back inside.

Robson stepped over to Caslow and crouched beside him. "You okay?"

Caslow hacked and shook his head.

"Here." Robson reached into his jacket pocket and pulled out a small plastic bottle of water, handing it to Caslow. "Rinse your mouth."

Twisting off the cap, Caslow poured some of the water into his mouth, swished it around, and spat it onto the cement, gagging in the process. He wiped his sleeve across his mouth. "The bus is clean. Are you done punishing me for what I did to my family?"

"You'll do a better job of that than I ever could." Robson offered his hand. "I made you clean the bus because it's time you started pulling your weight around here."

Caslow took the hand and raised himself off the ground. "Good, because I want to do more. I want to go with you guys when you raid the compound."

"No."

"Why not?" Caslow demanded.

Bastard is finally showing a little backbone, Robson thought. He still didn't want him along. "I already have enough people."

"Bullshit. It's because you don't trust me."

"It has nothing to do with trust. You don't know how to handle yourself. You'll get yourself killed."

"That's my decision, not yours."

"It *is* my decision because you might wind up getting one of *us* killed in the process. End of discussion."

Robson turned and headed back to the garage. Caslow raced ahead and cut him off. All the defiance had drained from him. "Please, listen to me for just a minute. You have to let me go. You have to give me a chance to redeem myself. I know what I did was selfish and fucked up. The only chance I have of ever winning back my family's trust is if I go with you. If you get them out while I'm waiting safely back here, I've lost them forever."

What Caslow said made sense, although Robson felt that redeeming himself was not Caslow's only reason for asking to go along. A part of him thought Caslow might be hoping for death by suicide mission. Not that it mattered. He had asked for a chance for recover his dignity with his loved ones, a chance Robson would never get, and as such he couldn't deny Caslow's request.

"Okay. You'll go in with me."

A sense of relief washed over Caslow. "Thank you."

"Don't thank me. You have no idea what type of a shit storm you've just volunteered for. Now come with me." Robson placed an arm around Caslow's shoulder and led him into the garage. "I'm going to teach you how to use your weapon."

CHAPTER THIRTY-NINE

Emily missed their target by twenty miles, not bad considering she had navigated solely by the stars. They had made land near Grand Isle on the southern coast of Louisiana, west of the Mississippi River. Cruising southeast, she soon found the river entrance. Natalie had expected the waterway to either be barricaded to traffic or so jammed with abandoned vessels as to be unnavigable. To her surprise, the river was clear. No ships, no debris, no rotters. It looked like no one had traversed the river for years. Natalie didn't question her luck. God knew they needed all they could get. However, as Emily steered the yacht up the Mississippi, Natalie had called the Angels on deck in full uniform and gear to deal with any potential threats.

It had taken them the better part of the afternoon to make their way along the hundred miles of river that snaked through the wetlands south of New Orleans. For hours, they had seen no signs of the living or the living dead, which only built up the tension. The afternoon sun had begun making its slow descent toward the western horizon when they saw the first signs of civilization, an oil refinery and warehouses mixed in with small bedroom communities. Down the river sat the suburban community of Belle Chasse and, beyond that, the New Orleans skyline.

"This is creepy," Amy mumbled.

"What?" Natalie asked.

Amy pointed to Belle Chasse along the port beam. "There's no sign of rotters. You'd think so close to New Orleans we'd see at least a few of them roaming about."

Natalie raised the binoculars. She saw no activity. She crossed to starboard and found Ari. "Have you seen any rotters?"

"Not since we entered the Mississippi. Why?"

"The girls haven't seen anything on the other side of the river either."

"That's not good."

"Yeah." Natalie scanned the river bank. "Where the hell are they?"

"Let's hope we don't find out."

The Mississippi turned sharply to the right and entered a long U-turn before flowing into New Orleans. Here the suburbs showed signs of having experienced the outbreak. Roads barricaded and clogged with abandoned vehicles, some bearing witness to vicious rotter attacks with shattered windows and blood streaks. Houses boarded up or ransacked. Blood smeared across building facades. An entire neighborhood burnt to the ground. Along the shore, dozens of small boats remained tied to the docks, some partially sunk. Skeletons lay scattered along the water's edge. Still no signs of rotters.

All that changed when Emily turned the yacht around the southern bend and sailed into the downtown area. The incessant moaning caught their attention first. It was low key yet overwhelming, like the buzz that emanated from a large beehive. As the yacht approached the Cross City Connector Bridge, Natalie noticed a series of boards attached to the structure. Several had fallen off, but the basic message remained intact: a red-painted arrow pointing to the left with the words SAVE US!!!!! As they drew closer to the bridge, she saw where the moaning came from.

Thousands of rotters filled the southern bank of the Mississippi, stretching for several hundred yards along the waterfront and inland. They didn't shamble aimlessly. The attention of every one of them was directed toward a brick warehouse located six hundred feet before the bridge and one hundred fifty feet inland. Each wall of the building had inscribed across the top in bright red paint the words HUMANS INSIDE – HELP US. The living dead swarmed the structure, shoving and pushing their way forward.

"Oh, dear God," said Sandy. "On the roof."

Natalie raised the binoculars and, as she focused in on where Sandy gestured, she felt the nausea fill her stomach.

Five people stood on the roof – three men, a woman, and a little girl of about six. Even from this distance she could tell they were in terrible shape. Their bodies were emaciated and their worn clothes hung off of them. The three men jumped up and down and screamed. The woman pointed to the yacht and said something to the little girl, and then both began waving. Below them, the rotters grew excited. As one, the horde of thousands surged toward the warehouse, their hands groping toward the food. Their moaning increased until it became a roar that drowned out the yacht's engines.

All the Angels moved toward the port gunwale. Tiara shook her head. "I can't imagine what they must be going through."

"The warehouse is surrounded," said Josephine. "We'll never get near it."

"How are we going to get them out?" Ari asked.

"We're not," Natalie stated.

"What do you mean?" Amy asked.

"We can't just leave them there," protested Stephanie.

"We can and we will." Natalie took a step forward. "There's no way to save them without all of us getting killed, and I'm not even going to risk it. I feel sorry for them, but our job is to get this vaccine to Omaha. If we don't, a lot more people than those five are going to die. Understood?"

A despondent chorus of approvals came from the Angels.

"Good. Now get back to your stations and ignore them."

The Angels went back to guarding the yacht. Natalie raised the binoculars and looked one final time at the warehouse. The woman had dropped to her knees and was crying, clutching the little girl in her arms. Two of the men had sat down on the roof, one of them holding his head in his hands and shaking it. The third one screamed at them and raised the middle fingers of both hands high above his head. Not that she blamed them. She would feel the same way under the circumstances. That wouldn't do anything to assuage her guilt over leaving them to die.

She waited until the support columns for the Cross City Connector Bridges blocked her view of the warehouse before turning her back on the scene.

CHAPTER FORTY

By now the feeding of Lee had become routine. Windows would come in with his meal, Lee would sit up and make himself as presentable as possible, and Cindy would scurry off and sit in the corner. She had closed off even more than usual following the attack in the kitchen, undoing all the progress Windows had made to break her out of her shell. Lee would glance over at Cindy every so often, concern on his face. Usually they kept the conversations casual, focusing on any topic that would get their minds off of the hell they were going through, even if for only a few minutes. Today, Windows wanted to share the news.

"Did you hear?" Windows asked as she fed Lee his dinner. "We're moving."

"You and Cindy?" he asked with a tremble in his voice.

"The whole camp. One of your son's foraging parties found an empty gated community not far from here. There are houses that haven't been ransacked and a wall that can keep out rotters. We'll be moving in a few days. The best part is you'll finally get out of this box."

Lee frowned. "I'll just be trading this prison for a nicer one."

Windows' wanted to yell at him for being so negative, then realized he was right. Nothing would change for them. Price would shove his father into the damp basement of one of the homes, and she would still have to fuck Meat, only now it would be in a bed rather than on a mattress on the floor. And Cindy would still be in danger. Physically, the girl might survive the coming winter; emotionally, Windows was about to lose her forever.

Windows fed Lee a forkful of beans. Chewing, he glanced over at Cindy and back to Windows. "You two can't go with the others when they move."

"That's easier said than done."

"If you want to live you'll find a way." Lee said it with such force it took Windows by surprise.

"What do you mean?"

"Price isn't doing this because he's had a change of heart about the camp followers. He's making this move to keep his men alive. He'll leave behind anything that is no longer of value to him. That includes everyone on the Line and half the women inside camp, at least the ones they're bored with. Knowing my son, he won't let them just walk away. He's used to murdering those who he no longer has a use for."

Windows' hands shook. She placed the plate down on the blanket and tucked her hands under her arms so the tremors wouldn't show. "Do you really think he'll kill us?"

"If not, he'll take you with him where you will wind up servicing the entire camp." He met her gaze and mouthed the words, "And probably Cindy, too."

Windows began to cry. How could she have been so naïve? Things would not get better. In fact, her situation would become infinitely worse. And now Cindy would be dragged into it. Fear for their safety mixed with the desperation that flooded her emotions. She understood why Debra committed suicide.

"Don't cry." Lee placed a deformed hand on her shoulder. "There's a way out."

"No there isn't!" she sobbed.

Lee grinned. "What if I told you I had hidden a car less than five miles from here with a full tank of gas and three days' worth of supplies."

"Are you serious?"

He nodded. "When the others were getting ready to take down Price, I prepared a Rav-4 for escape just in case things went wrong. It's fully gassed and has four backpacks in it, each with a three-day supply of dried food and water. I'm the only one who knew about it, and when we got ratted out I kept quiet, hoping someday I might be able to use it to get out of here. I can't use it anymore, but you can."

Windows rubbed the back of her hand across her eyes and sniffed. "You're going with us. I won't leave you here."

"You have to."

"No."

"Listen to me. If you and the girl disappear during the move, Price probably won't even notice, and if he does, I doubt he'll send anyone after you. If I go missing, he'll hunt me down and kill anyone who's with me. You stand a much better chance if you leave me behind."

"I can't—"

Lee held up his hand to cut her off. "You know I'm right. I'll be okay if I stay here. You two won't survive much longer. End of argument."

Windows fought back the tears. She knew her only chance of saving Cindy was to sneak off on her own. She also knew that she would be condemning Lee to misery. The thought of it tore her up inside. However, she had her priorities. She forced a smile.

"Getting to the car is easy," Lee whispered. "Route 28 is right outside the compound. Head north, take the second street on your left, and follow it for about two miles. You'll come to an old construction site. There's a metal garage on the site. The Rav-4 is in there."

"Thanks."

"You can thank me by getting that little girl to safety."

The meal continued on as usual, only this time Windows noticed that Lee had a content expression on his face.

CHAPTER FORTY-ONE

"Television." Wayans thought about it for a moment and nodded. "I miss television the most."

"That's it?" laughed DeWitt. "Of all the things you could miss from the pre-outbreak days, you miss television the most?"

"What's friggin' wrong with that? I used to love the SyFy Channel, though that sounds pretty lame now."

"What about you?" Jennifer asked Simmons. "Excluding family and friends, what do miss most about life before the outbreak?"

"Crime."

"Stopping it or committing it?" chided Frakes.

"I know it sounds weird. A better answer is probably solving crime. It kept me busy. The worst part about being here is I'm bored out of my mind. I now understand why so many cops can't handle retirement." Simmons leaned forward in his chair and smiled good-naturedly at Jennifer. "What do you miss?"

"Drinking a hot cup of peppermint tea while reading a book."

"I didn't picture you as the nerdy type," Robson remarked.

"Would it make me less nerdy if I told you I did that in silk pajamas?"

"No," he lied, enjoying the mental image.

"Your turn."

Robson thought a moment. "The beach."

"The beach is still there, man," said DeWitt.

"I mean enjoying the beach. When I was with the sheriff's department, I'd always stop by the coast on the way home, park for a few minutes, and just listen to the waves rolling in. I found it relaxing. It used to give me a few moments of solace. Now it just reminds me of how alone we are."

Jennifer reached out for his hand and squeezed, and then steered the conversation back on track.

"DeWitt?"

"Dunkin Donuts iced coffee."

"Oh, my God. Yes." Allard closed his eyes. "With a half dozen honey dipped Munchkins."

Frakes shook his head. "Ever been to Revere Beach down in Massachusetts? Kelly's makes the best roast beef sandwiches in the world. We used to drive down there every Friday night for dinner. That's a meal to miss."

Seeing that Roberta appeared ill at ease, Jennifer asked, "What's wrong?"

Roberta's eyes went from Jennifer to the two cops and back again. "I don't know if I should say."

"We're all friends here. Go on."

Roberta shrugged. "I'd kill right now for a joint."

Wayans threw his head back and laughed. "You and me both."

Roberta showed her surprise. "But you're a cop."

Even Simmons laughed now. "That doesn't mean we don't know how to have fun."

Allard nudged Roberta in the arm. "I bet you those two could hook you up."

She flushed red from embarrassment.

Jennifer glared at Caslow, who sat separated from the others, staring at his plate. "What do you miss most?"

Without lifting his head, he responded, "My wife and daughter."

"Family and friends are excluded."

"I don't care." He fixed his eyes on Jennifer. "They're the only things I miss from my past life."

The joyous mood drained away as everyone remembered a loved one who didn't make it past that first week. After a minute of morose silence, DeWitt spoke.

"I have a question. Once we rescue Windows and Caslow's family, then what?"

"We bring them back here," Robson answered.

"I mean, what about all the other people being held hostage at the compound? What are we going to do with them?"

Robson sat back in his chair. He hadn't thought about that.

The defense perimeter held thirty to forty people, none of whom could survive on their own for more than a few days. Most of them probably wouldn't last long even under his protection. And God only knew how many more were inside the compound that he wasn't aware of. He couldn't set up a new camp here. Although the garage served well enough as a temporary shelter, it would be inadequate to house another forty people. Setting out to find another location would be a death sentence for most of those who survived the raid. Without food and proper medical care, few of them would make it past the first week. He didn't even want to contemplate what would happen if rotters attacked the convoy. Best case scenario, even if most of them lived through the trip and they found an ideal location to reestablish camp, he still faced the prospect of fortifying, supplying, and defending the new compound with far fewer able bodied personnel than he would have mouths to feed. Christ, by trying to do the right thing he may have condemned them all to death.

What really sucked was that he could still change his mind about this raid.

"Boss?" DeWitt asked. "Did you hear me?"

"I did. I just hadn't thought about that before. I've been concentrating on saving Windows."

Simmons shifted uncomfortably in his chair. "I hate to be an asshole about this, but we can't accommodate so many people."

"You're not being an asshole," said Robson. "You've done more than enough for us already, and I wouldn't put that burden on you."

"Friggin' sorry, man."

"It's okay. Honest." Robson stood up. "If you'll excuse me, I need to figure this out."

Leaving the rectory, he took a slow walk up the road away from the garage, trying to find a solution between two unenviable options. If one existed, he couldn't come up with it. His choices sucked. If he did the right thing and tried to save everyone, more than likely he would get them all killed. If he saved only his own people, they had a pretty good chance of making it, yet the price would be his conscience.

He heard the footsteps approaching then Jennifer called out, "Wait up."

He turned around as she raced up. "I need to be alone."

"I know. I want to say something. You have a tough decision to make, and either way you're going to feel guilty about what you do. I've been there. Dr. Compton and I agonized for days over whether we should try the vaccine on human volunteers, fully aware of the risks. Every time a volunteer turned, we felt horrible."

"Thanks." Robson turned to walk away.

Jennifer grabbed his hand and pulled him around to face her, keeping a grip on his palm so he couldn't leave. "I'm not finished. We did things we would never have done under normal conditions, made decisions we knew would cost lives. We had to under the circumstances. Things have changed. As difficult as it is for any of us to grasp, sometimes we have to sacrifice people so humanity can thrive. It's not easy, but the tough decisions have to be made. Do you think any less of me because of what we had to do to create the Zombie Vaccine?"

"Of course not."

"Then you shouldn't think any less of yourself. All I'm trying to say is, do what you think is best for all of us, not what you think a society that died nine months ago would want you to do. Whatever, decision you make, we'll support you."

"Thanks. I mean that. It does put things into perspective."

"I'm glad." Jennifer gave his hand a squeeze and broke the grip. She turned to leave, throwing over her shoulder, "I'm here if you need *anything*."

Robson watched her walk off until she disappeared into the dark. For the first time in weeks, he had thoughts of being intimate with someone. Only this time those thoughts were not of Natalie.

CHAPTER FORTY-TWO

"We're not going anywhere," Emily said.

"This can't be the end of the line," protested Ari. "There has to be a way around."

"Maybe on foot," replied Emily. "There's no way we're getting the yacht past that."

That referred to the pontoon bridge one hundred feet in front of them that stretched across the Mississippi River a few miles north of St. Louis.

Natalie stood on the flying bridge between the two women, scanning the area with her binoculars. On either bank, the approaches for both the Chain of Rocks and New Chain of Rocks Bridges stood intact; however, one of the central spans on each bridge had collapsed or, judging from the jagged edges of the surrounding spans and the burnt marks on the concrete abutments, had been blown away. Between the two damaged structures, the military had erected a pontoon bridge across the Mississippi that blocked further access along the river. To the north of the pontoon bridge, dozens of boats of various sizes had been abandoned, either stacked against the bridge, moored to the supports of the New Chain of Rocks Bridge, or run aground on the sandbar that stretched for half a mile along the west bank of the Mississippi. Fortunately, she saw no signs of rotters.

Natalie scowled. "How far are we from the Missouri River?"

"It's less than two miles north of us," Emily replied.

"And how far to Omaha?"

"Another four hundred miles."

"Shit." Natalie used the binoculars to scan the boats along the sandbar.

"What if we removed the center span of the pontoon bridge?"

suggested Stephanie. "We could let it flow downriver, along with the boats clogged up behind it. That would open a way for us."

Emily shook her head. "The only problem is we don't have the tools or the know how to do something like that."

"Maybe we could use explosives to blow it away?" Ari grasped at ideas.

"Do you know where we can get explosives?" Emily had a tinge of frustration in her voice.

"No."

"Both of you, can it." Natalie placed the binoculars on the console. "There's no way of getting past that bridge."

"So this is it?" asked Ari. "We're stuck here?"

"Nope. We're just changing boats." Natalie stepped over to Emily. "Can you sail anything?"

"Pretty much. Why?"

Natalie pointed to the sandbar. "There's a couple of dozen vessels beached up there. I'm sure we can find one that still works that'll take us to Omaha."

Emily grinned. "That sounds like a good plan."

"Of course it is. It's my plan." Natalie winked at her. "Ari, go below and tell the rest of the Angels to get ready. Bring all the ammo and as much food and water as they can carry in their backpacks. And bring our gear. We meet on deck in fifteen minutes."

Ari headed below, and Natalie grabbed the binoculars, scanning the sandbar one final time. Nothing stirred, not even wild animals.

Dear God, please let us pull this off.

* * *

Emily maneuvered the yacht alongside the pontoon bridge and cut the engines. Ari jumped off, used a dock line to anchor the bow to the bridge, and then ran astern to do the same. Once she had moored the yacht, she climbed back on board.

The twelve Angels stood in a semi-circle on the main deck near the transom. Each wore their leather jackets unbuttoned and had a backpack strapped over their shoulders. Ari held the briefcase containing the Zombie Vaccine in her left hand. Natalie took Ari's M-16A2 and swung it over her shoulder.

"Okay, ladies. This should be easy. I've been watching that beach for twenty minutes and haven't seen any rotters. I have no idea if there are any in the boats. So when we get to the sandbar, don't talk unless it's necessary. Emily and I will check each boat until we find one that works. Ari, keep close to us. The rest of you stay on the sandbar and keep your eyes open. Any questions?"

None.

"Then let's rock, ladies."

The Angels disembarked from the yacht and onto the pontoon bridge. Before she left, Emily bent over and patted the gunwale. "I'm gonna miss ya, honey."

They walked along the pontoon bridge for a few hundred feet. Natalie noticed that the girls maintained a defense stance, with half of them on each side of the span on the lookout for danger. The women jumped down from the bridge and, as they made their way down the sandbar, formed a circle around Natalie, Emily, and Ari. They proceeded along the bank closest to the river where most of the boats were beached. Emily stopped after a few minutes and studied each of the vessels.

"What are you looking for?" Natalie asked.

Emily ignored her and took off. "That."

Maintaining formation, the Angels followed her until she stopped fifty feet from the end of the sandbar in front of a police boat emblazoned with the logo of the Missouri State Water Patrol. It was thirty feet long, with a cabin on the centerline and an exposed deck to the rear, and no lower deck. Emily walked around the exterior, checking the portion of the hull lodged on the sand. When she reached the stern, ten feet of which extended into the river, she waded in up to her hips and viewed the hull. When she came ashore and rejoined Natalie, she had a grin on her face.

"I don't think there's any damage to the hull or propellers, so she should be seaworthy."

"Are you sure?" asked Natalie. "It looks awfully small."

"It's not as comfortable as the yacht. It's faster, though, and should get us there by morning."

"I'm sold. Let's just hope it runs," Natalie said. "Doreen,

you're with us. Tiara, keep an eye on and Ari. The rest of you, spread out."

The Angels formed a semi-circle that extended out one hundred feet. Natalie and the others approached the patrol boat. Doreen peered over the gunwale and, finding it empty, climbed aboard and waved on the others. Natalie and Emily joined her and made their way forward to the bridge, with Emily positioning herself in front of the console. The key was still in the ignition. She turned it to the right, and the gauges came to life.

"That's good," she said. "The battery works."

"Check the fuel gauge," Natalie responded. "It's half empty."

"Not to worry." Emily pointed to the bow. Four fifty-five gallon drums had been lashed to the deck, with a hand pump protruding from the top of one of them. "We have plenty of refueling capability. Whoever owned this boat had prepared to make a run for it. I don't think they anticipated finding a pontoon bridge blocking their path."

"Good news for us."

"That's for sure, honey." Emily placed her finger on the starter button. "Keep your fingers crossed."

* * *

Josephine stood in the center of the perimeter, watching the Missouri side of the Mississippi River for any activity when she saw something protruding from the sandbar two hundred feet away. She squinted to see it more clearly. Only a small portion stuck up above the surface. Josephine snapped her fingers to get the attention of Tiara's, who stood on her right. When Tiara turned to her, she said, "Cover me."

"Why?

Josephine pointed to the object. "Something's in the sand. I want to see what it is."

"Forget about it."

"It might be something we can use."

Tiara sighed. "Be careful."

Josephine left the perimeter and crossed the sandbar. She was surprised she had even spotted it considering only an area the size of a baseball was visible, and even that only stuck out an inch or so. The dark color had attracted her attention because it contrasted against the surface. When she reached it, it looked like an old piece of leather. Kneeling, she brushed away the sand covering the object, exposing what lay—

Josephine drew back in horror.

The object was a decayed, mummified hand.

And the index and forefinger twitched.

CHAPTER FORTY-THREE

Emily pressed the starter button. The engines sputtered and protested.

* * *

The groan of the patrol boat's engines cut across the sandbar. The fingers on the dead hand closed in on the palm. Josephine spun her head toward the patrol boat and screamed, "Don't start those engines!"

* * *

Natalie heard Josephine's cry and turned toward her just as Emily pressed the starter button again. This time the engines roared to life. Emily throttled them forward to make certain they didn't stall. In the quiet along the Mississippi, the noise was deafening.

All along the sandbar, decayed hands shot out from under the sand as the living dead woke from their rest. And the Angels were in the middle of them.

* * *

The hand grabbed Josephine around the wrist and held her tight. Startled, she fell backwards and dropped the M-16A2. When she tried to crawl away, the backpack dug into the sand, hindering her movement. She succeeded only in pulling the rotter free. Clumps of wet sand broke off and crumbled. It wore a National Guard uniform. Its chest had been torn open and emptied of organs, leaving a dozen crabs crawling around the empty cavity. The rotter snarled, exposing grit-encrusted teeth. With its free arm, it grabbed her by the left ankle and pulled itself out further. Josephine reached for her semi-automatic rifle, but the rotter lay between them. Twisting to one side, she kicked at its head, driving the heel of her boot into its face. With each strike, shattered teeth flew from its mouth. The third kick tore loose a large chunk of its upper lip, revealing the decayed jaw underneath. On the fifth, its lower jaw broke loose, dangling from the right side of its face by a few tendons and strips of skin.

Still, the rotter would not release its grip and continued to crawl onto Josephine.

* * *

One rotter that had been face down pushed itself to its hands in knees in front of Sandy. She took a step back, aimed her M-16A2 at its head, and pulled the trigger. The rotter shuddered and collapsed, the sand beneath it absorbing the gore. She switched her aim to another of the living dead rising five feet to her left.

Sarah went to help Josephine when three of the living dead rose out of the sand in front of her. She took down the ones on the right and left with double taps to the head; shooting the one in the center would put Josephine in the line of sight. Stepping forward, Sarah kicked the rotter in its face, knocking it on its back. She shoved the barrel of her M-16A2 into its mouth and fired.

Stephanie felt the ground bulge beneath her. Looking down, she saw one of the living dead trying to push itself free under her feet. She stomped on its head three times until the skull caved in.

Amy stood on the far right end of the perimeter, away from the rotters. Ten of them emerged from the sandbar between her and the police boat, and she could not shoot them without the risk of hitting the other Angels. Holding the stock in her right hand and the barrel in her left, she surged forward, ready to club her way to safety.

Four of the living dead broke through the sand around Katie, encircling her. One by one, she stepped up to each rotter, placed the barrel against its head, and took it down with a single shot. When she glanced around, an increasing number of the living dead were rising all along the sandbar. Some had already stood and staggered toward the perimeter.

Tiara raised her M-16A2 and took careful aim at the rotter attacking Josephine. Inhaling deeply and holding it, she applied pressure to the trigger, waiting for the clear shot. She tuned out everything around her.

Including the hand that pushed its way through the sand by her right foot.

* * *

Natalie watched in horror as rotters pushed their way to the surface all along the sandbar, surrounding the Angels. At least twenty stood between her girls and the police boat, with another thirty beyond them.

Emily shifted the throttles into reverse and gunned the engine. The boat shuddered, yet remained lodged on the sandbar.

"What are you doing?" Natalie asked.

"Trying to get us off this thing. We're stuck. I need you three to push us loose."

"We have to help the others."

"Honey, if we don't free this boat before the rotters reach us, none of us are getting out of here alive."

"Fuck." Natalie reached over the gunwale. "Ari, give me that briefcase. Then you and Doreen get to the bow and get ready to push."

Ari handed it over as Doreen jumped off the boat, and the two women moved to the bow. Natalie laid the briefcase between two seats and joined them. When all three were in place, she yelled out to Emily.

"Ready!"

The engines roared. The three women pushed against the hull, digging furrows in the sand with their feet. The boat would not move. Natalie glanced over her shoulder. The commotion had attracted the attention of seven rotters that shambled toward them.

* * *

The National Guard rotter had Josephine pinned. She couldn't roll to the left because of her backpack, and if she rolled to the right the rotter would fall on her. It climbed onto her chest, its weight pushing her down. She placed her hands on its shoulders and shoved it away. That wouldn't save her for long.

Then its head exploded, spraying the sand to her left with gore and skull fragments. Rolling to the right and pushing, she knocked the body to one side, and crawled on hands and knees to retrieve her M-16A2. She turned to Tiara to thank her, and her heart sank.

* * *

Tiara gave herself a mental high-five when the headshot brought down the rotter attacking Josephine. Her friend threw off the corpse and scurried to get her weapon.

A hand grabbed Tiara around the right ankle. Before she could react, a second hand reached out and clutched her pants leg. Layers of sand poured off, revealing a female rotter in a police uniform. It climbed up Tiara, grasping her belt, then her arm, and then her shoulder. Its weight knocked Tiara down, pinning her free arm. The rotter dragged itself across Tiara's body. Placing one decayed hand on her shoulder and the other on her face, it exposed her neck and lunged.

Tiara screamed when she felt its teeth slice through the skin and bite deep into muscle.

* * *

Natalie and the others continued to push, and the boat refused to budge. The rotters were only fifteen feet away now. Unslinging her M-16A2, she stepped up to the closest one, placed the barrel against its forehead, and fired. Before it even hit the ground, she moved toward the next closest. Doreen raced up beside her and started shooting the living dead. It took only a few seconds to bring all seven down. Things had changed dramatically in those seconds.

When Natalie glanced out at the perimeter, she saw the rest of the living dead threatening to swarm her Angels.

"Everybody fall back to the boat! Now!"

* * *

Josephine could tell by the spray of blood that the rotter had severed Tiara's carotid artery. Even though Tiara wouldn't come back as one of the living dead, she would not survive the attack. Raising the M-16A2, she emptied her magazine into both her friend and the rotter. Bullets churned up the sand and thudded into living and dead flesh. When Josephine finished, neither one moved.

She silently said goodbye to her friend and climbed back to her feet.

* * *

Upon hearing Natalie's order to fall back, most of the Angels obeyed. Only a few rotters now stood between them and the boat, all of which were shot through the head on the Angels' retreat. One grabbed Katie's backpack and nearly dragged her down. She dropped her M-16A2 and shoved back. The rotter tumbled over, still clutching the backpack, and Katie arched her shoulders, sliding the backpack free. She grabbed the automatic rifle and dashed for the boat.

The rotters from outside the perimeter drew closer, their moans incessant as they neared their food.

When each of the Angels reached the boat, Natalie had them throw their backpack on deck and join in dislodging it. Soon most of the Angels were gathered around the bow, trying to shove it into the river.

Except for Josephine and Amy.

Josephine noticed that the rotters between her and the boat concentrated on the Angels gathered around the bow. She calculated the path of least rotter presence, took a deep breath, and made a dash. Josephine dodged between the living dead, constantly changing direction to stay as far away from danger as possible. Several rotters turned and lunged, and she swatted their hands away as she raced past. Within seconds, she had made it through the horde and reached her friends.

Amy had waded into the approaching rotters, slamming the butt of her M-16A2 several times into the face of the closest rotter before it collapsed. She paused to catch her breath, and saw the other nine bearing down on her. At this rate, she would never make it through. Even if she did, too many rotters converged around the police boat. Amy searched for another escape route and found it in the row off abandoned boats that sat along the bank of the sandbar. She counted ten between her and the police boat. Racing for the nearest one, a small six-seat pleasure craft, she climbed over the gunwale onto the main deck. When she turned around, the nine rotters had changed direction and approached the pleasure craft. Jumping to the adjacent barge, she made her way along the sandbar one boat at a time.

* * *

Emily cut back power to the engines and swore to herself. Thirty rotters drew closer. Her fingers wrapped around the throttle.

Come on, honey. Don't let me down.

Emily yanked the controls into reverse.

At the bow, the Angels pushed with all their strength. Sweat poured down their faces and backs, and their feet dug up the sand until they began to lose their footing. The police boat would not move. Then, just as they were about to give up hope, it lurched back a foot. The Angels pushed even harder.

Natalie glanced over her shoulder and saw the nearest rotter ten feet away. It wore a sweatshirt whose design had been blotted out by dried blood and sand. Breaking away from the others, she unslung her M-16A2 and aimed. The first bullet struck the rotter's forehead at a range of less than three feet. The others were too close to aim properly, so she settled for three-round bursts until the bolt stuck open. Two more rotters dropped. The rest kept closing in.

She turned around to see that the police boat had moved another few feet down the sandbar. "Stephanie, Sandy. Spot me."

The two Angels broke away and took up firing position. Natalie joined the others in pushing against the hull. Finally, it slid into the river. Emily maneuvered the boat parallel to the sandbar. The Angels hopped aboard one at a time while Stephanie and Sandy provided covering fire. When they had run out of ammunition, they fell back and climbed on board. Natalie joined them last.

"Let's get out of here," she ordered.

"With pleasure, honey."

"Wait!" yelled Doreen. "Where's Amy?"

"Where was she last?" Emily asked.

"Down the other end," answered Stephanie.

"There she is!" shouted Sandy, pointing to the row of abandoned boats.

Amy swung over the side of a tugboat and climbed down the port ladder, dropping onto the deck of a low keeled fishing skip. Emily flipped on the siren to get her attention. Amy stopped and waved. The rotters along the sandbar moaned and waded into the Mississippi. Turning the police boat toward shore, Emily pulled up alongside the rear of the fishing skip. Amy climbed on board, helped by Doreen and Stephanie. Emily steered the boat back into the river and gunned the engine, accelerating away from the sandbar. A few minutes later, she reached the fork where the Missouri River poured into the Mississippi. Turning to port, she entered the mouth of the Missouri.

"Like I said before, a little over four hundred miles to Omaha," Emily said. "With luck, we should be there by morning."

Natalie slumped into one of the seats in front of the console.

"Are you okay?" Emily asked.

"No."

Emily reached over and squeezed her shoulder. "We'll be in Omaha soon, and all this will be behind us."

"I hope you're right."

"I usually am." Emily smiled. "I'll take it from here. You get some rest. You can spot me later."

"Sounds good." Natalie moved to the bow, taking her backpack with her and wedging it between two of the fuel drums to use as a bed. She really wanted to cry, an impossibility in front of the other Angels. So instead she fell into a deep sleep.

CHAPTER FORTY-FOUR

Tibor seemed pleased when he showed the others the renovations he had made to the school bus. For the first time since leaving Site R, he appeared to want to be part of the group, which pleased Dravko and Robson. Jennifer, Caslow, Simmons, and Wayans stood with them at the end of the bus, while the others lingered in the background.

"As you requested, I removed the rear door and replaced it with a ramp." Tibor stood on the ramp and jumped on it to show it would hold weight. He grabbed one of the chains connected to the end of the ramp that stretched to the top of the bus and through a series of loops welded onto the roof before finally disappearing into the driver's compartment. "You can use these to raise and lower it. The other end is by the driver's seat."

Tibor walked up the ramp into the bus and waved for the others to follow. All the seats had been removed. Making his way to the front, he stood by the exit stairs and pointed to a metal cage that had been erected across the interior behind the driver's seat. It consisted of dozens of rebar spikes running horizontally and vertically, each welded to one another. The space between each bar was only a few inches. A steel door and frame had been welded into the center. Tibor closed the steel door and secured it on the driver's side by dropping a four-foot long two-by-four into the twin brackets on either side of the door mount.

Tibor stepped back and smiled, immensely proud of his work. "Once you're up here, nothing can get to you."

"You're sure it'll hold?" asked Dravko.

"Try it."

Dravko stepped up, wrapped his fingers around the bars, and pulled. The cage did not move. Morphing into his vampire form, he tried again. The cage still did not give. Dravko returned to his human state. "That's built strong."

"It needs to be," Tibor replied with a broad smile. He removed the two-by-four and opened the door, then motioned to the chain dangling from the roof and ending in the cage area. "This is how you control the ramp."

He grabbed the chain and pulled, raising the ramp until it covered the open doorway in back. A crowbar had been welded to the driver's side of the cage, with the hooked portion pointing down. Tibor wrapped the chain several times around the hooked end of the crowbar and secured one of the links through the tip. "When not in use, you secure the chain here."

Caslow stepped forward and pulled on the chain. "It looks difficult to operate. Are you sure it'll work?"

"It'll be okay for an hour or so."

"It'll do just fine." Robson patted Tibor on the shoulder. "Thanks."

"I even reinforced the plow up front. Once you're up here, you'll be safe from everything except gunfire."

"Hopefully no one will be shooting at me." Robson turned to the others. "We're all set to go. We do this tomorrow night."

Everyone nodded halfheartedly, not because they didn't feel the need to rescue Windows, they all knew the odds. By this time tomorrow night, most of them would probably be dead. One by one, everyone wandered off.

Once alone, Robson made another tour of the exterior of the bus and entered the driver's compartment. Using the chain, he lowered and raised the ramp to get an idea of how it would handle. He also tested the cage, grabbing it in several places and pulling with all his strength. The welds were solid. He might have a chance after all.

How things had changed. Two weeks ago, he had a cohesive unit that had fought its way to Site R and back, retrieving the Zombie Vaccine and battling hundreds of rotters along the way. Now his team had been whittled down to a ragtag group of survivors. Only Dravko and Tibor remained from the original raiding party, and the latter's loyalties remained in doubt. He counted Jennifer as one of the original team because she had accompanied them; however, as a scientist she had never been trained for combat. Not that it mattered. He knew she would throw a fit if he tried to leave her behind, even though putting her in harm's way was irresponsible. Christ, everything about tomorrow night's raid was irresponsible. DeWitt's people had been trained to defend Fort McClary, not go into combat against well-armed killers. Simmons and Wayans possessed the skill set, and were placing their lives on the line for someone they had never even met. And Caslow would be next to useless; the best Robson could hope for was that when Caslow got himself killed he didn't take anyone else with him. They would have stood a much better chance with Natalie and the Angels, even with their shattered morale. Necessity had dictated he send them west with the vaccine, otherwise everything they had endured would have been for nothing. The deaths of Mad Dog, Daytona, Whitehouse, Caylee, and Leila. Of Sultanic and Tatyana. Of those assholes Compton and Thompson. And especially the destruction of their compound and the murder of everyone in it. All of it would have been a fucking waste.

Robson dropped into the driver's seat and leaned back, closed his eyes, and took a deep breath. Maybe this raid on the gang's compound was a horrible idea. Ever since coming up with this plan to save Windows, he had asked himself if rescuing her was his true intention, or just an excuse to justify revenge. Or worse, maybe he sought suicide by vendetta, and was selfishly bringing along the others to die with him. That thought had crossed his mind a few times. He didn't know for certain, which bothered him. He now had an inkling of what Paul had gone through those many months running the compound, and had a newfound respect for him.

Someone stepping onto the bus broke him from his reverie, and he saw Jennifer standing on the stairs.

"I'm sorry," she said. "Did I disturb you?"

"No. I was just thinking. I haven't done a lot of that lately."

"I don't know. To me it seems like that's all you've been doing since we found your camp destroyed."

"Am I doing the right thing, or am I going after Windows for the wrong reason?"

"Let me ask you this." Jennifer moved up to the main floor. "If they had only destroyed the camp and murdered everyone, and hadn't kidnapped her, would you be staging this raid?"

Shit, he hadn't thought of it that way. Robson contemplated the question for a minute. He probably wouldn't be launching this raid if not for Windows. Getting some payback on the assholes who butchered his friends happened to be a plus. If Windows had been murdered along with the others, Robson would have placed the safety of the survivors over anything else, and would have headed north to put as much distance between them and the rape gang as possible. The realization took a weight off of his shoulders.

Robson made eye contact with Jennifer. "I guess I wouldn't."

"And you're not forcing any of us to accompany you. We're going because it's the right thing to do. We're going because we trust you." Jennifer moved closer. "I know that if it was me stuck in that camp, you'd come after me."

"Of course I would."

Jennifer smiled. She slid one hand behind Robson's neck and gently pulled him toward her. She kissed him with a tenderness that he had never experienced before, her tongue caressing his lips. An image of Natalie flashed through his mind. Sliding his hands along Jennifer's arms, he gently pushed her away.

"I can't do this."

"I'm not asking you to fall in love with me. I just want you to make love to me." Robson didn't protest when Jennifer unzipped him, dropped to her knees in front of him, and pulled out his erection.

CHAPTER FORTY-FIVE

The Omaha skyline poked though the morning mist, the glass of its many office buildings reflecting the sun. Natalie found it peaceful, yet surreal. Before the outbreak, she had always enjoyed cities early in the morning when only a handful of people milled about. That seemed like a lifetime ago. Now, every major city they passed swarmed with rotters. That was why Omaha was unusual. Nothing moved, either living or living dead. It was almost as if the death of mankind had bypassed the Midwest. A part of Natalie wanted to pull onto the nearest bank and spend the rest of her life here. In reality, she knew unimaginable horrors probably waited deep in the city.

Emily decreased the patrol boat's speed to ten knots. Natalie glanced over at her. "Why are you slowing down?"

"We reached the end of the line."

Ahead of them, a trestle-style bridge spanned the Missouri River. It looked like the dozens of bridges they had passed underneath since leaving New Orleans, with one major difference: this one was clear of debris. Barricades had been erected on both approaches, preventing any vehicles from crossing. On the western bank, a chain link fence topped with barbed wire ran for two hundred feet along the river on either side of the bridge before turning at a ninety-degree angle toward the city. Plywood boards had been attached to the structure to form signs. The one on the western approach said BELLEVUE BRIDGE/MISSION AVE. The one on the eastern approach read THIS WAY TO SAFETY accompanied by an arrow pointing to a rope ladder that dangled from the central span along the central support column.

"What do you think?" Emily asked. "Should we stop?"

Natalie didn't know what to do. Nothing indicated that this was a check-in point for the government-in-exile. She would hate to walk into a trap at this late stage. Then again, if this proved legitimate and they passed it by, they could wind up missing their opportunity to find a safe refuge. She opted to play it safe.

"Stephanie, wake up the rest of the Angels," Natalie said. "We're going to check this out."

* * *

Ten minutes later, the police boat pulled up alongside the bridge's central support. Emily remained at the controls, ready to escape the area if necessary. Amy, Sarah, and Doreen joined Natalie while the other Angels stayed on board covering the two banks and the approaches to the bridge.

While Doreen provided cover, Amy and Sarah held the rope ladder for Natalie. She climbed quickly, expecting at any moment for a bullet to slam into her. Nothing happened. When she reached the central span, she swung her legs over the guard rail, unslung her M-16A2, and scanned the area. No sign of danger. Hell, no sign of anything. Leaning over the guardrail, she waved for the others to climb up, and crouched into a firing position by the ladder. After the other three girls joined her, they formed a semi-circle. Natalie directed Doreen and Amy to the eastern side of the bridge, and she and Sarah made their way in the opposite direction toward the barricade at the western approach.

They were fifty feet from the barricade when a male voice called out. "Stop right there. Slowly place your weapons on the ground and raise your hands above your head."

Natalie veered to the left and slid up beside a steel girder, then crouched and aimed toward the barricade. Sarah jumped over the pedestrian walkway and stooped behind the rail. On the opposite side of the bridge, Doreen and Amy dropped prone and aimed their M-16A2s at the barricade.

"I said, place your weapons on the ground and raise your hands above your head. I promise, no harm will come to you."

"How do I know you're telling the truth?" Natalie yelled.

"Ma'am, this is your last chance. Drop your weapons or we will be forced to open fire."

"Okay. We're putting them down." Natalie stood and raised the M-16A2 over her head. She took three steps from the girder, crouched down, and placed the automatic rifle on the span in front of her. Dropping to her knees, she lifted her hands above her head. The other Angels stared at her incredulous, but went along.

Once the women had surrendered, two soldiers in camouflaged uniforms emerged from behind the barricade. The larger of the two, a black man, stayed partially covered and trained his weapon on the women. The other approached, his M-16A2 raised and ready to fire. As he neared, Natalie noticed the name LOPEZ stitched to his breastplate.

"Please unzip your jackets, slowly and with one hand. Do not make any sudden movements or reach under your jackets. Is that clear?"

The Angels obeyed. Lopez moved closer. He paused a few feet from Natalie. "I'm going to frisk each of you for weapons. Do not resist or make any sudden movements. Understood?"

Each of them nodded, and Lopez moved in. His search was thorough but unobtrusive, and he didn't inappropriately touch any of them. When finished, Lopez stood back, his weapon now pointed toward the ground. "Sorry, about that. You can stand up."

"Thanks." Natalie got off her knees. "What about our weapons?"

"You can keep them for now. Remove the magazines and make certain a round isn't chambered. Then have the rest of your party in the boat come on up, with their weapons unloaded."

Fifteen minutes later, all the Angels stood on the bridge and had been searched. While Lopez seemed relaxed throughout the procedure, Natalie noticed his friend never took his weapon off of them.

When they finished, Lopez asked, "I'm curious. Why did you back down so easily?"

"I knew I wasn't in danger when you called me 'ma'am'."

Lopez looked confused. "Why?"

"I figured you were military or law enforcement. Most others we run into who are a danger call me 'bitch' or 'whore'."

Lopez laughed. Even the black soldier smiled and pointed his weapon away from them.

"What brings you ladies to Omaha?" Lopez asked.

Natalie pointed to the briefcase Ari held. "We have the Revenant Vaccine that Dr. Compton created."

"Dr. Compton?"

"That's the scientist on the East Coast," said the black soldier. "He's the one who supposedly had developed a cure for the zombie outbreak."

"He succeeded. With this, none of us will ever have to worry about being turned if we're bitten."

"Are you serious?" Lopez asked. "It really works?"

Natalie nodded. "We're here to give it to the President."

Lopez snorted. "In that case, ma'am, you're screwed."

CHAPTER FORTY-SIX

Lopez didn't elaborate. He and the other soldier, who had introduced himself as Private Carver Duncan, escorted the Angels back to Offutt Air Force Base to meet the commanding officer. They approached the facility after walking south along the river and turning west, which meant that the group had to traverse the entire length of the runway.

Two things struck Natalie. First, the diversity of aircraft lined up on either side of the runway and scattered around the tarmac: Air Force One; Air Force Two; Marine One; several dozen military aircraft, a score of private jets; an Airbus 310 with the palm tree and crossed swords logo of Saudia on the tail. These planes had been left unattended for months. Many had flattened tires, a few had engine cowlings or access doors left open, having been scavenged for parts. All of the aircraft, even Air Force One, had months of soot and grime covering their wings and fuselage. It reminded her of an outdoor air museum where no one maintained the exhibits.

Second, she noticed the lack of activity around the air base. Other than themselves, Natalie saw no one else. With so many aircraft crowded onto the field, she figured there would at least be maintenance personnel servicing them. She reasoned that the lack of crews explained the poor condition of the aircraft. Only when they reached the far end of the runway did she see a lone figure in a leather jacket. He walked around a C-130 military transport that stood separate from the other aircraft and sat between two hangers set fifteen hundred feet from the runway.

Lopez headed for the C-130 and led the group toward a two-story building on the opposite side of the twin hangers. A sign on the building read HOTEL AIR FORCE. The corporal entered and made his way to the dining room.

"Hey, Lieutenant. We got company."

A young woman in green Air Force cammies emerged from the kitchen. Natalie guessed her to be no more than thirty. She had the petite body of someone in their late twenties, with a haggard appearance that made her look years older. Her red hair, which hung down to her shoulders and had not been trimmed in months, contained streaks of white. Furrows ran across her forehead, and black circles highlighted her glazed eyes. She showed no expression upon leaving the kitchen until she saw the assault rifles slung over the Angels' shoulders. Then she turned on Lopez.

"Why the fuck are they still armed?"

"It's okay, Lieutenant," Lopez defended himself. "They're friendly."

"Not that it matters anymore." The woman's defiance evaporated with an exasperated shrug. She approached Natalie, extending her hand. "I'm Lieutenant Jane Pandelosi, United States Air Force. I'm in command of what's left here."

"Natalie Bazargan." She gave the hand a single pump. "We have the vaccine Dr. Compton prepared against the Zombie Virus. We're here to pass it to the President."

The lieutenant sighed. "You wasted your time, lady."

"Why's that?"

"Revenants overran the President's bunker thirty hours ago."

* * *

After dropping that bombshell, Pandelosi refused to explain until they had breakfast. Although Natalie had been stunned by the lieutenant's indifference, she withheld asking any questions until the appropriate moment. The Angels followed the lieutenant through the chow line, grabbing trays and getting themselves a hot meal.

Besides Pandelosi, Lopez, and Duncan, three others joined them for breakfast—Privates Curtis Harrington and Michael Kim, and Sergeant Ray "Sarge" Batchelder. Natalie waited until everyone had started eating before broaching the topic.

"Is this all your people?"

"For the most part," Pandelosi replied. "I have three people north of the base in case anyone staggers south from the bunker."

"And The Butcher," added Harrington.

"Knock that shit off, soldier," ordered Pandelosi. "Mouth off like that again and you'll do guard duty up north."

"Yes, ma'am."

Lopez leaned closer to Natalie. "They're referring to Captain Everett, the pilot of the C-130. You saw him on the way in earlier."

"Isn't he joining us?" asked Ari.

Pandelosi shook her head. "He avoids us because most of my people can't stand him."

"Because he's a butcher," said Harrington under his breath.

Pandelosi cast the private a withering stare, and then went on to explain. "When the outbreak first occurred, Captain Everett flew an AC-130 Specter to run strafing missions against revenants in Illinois. They're armed with a 105mm Howitzer, a 40mm Bofors gun, and a .30 caliber chain gun. On his last mission outside of Chicago, to stop a swarm of revenants from escaping the city, the fire control team aboard opened up on a bridge that contained several hundred civilians trying to flee the horde. It only slowed down the dead and killed off most of the survivors. Everett jockeyed the ship; the fire control team did the killing. That didn't matter, though. The media placed the blame for the massacre on his shoulder and gave him the nickname The Butcher. He has never lived it down, nor has he forgiven himself. That's why he never eats with us. It's also why he refused to take command of this base when the President downsized it."

"It's not a very large command," said Emily. "No offense."

"Not now. After the outbreak, the military expanded our ranks to five hundred people under a major general. We're the closest air base to the bunker where the government-in-exile was established. Those first few weeks, everyone in Washington who had survived the outbreak made their way here, mostly by plane. The Vice President and some others had been ordered to Colorado Springs to set up a shadow government in case something happened here. We lost contact with them after five weeks. No one knows what happened."

"And nobody around here gave a shit," added Sarge.

"That's harsh," said Natalie.

"It's true." Pandelosi vented a lot of frustration in that response. "We had a lot of good men and women here, people with their own loved ones they were concerned about, who stayed put to keep this air base open so we could ensure continuity of government. Our elected officials, however, were more concerned with saving their own asses. Over a thousand people landed at this airport, and half of them weren't even government officials. I watched staffers, lobbyists, Hollywood celebrities, CEOs, media personalities, and a whole host of non-essential personnel fly into here before heading north. There are even twenty-five members of the Saudi royal family up there.

"About a month after the outbreak, when everybody was who going to make it out alive had already arrived, the President downsized Offutt to just under one hundred people. That's when I took command. The rest were sent east to battle the revenants along the Mississippi. There wasn't much for us to do after that. We got a hundred or so survivors coming through here, fed them, and sent them on their way."

"Why?" asked Natalie.

"Officially they're 'a drain on resources'." Pandelosi grimaced at the words.

The Angels did not fully understand.

"Did you notice Omaha is deserted?" Sarge asked. "That's because, under orders of the President, the governor declared martial law and evacuated everyone from the city. The President wanted to avoid any local infestations that could threaten the bunker. Tens, maybe hundreds of thousands of innocent people died because they were forced out of their homes and sent south. Not that it did any good in the long run."

"What happened?"

"In the bunker?" Pandelosi shrugged. "Who knows? The rules on containment security were supposed to be very strict. Everyone who landed here was supposed to undergo a complete physical before being allowed to proceed up north, and if you had a wound of any kind, then you had to undergo a forty-eight-hour quarantine."

"I assume those rules weren't adhered to?" Emily asked.

"Staffers, military personnel, and family members obeyed them. The principals and Congressmen refused to submit to such an indignity, and the President waived the rules for them, and for most of the other special guests."

"Is that how the infection reached the bunker?" This time Natalie asked the question.

"We don't know." Pandelosi stared down at the table and swallowed hard. When she didn't speak after several seconds, Sarge picked up the conversation.

"The lieutenant had a good friend in the bunker's radio room who she used to chat with every day. They exchanged gossip on what was going on inside and out here in the real world. Two days ago, he contacted us to say an outbreak had taken place inside the bunker, and that they were trying to contain it. Seven hours later, he called back to say they had been overrun, that almost everyone had been infected, and that he and the few survivors left would try and make their way to Offutt. That was the last anyone heard from them."

"I'm sorry," said Natalie. "Did your friend make it?"

"No." Pandelosi raised her head. Tears filled her eyes. "And he was my fiancé."

An awkward silence fell over the group.

"I ordered everyone here to get out while they could," Pandelosi resumed after composing herself. "We agreed to stay behind for a few days in case anyone made it out of the bunker alive and managed to get this far south. We're flying out first thing tomorrow morning, which is why it's good you showed up when you did. You're welcome to go with us, if you want."

"Is there anyone left from the government?" Ari asked.

"That depends on who you talk to," answered Kim.

"What do you mean?" Ari asked.

"Go ahead," Pandelosi said to Kim. "You're the political science major."

Kim smiled. "According to the Constitution, the highest ranking surviving official still alive who can take over the government now that the President is dead is the Secretary of Defense. But he's in Canada. He was flying back from a summit in Europe and made it as far as Montreal before the United States banned all air travel. Now there's a huge debate going on within the remnants of the government over whether or not his being in a foreign country makes him ineligible to take over the Presidency."

"Do you believe it?" Harrington snorted. "America is dead and these assholes are still fighting over power."

"What are the other options?" Natalie asked.

"We could go to Wyoming," joked Duncan.

"Too cold for me," Lopez remarked.

"What's in Wyoming?" asked Emily.

Pandelosi rolled her eyes. "This past spring, the governor of Wyoming declared himself the most capable official to deal with the revenant threat. The winter was so cold and the snow so deep that it stopped the spread of the revenants for several months, giving the governor time to regroup and organize his defenses. By the time the thaw hit, he had cleared out most of the state of the living dead and had set up fortified enclaves throughout the region. He doesn't have the legal authority to be President, yet he has the street creds. That's not where we're heading. We're flying to San Francisco. The Secretary of Education has established a bridgehead that has withstood the revenants for eight months. From what we've heard, a lot of survivors have been making their way there. Rumor has it he's getting ready to launch a counteroffensive. That's the reason we're going, to be part of that. If you have the vaccine, you guys will be welcomed as heroes."

A flurry of excitement passed among the Angels. Natalie quieted them down, and then asked Pandelosi, "You don't mind taking us along?"

"Not at all. We have plenty of room on the C-130. We already have clearance to land at Alameda Airport. Lopez, call Alameda and let them know we'll be bringing eleven extra people with us. Then set these women up in the empty rooms. Make sure they have bed linen and towels for the showers."

"Showers?" Stephanie asked.

"*Hot* showers." The lieutenant grinned for the first time.

Natalie smiled as the Angels talked excitedly amongst themselves like teenagers discussing the prom. "I don't know how to thank you for this," she said to the lieutenant.

"Be on time tomorrow," Pandelosi responded. "Breakfast is at

0800. We take off at 0900."

CHAPTER FORTY-SEVEN

Price strolled around the facility, ostensibly checking on the progress of the pack up. It had not taken as long as anticipated because his people had so little. As he walked into each storage unit that had served as private quarters, he noticed his guys had left behind a lot of their belongings in the hopes that they would have better stuff at the new place. Sure, he knew this wouldn't be the case since the new homes were unfurnished, but he wasn't going to tell them that. This move had given them incentive, something to work toward. Something he could use to keep them in line. Price knew that their future depended on his being able to refocus their energies from raping and violence to rebuilding, and he felt confident he could pull it off.

He also made his rounds out of a sense of nostalgia. Not for the place itself, but for what it represented. Respect. For the first time in his life, Price was someone other than the local thug or the problem case that the police and courts didn't know how to handle. People had always feared him. Now that fear was combined with power, and the combination had earned him the trust and respect of his men. These guys followed him. Sure, part of it came from him letting them do what they wanted to the women in camp. Sometimes you have to allow the boys blow off some steam to let them know you understand where they're coming from. Now that he had their loyalty, he could start making something of himself. Rather than be a small cog in society, he would build that new society. And it wouldn't be a flawed one where the weak flourished at the expense of the strong. That was why mankind couldn't stand up to the deader outbreak. No. His society would be built on strength, like the Old West. When everything had blown over—

"Excuse me, sir."

Price turned around to see Carter approaching. "What's up?"

"We're all set to go except for the kitchen. Considering that it's noon, I didn't know if you wanted us to pack that up and head out now or wait until morning."

Price contemplated the idea for a moment. They still had enough time to get to the new location by nightfall if everything played out according to plan. If anything went wrong, they ran the risk of being stranded between camps at night, which could be fatal. Better to be safe than sorry.

"Let's wait until tomorrow. It'll give the guys a chance to rest and give us plenty of daylight to set up in the new place."

"You're the boss."

You're damn right I am, thought Price. *Soon I'll be the boss of this entire region.*

* * *

When Carter stuck his head into the kitchen the women were completing the morning clean up. "It's official. We're leaving for the new compound tomorrow morning. So after dinner tonight, pack up everything you won't need for breakfast. That'll make it quicker for you in the morning. Understood?"

"Whatever," Tracey sighed.

Carter stormed into the kitchen. He grabbed her by the hair and yanked her head back so he could look into her face. "What'd you say, bitch?"

Tracey cringed. "I said 'yes'."

"That's better."

"I'm sorry."

"You are sorry. And pathetic." Carter whipped his hand to one side, tossing her to the cement. "You better adjust your attitude in the new place or you'll find yourself deader bait."

"Yes, sir."

Carter stormed out, leaving Tracey on her knees sobbing. The other women ignored her, grateful it wasn't them. For Windows, Carter's comment about making Tracey deader bait reinforced her decision to escape before Price moved, which meant she would have to do it tonight.

Windows stepped into the rear of the unit where the food supplies were kept to get a bottle of water. As she pulled one of the last bottles from the package, something caught her eye. A pair of wire cutters had fallen beside the wooden pallet the food had been stored on. One of the gang members must have dropped it when they were breaking down the remaining stock to load for the move. The cutters were only nine inches long and intended for small wires, yet she should be able to use them to get through the chain link fence surrounding the compound. Making certain no one was paying attention, Windows crouched down and moved the cutters so they were hidden between the slats.

She and Cindy would sneak back to the kitchen later tonight to retrieve the cutters and to steal the fifty-five gallon drum, maneuver it against the wall, and use it to climb up and over. She had done the calculations yesterday, and the barrel would give her enough height to hoist Cindy to the top and pull herself over. All she would need was about an hour to make it to the vehicle Lee had told her about. Considering the entire compound would be moving in the morning, she doubted Price would send anyone after her.

At least, she hoped so.

Not that it mattered. Windows knew the two of them would be murdered if they stayed here. At least on the run they had a fighting chance. She had made up her mind.

They would escape once everyone else had settled down for the night.

BOOK THREE

CHAPTER FORTY-EIGHT

Natalie lay naked in the sand. Robson knelt over her, wearing only his pants. She enjoyed the way he explored her body. He was slow and gentle, gliding his hands up and down along the outside of her legs, occasionally teasing her by sliding up to her hips, moving over to her inner thighs, and back down. All the while, he never broke eye contact. Their gaze remained locked, which turned her on more than his touch. She reached up, gently clasping his cheeks. He shifted his gaze long enough to kiss the palm of her hand. His blue eyes took her in, cherished her. She saw that they mirrored her own emotions. A twinge of passion flashed between Natalie's legs.

Clutching Robson by the hair, Natalie pulled him on top of her. She let out a throaty moan when she felt the bulge in his crotch burning against her. His mouth felt so warm and inviting. She kissed him, running the tip of her tongue along his lips. He groaned and ground against her, sliding across her wet lips. Natalie gasped. She wanted him more than anything. Holding his face in her hands, she stared into his eyes. "I love you."

Robson smiled and opened his mouth to say those precious words back to her.

And screamed.

Not a scream, exactly. More like a howl. Or a piercing wail.

Natalie bolted upright, momentarily disoriented. She wasn't naked on the beach with Robson. She had been sleeping fully clothed, alone in a hotel bed. The sound wasn't a cry.

It was a siren.

An air raid siren.

Natalie heard yelling and screaming in the corridor. All of her senses went onto high alert. Ripping off the covers, she jumped

271

out of bed and gathered her gear. She had finished when something banged against the door. It started to open. Natalie grabbed her M-16A2 and swung it around.

Pandelosi stood in the doorway, her emotions under control despite the fear in her eyes. "We have to get moving!"

"What's wrong?"

"Just haul ass!"

Natalie didn't need to be told twice. She slid on her leather jacket, grabbed her backpack and automatic rifle, and ran out of the room.

Panic reigned in the corridor. Lopez stood at the far end of the corridor, waving on the Angels and directing them out the rear door. Her girls followed orders, even though they had no idea what was going on, which only added to the uncertainty and terror. His voice was barely audible over the siren. Natalie heard him yelling, "Get to the plane! Go! Go! Go!"

She ran up to him. "What's going on?"

"Our advance team up north called in that swarmers are heading this way."

"How many?"

"Over a thousand. Best we can tell, everyone infected in the bunker is on their way here."

"How long before they get here?"

"They're already here." Lopez grabbed Natalie's shoulder and shoved her toward the door. "Now move!"

Outside, Natalie witnessed complete chaos. The C-130 stood between the two hangers, its propellers spinning and its loading ramp down. Sarge and Duncan had positioned themselves on either side of the aircraft's rear opening, their weapons ready, while Kim stood at the top of the ramp urging the others forward. Everyone else raced for the aircraft as if their life depended on it.

Which it did.

Sarge and Duncan raised their M-16A2s and began firing at the hotel. Natalie looked over her shoulder as she ran. A score of swarmers crossed the parking lot and raced along the right side of the building. Lopez remained by the rear door, yelling to someone inside the building. When he heard the gunfire, he spun around in time to see the first swarmer rush around the corner. It wore a black suit and white shirt stained red with blood from a vicious neck wound. It saw Lopez and charged. With one motion, Lopez stepped out of the doorway, raised his M-16A2, and put a single shot through the swarmer's forehead.

Harrington burst through the doorway, with Katie right behind him. Lopez joined them, and the three made a mad dash for the plane.

They didn't stand a chance.

The swarmers surged around the corner of the building and bore down on the three. Lopez and Harrington stopped and fired into them, hoping to buy Katie some time. They took down a few of the living dead before being tackled. Four brought down Harrington. The private screamed so loud Natalie could hear it over the siren and the roar of the C-130's engines. He tried to crawl away, shredding the skin off of his fingers on the concrete. The swarmers ripped into him, tearing open his abdomen and gorging on his insides until Harrington's screams died off.

Lopez crouched when the closest swarmer reached him. It tripped over him and fell face first onto the tarmac, shattering its front teeth. Lopez swung his legs around, kicking down the next closest, which toppled to the side. Jumping to his feet, the corporal charged a swarmer ten feet away, driving his shoulder into its abdomen and pushing it back against two others. Lopez tried to run, but two swarmers grabbed him from behind. He attempted to throw them off . Being off balance because of the tackle, they forced him to his knees. The corporal still wouldn't give up. He shoved the first swarmer away, and then wrapped his arms around the second one's legs and pushed forward, knocking it over his shoulders onto the tarmac behind him. By then, the others he had knocked down had gotten back to their feet and lunged. Six sets of dead hands pinned Lopez to the ground and tore him apart.

The last two swarmers honed in on Katie. Lugging her backpack over one shoulder slowed her down. Glancing behind her, she saw a female swarmer in blue nurse scrubs closing in. Katie slipped off the backpack and dropped it on the tarmac in front of the swarmer. It bounded over the backpack and leapt at Katie, landing on her shoulders and knocking her to the cement. Katie cried out and struggled to break free as the second swarmer in a tattered and blood-stained *thawb* dived onto her. Each took a bite out of her neck, one tearing meat off of her shoulder, the other rupturing her larynx. Thankfully, the end came quickly.

"Lady, hurry the fuck up!"

Natalie turned around. The C-130 had begun to taxi toward the runway, the ramp now raised a foot off the ground. Sarge stood on one side, pumping his fist up and down to hurry her up. Duncan stood opposite him, helping on board the others as they reached the aircraft. Pandelosi jumped onto the ramp and lost her balance. Duncan steadied her, and then reached to help Emily. Her foot slipped on the metal ramp and she landed with a thud, her legs dangling over the side. Duncan grasped her hand, preventing her from falling off. Pandelosi grabbed Emily's belt and pulled, dragging her up the ramp until Kim came down to help her inside.

Natalie was now the only one still on the tarmac.

She increased her speed, knowing that with swarmers bearing down on them, the others couldn't risk stopping the aircraft. As she closed the distance with the C-130, she felt her legs getting weak and her breathing becoming labored. Pandelosi stood on the ramp and screamed something to the pilot. The C-130 decreased speed. Not by much, but enough to let Natalie catch up. Summoning all of her strength, she sprinted forward. When she reached the end of the ramp, Sarge and Duncan each grabbed an arm, lifted her on board, and shoved her toward the cabin.

Pandelosi rushed forward. "Raise the ramp and get us out of here!"

Everett pushed forward the thrust levers. The C-130 shot ahead, knocking everyone off balance, and raced along the tarmac.

Natalie caught her breath, slipped off her backpack, dropped it and her M-16A2 to the deck, and made her way to the cockpit. Pandelosi sat in the co-pilot's seat and strapped herself in. Everett focused on the tarmac ahead of him, swerving around parked aircraft. Checking the airspeed indicator, she saw that the C-130 had obtained a speed of sixty-three miles per hour.

"Thanks... for slowing down... for me," Natalie rasped.

"No problem. I just hope it doesn't let them catch us."

"There are... only a few swarmers... behind us."

"They aren't the problem." Everett pointed to his right. "I'm concerned about them."

Natalie followed his finger and uttered the only word that came to mind. "Fuck."

A thousand swarmers flowed around the main terminal and spread out across the surrounding tarmac like a tidal wave of living dead. They ran between the parked planes, crouching under the fuselages of the larger aircraft or racing around the smaller ones. They all converged on the only moving object in the airport.

Their aircraft.

Everett pushed the thrust levers to their limit. The four turboprop engines roared as each one strained to put out maximum horsepower. The C-130 picked up speed, approaching eighty miles per hour when it reached the runway. Natalie expected Everett to slow as he made the turn. Instead, he whipped the aircraft onto the runway. The tires screeched and the fuselage listed to one side, throwing Natalie against the bulkhead. The maneuver prevented them from losing significant speed. The C-130 barreled down the runway.

The swarmers had closed to within two hundred feet.

Everett gestured to the control yoke in front of Pandelosi. "Pull it toward you."

The lieutenant raised her arms beside her and physically backed into the seat. "I don't know how to fly."

Everett grabbed her left hand and forced it onto the yoke. "Just pull the fucking thing back for all it's worth!"

Pandelosi grabbed the yoke and yanked it toward her until she practically stood in the seat. Everett pulled back on his with his left hand while shoving the thrust levers forward with his right. His knuckles clutched the levers until they turned white, as if the effort would push a few extra miles per hour out of the C-130. The swarmers were less than one hundred feet away. Natalie swore she could hear them snarling even over the roar of the engines.

She felt a slight lurch when the C-130 lifted off the runway. She closed her eyes to thank God. Her relief was short lived.

Something thudded against the fuselage, and she felt the aircraft shudder.

Everett muttered, "Fuck."

She opened her eyes to find the starboard windows splattered with blood and gore. The first wave of swarmers had reached the C-130, only to be shredded by the propellers. A length of intestine dangled from the cowling of the inner engine. Black smoke flowed from the outer engine.

"Let go of the yoke!" Everett ordered.

Pandelosi sat back in her seat and moved her arms away. "Are we going to make it?"

Everett ignored her. He kept his yoke pulled back and to the left, trying to compensate for the drag of the right wing. "Come on, baby. Don't let me down."

They were not gaining altitude.

Everett let go of the thrust levers long enough to hit the switch to raise the landing gear and the hydraulics whirred. There was a thump as the port gear retracted into its bay. The whirring continued on the right, only now it sounded strained.

"The starboard gear is stuck!" Everett shouted to her. "What's wrong with it?"

Natalie peered out the side window. A swarmer was lodged between the twin tires, its torso leaning to the right and hooked on the bay's outer rim, preventing the gear from retracting. It clawed at the metal, trying to free itself.

"We have a rotter stuck in the landing gear."

"God fucking damn it!"

Everett shut down the outer starboard engine and feathered the propeller, preventing it from catching on fire. When he did, the plane veered left and lost altitude. Natalie gasped. Everett quickly corrected and leveled out. He reached out and flipped the starboard landing gear switch.

"How's our stowaway?"

Natalie glanced out the window. When the gear descended, the swarmer slipped from between the tires and plummeted behind them. "He's gone."

Everett retracted the gear and then concentrated his energy on flying. The C-130 still could not gain altitude. He pulled back on the control yoke. "Come on, baby. You can do this."

Natalie closed her eyes and braced herself for death.

"Come on!" Everett slammed his hand against the yoke. "Give me some height, you stupid whore!"

The C-130 steadily gained altitude. After a few minutes, Everett physically relaxed. He brought the aircraft into a slow U-turn to starboard and leveled off at an altitude of three thousand feet. Omaha passed by on their right.

Natalie waited until everything seemed under control then asked, "I assume we're going to make it?"

"If you're referring to staying airborne, yeah, we're going to make it. If you mean are we going to make it to San Francisco, that's another story."

"Why?"

"We have nothing to navigate by other than visuals, and when the sun goes down in half an hour we won't even have that." Everett pointed to a major highway running southwest from the city. "That's Interstate 80. It goes right into San Francisco. As long as I don't lose that, we should be there by morning."

"And if we do lose it?" Natalie asked, not sure if she wanted to hear the answer.

Everett tried to sound reassuring. "Then when she runs out of fuel, we'll put her down and hope for the best."

CHAPTER FORTY-NINE

Everyone stood outside the garage waiting for sundown, engaging in small talk and banter. Even the friendly atmosphere could not conceal the underlying nervousness. They all knew what was going to happen in the next few hours, and were equally aware of the chances of several of them getting killed. However, no one mentioned it. They chatted about the dinner they just had eaten, life before the outbreak, and even plans for the future. Jennifer stood beside Robson, occasionally brushing her fingers against his hand as they talked.

The banter came to an end when the sun set below the horizon. A few minutes later, Dravko and Tibor emerged from the garage. No one spoke when the vampires joined the others. An awkward silence fell over the courtyard, the specter of impending death looming over them.

After several moments, Dravko finally said, "I guess this is it."

The others mumbled in the affirmative.

Robson stepped into the middle of the group, making eye contact with each member as he spoke. "Before we go any further, I want to offer a final chance for anyone to back out. Let's be honest, the odds of success are not good. And for some of you, this isn't even your fight. If anyone wants to walk away now, I promise you no one here, especially me, will think any less of you."

No responses.

"Are you certain?"

"I think Toby Keith said it best," said Simmons. "A little less talk and a lot more action."

The others nodded in agreement.

Robson smiled. "All right, let's do this."

The group moved off to their respective vehicles. Robson followed Simmons and Wayans over to their Suburban.

"Do you have any handcuffs?" Robson asked.

"Sure." Simmons leaned forward, removed a pair from his belt holder, and passed them to Robson. "I thought we weren't arresting anyone?"

"We're not. These are in case one of the hostages panics and has to be restrained." Robson slid the handcuffs into his pocket and passed Simmons a radio. "Take this. When you get into position, if you see anything different that we should know about, or any reason why we need to call this off, let me know and we'll abort."

"You sure about this?"

"I trust you."

"You're the boss." Simmons took the radio and climbed into the Suburban. "And don't worry. We've got you covered."

"I know. See you back here in the morning."

Robson waited for the two to drive off before approaching the others. "Is everyone clear on what they have to do?"

His people nodded.

"Caslow, you're with me. DeWitt, your team and Jennifer will follow in the Hummers and provide backup. Dravko and Tibor, you know what to do. Let's rock."

Every climbed into their respective vehicles. Robson pulled out of the courtyard first and led the way to the main road, with the others close behind. The vampires brought up the rear in the Ryder. The convoy turned west onto Suncock Valley Road. After proceeding for several miles, it turned left onto Route 126. The vampires took an immediate right and headed down Parade Road toward the storage facility. The remainder of the convoy continued on ahead in the direction of Dover.

CHAPTER FIFTY

When Robson led the convoy through Dover on the way down to Site R, it had been their first foray into a rotter-infested city outside of Kittery. It nearly got the vampires killed and almost derailed the entire mission. Now Dover would be their savior.

Just outside the city limits, DeWitt and Jennifer pulled the two Humvees off to the side of the road and reversed direction.

Caslow stared out the front window. "Are you sure there are rotters here?"

"Trust me."

The bus continued along Route 9 and traveled over the Spaulding Turnpike overpass. Now the living dead presence became apparent. The headlights illuminated more than a dozen of the living dead meandering along the road, with countless more visible in the shadows. Robson raced past them.

"What are you doing?" Caslow asked. "We just passed some."

"Not enough."

"What do you mean?"

Robson nodded his head toward the rear of the bus. "We have to fill the back. It'll take too long here. We're heading into town where they're thickest."

"Screw that. That's not what I signed up for."

"I can let you out here if you want."

"No!"

Robson shot him a withering glance. "Then shut the fuck up."

The deeper they headed into Dover, the heavier the rotter presence became. Robson noted the streets were more congested, with both abandoned vehicles and the living dead. He also came across a few areas where the convoy had originally plowed their way through on the first trip. The farther in he traveled, the greater the number of rotters and, by consequence, the more attention they brought on themselves. An increasing number emerged from side streets and buildings, attracted by the sound, more than enough around to fill the bus. Robson needed a place where he could park without becoming trapped.

He had driven just under a mile when a strip mall came into view on the right. A hundred rotters shambled around the parking lot. Robson pulled off the main road into the nearest entrance. The engine attracted the living dead and, as one, they closed in on the bus. Pulling to the opposite end of the lot where the numbers were fewer, and from where he could escape, Robson stopped. The horde lumbered toward them. He grabbed the chain attached to the ramp and released it from its mounting. The clanging of metal reverberated through the vehicle, followed by a heavy thud when the ramp dropped.

"You're on," he said to Caslow.

Caslow opened the gate leading to the rear and rushed toward the ramp to stand by the opening. Dead hands clutched at him. Caslow did nothing. Robson cursed to himself. Caslow was supposed to lure them on the bus. Robson unholstered his Colt. If that little prick chickened out now, Robson would shoot him and let his body serve as bait.

"You'll have to move forward a few feet," Caslow said.

"Why?"

"You dropped the ramp on one of them. The end is a foot off the ground. None of them can get up."

Robson shifted into first gear. The bus lurched forward, pushing aside several rotters that had gathered around the front end. When he heard the clang of metal striking cement, he stopped.

The incessant moaning grew more intense. Robson spun around to see Caslow standing in the center of the entranceway, taunting the living dead. Several converged around the door, clawing against the floor or door jamb to get at him. One or two tried to crawl into the bus. It dawned on Robson that this might not work after all, that he had miscalculated how easy it would be to lure them onto the bus. If he couldn't do that, his entire plan fell apart.

While he was attempting to formulate a new idea, a rotter in a soiled hospital gown staggered onto the end of the ramp. Its balance was precarious, and for a moment it seemed as though it would fall off. The rotter looked around uncertainly and started to turn. Caslow stepped out onto the ramp and stamped his foot. The vibrations caught its attention, and its dead eyes landed on him.

"Meat sack!" Caslow stamped his foot again, coming dangerously close to being grabbed by several pairs of grasping hands. "Come on. There's a hot meal here if you want it."

The rotter snarled. Realizing there was food in the bus, it shuffled up the ramp. Others followed.

"It's working," Caslow called out to Robson.

"Get up here where it's safe."

Caslow ignored him. He stood by the open door, calling out to the living dead. A horde gathered around the back, with scores of hands reaching for him. With all the attention drawn to Caslow, only a few rotters gathered around the front of the bus, which would make their exit easy. When the rotter in the hospital gown reached the top of the ramp, Caslow moved toward the front and hovered a few feet from the gate. Two more climbed the ramp.

"Get your ass up here now!" ordered Robson. "We need time to close the cage."

Caslow raced into the driver's area, slammed the door shut, and dropped the two-by-four between the brackets to lock the door into place. As he finished, a set of fingers thrust through the openings in the rebar, the tips brushing against his face. Caslow yelped and jumped back, stumbling down the exit stairs.

"Relax," said Robson. "They can't get to you."

"Are you sure?"

"If I'm wrong, then we're both fucked."

Rotters continued to enter the school bus until it was half filled, those farther in back shoving against the ones already stacked up along the cage. More and more fingers reached through the openings in the rebar, scraping off strips of decayed flesh against the metal. The hospital gown rotter chewed at the metal to get to them, each bite dislodging decayed teeth from rotted gums. The moaning was deafening, although it did not bother Robson as much as the stench and the insects. Jostled about by the pushing and shoving, dozens of flies and a few wasps that fed off of the decayed flesh flew into the front part of the bus and buzzed around his head.

Caslow gagged. "Aren't we ready yet?"

"Not until we're full."

"Do we really need so many?"

"Trust me," Robson swiped his hand in front of his face, providing a momentary reprieve from the insects. "You'll appreciate them soon enough."

Glancing into his rearview mirrors, Robson noticed an increasing number of rotters along the side of the bus, with more gathering near the front fenders. One of them reached the folding exit doors and slapped the glass, leaving a bloody streak along its surface, and making Caslow jump again. Robson checked in back. The rear was more than three quarters full. He would have liked to collect more, but thought better about it. He didn't want to get hemmed in.

Robson shifted into first gear. "Let's go."

"Thank God."

The school bus lurched forward and stalled. Caslow freaked. "What the fuck happened? Are we stuck here?"

Robson shifted into first, this time applying more gas to compensate for the extra weight. The bus lurched forward again, and this time the gears caught. It inched across the parking lot, gradually pulling away from the horde. Those rotters still on the ramp fell off, tumbling onto the others around them. The rest staggered after the bus, arms outstretched, grasping at the escaping prey.

"Lift the ramp," Robson ordered.

Caslow grabbed the chain and pulled. Robson maneuvered the bus through the approaching rotters. By the time he reached the main street, he had it in third gear and Caslow had the ramp fully retracted.

Ten minutes later, they met up with the rest of the team outside of Dover. Jennifer and DeWitt walked over when the bus pulled up. Robson opened the folding door, and Caslow ran out, fell to his knees, and puked. A cloud of insects followed him. Jennifer and DeWitt stepped back several paces.

Jennifer placed a hand over her mouth. "Jesus, that smells horrible."

"Try being in here."

"No, thanks."

Robson gestured toward Caslow. "Get him and follow me. You know what to do when we get there."

DeWitt replied, "Roger that."

"See you guys on the other side." Robson closed the door to the school bus and headed for the storage facility outside of Barnston.

CHAPTER FIFTY-ONE

Price had made his final round of the facility and was heading back to his office when he heard Carter come up behind him. "Got a minute?"

"Sure. Walk with me." When Carter fell in beside him he asked, "What's up?"

"We're ready to go. Most of the camp will move out right after breakfast. I'll stay behind, oversee the cleaning and loading of the cooking gear, and then take care of the whores."

Price arrived at the door to his office and reached into his pocket for the keys. "What about their cooking skills?" he laughed.

"They cook as bad as they fuck. Once we get to the new place, I'll train someone else on kitchen detail. Besides, those bitches have been nothing but trouble. One of them has begun mouthing off to me, so I made sure they'll have a nice going away party. My way of saying thanks. Tomorrow morning, once the others have departed and they're done loading up everything from the kitchen, I'll shoot 'em, including the little brat."

Price unlocked the door and entered his office. "What'll you do with the bodies?"

Carter closed the door behind him. "I'll dump them somewhere along the road on the way to the new compound. I'll tell Meat that we got a flat tire and they ran away while I was fixing it. It won't be a problem. I'll keep him busy with chores until he finds another cunt to shack up with."

Price sat down behind his desk and offered Carter the chair in front. "What about the Line?"

"We're just going to leave them."

"You're not even going to put them down?

"Why waste the ammo? They'll be dead in a few days."

"Man, I thought I was heartless."

Carter smirked.

"You seem to have everything under control."

"Thank you."

Price reached into his desk drawer and pulled out the half-empty bottle of whiskey. "So let's you and I celebrate by finishing this off."

"With pleasure."

* * *

From his position behind a clump of bushes on the hill overlooking the storage facility, Simmons scanned the compound with his night-vision scope. He noticed an unusual lack of activity. In addition to the normal twin guards at the main gate, plus the one who made his rounds through the facility, he saw only two men entering the main office and three women wandering around near the rear of the compound. Good. That would give Robson the element of surprise.

Swinging his sniper rifle to the right, Simmons scanned the far end of the hill looking for Wayans. After a few seconds, he found his friend prone behind a rock formation, using a small boulder for cover. Wayans was examining the compound through his scope, ready to rain down hell on the gang.

* * *

"What does Price want to see us about?" asked Lisa as they walked to the rape room.

Karen nervously ran her hand through her close-cropped blonde hair. "Did we do something wrong?"

"I don't know any more than you do," Tracey snapped. "Carter said Price wanted to see us and show his appreciation for all we've done."

Lisa was confused. "Then why not call us to his office?"

"Ask him yourself when you see him." The anger in Tracey's voice shut Lisa up. It did nothing to assuage her own concerns. She hoped the move to the new community would also mean a change for the better in their circumstances. After all, if the guys lived less like animals, maybe they would also act that way. The entire kitchen staff had been talking about it for the past few days. This might actually be a good thing.

Any confidence Tracey had in a better future fell apart when the three women entered the rape room. Most of the gang members stood around drinking beer. Earl looked at Tracey and the others and grinned. "The entertainment's here, guys."

Karen tried to run. A burly guy in a leather Harley Davidson vest who had been standing by the door slammed it shut and blocked it with his body.

"Jake," she pleaded, "please let me go."

"Why, you in a hurry? The party's only beginning."

Two guys stepped up behind Karen, grabbed her by the arms, and dragged her over to the table. They held her down and pinned her shoulders, while two others grabbed her by the legs and ripped off her jeans. Karen screamed and kicked, trying to shove them away, which only made her attackers laugh. A line formed in front of her.

A tall gang member with a beer belly clutched Lisa by the arm and tried to drag her to the table. The teenager lurched free and spit in his face. He punched her in the mouth, breaking Lisa's nose and shattering her two front teeth. The tall gang member clutched the back of her neck and slammed her face down on the end of the table not being used, pinning her there with his left hand while he used his right to unzip and pull down her pants. Lisa offered no resistance.

Seven gang members neared Tracey. She backed up. Someone clutched a handful of her hair, and she saw it was Jake standing beside her. Yanking down, he forced Tracey to her knees. Earl stepped in front of her and unzipped his pants.

"Carter says you have a real dirty mouth, girl. Let's see just how dirty it is."

* * *

The three-vehicle convoy raced through Barnston. For the hundredth time since leaving Dover, Jennifer checked her rearview mirror. The school bus maintained a steady pace behind her. She wanted to call Robson on the radio even though he had ordered a strict radio silence to be broken only if they needed to abort. Jennifer refocused her attention back on the main road.

Just north of town, the convoy slowed to make the left turn onto Parade Road. DeWitt pulled his Humvee onto the shoulder and waited, with Jennifer doing the same. Robson slowed the school bus to a crawl and cautiously made the turn, careful not to flip the vehicle because of the excess weight. Once on Parade Road, he picked up speed and drove past. According to the plan, they couldn't follow for another three minutes. Knowing what Robson was about to do, those would be the longest three minutes of her life.

Jennifer watched the bus' taillights until they disappeared.

* * *

Lee fought back his tears. He knew he would never see Windows or little Cindy again because of how she acted when she had fed him dinner. She had a sad tenderness to the way she cared for him, the way she chatted with him, the way she held his cheek for a few extra seconds when she wiped his mouth. What cinched it was the hug she gave him just before she left, a gesture she had never done before, and that confirmed she would be making her escape tonight. He was happy for Windows, and prayed she and Cindy would make it.

However, their success would condemn him to a life of loneliness because only Windows had ever shown him any kindness.

Bowing his head, Lee sobbed.

* * *

Dravko crouched in a ditch opposite the main gate of the storage facility. The heat signatures of the humans tied to the perimeter defense burned bright against the cold night.

"They look delicious," said Tibor.

"Can it," Dravko snapped. "We promised Robson we'd help him."

"Half those people won't make it through the next few days."

"I said no."

Tibor growled. "If we were fighting with them inside the compound, at least we'd have a chance to feed."

Dravko didn't respond, although he agreed. A part of him hoped some of the gang members would try to escape.

* * *

Meat rolled over on his sleeping bag and wrapped a fat arm around Windows. His erection strained against his pants and pushed against her ass.

"Come on, baby. It's our last night in this dump. Let's celebrate."

"That sounds great." Windows could already feel herself heading into that cold, emotionless void that allowed her to survive the constant molestation.

Meat stood up and slid off his pants. "Tonight I want a three-way."

"I'll get one of the other girls. Do you have anyone particular in mind?"

"Yeah." Meat pointed to Cindy. "Her."

Windows' fight-or-flight senses cranked into overdrive. "Are you serious?"

"Yeah. She's watched us enough times to know what to do. Besides, she's the only virgin around."

Windows glanced over at Cindy, who sat in the corner of the unit, her legs pulled against her chest until the knees touched her cheeks. The girl's eyes widened with fear. Windows turned back to Meat. "You promised you wouldn't touch her."

"I never made no such promise. I've just never wanted to tap that shit until now." Meat spoke slowly, his tone deep and menacing. He picked up his pants as he spoke and slid out the belt through the loops. "She's gettin' fucked tonight. It's your choice whether it's gentle or not."

Windows stiffened and placed herself between Meat and Cindy. "I'm not going to let you tou—"

Meat slapped her across the face with the belt. The buckle hit her left cheek, gouging out a chunk of skin. Pain and shock shot through her body. Meat wrapped the belt around his right hand, with the buckle on the outer knuckles.

"All right, ya cunt. I'm goin' to beat the fuckin' shit out of ya, and then you're gonna watch me take the bitch's cherry."

* * *

Robson breathed through his mouth, though it barely helped. The stench of decay had become so thick inside the school bus he could taste it. When he did open his mouth, flies crawled in. He had already swallowed back vomit half a dozen times, as well as God only knew how many insects. When he broke through the woods at the end of Parade Road into the open and saw the storage facility off to his right, his relief was palpable. He didn't have any fears about entering the battle of his life. He just wanted to get out of this rolling carnage house.

Veering right, Robson pushed his foot down on the accelerator, shifted into second gear, and steered toward the main gate of the outer defense perimeter. The bus slammed into it at over sixty miles per hour. The cowcatcher hooked the gate in the bottom right quadrant, slicing through the chain links and impaling the metal frame. Because of its momentum, the bus ripped the gate off its hinges and bent it over the hood. The upper left quadrant curled over and crashed into the driver's side windshield. Robson closed his eyes. He heard the shattering of glass and the scraping of metal against metal. When he opened them again, a piece of the upper gate support and the barbed wire strands stuck through the windshield.

Ignoring the damage, Robson kept his foot pressed on the accelerator and aimed for the metal security gate built into the brick wall of the storage facility. The bus slammed into it, and Robson felt his senses being overwhelmed: the sudden deceleration distorting his equilibrium; the pain of the seat belt digging into his chest and shoulders; the sound of metal grinding against metal; of rotters being tossed around the back; of flies and wasps being stirred into a frenzy; and of people yelling. When Robson opened his eyes, he was staring into the barbed wire. The crash had shoved the gate section through the windshield until it sat only a few inches from his face. He had busted through, and the front third of the bus sat inside the storage facility.

Robson unbuckled and slid out of his seat. He opened the folding doors, and then spun around and lifted the two-by-four from its mounts. The cage door popped open. Grabbing his AA-12, Robson jumped off the bus.

"Freeze, motherfucker!"

Two gang members stood ten feet away, their weapons aimed at his face. Cries and yells could be heard all over the compound. The larger of the two men leveled a Remington hunting rifle at Robson.

"Drop your weapon and get on your knees!"

"Whatever you say." Robson tossed his gun back and to the side so it landed beside the bus, and knelt down.

"Jesus Christ!" said the younger guard.

"What's wrong, Billy?"

"That's him!" He gestured with his shotgun at Robson. "The one I was telling you about. That's the guy with the vampires down by—"

The first rotter stumbled off the bus.

CHAPTER FIFTY-TWO

The two guards shifted their weapons from Robson to the lead rotter, a male in a soiled hospital gown. Robson used the opportunity to drop to the ground and roll under the school bus, grabbing his AA-12 in the process. The guards ignored him, concentrating on the main threat. They each fired a round, blasting apart its head and upper torso. It tumbled off the stairs and dropped to the ground, and two more took its place. The guards also took these down. While Billy reloaded, three more of the living dead staggered off the bus.

* * *

Price and Carter heard the school bus approaching seconds before it slammed into the outer gate. Both men jumped out of their seats and headed for the compound. Price saw his guards get the drawdown on the driver and heard Billy yelling, "That's him! The one I was telling you about. That's the guy with the vampires down by—"

Price could barely control his anger. "Shit. Those motherfuckers came for us."

"And they brought hell with them." Carter pointed to the first rotter stumbling off the bus before taking off toward the rear of the compound.

Price ignored his second in command, focusing instead on the intruders.

* * *

From his position on top of the hill, Simmons watched the

295

opening minutes play themselves out. He had to admit that so far this crazy scheme seemed to be working. Robson had inserted a dead horde into the compound and, as expected, now faced the compound's security detail. That's why he and Wayans were there.

Simmons centered his scope on the younger of the two guards by the bus. Before he could pull the trigger, he saw two men emerge from the office. He quickly calculated their threat potential. Neither carried weapons, and one of them got scared and ran off. This would be simple.

Switching back to the younger guard, Simmons realigned his scope on the side of his head. Tightening his finger against the trigger until he felt tension, he took a deep breath, steadied the rifle, and squeezed. The bullet struck the left temple and exploded out the right side of the guard's head. The kid dropped to the ground. A shot echoed from his right, and the other guard died a quick death.

Simmons swung his rifle toward the lone figure standing by the office door and centered the crosshairs on his face.

* * *

Price heard the twin thuds of bullets striking flesh and saw his guards go down. He immediately knew what was happening. Ducking and dodging to the right, he dove through the office door as two rounds ricocheted off the wall where he had been standing. Once inside, he slammed the door, half expecting another barrage of bullets to follow him. Nothing happened. Crawling to the back room, he grabbed his M&P15-22LR semi-automatic. If these assholes wanted to make this a blood feud, he would spill as much of theirs as possible.

First, he had something to take care of.

* * *

Simmons saw his target move out of the way at the last second and his bullet fragment against the wall. He kept the scope trained on the door until it closed. Not that it surprised him. No one would be stupid enough to come back out with snipers present.

Simmons panned his scope across the compound, searching for his next target.

* * *

"What the fuck is all that racket?" Earl asked, stepping away from Tracey. He went over to the door and stepped outside. He nearly shit when he saw the bus imbedded through the front gate spewing out deaders.

"What's wrong?" asked Jake.

"We're under fucking attack. There's deaders in the compound." Earl came back inside. "Grab your weapons and get out there. Now!"

Earl yanked away two of the gang members standing around Tracey and forced them through the door. They never made it outside. The moment they stepped through the opening, a pair of bullets caught each one in the head, spraying the others in a cloud of blood.

"What the fuck are we gonna do?" demanded a Hispanic gang member.

"We're going to have to make a break for it."

"Fuck that, man. They'll gun us down before we get twenty feet."

"No they won't." Earl grabbed Tracey by the hair and yanked her to her feet. "We'll have cover."

* * *

"What's goin' on out there?" Meat stopped beating Windows and stared at the door of his unit.

Windows tried focusing on the floor through her blurred vision. When Meat began his assault, she had lowered her head so the blows struck the back of her neck and would cause less damage. He had only hit her three times, yet it had taken a toll, leaving her dazed. Gradually, she became more aware of her surroundings, and knew she only had one chance. If she screwed this up, Meat would kill her.

When Meat turned from the door, Windows lunged forward

on her hands and knees. She bent her head to the side, sucked one of his testicles into her mouth, and bit. It crunched between her teeth. Meat howled. Windows opened her lips enough to let the ball sac slide into her mouth, bit down again, and whipped her head to one side, tearing it off. Meat emitted a muffled croak. He collapsed to his knees, his hands clutched to his groin, blood pouring through his fingers.

Windows spit out the bloody segment and staggered to her feet. Meat's shotgun stood in the corner. She raced over and grabbed it, and then circled around the unit to get Cindy, keeping the weapon trained on Meat.

"Ya fuckin' cunt!" he sobbed, looking down at his tattered groin and the growing pool of blood on the cement between his knees. "I'm fuckin' gonna beat ya to fuckin' death."

"You're not going to do anything to me ever again, asshole."

Meat saw Windows holding the carbine. "I took good care of ya. I kept ya safe from the others."

"You raped me, fucker."

"Go ahead and kill me, cunt."

"I'm not like you. I'm not going to kill you." Windows lowered the barrel and fired two rounds that tore through Meat's upper legs and thighs. He screamed and fell over on his side, crying so hard from the pain he could not breathe. "I'm just going to leave you here and let your friends dispose of you."

Windows dropped the shotgun. Taking Cindy by the hand, she led her out of the unit and toward the kitchen.

* * *

Gunfire in the distance broke the silence, starting with only a few shots and increasing in intensity within seconds. Jennifer knew what that meant. Robson had made it into the compound and had engaged the gang. DeWitt pulled his Humvee off the shoulder and headed for the security compound, with Jennifer behind him. Soon they'd be joining the fight.

She hoped Robson would be safe until they got there.

* * *

Dravko tapped Tibor on the shoulder. "Let's go."

The two vampires climbed out of the ditch, dashed across the road, and entered the outer perimeter through the ripped-apart gate. Dravko headed for the first human staked to the ground, an emaciated middle-aged woman whose long brunette hair hung in straggly clumps. Dravko noticed her life signs were weak. As he approached, she cowered against the ground and wrapped the blanket around her for protection.

"Don't hurt me."

"I'm not." Dravko slipped up beside her while Tibor moved along to the next person. He placed a comforting hand on her shoulder. "We're getting you out of here."

"Really?" Her voice was mixed with joy and disbelief.

"Yes." Dravko grabbed the chain as close to her wrist as possible and snapped the links.

"How did you do that?" she asked warily.

Dravko ignored the question. He pointed to the ditch across from the main gate. "Wait over there where you'll be safe. Understand?"

"Yes." The woman threw her arms around Dravko and hugged him. "Thank you."

"You're welcome." He patted her shoulders and broke the embrace. "I have to save the others."

* * *

Crawling out from underneath the opposite side of the bus, Robson got to his feet and rushed down to the front fender where he paused to survey the area. Across from him and to the left was the parking area. He counted a dozen vehicles, from cars to pick-up trucks and Humvees, all packed with boxes and supplies. To the right sat two parallel rows of buildings, two buildings to a row. These contained the storage units. The buildings ran the length of the compound. Robson peered around the bus. The guards who confronted him were being feasted on by rotters. The rest of the living dead sauntered around between the first building on the right and the perimeter wall.

Robson dashed across the open space to the first row of

buildings and stopped with his back to the wall. He moved down to the corner closest to the center path, raised his AA-12 into firing position, and peeked around the edge. He didn't see anyone. After turning on the barrel-mounted flashlight, he moved into the path between the two rows of buildings, staying close to the wall.

When Robson reached the first unit, he crouched down and wrapped his hand around the handle of the sliding door. Taking a deep breath, he lifted it. As the door slid up along its rollers, Robson did a quick pan with his AA-12, ready to fire on anything that didn't appear friendly. He found only a sleeping bag and a wooden crate with an unlit lantern on it. Removing a piece of chalk from his pocket, he etched an X onto the bricks to the left of the door and moved to the next unit.

* * *

The twin Humvees emerged from the woods along Parade Road. Jennifer followed DeWitt as he pulled off to the side, passed through the broken outer gate, and circled behind the school bus to race along the perimeter wall, careful not to run over any of the people tied to the ground. When DeWitt reached the far right corner along the front facade, he stopped his Humvee against the wall and let Jennifer go on ahead. While his team disembarked, a few of the victims trapped on the defense perimeter called out to them, begging for help. DeWitt ignored them and ordered his people to climb onto the Humvee. When everyone was in position, he and Roberta hoisted Allard up to the top of the wall. Allard straddled the wall and reached down to help up Frakes.

Jennifer drove her Humvee around the corner and stopped near the far rear corner. She crawled through the access hole in the roof, followed by Caslow. Cupping his hands together and holding them in front of him, Caslow assisted her in climbing up to the top of the wall. Once there, she helped up Caslow, and then the two dropped down on the other side into the compound.

* * *

Carter ran into his unit and grabbed his Macmillan TAC-50 .50 caliber long range sniper rifle, a pouch of ammunition, and a pair of night vision goggles. It took him only a few seconds to gear up and race back to the compound.

He assumed by now that the deaders had swarmed the cherry picker located by the main gate, so he wouldn't be able to use it to gain a vantage point. His next best option was the roof of the office building. Several months ago, he had placed three empty crates by the end wall to use as stairs. They came in handy now, and Carter climbed onto the roof, taking up a firing position. The swarm of deaders passed beneath him in front of Price's office. Carter loaded a round into the chamber and studied the horde beneath him. It would be like shooting fish in a barrel.

* * *

Earl exited the rape room clutching Tracey by the hair. Holding her in front of him as a human shield, he moved toward the main gate. Several other gang members followed on either side, firing their weapons indiscriminately into the hill above the compound. Two other guards followed, using Karen and Lisa as shields.

* * *

Shit, muttered Simmons as he watched the three groups make their way through the compound. *This is going to make it difficult.*

He lined up a shot on the asshole holding the brunette. He had his crosshairs centered on the bridge of his nose, waiting for a clear shot, when the head of the gang member on the right erupted with blood and gore. The group froze, all eyes focused on their dead comrade. A moment later, a second gang member spun around and fell to the ground as a sniper round pierced his chest.

Damn, Wayans is kicking ass.

* * *

Allard and Frakes were still straddling the wall when they heard the gang members leave the building and make their way down the compound. They didn't notice the women being used as human shields; they saw only enemy combatants. Raising their weapons, they fired into the gang.

The next twenty seconds took place in a blur.

Each man carried an M-16A2 automatic rifle. They fired into the group closest to them, not caring where they aimed. None of the gang members knew what hit them. The barrage ripped through their ranks, killing six within the first few seconds, including Lisa, and wounding three others. Two of the wounded lay on the ground, writhing in agony from shots to the abdomen and chest. The third had taken a round to the shoulder.

The middle group returned fire, raking the top of the wall. Allard took the full brunt of the assault, the gunfire nearly cutting him in half. Frakes tried to escape as eleven rounds slammed into his chest, propelling him backwards. What remained of his body crashed onto the Humvee's hood in a bloody heap.

The group around Earl panicked. Most fired blindly into the night sky in a desperate attempt to hit the sniper. Some looked around at the multiple targets, not having any idea what to shoot at. A few off to his right began firing at the approaching deaders, the nearest one now only a hundred feet away. Every few seconds, someone around him went down with a well-placed shot to the head.

Fuck Price and fuck this shit, thought Earl.

He made his way to the path that cut between the two buildings, dragging Tracey in front of him. He called out to the gang member in the leather Harley Davidson vest. "Jake, follow me."

Jake fell in beside Earl, staying as close as possible to Tracey to benefit from her protection. He kept his weapon raised, scanning it from left to right, aiming at nothing in particular. "Where are we going?"

"We're getting the fuck out of here."

* * *

Carter saw a flash on the hill above them, and heard the death moan of one of his men who absorbed the bullet. Ignoring the deaders, he concentrated on a new target. A human target.

Carter dropped prone on the roof, kicked out the supports for his sniper rifle, placed them on the tar, and aimed in the general direction of where the gunfire had come from. It took only a few seconds before the target fired another round. In Carter's night vision goggles, the shot glared like a beacon, giving away the shooter's position. He was hidden behind a boulder off to the left, and Carter could see movement between a curve in the rock and the ground. The target had done a good job of concealment, but not good enough because he had to expose himself to shoot. Carter bided his time.

He did not have long to wait. The target moved around the boulder and set up his next shot.

Before the target could get off a round, Carter squeezed the trigger.

* * *

Simmons saw the flash of gunfire and involuntarily ducked. The sound of the bullet striking to his right put him at ease, until he heard Wayans moan. Simmons scanned the roof with his scope until he saw the sniper lying prone. Holy fuck! The guy was using a .50 caliber sniper rifle. He watched the sniper load another round into the chamber and line up his next shot.

Simmons wouldn't give him that chance.

* * *

Carter cursed when he saw the sparks generated by the bullet ricocheting off the boulder. However, rather than disappear under cover, the target rolled back and forth. He must have wounded him. Carter reloaded and sighted in on the target again, taking extra time to aim and steady himself. His finger closed around the trigger until it caught. He took a deep breath and held it, adjusted the aim, and—

The pain lasted a split second, not even long enough for Carter to register that he had been shot. The bullet entered just above his right eye and flattened out. The misshapen hunk of metal continued on its trajectory, tearing a path of destruction through his brain. Carter felt none of it. He died before the projectile punched its way through the back of his skull, leaving a cloud of blood and brain matter to follow behind it.

* * *

Simmons smiled when he saw the sniper's head explode in the green light of the night vision goggles. He kept his scope trained on the compound, searching for more targets of opportunity, calling out to his friend in a low voice.

"Wayans, are you all right?"

No answer.

"Wayans?" he called again, louder.

Still no answer.

"Are you okay?" Simmons yelled.

"Friggin' shut up, man," Wayans whispered fiercely, more in frustration than anger. "You want that friggin' sniper to get us?"

Simmons breathed a sigh of relief. "I took care of him. How are you doing?"

"A chunk of that last bullet ricocheted and caught me in the chest. Hurts like friggin' hell."

"Do you need my help?"

"I'm fine. Cover Robson."

* * *

Neither DeWitt nor Roberta was prepared for the gunfight with the gang members. They both stood on the roof of the Humvee, waiting to be pulled onto the wall, when Allard and Frakes got caught in the crossfire. DeWitt grabbed Roberta by the shoulders and forced her into a crouch. A few seconds later, Allard's partially-severed torso and Frakes' bullet-riddled corpse dropped onto the Humvee, splattering the two in blood. DeWitt rolled off the roof onto the ground, pulling the stunned Roberta with him. She sat with her back against the vehicle's door while DeWitt kept an eye along the top of the wall, ready to fire if any gang members tried to climb over it.

When he glanced over at Roberta, she stared numbly at the blood covering her clothes. He spoke her name, but she did not hear him. He reached around with his left hand and shook her shoulder.

"What?" Roberta yelped as he jerked her back into reality.

"Snap out of it."

"For Christ's sake, I just saw two of my friends gunned down."

"Yeah, and we're going to lose Robson and the others if we don't find a way to get back into this game."

Roberta mumbled the word "bastard" under her breath. She grabbed her M-16A2 and knelt beside DeWitt. "Obviously we can't get into the compound this way, so how do you propose we break in?"

DeWitt sighed and shook his head. "I haven't figured that out yet."

* * *

The eruption of weapons fire on the other side of the compound caught Jennifer and Caslow off guard. She crouched and raised her weapon in case the gun fight moved in their direction. Caslow took several steps back until he bumped into the wall. When the battle didn't spill toward them, she relaxed a little. The contemptuous glare she shot at Caslow caused him turn his head.

Jennifer pointed to the storage units opposite the perimeter wall. "I'll search this row. You take the ones in the center. Be careful. We have no idea what we'll find in there. And for God's sake, don't panic and shoot any of our own people."

Before he could respond, Jennifer ran off, headed for the first storage unit in her row.

* * *

Price entered Meat's quarters, hoping to find Windows and the girl. Instead, he found Meat lying in a near fetal position on the floor in a pool of blood, naked from the waist down, groaning and holding his groin. When Price walked over, he saw the blood-stained belt tossed to one side and the severed testicle sitting on the cement. He surmised what must have taken place. Price hovered over Meat.

"What happened?" he asked in a voice devoid of sympathy.

Meat rolled onto his back. Fear and relief filled his eyes on seeing Price standing above him. "The cunt attacked me. She took that bitch kid and left me here."

"Where did they go?"

"Ya gotta help me, boss."

"Where did they go?" Price asked, this time emphasizing each word.

Meat removed his hands and pointed to his groin. "I'm hurt bad," he whined.

Price placed the toe of his boot against the wound and pressed. Meat screamed and tried to roll away. Price held him in place with his foot.

"I'm not going to ask again. Where did the bitch go?"

"I don't know. I don't know. I don't know." Meat's voice trailed off into a muffled sob.

Price removed his foot and wiped the sole on the man's pants. Meat reached a hand up to him. "Ain't ya going to help me?"

Price turned and made his way to the door.

"Boss! Please!"

Ignoring the pitiful calls for help, Price stepped into the compound. Meat had created his own hell, and now he could spend the rest of his life in it. Price didn't have time to help those who wallowed in sin. He had to find Windows and that bitch kid, and he had a good idea where they went. Now he could kill two birds with one stone.

Price made his way to the far corner of the compound.

* * *

Windows hurried Cindy between the buildings. Every time the girl asked a question, Windows would hush her, partly to keep her quiet, and partly because she needed to concentrate on making certain no one noticed them. The commotion by the main gate made that easy because it kept the camp preoccupied, and she prayed it stayed that way. If Price ever caught them trying to escape... well, she didn't even want to think about that.

They finally reached the kitchen. Windows took one last look around and, certain no one saw them, raised the sliding door halfway up. She ushered Cindy inside and reclosed it. It took her a few minutes of fumbling around in the dark to find the lantern and light it.

"Did I do something wrong?" Cindy asked. "Why don't you want me to talk to you?"

"Honey, you did nothing wrong." Windows hugged Cindy, wrapping her arms around the girl and cradling her head. "We just have to make sure no one sees us or knows what we're doing."

"What *are* we doing?"

"We're getting out of here."

Cindy broke the hug. Windows saw a glimmer of hope in her eyes. "You mean forever?"

"Yes."

"And I won't have to watch them hurt you anymore?"

Windows nodded.

"Okay. I'll be quiet."

"Good girl." Windows rubbed Cindy's cheek. "Stay here."

Crossing over to the empty pallets that once held the compound's food supplies, Windows removed the wire cutters she had hidden there and slipped them into her back pocket. She stepped over to the fifty-five gallon drum and tipped it onto its side, being careful not to drop it, and rolled it over to the sliding door.

"Okay, Cindy. We're going to roll this over to the wall and use it to climb over the top. Are you up for that?"

"Yes."

"Good. Now stay quiet and do as I tell you, and we'll be fine. Can you do that for me?"

Cindy nodded.

Windows extinguished the lantern and raised the door. The gun battle still raged near the main gate. She rolled the barrel out and steered it toward the end of the building.

* * *

Robson made his way down the row of storage units, checking each one and finding them empty except for scattered personal belongings. He marked each one with a chalked X by the door. When he lifted the sliding door to the sixth unit, a female voice asked from inside, "Kyle, is that you?"

"I'm not Kyle." Robson scanned the room with the barrel-mounted flashlight until the beam fell on two women huddled in the rear corner. One had long red hair, the other close-cropped blonde hair. Their clothes were threadbare and, like the women themselves, filthy. Both looked emaciated and terrified, especially when they saw Robson's face in the backwash from the flashlight and realized they didn't know him. They wrapped their arms around each other. The redhead begged, "Don't hurt us!"

"I'm not going to hurt you." Robson shifted the barrel of the AA-12 away from the women, but still kept them in the beam of light. "We're getting you out of here."

The blonde perked up. "Really?"

"Yes." Robson moved forward, stopping ten feet away so as not to pose a threat. "What are your names?"

"I'm Michelle," the blonde answered and pointed to the redhead. "This is Kay."

"My name is Mike. Now I need you to do me a favor. Close this door behind me—"

"No!" Michelle broke away from the other woman and crawled toward him. "You can't leave us! What if Kyle comes back?"

Robson held up his hand to calm down and reassure Michelle. "Do you hear that gunfire? We're taking care of the gang members, so I promise, Kyle is not coming back. I need you to close this door because there are rotters on the compound. You'll be safe here until someone comes and gets you."

"You can't leave us!" begged Kay.

"Are there others like you on the compound?"

Both women nodded.

"Then I have to check on them and make sure they're safe. I'll come back for you. Right now I need you to close the door and don't open it for anyone except me. Understand?"

They both stared at him blankly.

"Ladies, do you understand?"

"Y-yes," Michelle stammered.

"I'll return in a few minutes." Robson made his way to the door and looked out, checking the compound for signs of gang members or rotters. When he turned, neither woman had moved. "Close this behind me."

Michelle jumped up and ran over. Robson stepped out and waited until she slid the door shut. She stopped halfway, her eyes pleading. "Please come back for us."

"I will."

After Michelle closed the door, Robson used the chalk to mark the cement with an X and the number "2" beside it. He moved on to the next storage unit.

* * *

Earl moved so fast Tracey could not keep up, so he practically dragged her through the compound. She had complained once or twice, and each time Earl clutched her hair tighter and jerked her head to one side to shut her up. Now she kept quiet and endured the lesser of the two pains. Jake followed ten feet behind them, walking backwards and facing the battle zone to make sure no one pursued them. The trio made their way to the opposite wall of the compound, turned left, and after a minute arrived at the parking area.

Earl walked down the line of vehicles, checking the steering columns of each one until he found an SUV with the keys in the ignition. Even better luck, this one held enough food and ammunition to keep them supplied for a while. Stepping toward the rear fender, he opened the back door and shoved Tracey toward the vehicle.

"Get in, bitch."

"Please," Tracey pleaded, "leave me here."

"Get in the fucking car."

When she hesitated, Earl grabbed her by the throat, pushed her into the backseat, and slammed the door. Tracey's leg was not all the way in and the door closed on her shin. Earl opened it, grabbed her leg, and shoved it inside. She lay on the back seat, wailing. He slammed the door shut again and spun around to face Jake.

"Go move the school bus so we can get out of here."

Jake shook his head. "No fucking way, man. That thing is full of deaders."

"Move it or I leave you behind."

It took a moment for Jake to realize Earl was serious. Rushing across the parking lot, he climbed up into the bus, checking the back to make sure no deaders remained inside, and slid into the driver's seat. The engine was still running, so he shifted into reverse.

As Jake cleared the entranceway, Earl crawled into the driver's seat of the SUV, started the engine, and pulled out of the parking space.

* * *

Dravko and Tibor had released close to twenty prisoners and made their way down the western side of the Line when Tibor heard the school bus shift into gear and its engine rev. He stood up, the chains of another prisoner clutched in his hands.

The human stared at him. "What's wr—?"

"Shh!" Tibor silenced him and called over to Dravko. "Do you hear that?"

"Yeah."

"Something's not right. Moving the bus is not part of the plan."

"Let's check it out."

Tibor rushed away, and everyone on that segment of the Line who had not been freed shouted for them not to go. When Dravko stood, the middle-aged man who he was attempting to release grabbed his arm and clutched it tight. "Don't leave me here. I can't take it any longer."

Dravko patted the man's hand. "We'll be back in a minute."

The man held Dravko's arm for another few seconds before letting go. Dravko set off after Tibor and caught up with him at the corner of the wall. Someone had moved the bus fifty feet from the main gate and backed it between the compound wall and the perimeter fence. "What's going on?"

"Someone moved the bus, but it's not one of our people."

"Why would they do that?"

"I think they're trying to escape." Tibor pointed to the gate. An SUV exited the compound and stopped. A person in a Harley Davidson leather vest ran off the school bus and over to the passenger side of the SUV. Tibor glanced over at Dravko. "Should we stop them?"

"Yes."

"And feed?"

Dravko hesitated for a moment. "Yes."

The two vampires rushed the SUV and caught up with it as it passed through the outer gate and turned onto Parade Road. They morphed into their vampiric forms and jumped onto the vehicle's roof, with Tibor landing on the passenger's side and Dravko above the driver.

* * *

"We made it." Earl high-fived Jake as they sped away from the compound, only to have the elation drain away when something heavy dropped onto the roof.

"What the fuck is that?" Jake asked.

Three-inch-long talons penetrated the metal above his head. Jake froze, watching in horror as the vampire tore back the front section of roof and hovered over the opening, glaring down at them. It had elongated ears, a furrowed forehead, and a flared nose. Tracey screamed and tried to push herself into the corner of the backseat, ignoring the throbbing in her leg. The vampire snarled at Jake, exposing a mouth full of fangs. Reaching in, it yanked Jake to his feet, plunged its fangs into his neck, and began to drink. Jake whimpered and his body shuddered. After a few seconds, the vampire lifted Jake out of the compartment and tossed him aside, the body disappearing into the dark along the side of the road. The vampire snarled at Earl.

Earl whipped the steering wheel to the right and back again. The vampire lost its balance and tumbled off the roof on the passenger side. It reached out at the last second and grasped the SUV's roof rack, trying to regain its footing. Earl swerved right, aiming for the trees along the side of the road, hoping to rip the son of a bitch off the roof.

A taloned hand smashed through the driver's side window.

Earl waited for the vampire to claw at him. Instead, it grabbed the steering wheel and pulled. The SUV made a sharp left turn toward the woods. Earl stiffened his arms against the steering wheel as they crashed into a tree head on. He experienced an incredible bolt of pain as his arms snapped and his chest smashed into the steering column, and then everything went black.

* * *

Dravko pulled the mangled body from the driver's seat and threw it onto the grass. Blood poured from the twin compound fractures in the arms, draining away precious life fluid. Desperate for a meal, he dug his talons into the human's chest and ripped open the ribcage, revealing its heart. He had not tasted human blood in weeks, ever since he had turned Dr. Compton. Bending over, he plunged his fangs into the meat and drank, savoring the taste. Terror sweetened human blood, the adrenaline adding a special flavor. Because this human had already lost so much due to the accident, he faded quickly. Dravko sucked as the heart slowed and finally stopped beating. Rising to his knees, he wiped his mouth with the back of his hand and licked the last few drops from his fingers. This one body barely satisfied his hunger. How he missed preying on humans.

Dravko heard a noise from the rear of the SUV. Tibor crouched in the back on top of a young woman. He had her pinned to the seat, his knees resting on her pelvis and his hands holding her arms by her side. She didn't struggle, probably from being stunned from the accident, although she did quietly plead for Tibor to leave her alone. He ignored the woman and drained her blood from her carotid artery. Dravko had to stop him. After all, this woman did not belong to the gang. The vampires had to rise above their instincts if they wanted to live among humans. He moved around to the other side of the SUV and opened the rear passenger door. He reached in, and for the first time he noticed the woman's injuries. The right front of her face was a bloody pulp from where she had smashed it against the window during the accident, and her collar bone protruded from her shoulder. She would die soon, so why let good blood go to waste?

Leaning in, Dravko sank his teeth into the other side of the woman's neck and fed.

* * *

DeWitt and Roberta also heard the commotion by the main gate. Someone backed the school bus into the perimeter zone and then jumped into an SUV that raced off down Parade Road, with the vampires in pursuit.

DeWitt stood up and headed toward the gate.

"Where are we going?" Roberta asked.

"To make sure no one else escapes."

* * *

The battle between the rotters and gang members intensified, and it slowly became apparent the humans were not going to win.

They maintained a steady barrage against the living dead, taking several down, but their numbers were too great. They also had to contend with Simmons in the hill above them, who had thinned out their own ranks by seven. Several attempted to retreat to the opposite end of the compound. Simmons took down each one who tried. He allowed Karen to escape when she broke away and ran for safety. One of the gang members went after her, making it only ten feet before Simmons put a bullet through the side of his head. A few tried to cut between the two buildings and escape to the rear wall of the compound. By then, Robson had reached the end of the first row of storage units and positioned himself at the corner, shooting anyone who tried to get by him. With the only avenues of escape closed off and the rotters closing in, the gang members fell back to the rape room. Even here they could not find safety because Simmons shot anyone who tried to close the door.

Simmons ceased sniping when the first deader wandered inside, though he continued to watch through his scope. The gang members blew it apart as it sauntered through the open door. The gunfire attracted more of the horde. In less than a minute, fifteen deaders had swarmed the room. The intensity of the gunfire increased, followed by screams of terror and pain as the rotters overwhelmed them. Simmons could not see inside because of the angle, although he could imagine what was going on by the silence, and wished he could watch those assholes suffer.

A score of deaders ignored the rape room entirely. Some passed it and shambled among the perimeter wall, while most turned left between the two buildings and wandered into the compound.

Simmons switched his mission from neutralizing gang members to protecting his people. Moving his scope away from the rape room, he scanned the area for Robson and the others.

* * *

Making his way along the middle left row of storage units, Caslow fought back the panic threatening to overwhelm him. He didn't know what scared him more—the sound of the gun battle raging on the other side of the building, or the fact the firing had become less intense, which meant that either the gang members or the rotters had been wiped out, and whichever side had won would soon be roaming the compound. Instead, he tried to focus on finding Debra and Cindy. At each unit, he paused for several seconds to summon up his courage before raising the sliding door. It had taken him five minutes to check out only three of them. At this rate, he would never find his family. He could not move any faster, being paralyzed by fear.

Caslow raised the door to the fourth unit and swung his flashlight from one wall to the other. This time he almost pissed himself when he saw movement in the corner. He raised his Heckler and Koch 223 to confront the threat, and in the process dropped the flashlight. It rolled one hundred eighty degrees, directing the beam behind him. He held the weapon in the direction of where he had noticed the movement, his aim unsteady.

"W-who the fuck is there?" he asked.

"Don't shoot," said a female voice. It did not belong to Debra or Cindy. She sounded more scared then him, if that was possible. He relaxed a little. Keeping the semi-automatic trained in the direction of the voice, he bent down, picked up the flashlight, and shined it in the corner. A filthy, sickly woman sat with her back to the wall, clutching a soiled blanket against her chest. He couldn't even begin to imagine what she had gone through.

"I'm not one of them," she said. "My name is Patty."

"I won't hurt you." Caslow stepped a few feet closer. "I'm looking for Debra."

"You mean the woman with the little girl?"

"Yes," he answered hopefully. "Do you know where she is?"

The expression on the woman's face said it all. Caslow fell to his knees, bowed his head, and cried. He had let them down. His family was dead because of him, because of his cowardice. For a moment, he thought of placing the barrel of the Heckler and Koch into his own mouth and pulling the trigger.

"I'm sorry," said Patty. "The little girl, Cindy, is safe though. One of the new girls is looking after her. I think her name is Wendy."

"Where are they?" Caslow asked excitedly.

"I'm not sure. When the fighting broke out, all of us women went into hiding. You could try Meat's quarters."

"Where is that?"

"To your left and...." Patty's sentence dropped off, and her eyes widened in terror.

Caslow spun around to see a rotter in a tattered brown UPS uniform enter the storage unit. Two more approached from fifty feet away. Caslow tried to stand, but the rotter was too close. Spinning around on his knees, he raised the Heckler and Koch at an angle across his chest as it lunged. The UPS rotter knocked Caslow onto his back and fell on top of him, pinning him to the floor. The semi-automatic Caslow held outstretched in his arms prevented it from getting to him. He wouldn't be able to hold it off for long, and had no way of defending himself from the other two.

Keeping his left arm outstretched, Caslow lowered the right until the stock rested on the floor. The rotter's dead hands clutched and scratched at his face. He reached down to his holster, withdrew his Smith and Wesson, and stuck the barrel in the rotter's mouth.

"Fuck you!" he yelled and pulled the trigger.

The trigger did not budge.

Shit, he had forgotten to release the safety.

Out of the corner of his eye, he saw Patty rush out the door. The two living dead had closed to within ten feet, and grabbed her as she tried to push pass them. One latched on to her right arm and bit into it. She screamed and flailed to break the grip, to no avail. The second rotter moved up behind her. Clutching Patty by the hair, it pulled her head to one side and plunged decayed teeth into her neck.

Caslow felt his left arm giving way. Pulling his right hand back, his thumb fumbled around on the stock until it found the safety. Switching it off, he shoved the sidearm back into the rotter's mouth just as his left arm collapsed. The rotter fell forward, its weight crushing into Caslow's chest, its mouth only inches from his face, and with the Smith and Wesson still lodged down its throat. It gagged out a moan.

Caslow pulled the trigger.

A cloud of blood and skull fragments mushroomed above the rotter's head. Some of the gore dripped onto Caslow's face. The rotter went limp and collapsed onto him. Caslow rolled to his right, throwing the carcass to one side. Crawling on his hands and knees into the corner, he vomited, retching until he could only dry heave. When he stood, the room spun a little, forcing him to lean against the wall until everything returned to normal.

From where he stood at the rear of the unit, he saw the other two rotters rip chunks off of Patty and devour them. Once again, someone had died because of his own cowardice and stupidity.

Pushing himself away from the wall, Caslow crossed over to the living dead. With a steady hand and clear aim, he fired off three rounds—one into the head of each rotter, and the third into Patty's face. He then stepped back inside the unit, closed the door, and sat with his back against the metal.

* * *

Jennifer had made her way to the end of the row of storage units because she wanted to check the situation at the center of the compound where the fighting was taking place. Once certain that the gun battle posed no immediate threat to her, she made her back along the row, checking each unit and marking them with an X since all were empty. The last one had the words KEEP OUT written in red paint across the sliding door and a padlock securing it to the frame. She slammed the stock of her semi-automatic rifle against the padlock until it broke off, and then crouched down and wrapped her hand around the handle. Raising the door four feet, she scanned the inside of the unit with her flashlight. The beam fell on an old man wrapped in a blanket seated in the corner. He raised his deformed hands level with his head.

"Trust me, I'm no threat."

Jennifer lifted the sliding door all the way and stepped inside. He appeared harmless enough. Still, she kept the M-16A2 trained on him. "Keep your hands where I can see them. I'm not taking any chances."

"I understand."

Jennifer approached and pulled aside the blanket to make certain the old man hadn't any concealed weapons. "We don't want to hurt anyone if we can help it."

"It sure sounds like someone is getting hurt."

"We're here to save our friend and get the rest of you to safety."

The old man's eyes lit up. "You're a friend of Windows?"

"Yes! Is she safe?"

"God, I hope so."

"Where is she?" Jennifer asked.

"I'd like to know the answer to that one myself." The voice came from the doorway.

Jennifer spun around to see a man dressed in black standing ten feet behind her. He had a Smith and Wesson M&P15-22LR trained at her head. "Put the weapon down. Slowly."

She knelt and placed her M-16A2 on the floor.

"Good girl. Now step back."

Jennifer obeyed.

Price stepped forward, took the M-16A2, and slung it over his shoulder, all the time keeping his eyes and his semi-automatic fixed on Jennifer. When finished, he moved back five feet.

"So, old man, answer her. Where is the bitch?"

"Why do you care?"

"Because her and that little brat have been nothing but trouble since they got here."

"So you're the one who runs this rape camp?" spat Jennifer.

"The name is Price," he smiled. "And it's not a rape camp. Everyone has to contribute something to eat, and for most of the women here, that's all they have to offer."

"You're a sick fuck." Jennifer took a step toward him.

Price raised the M&P15-22LR and leveled it at her face. When she moved back, he shifted the weapon onto Lee. "Okay, old man. I don't have time to fuck around. Where is she?"

Lee refused to answer.

"Why are you always causing problems for me?" asked Price.

Lee remained silent.

Price shrugged. "Suit yourself."

He raised the semi-automatic again and fired.

* * *

The decreasing sound of gun fire concerned Windows. It meant that if she and Cindy didn't make it out of here soon, they would never get out alive. She rolled the fifty-five gallon drum faster, not caring if they made noise, the desire to escape now paramount. When she reached the rear wall of the compound, she maneuvered the drum against the surface and tilted it over so that the open side faced down. She lifted Cindy on top and climbed up herself. The drum wobbled.

"Okay, honey. I'm going to lift you to the top of the wall."

"I'm scared."

"I know you are. So am I." Windows brushed the hair off of Cindy's face. "You want to get out of here, don't you?"

The little girl nodded.

"Then we have to do this. It'll be over soon. I promise."

Grabbing Cindy by the hips, Windows lifted, being careful to distribute as much weight as possible against the wall. "Tell me when your hands can reach the top."

"They can."

One at a time, Windows moved her hands down to Cindy's

ankles and lifted. The weight in her hands lessened, and when she looked up Cindy sat on top of the wall. "Scoot over a few feet so I can get up."

As Cindy obliged, the sound of a gunshot rang out from behind her. The door to Lee's storage unit was open. She wanted to check on him, but knew better. If she went to help Lee, she would blow her only chance to get Cindy out of this hellhole, and keeping her safe was the main priority.

Jumping up, Windows grabbed the end of the wall and pulled. Her muscles strained, and she could only make it up so far. She dug her shoes into the wall, trying to find a foothold that would give her leverage. A small pair of hands wrapped around her shoulders as Cindy grabbed her shirt and helped lift. It took several seconds, and for a few of them Windows thought she would not make it. Eventually she reached the top of the wall. Sitting beside Cindy, she paused for a minute to catch her breath.

"Are you okay?" Cindy asked.

Windows nodded. "Let's get going. We'll be free in a few minutes."

* * *

The bullet tore its way through Jennifer's abdomen. She dropped onto the cement floor, clutching her wound and whimpering in pain. Blood poured through her fingers.

"Why'd you do that?" Lee yelled.

Price ignored the question and leveled the semi-automatic at Jennifer. "Tell me what I want to know and I'll finish her off. Otherwise I'll leave her this way. It could take hours to die from her wounds, maybe a day or more. I don't think you want that."

"You're sick."

"This is a whole new world, old man. A world in which you have to be strong to survive. That's why you're in the position you're in." Price stepped over to his father and knelt down so he could make eye contact. "You've always worried too much about other people. Rather than support me, you were more concerned about those I culled from the pack. You don't know any of these people, and yet you'll screw me over to protect them. So I'm giving you have a choice to help out others. What's more important to you? Saving that bitch and her little kid, or putting this one out of her misery."

"I'm not going to play this game with you."

"Have it your way. This bitch can bleed out for all I care." Price stood up, stepped back, and rested the barrel of his M&P15-22LR on his shoulder. "I'm sure the other two are heading for the car you stashed away at the construction site."

Lee's eyes widened, and Price knew he had won. "You know about the car?"

"Of course. I know everything that goes on around here. I never mentioned it before in case I needed it to get away. You just confirmed for me that you let her know about it. Checkmate, old man." Price smirked. "I'll just meet them there when they arrive and take care of my problem once and for all."

"You motherfucker!" Lee lunged at Price, or what served as a lunge for a cripple. The old man struggled to his feet, stumbling once and landing on his hands. He struggled to stand upright and lumbered toward his son. Price fired a round directly into Lee's face. The shot blasted away most of the old man's head, leaving only a draping portion of the bottom jaw and a segment of the rear skull attached by a sliver of skin. The body hovered for a second before collapsing onto the soiled blanket.

"No," Jennifer moaned. She tried to go to Lee's aid. The moment she moved, she cried out from the pain.

Price walked over to her, crouched, clutched her hair, and yanked her head off the floor. "As for you, I'm leaving you alive. Those deaders your friends introduced onto my compound will be done with my men soon and will start looking for fresh meat. You'll make a nice little meal for them. Kind of ironic, don't you think?"

Price let go of Jennifer's hair, and her head fell to the floor. He left the storage unit and headed back to his office.

* * *

Once the rotters had overrun the gang members and forced them back into the rape room, Robson left his spot near the intersection of the four buildings and continued searching the units heading toward the rear of the compound. He heard a single gunshot from one of the nearby units. With all the other noises around him, he couldn't tell where the sound came from. He continued down to the end of the buildings near the perimeter wall when he heard a second blast. This time he determined it came from behind the set of buildings on his left. He headed for the end of that building. He turned the corner in time to see someone walk out of the last unit. Robson raised his AA-12.

"Freeze!"

The figure spun around and dodged to one side, firing off a round. Robson jumped back around the corner as the shell slammed into the cement wall where he just stood. A moment later, a burst of gunfire blew past the end of the building. Robson waited a moment and dived out, rolling into the center of the path, his AA-12 ready to fire. The gunman disappeared around the other end of the building. Jumping up, Robson rushed over to the storage unit.

He nearly threw up at the sight that greeted him. Jennifer lay on her side curled up, blood flowing from a gunshot wound to her abdomen. He rushed over and touched her shoulder. She jumped, both from pain and fear, until she opened her eyes and saw it was him. Despite the agony, she smiled.

"What happened?" he asked.

"The guy who runs this place... Price... was looking for Windows... to shoot her.... He shot me...." Jennifer gestured toward Lee's corpse, "...to get him to reveal... where Windows is. He didn't."

"Do you know where she is?"

"She's with a little girl.... there's a car hidden nearby... that she plans on using... to escape. But Price knows... where it is. Stop him."

"First I'll take care of you."

"We both know... I'm not gonna make it." Jennifer's body convulsed. She reached out and gently held Robson's left hand. Robson fought back the tears.

"It's okay.... leave me... your sidearm."

"No." Robson would not abandon another woman he cared about to die alone. Still holding Jennifer's hand, he used his right to unholster his Colt. He placed the barrel against her forehead. "I'll never forget you."

"Of course... you won't." Jennifer smiled and closed her eyes, an expression of contentment on her face.

Robson turned his head and squeezed the trigger. He felt Jennifer's hand tense around his own, and then go limp. He could not bring himself to look at her. He felt for a pulse on her wrist and, when he didn't detect one, gently put down her hand.

Robson raced out of the unit and set out after Price.

* * *

Windows and Cindy dashed across the open space between the compound wall and the outer perimeter fence. Those closest in the Line saw them and called out.

"What's going on in there?"

"Are we under attack?"

"What's going to happen to us?"

And the one question that cut into Windows' soul: "Will you help us?"

Windows ignored them. She couldn't save them all, and every minute she spent trying to help them lessened their own chances of getting away. The more she ignored them the louder they got. Some insulted and threatened her. Damn it, these people would wind up getting them all killed. Working quickly, Windows removed the wire cutters from her back pocket and used them to snap the links from the ground up, cutting a hole large enough so she and Cindy could sneak through. When finished, she dropped the cutters and pushed open one end of the fence.

"Go ahead. Climb through."

Cindy paused and stared at the people tied to the Line. "What about them?"

Windows placed her hands on the girl's cheeks, trying to be gentle but firm. "We can't take them with us."

"I know that." She bent down and picked up the wire cutters. "Can't we at least give them these?"

Windows smiled. Cindy may be only eight years old, but she still retained more humanity than the adults around her. Windows took the cutters. "Crawl through and wait for me on the other side."

While Cindy slid through the opening, Windows ran over to the nearest person in the Line, a teenage girl, and handed her the cutters. "Here. Use these to cut yourself free."

"I don't know if I'm strong enough to use them."

Windows clasped her hands around the teenager's and closed them around the cutters. "Sorry, that's all I can do."

Rushing back to the hole she had cut into the fence, Windows crawled through to where Cindy waited for her. The two ran as fast as they could down the road toward where Lee had told them he had hidden the car, never once glancing back at the compound.

* * *

Meat tried to crawl away to get help. He had only gotten as far as the sliding door before the pain became too great. Not only that, every movement caused the wound to bleed, leaving a trail across the floor. He had collapsed after making it ten feet and waited, hoping someone would find him.

Five minutes had passed before Meat heard someone enter his quarters. He rolled onto his side. "Thank God ya fou—"

A pair of deaders wandered into the storage unit. The closest wore a soiled policeman's uniform and had more than a dozen fresh bullet holes punched into its chest, the congealed blood oozing black streaks down its front. The other wore the remnants of mechanics overalls, the bottom portion shredded to reveal chewed legs, in some places all the way to the bone. They smelled fresh blood and already had worked themselves into a feeding frenzy.

Meat didn't even try to escape. As they fell to their knees and reached out for him, he braced himself for the inevitable.

* * *

Price ran back to his office and entered through the rear door, making sure to lock it behind him. His compound was falling to both the deaders and the attackers, and he needed to get out fast. Grabbing the emergency bug-out backpack he kept at the foot of his cot and throwing it over his left shoulder, and then stopping by his desk to pick up the keys to his Hummer H3, he entered the front part of the office. Price paused to glance out the window. He did not see any deaders near the vehicle. The only living dead he saw milled around the rape room.

Exiting the office, he headed for the Hummer. Holding the keychain in his right hand, he unlocked the doors.

* * *

Robson ran between the twin buildings trying to catch up with Price even though he had no idea where the latter had gone. When he reached the path that ran perpendicular to the buildings, he saw crates piled up along the end of one of the buildings, creating makeshift stairs. Rushing over, Robson climbed the boxes onto the flat roof and moved to the edge, searching for Price. A black Hummer H3 was parked in front of the main office. Reasoning that Price planned on escaping in it, he raced along the edge of the roof toward the vehicle.

When he got to within ten feet of the Hummer, Price exited the office and made his way to the vehicle, using the automatic keychain to unlock it. Robson dove off the roof and landed on top of Price, knocking the weapon and keys out of his hand and driving him face first into the rear of the Hummer. Robson grabbed the backpack and yanked, hoping to drag Price to the ground. Instead it slid off his shoulder, leaving Robson off balance. Price kicked out with his left foot, catching Robson in the outer right thigh and knocking him down. Price knelt and picked up his M&P15-22LR, swinging it around to fire.

Robson rolled to his feet. Realizing he didn't have time to close the distance before Price got off a shot, he hurled the backpack. Price ducked, causing his aim to be off. Robson lunged and punched Price in the kidney. Price huffed and doubled over. Robson grabbed the semi-automatic by the barrel and the stock ripped the weapon away from Price, and swung it back, slamming the butt into his face. He heard a crack and blood flowed down Price's forehead. Price fell back against the Hummer. As Robson hit him again on the shoulder, Price punched up with his right hand, aiming for Robson's balls but instead catching him in the groin. It still hurt like hell. Price punched twice more. Each time, Robson shifted his body so the blows landed on his pelvis; however, the maneuver knocked him off balance. Price grabbed the semi-automatic rifle, and the two men attempted to wrest it from the other, with Robson holding the stock while Price kept both hands wrapped around the barrel. Robson shoved Price into the rear of the Hummer, winding him. He removed his right hand from the stock, slid a finger around the trigger, and squeezed, firing the remaining bullets. The barrel instantly grew hot, forcing Price to release his grip. Robson swung his right arm wide and smashed his elbow into Price's face, stunning him. Jumping back, he kicked out with his right leg and smashed his heel onto Price's left knee, shattering the bone. Price screamed and dropped to the ground, holding his useless leg.

Removing a pair of handcuffs from his jacket, Robson slapped one end around Price's wrist and attached the other to the anchoring loop on the bumper. He crouched in front of Price, grabbed a handful of hair in his left hand, lifted his head, and slapped Price's face with his right.

"You know who I am?"

"Yeah." It took a moment for Price to regain his senses. "You're the fucker who came through here a few weeks ago, killed a bunch of my guys, and brought the deaders behind you."

"And you know that was my compound in Maine you destroyed?"

"So I destroyed your camp and you destroyed mine. How does that make what you did any different than what I did? How does that make you any better than me?"

"It doesn't." Robson glanced around the devastated storage facility. "I just wanted to make certain you knew who caused all this."

Price sneered. Robson had seen it dozens of times from convicts who kept on getting busted and who never saw themselves as the problem.

"What now?" asked Price. "Are you going to kill me?"

"That's too good for you." Reaching down beside him, Robson picked up the Hummer's key chain and pressed the alarm button. The horn blared, the siren wailed, and the lights flashed.

Every rotter in the compound turned toward the noise and started making their way in that direction. Those still in the rape room staggered out and fell in line with the others.

Price yanked on the handcuffs. When they didn't budge, he stared at Robson incredulously.

Robson stood up and took a head count. "I estimate about twenty rotters left."

"You're going to leave me here to be eaten alive?"

"That's the plan."

"Then you're no fucking better than me!"

"I never said I was. This is for fucking with me and my people. Payback's a bitch."

Standing up, Robson walked away, enjoying the terror in Price's eyes.

* * *

Price refused to beg for mercy. Fuck it, he would rather be eaten alive than show any weakness to that motherfucker. His best revenge would be breaking free and escaping. He tried shaping his hand into a funnel and slipping it through the cuffs, but Robson had attached them too tight. The nearest deader was less than fifty feet away.

Bracing himself for the pain, Price jerked on the handcuffs. Nothing happened. He kept it up, trying harder each time. When he glanced over his shoulder, the deaders had closed to within twenty feet. Placing his hand on the bumper and taking a deep breath, he summoned all his strength for one final yank. The cracking of bones accompanied the agony of his wrist being shattered, and his broken hand slipped out of the cuffs. Steadying himself on his one good leg and one good hand, Price stood up.

A hand clutched at his face, and he smelled decayed flesh. Jumping back, Price lost his balance and fell against the Hummer. The deader stumbled forward and pushed him against the vehicle. Price tried to run, but his leg gave out and he fell to the ground, the deader landing on top of him. He reached under the Hummer with his good hand, hoping to find something to grab on to so he could pull himself under the vehicle. Other hands grasped at his legs, more and more getting a hold until the horde dragged him away. Price tried to fend them off. Decayed fingers ripped at his clothes and dug into his flesh, while several sets of teeth bit into his limbs. Price screamed, a bloodcurdling cry that ended when several of the deaders ripped open his chest cavity and tore out his lungs.

* * *

Robson jogged away, wanting to put as much distance as possible between him and the approaching rotters. DeWitt and Roberta stood by the gate, wary eyes on the horde.

"Is everything okay down this end?" he asked.

DeWitt nodded. "No rotters or gang members, if that's what you mean."

"What happened to Allard and Frakes?"

"They were killed during the gun fight with the gang members. Did you find Windows?"

"No. Apparently she had an escape plan and put it into play when the fighting started. I don't know what it is, though. I want to take—"

Robson stopped when Dravko and Tibor approached from down Parade Road. He noticed the blood covering their clothes. "Where were you?"

"Two of them tried to escape," said Dravko. "We stopped them."

"Has anyone seen Caslow or Jennifer?" asked DeWitt.

The expression on Robson's face said it all. Roberta raised her hands to her mouth. "I'm sorry."

"Thanks. I haven't seen Caslow, though."

"What now?" Dravko asked.

"You and Tibor finish releasing the prisoners, and then bring the Ryder here and load them on board. DeWitt and I will clean out the rest of the compound. There's still a few civilians in here who need to be rescued. Roberta, grab one of the Hummers and see if you can track down Windows. She should be with a little girl."

"Do you really think we'll find her?"

"We have to try." Robson turned back into the compound

where the rotters swarmed around the Hummer H3. "Otherwise all this was for nothing."

* * *

Windows and Cindy did not stop running until they traveled far enough along Route 28 that they could no longer see the storage facility. Even then, the two maintained a brisk pace. Windows maneuvered them to the shoulder and kept her ears open for anything that might be following them, human or living dead. She only felt at ease when they turned onto the second road on the left. They followed it for what seemed like forever, and Windows began to think Lee must have been wrong, when off to the right she saw a chain link fence reflecting the moonlight. She broke into a jog, pulling an exhausted Cindy behind her. She almost cried when she saw that the fence surrounded a construction site.

The main gate was not locked. Pushing it open, they stepped inside and stopped. Windows listened for any unusual sounds, still wary of walking into a trap or a swarm of rotters. The only noise came from crickets. Taking Cindy by the hand and giving it a reassuring squeeze, the two entered the site.

It took only a few minutes to find the metal garage. Inside sat the Rav-4, just as Lee had said. Sliding open the garage door, she walked round the SUV. The tires were still inflated. Boxes of canned goods, bottled water, and weapons and ammunition were stored in back. She helped Cindy into the passenger side before sliding into the driver's seat. The keys dangled from the ignition. Taking them in her hand, she paused for a moment to say a silent prayer that this would work, and turned them.

The engine roared to life on the first try.

Windows burst into tears. She laid her forehead against the steering wheel and cried until a tiny hand patted her arm.

"Everything will be okay now," Cindy reassured her.

It may not be okay, thought Windows, *but it will be hell of a lot better than what we're used to.*

Using the back of her hand, Windows wiped the tears from her eyes and the snot from her nose. She smiled at Cindy. "Where do we go now?"

"As far away from here as possible."

"Deal."

Pulling out of the garage, Windows crossed the construction site, exited onto the road, and turned north.

CHAPTER FIFTY-THREE

Natalie had replaced Pandelosi in the co-pilot's seat an hour earlier. Not that she knew how to pilot an aircraft in case of emergency; her job was to make sure they didn't lose contact with Interstate 80 below them and to make sure Everett didn't fall asleep. She had tried chatting with him, but he was not in a talkative mood. He was pleasant enough when he asked her for the time or to keep an eye on the console while he checked navigational charts, but other than that, he shunned conversation. She tried a different approach.

"What do you know about the Beachhead and the new government-in-exile?"

"Not much more than what the lieutenant probably already told you. Why?"

"You seemed like the type of guy who'd have contacts who know things."

Everett chuckled, the first positive emotion she had seen from him. "I do, but everyone I know is pretty tight lipped. The GIE is afraid that if it becomes know how good they have it at the Beachhead, others might try and take it away. RUMINT has it that one of the local gangs that survived the outbreak has already made a move against the Beachhead and was driven back. Secretary Fogel is gathering forces to go on the offensive and take back the country, and he doesn't want to squander them on gang wars."

"How can he do that? Most of us have barely been able to survive the last nine months."

Everett shrugged. "Somehow the Secretary has established a viable, safe community. They've been rescuing anyone who can make it to San Francisco and survive the revenants and the gangs. One of the pilots who used to make commuter runs between the Beachhead and Omaha kept urging me to put in for the assignment. He said it was a lot safer than being stuck out in the middle of nowhere. I guess he was right."

"Well, you finally made it—"

A voice came across the speakers.

"This is Alameda Naval Air Station to unidentified aircraft approaching the Bay from the northwest. Please identify yourself. Over."

Everett leaned back to yell into the aircraft. "Lieutenant, we have Alameda on the horn!"

"This is Alameda Naval Air Station to unidentified aircraft approaching the Bay from the northwest. Identify yourself. Over."

Pandelosi joined them in the cockpit. Everett switched the audio to the speakers. "Alameda, this is Flight 98 from Omaha. Landing designation Alpha Echo Bravo. Requesting permission to land. Over."

"Hang on Omaha 98. Over."

The moment of radio silence that followed felt interminable.

"Omaha 98, we have you scheduled for a 1400 arrival time, which is almost eight hours from now. Over."

"We had to leave Omaha early because of a swarm of revenants. We are requesting permission to land. Over."

"Permission denied, Omaha 98. Over."

Everett stared at the speaker. "Could you repeat that, Alameda?"

"Permission to land at Alameda Naval Air Station is denied at this time. We do not have the support personnel, medical staff, or containment facilities set up at this time to handle your arrival. Come back at the designated time when we are set up and permission will be granted. Over."

Everett stared at the women in disbelief. "Alameda, what the fuck do you mean come back at the designated time? We've been flying all night and are almost out of fuel, and I lost an engine. We land now or we crash into the Bay."

"We appreciate your situation, Omaha 98, but we cannot grant permission at this time. Over."

"Can we at least land and remain in quarantine at the far end of the runway until 1400?"

"Negative, Omaha 98. If there are infected on the plane, there is the potential risk of spreading it through the community. Sorry. If you attempt to land, we will shoot you down without warning. Is that understood, Omaha 98? Over."

"Yeah, Alameda. And fuck you. Out." Everett ripped off the headphones and flung them across the cockpit where they shattered against the windscreen.

"Now what?" Natalie asked.

Pandelosi opened the map. "What's the next nearest airport?"

"That would be San Francisco International. It's ten miles south of the Beachhead, with the entire city between us and sanctuary. We wouldn't make it two miles."

"So we're screwed," Pandelosi sighed.

"Not yet." Everett turned the C-130 a few degrees west. "A couple of the other pilots I knew told me about an emergency improvised airstrip not far from here. They used it mostly for choppers and small aircraft."

"Can a C-130 land on it?" Pandelosi asked.

"They say if you're really good or insane you can." Everett grinned. "That just doubled our odds. Go back and tell everybody to buckle up. The next few minutes are going to be tricky."

Everett held Natalie in place. "I need you up here with me."

"I don't know how to fly."

"You have to make sure there's nothing on the runway."

"And if there is?"

"Let me know before I hit it."

Natalie buckled herself in and looked out the starboard window. San Francisco Bay passed beneath them and got closer as Everett began his descent. A few minutes later, they made landfall. She calculated their altitude as no more than two hundred feet. The C-130 turned to port.

"Keep your eyes open, ma'am."

Natalie leaned forward to better see out the windshield and gasped. The improvised airfield Everett had mentioned turned out to be a two-thousand-foot length of an eight-lane highway that had been cleared of vehicles and obstructions. Cars, trucks, guard rails, signs, and lamp posts lay in twisted heaps of metal along the outer shoulders. At the far end of the makeshift runway, less than two thousand feet away, sat a collection of helicopters and small aircraft. On either side, the hills loomed large in the night sky, their shadows precariously close to the wings.

Everett lowered the landing gear and pulled back on the thrust levers. The C-130's speed and altitude dropped. For a second, it felt as if the aircraft would fall out of the sky. Natalie glanced at the air speed indicator. It read forty miles per hour.

"Eyes on the highway, ma'am. Let me worry about not stalling her."

Everett brought the C-130 down with a heavy thud that shook the entire aircraft. He throttled back the engines, dropped flaps, and applied the brakes.

She saw the rotter a split second before they struck it. It staggered along the highway, and had turned toward the noise when the left landing gear ran over it. The entire plane lurched as the rotter went under the wheels. Two more appeared ahead and to the right. Instinctively, Everett pulled the yoke left to avoid them. He didn't see the military Humvee sitting on the third lane. The outer port propeller clipped the vehicle, and both exploded in an array of sparks and twisted metal. Natalie flinched when she heard the chunks slam against the fuselage. Everett brought the C-130 to a stop two hundred feet from the other aircraft and shut down the engines.

Natalie peered out the starboard windshield. The two rotters they had tried to avoid were splattered across the highway after having been shredded by the starboard engine. She saw a few figures along in the shadows, although not enough to be a concern.

"Is everyone all right?" Natalie asked.

"I think so," responded Pandelosi.

"There's a few rotters in the area. Have my girls set up a perimeter and take them out with knifes rather than shoot them. I don't want to make any more noise than we already have."

"Aye, aye, honey," she heard Emily respond.

"Everett," Natalie said, "that was impressive. I mean it."

"I've had better landings," he gasped.

"They say any landing you can walk away from is a good one."

"For me it won't be that good." Everett motioned toward his left leg. A piece of metal was imbedded into his thigh directly across from a basket ball-sized hole in the fuselage.

"Oh my God, you're hurt!"

"I'll live."

Natalie unbuckled herself and reached over to unstrap Everett. "We have to get you medical attention."

Everett stopped her. "You can't take me with you."

"I'm not going to leave you here."

"I'll be fine. Just be sure to close up the plane behind you so nothing can get in."

Natalie hesitated.

"You know I'm right," said Everett. "If you take me with you, you'll either have to leave me exposed out there or die trying to defend me. Once you reach the Beachhead, tell them where I am. They'll send someone after me."

"How do we get to the Beachhead?"

Everett pulled the maps out of his pocket and handed them to Natalie. "Continue straight down this road and you'll know exactly where you are. It's less than four miles from here. Now hurry."

Natalie left the cockpit and headed for the exit hatch. Before she closed it behind her, Everett called out, "Don't forget to send help."

Other than some bumps and bruises, and some reinforced fear of flying, everyone in back had made it through the landing safely. The Angels had formed a perimeter around the C-130, and so far only had to deal with four rotters. Pandelosi was helping Ari load the briefcase with the Zombie Vaccine into a backpack to keep her hands free for the trip.

"Where's the pilot?" asked Duncan.

"We'll have to come back for him. He took a piece of shrapnel when the engine shredded the Humvee, and can't walk." Natalie noticed that none of the military folks seemed concerned about leaving him behind.

"So where do we go from here?" Pandelosi asked.

"Everett says just follow this road straight and we'll know where we are, and then we can follow the maps to the Beachhead." Natalie deferred to Pandelosi. "Do you want to lead?"

The lieutenant hesitated, but then her military bearing took over. "All right people, listen up. Stay single file, with ten feet between us. Keep your eyes open for revenants." She faced Natalie. "Are your girls okay with taking orders from me?"

"They are."

"Good. If we get separated, we make our own way to the Beachhead and meet up there. Any questions?"

None.

"Let's move out," Pandelosi said. "Natalie, you're with me."

The group made its way through the parked aircraft. At the end of the makeshift airstrip, four rows of Jersey barriers blocked all eight lanes of the highway, arranged in such a way so as to create a staggered passage through them to slow down rotters. The going was easy because no vehicles clogged this road. Once past the barricade, they headed toward the bend in the highway. Off along the eastern horizon, the first rays of sunlight reflected off the bottom of the clouds, creating a perfect sunrise.

Pandelosi went through the maps Everett had given them, opening and closing them, growing more and more frustrated. As they rounded the bend in the highway, she refolded them and shoved them into her pocket.

"What's wrong?" Natalie asked.

"These maps are fucking useless. I can't figure out where we are."

Natalie pointed ahead of them. "Maybe that will help."

The highway led to the Golden Gate Bridge.

CHAPTER FIFTY-FOUR

"You gotta be kidding me," said Duncan. "How the hell are we going to get across that?"

"We walk," snapped Pandelosi. "Do you think they would have set up an emergency airstrip on the Sausalito side of the Bay if they hadn't secured the bridge first?"

"I guess," replied Duncan somewhat contrite.

"This is going to be a cakewalk compared to what's ahead of us." Pandelosi waved them forward. "Move out, people."

Approaching the bridge, Natalie surveyed it for potential danger. She noticed a set of Jersey barriers arranged across the entranceway in the same way as at the airstrip and open in the center to allow traffic through. On the other side of the barricade, vehicles were neatly lined up along the two outer lanes on either side of the bridge as though someone had parked them there, leaving the four center lanes unobstructed. The two pedestrian walkways on either side of the bridge were also clear. No rotters were visible.

When they reached the barricade, Pandelosi stopped and faced them. "Split into four groups as we cross."

"I thought you said this was going to be a cakewalk," chided Duncan.

"No sense being bunched up and an easy target in case we run into something. Since you like to second guess me so much, you can join me down the center of the span. Kim, you take the left walkway. Batchelder has the one on the right. You ladies can team up with us as you see fit. Keep ten feet between you. Let's roll."

The military personnel spread out. Pandelosi walked down the left side of the four center lanes and Duncan took the right.

Kim and Batchelder swung over the guardrails and moved along the east and west exterior walkways, respectively. Amy and Sarah followed Kim. Sandy and Doreen fell in behind Batchelder. The rest of the Angels stayed in the center, with Josephine and Emily trailing Duncan and Natalie, Stephanie, and Ari following Pandelosi.

As they approached the north tower, Pandelosi waved for Natalie to join her. When Natalie caught up, the lieutenant pointed to the cars lining the outer guard rails. "What do you make of the fact that the cars look like they had been parked here rather than abandoned, and that there's no blood or bodies around?"

"I'm taking it as a good sign."

"How so?" asked Pandelosi.

"Every other city we've encountered completely fell apart during the outbreak. So far we haven't seen any rotter activity here. Secretary Fogel knows what he's doing. Maybe we finally found a place that's really safe."

"I hope you're right." The lieutenant glanced over her shoulder and saw most of her unit and the Angels gazing up at the North Tower that stood five hundred feet above them. "Pay attention, people. You can sightsee on your own time."

Duncan replied with, "Hooyah."

When they reached the middle of the center span, a knot of traffic blocked the bridge a thousand feet ahead of them. Pandelosi raised her hand for the others to halt, and checked her flanks to make certain Kim and Batchelder saw. When everyone had come to a stop, she pointed to Duncan and Natalie. "You two are with me."

Duncan stayed to the rear, scanning the span for danger. As the women approached, they saw a tour bus on its side at an angle and blocking the right four lanes, its roof facing their direction. There were no indications of a struggle, no blood smears or broken windows. Abrasions in the concrete near the rear end of the bus and accompanying dents in the roof indicated the bus had originally blocked six lanes and had been moved. The parked vehicles on either side of the bridge ended one hundred feet before the accident, leaving a path that veered to the left and disappeared around the bus. Raising their weapons, the two women made their way around the overturned vehicle.

Traffic crowded the southern span and stretched back as far as Natalie could see. Hundreds of cars, SUVs, a few buses, and even a propane truck sat stalled along the southern span. Two lanes on the eastern side of the bridge were clear. Natalie assumed that the cars dispersed along the northern span had been removed from the southern portion to make a path. A single rotter stood fifty feet away staring at the windshield of a taxi. Its back was to them, and it did not appear to be aware of their presence. Pandelosi raised her M-16A2, took aim, and fired off a single round. Its head jerked and its body stiffened for a second before falling to the cement. Pandelosi gave Natalie a thumbs-up, and they rejoined the others.

"We heard a gunshot," said Duncan. "What's up?"

"Just a stray revenant." The lieutenant spoke so all four groups could hear. "We're halfway home. There's a lot of traffic on the other side of the bus, but for the most part it looks clear. Stay alert. Let's move out."

The four groups set out. They had gone about one hundred yards when Duncan called out, "Revenant."

A rotter in the remnants of a woman's business suit staggered between two lanes of parked vehicles, its gait swaying and uncertain because it still wore a single high heel, its head twisting from side to side as if searching for something. Duncan raced forward, closed to within ten feet, and took it down with a single shot to the forehead. Raising his right arm, he waved the others forward.

After another several yards, Natalie spotted a rotter moving down the unobstructed lane toward them, this one shirtless from the waist up, its abdomen exposed and decayed flesh dangling off its ribcage. At that moment, off to the right, she heard Duncan call out, "Revenant." He didn't refer to the shirtless rotter, but to a second one in a bicyclist's outfit that stood up from between two stalled cars and lumbered toward him. Duncan took it down with a single shot. Pandelosi raised her M-16A2 and put a bullet through the head of the shirtless rotter.

Natalie stepped up to her. "Maybe we shouldn't be firing on them. The noise is attracting them."

"What do you suggest?"

"My girls have hunting knives. We can take them out quietly."

Pandelosi nodded and called out to Duncan. "Let the women lead."

Natalie and Stephanie moved ahead, leaving Ari to mind the backpack containing the briefcase. Emily and Josephine took the lead on the left. Each of them slung their weapons and removed their hunting knives. After another few yards a rotter in a chauffeur's uniform appeared on the right from behind a tour bus and stumbled toward Josephine. Josephine moved quickly. Slamming her arm against its chest, she drove it back against the front of the bus and plunged the blade into its right eye, twisting once to scramble its brains. The rotter went limp. It dropped to the ground, sliding off of Josephine's knife. She circled around the bus to the right. Emily moved along the left.

"Hey!"

The yell came from the left. Kim and Sarah were waving. When they had Natalie's attention, they pointed toward the south span.

Pandelosi walked up to her. "What's going.... Jesus Christ on a fucking bicycle."

A thousand feet ahead of them, hundreds of rotters filled the entire southern span of the bridge, all heading in their direction.

CHAPTER FIFTY-FIVE

"What should we do?" asked Duncan.

"Fall back," answered Pandelosi.

"To where?" Natalie protested. "Those things will just follow us. The farther we retreat, the harder it'll be to reach the Beachhead later."

"What do you suggest?"

Natalie pointed to the southern end of the bridge. "We go forward."

"We can't fight them all," said Duncan.

"We don't have to. We can bait-and-switch them."

* * *

"What are they doing?" asked Amy.

"We should join them." Sarah headed for the guardrail to join Natalie and Pandelosi.

Kim stopped her. "Don't expose yourself yet. Wait and see what they plan on doing."

Amy looked toward San Francisco. "I don't see any rotters on the walkway. Why don't we make a break for it?"

"The left two lanes are wide open. The revenants will spot us and swarm the walkway, and if they get across that guardrail we're trapped."

Amy sighed. She felt trapped already.

* * *

On the western pedestrian walkway, Batchelder and the others didn't see the approaching horde of rotters or the central group stop to confer. They continued ahead, and soon were several hundred feet ahead of the others.

* * *

Josephine's view of the approaching rotters was obstructed by the tour bus. Emily noticed them and paused to gape. Being distracted, she didn't see the rotter in a 49ers sweat suit inside the tour bus. It followed her along the center aisle, tracking her from the shaded windows. When it reached the open rear door, it turned onto the stairs, lost its footing, and fell off. Emily heard it moan an instant before it crashed into her. The two slammed into the adjacent Toyota and slid to the cement. Emily cried out as she felt the femur in her left leg break. The rotter clawed and bit at her right leg, unable to penetrate the leather. She took her hunting knife and plunged it into the back of the rotter's skull, twisting the blade. It went limp and collapsed across her legs, sending bolts of pain through her body.

Natalie and Pandelosi rushed over. Duncan, Ari, and Stephanie raced ahead of them and took up firing positions.

"Are you okay?" Natalie asked.

"No. My leg is broken."

"We'll carry you." Natalie helped her up.

Emily gasped and fell back against the Toyota, breathing heavy. "I'm not going anywhere today, honey."

"We're not leaving you."

"You have to." Emily held up her hand to cut off further discussion. "I'm not trying to be a martyr. Get me somewhere safe. I'll distract the rotters and give the rest of you a chance to escape. When you come back for Everett, pick me up on the way."

Natalie hesitated.

"It's the only way. I can't move, and if you guys try to carry me it'll get us all killed."

"She's right," said Pandelosi.

"Okay. Where around here is safe?"

"Right there." Emily pointed to a propane truck two lanes over and three vehicles down. "Every rotter on this bridge will see me, and none of them can get to me."

"Are you sure about this?" asked Natalie.

Emily nodded.

Natalie and Pandelosi threw one of Emily's arms around each shoulder and escorted her to the tanker, the latter wincing with every step. The women helped her onto the ladder and waited until she had a good handhold. The horde was three hundred feet away.

"Are you sure you'll be okay?" Natalie asked.

"It'll be better than the alternative, honey," Emily said. "Now get out of here so you can send back help soon. It's going to get cold up here when night hits."

Natalie hesitated, wanting to say something profound. Instead, Pandelosi grabbed her by the arm and pushed her back toward the bus, yelling for the others to follow.

When they gathered behind the tour bus, Duncan asked, "Are we falling back?"

"No. We're going to cut over to the walkway and follow Batchelder's team. Use the bus as cover so those things don't see us."

"Wait," said Ari. "What about Emily?"

"She broke her leg," explained Natalie. "She's going to draw the rotters' attention while we sneak away. We'll come back for her later."

"Enough chatter. Move out." Pandelosi pushed each of her team toward the western walkway. Once the others moved out, she caught Kim's attention and pointed to the southern edge of the bridge. When he nodded his understanding, the lieutenant set off after the others.

* * *

"Is she nuts?" asked Amy.

"The lieutenant knows what she's doing." Kim did not sound convinced.

"They're heading to the other side where there's more shelter, " argued Amy. "If we go this way, half the rotters on this bridge will swarm us."

Kim sighed. "I can't disobey an order."

"We can." Amy patted Sarah on the shoulder. The two ran

back the way they had just come.

"Shit!" Kim hesitated for a minute, and then followed Amy and Sarah.

* * *

Climbing to the top of the tanker was excruciatingly painful and slow. Emily would clasp a rung with both hands before hopping up with her good leg. With each rung, her dangling bad leg would throb from the concussion of the hop or from banging against the ladder. The last time she almost passed out from the pain. Emily paused three rungs from the top to catch her breath and let the throbbing die down.

"Hey! How about a southern hot meal?"

The horde moved quicker, especially those in the unobstructed lanes. Emily heard their collective moaning despite the constant wind from the Bay whipping across the bridge. They were less one hundred feet away. Preparing herself for the inevitable, she hoisted herself up the last three rungs, grimacing against the pain and grinding her teeth to counter the agony in her leg. Once on top of the tanker, she placed her weapon on the walkway and unslung her bag of ammunition. Unbuckling her belt, she pulled it through the loops, threaded it under the metal railing that ran along the walkway, and secured the rest of the belt around her good leg so she wouldn't fall off if she passed out. Dragging the bag of ammunition in front of her, she opened it. She had seven magazines left.

The horde had reached the propane tanker and swarmed seven deep around its rear, while others gathered along the sides. Hundreds of dead hands reached up to her, scraping fingers and palms against the metal tank. The cross winds from across the Bay helped to dissipate the nauseating stench of decay and the swarm of flies and wasps feeding off the carcasses. It did nothing to muffle the incessant moaning. More rotters approached from farther along the span.

Emily picked up her M-16A2 and took aim on one of the rotter's beneath her, a female in a short leather skirt.

This was going to be a long afternoon.

* * *

"Rotters," Sandy whispered, rushing up beside Batchelder. "Hundreds of them."

He turned and saw the horde making its way north along the bridge. He crouched so he would be hidden by the vehicles. Sandy and Doreen did the same, the latter crawling on her hands and knees to catch up.

"What do we do now?" Doreen asked in a hushed voice.

Batchelder didn't know. Common sense told him to proceed ahead while they still had a chance; however, his training told him not to leave the lieutenant and the others behind. But where were the others? They had to have seen hundreds of revenants heading their way. The Angels expected him to offer guidance. Damn it, basic training never prepared him for this.

"We're safe for the moment, so we wait here and hope the others catch up."

* * *

Duncan reached the guardrail first. He jumped over it and assumed a firing position, waiting for the others to join him. Pandelosi was the last one off the span.

"Okay," said the lieutenant, "stay low and head for shore. Don't stop for anything. Duncan, you lead. I'll bring up the rear."

"What about them?" he asked, pointing south.

Pandelosi saw Batchelder's team four hundred feet ahead of them. He waved to her. She held her hand over her head, pointed to the city, and mouthed the word, "Go."

She turned her attention back to her own team. "What are you waiting for? An engraved invitation? Move out."

* * *

Batchelder felt relief when he saw Pandelosi and the others jump onto the walkway. He especially appreciated the order to move out and get the hell off of this death trap.

"Follow me, and leave ten feet between us," he said to Sandy and Doreen. "Stay low so you don't attract attention."

* * *

Backtracking to where the bus accident blocked the bridge, Amy and Sarah jumped the guardrail and crossed over to the western side.

"Wait up."

They stopped. Kim was following them.

Amy smiled. "I thought for a minute there you were going to head off on your own."

"Screw it. This is safer. The lieutenant can court martial me if we make it through this."

"Don't worry. We'll make it," said Amy. She hopped the guardrail onto the pedestrian walkway. "We've seen worse."

"Really?"

Sarah joined her friend. "Yeah."

"Wow." Kim vaulted the guardrail and followed the two women.

A few seconds later, he heard gunfire. Off to his left, one of the leather-clad women sat on top of a propane tanker truck firing into a swarm of revenants massing around the vehicle. He admired her courage, and thanked God it wasn't him stuck up there.

The three raced toward the southern bank.

* * *

With so many rotters surrounding the tanker, Emily could not possibly miss. Still, she lined up each shot, the mental exercise taking her mind off the throbbing in her leg. So far she had fired ten rounds and achieved ten head shots. Pulling out the empty magazine, she dropped it in the bag and removed a full one. That left her with six remaining. At this rate, she would expend the rest of her ammunition in half an hour, which should be more than enough time for the others to escape. Then she would wait for them to rescue her.

Emily did not notice that several of the rotters at the back of the truck kept bumping their arms against the distribution valve on the back of the propane tank, a metal fixture that had been corroded by nine months of exposure to the wind and salt air.

The repeated jostling broke the valve, allowing propane to escape. Emily didn't see the spreading cloud of gas, nor could she smell it because of the stench of the living dead. She slammed the magazine into her M-16A2, pulled back the charging handle, and aimed at a rotter in a jogging outfit with its bottom jaw missing. When she fired, the muzzle blast ignited the propane cloud. Flames engulfed the rear end of the tanker, incinerating Emily. It also set ablaze the first few rows of rotters. The fire followed the cloud through the valve and inside the tank.

Ten thousand gallons of propane ignited.

A giant fireball billowed into the sky and spread outward. Those rotters not vaporized were ripped apart by the blast. The shockwave spread down the bridge, wrecking nearby vehicles and scattering them in every direction. It also blasted through the span, tearing it free from its suspension cables. The section of bridge underneath the tanker collapsed, plunging more than two hundred feet into the frigid water below, and ripping loose several of the spans on either side of it. One by one they broke free, some twisting off and plummeting into the water, others dangling for a few moments before breaking free. Vehicles and rotters rained into the Bay. The last section to separate was four to the south of the initial blast. The southern and eastern supports broke loose first, and it dropped vertically, spilling its contents. It swung back and forth for several seconds before its weight tore it free. It fell into the Bay, pulling a lengthy section of the western pedestrian walkway with it.

* * *

Sandy had no idea what had happened. For a split second she thought the world had ended. The shockwave had dissipated by the time it reached them, having been absorbed by distance and the surrounding vehicles. However, the concussion and the collapse of the center sections set in motion a chain reaction throughout the rest of the structure. The span swayed several feet in each direction, accompanied by the unnerving sound of straining steel. Someone screamed. Sandy was so terrified she couldn't be certain if it was her or someone else. She fell onto the walkway, her fingers clutching the wood, praying it didn't give way beneath her.

* * *

For Kim, it was the end of the world. One second he was rushing toward the southern bank, and the next everything around him exploded, knocking him off his feet and deafening him. He felt the bridge swaying. Rolling onto his side, he saw the center sections break away and drop into the Bay. When the last piece of bridge collapsed, it pulled several additional sections of walkway with it, like a piece of yarn being unraveled from a sweater. Kim scrambled to his feet and raced forward as the section under his feet gave way. He plummeted two hundred feet into the Bay, his body splattering when it impacted against the chunks of walkway underneath him.

Sarah's section of walkway collapsed beneath her, but did not break free. She had the presence of mind to drop her weapon and grab the outer guardrail. It stopped her fall, nearly yanking her arms out of their sockets. Sarah hung on tight and kicked her legs forward until she got a foothold on the slats in the outer guardrail. Pausing to catch her breath, she climbed the guardrail like a ladder. With each movement, the dangling piece of structure gave way a little more.

Amy was ahead of the last section of walkway to collapse. She continued running until she noticed that neither Kim nor Sarah were behind her, and went back to check. Cautiously approaching the end of the walkway, she leaned forward. Sarah clutched a dangling piece of guardrail ten feet below her.

"Climb up. I'll pull you to safety."

"I can't. Every time I move, this thing loosens up."

Amy lay prone on the walkway. Holding on to the guardrail with her left hand, she stretched her right as far as possible toward her friend.

* * *

The explosion threw Natalie off her feet, flinging her to the right. She hit the outer guardrail and bent over the top, staring down into the dark gray waters of the Bay. As the bridge swayed, she experienced the sensation of falling. Natalie closed her eyes and clutched the railing tight, praying the end would be quick. After a few seconds, she realized she was not plummeting to her demise. She was not going to die, at least not at this moment.

Turning behind her, Natalie gasped. A major portion of the center span had collapsed, including the section where Emily had been. She also saw Amy prone on the walkway, talking to someone. Natalie called to the others. "I need help!"

"I'll go," said Pandelosi. She caught Duncan's attention. "Get these people off this bridge. Now!"

The two women ran off to help Amy.

* * *

The explosion disoriented the mass of living dead. One minute they were shambling toward the sound of gunfire, which they now associated with food. The next, their primitive senses were overloaded with loud, unusual noises and strange motions. Many of the rotters close to, but not destroyed outright by the blast, had been knocked over by the shockwave. In the eerie silence that followed, every rotter on the bridge looked around aimlessly, not knowing what to do. Then they heard yelling and screaming, sounds associated with food. The horde tried to get their bearing, until a female rotter in a gore-encrusted "Keep calm and leave your heart in San Francisco" sweatshirt realized the noise was coming from the edge of the bridge. It staggered toward the sounds. The rest of the living dead followed it, maneuvering between the four lanes of stalled vehicles, swarming toward the western pedestrian walkway.

* * *

Duncan stepped between the members of his team. "Let's move."

Ari knelt on the wooden walkway, her eyes closed tight and her arms clutched around a lamppost. "I'm scared."

"We're all scared, ma'am. You need to move your ass."

Opening her eyes, Ari could only focus on the Bay more than

two hundred feet beneath them. "I can't."

"Then give me the backpack."

Her eyes widened. "What?"

"You're not important. What's in that backpack is. If you want to stay here and be revenant bait, go ahead. Just give it to me."

"No."

Duncan grabbed the shoulder strap. "That backpack is coming off this bridge. Either you carry it or I will. I don't care."

"Asshole." Ari's fear of being left behind overrode everything else. She stood up and secured the backpack on her shoulders, and then met Duncan's eyes. "Thanks."

He smiled. "You can buy me a beer if we live through this."

* * *

When Natalie and Pandelosi reached Amy, they saw her trying to save Sarah. Sarah saw Natalie and smiled, knowing everything would be all right now.

Pandelosi knelt down and called out to Sarah. "Come on, kid. Climb up."

"The guardrail will give way if I move."

Without hesitation, the lieutenant stepped over to the guardrail and clasped the last rung of the uncollapsed section. "I'm going to lower myself down. When I do, climb as fast as you can and grab my hand. Got it?"

Sarah nodded.

Pandelosi swung her body over the edge of the walkway, planting her left foot on an exposed metal beam for support, and leaned as far to the right as possible and stretched out her hand. Three feet separated her and Sarah.

"Now."

Sarah climbed. The steel groaned and twisted. As Sarah wrapped her right hand around Pandelosi's wrist, the guardrail snapped free and spiraled into the water. The lieutenant still had a hold on the woman, who dangled in the air, kicking and screaming.

Pandelosi felt her grip loosening. "Hold still!" she yelled to Sarah. Then to Natalie and Amy, "How about a little help?"

The two surged forward. The excess weight caused the section of walkway to buckle, and it tilted at a thirty degree angle toward the Bay. Instinct took over, and Natalie and Amy rushed back.

"Natalie, don't leave me!" Sarah cried, a heartbreaking plea in her voice.

Pandelosi knew she had a chance of saving herself if she let go of Sarah, but refused. She tightened her grip and pulled the woman up. Sarah let go of the lieutenant's arm with one hand and used it to grab for the rungs of the portion of guardrail. When her fingers wrapped around it, she let go of the lieutenant with the other hand and began to pull herself to safety. Pandelosi felt her muscles loosen with the excess weight gone. She also grabbed hold of the rungs and climbed.

They had made it only a few feet when the section underneath them broke loose and tumbled into the Bay.

* * *

Sandy got to her feet and looked behind to see what happened. Her mouth fell agape when she saw a huge portion of the bridge missing. She spotted two of the other teams farther down the walkway, and wondered who they had lost.

A hand grasped her shoulder. She yelped and spun around. Batchelder stood behind her.

"We have to get moving."

"What about the others?"

"If this bridge collapses, there's nothing we can do to help them. Our best chance of surviving is if we all get off as fast as possible."

Not waiting for a response, Batchelder turned and headed for the southern bank. Sandy and Doreen followed.

* * *

Natalie reached out for Sarah, but Amy held her back. She watched helplessly as her friend plummeted through the air and crashed into the water, creating a small geyser in her final resting place.

Amy nudged her. "Come on. We have to go."

351

Without a word, Natalie raced off to join the others.

* * *

Stephanie followed a few paces behind Duncan. She glanced over her shoulder to see if Natalie and the others were all right. A pair of hands grabbed her by the shoulders and dragged her toward the inner guard rail. A rotter in a fire fighter's coat was pulling down on her, threatening to topple her onto the highway portion of the bridge. Half a dozen other living dead closed in from different angles. With her right hand, she punched the rotter in the face. Since it felt no pain, it didn't release its grip.

Stephanie heard a burst of gunfire and felt a splatter of gore across her face. A second pair of hands grabbed her by the collar. Rather than drag her into the horde, it yanked her back onto the walkway. Ari held her by the collar, and Josephine stood to her left, firing into the horde.

"You okay?" Ari asked.

Stephanie nodded. "Thanks."

"Don't ment—"

"Fuck."

The Angels turned to see what Duncan was swearing about. Swarms of living dead pressed along the guardrail. Even more filled the spaces between the vehicles. In several places, the mass pushed those closest to the guardrail over the top and onto the pedestrian walkway, where they crawled to their feet. Within a few seconds, a dozen rotters converged on them from both sides.

"Should we make a run for it?" Josephine asked.

"We'll be swarmed before we make it a hundred feet," Stephanie responded.

"We need maneuvering room if we're going to get out of here," Duncan said. "Have you ever been in a running gun battle?"

The Angels shook their heads.

"You're about to be."

Duncan scanned the area. Ten feet down sat a Dodge Ram parked close to the outer lane. He ran down and vaulted over the guardrail into the bed of the pick-up. A dozen rotters grasped for him. He stayed far enough away that they couldn't reach him and waved for the Angels to follow. Stephanie joined him in the bed.

"What do we do?"

"Make your way to shore by going from car roof to car roof."

"You're joking," she said.

"If any of you have a better idea, now's the time to let me know." Duncan climbed up onto the roof of the Dodge and hopped over onto the roof of a Prius. The horde turned to follow him. He raced off the Prius, jumped the gap onto the hood of a BMW, and stopped on its roof. Twenty sets of dead hands clutched at him.

"Just keep going and make sure of your footing before you jump," he called back. "And don't shoot them unless you need to clear a path." When none of the women moved, he prodded, "Go! Now!"

Stephanie followed Duncan's path to the Prius. From there, she continued straight ahead, jumping onto the roof of a Forester and then again onto the roof of a Camry. Most of the rotters turned their attention to her.

"Come on," Ari said, tapping Josephine on the shoulder. "Now's our chance."

* * *

There were at least thirty rotters on the walkway in front of Natalie and Amy, with the number increasing by the second. Duncan led the other Angels onto a pick-up truck and into traffic. She and Amy found a Charger that had swerved left, the hood at an angle to the lane and flush with the guardrail. A single rotter stood in the apex of the angle. She fired one round into its face, dropping it. With the path clear, she and Amy vaulted onto the Charger, up onto the roof, and split off to separate vehicles.

* * *

None of the rotters spotted Batchelder, Sandy, or Doreen, partly because the team stayed low and quiet, and partly because the attention of the living dead was drawn to commotion near where the bridge had collapsed. By the time the others had moved onto the highway portion of the bridge, Batchelder and the Angels had passed the southern tower and were less than two thousand feet from shore.

* * *

Duncan led the way, bounding from vehicle to vehicle, pausing just long enough to make certain of his footing, and occasionally to turn around to check on the others. He pre-planned his next three or four moves, wanting to make certain he didn't trap himself and have to fight a last stand against the living dead from the roof of a Mini Cooper. The horde grew thicker, the living dead shoving their way between the vehicles to get at him. If one blocked his way, he would shoot it in the head and jump over the corpse. Never did he stay on any vehicle more than four seconds.

Stephanie followed Duncan, reasoning that he would find the best path to safety. That plan worked for about a minute before she realized that rotters swarmed around him and, as he made his way from car to car, he left the mass of living dead in his wake. Since Duncan made his way straight down the center of the abandoned vehicles, she veered to the left. For a few minutes the strategy worked, then the rotters from the unobstructed lanes moved toward her, forming several rows along the line of traffic and pushing their way through the vehicles. Stephanie was about to be surrounded.

She emptied an entire magazine into the heads of the rotters to her left, clearing a path of escape. Jumping off the car onto the unobstructed lanes of highway, she wove her way through the horde and hurdled the guardrail onto the eastern pedestrian walkway. Over a hundred rotters stumbled after her. Knowing she only had a minute at best, she broke into a run and headed for shore.

Ari stayed to the right, following the vehicles lined up closest to the western pedestrian walkway. There were fewer of the living dead here, most having turned back to go after Duncan and Stephanie. Carrying the backpack with the vaccine slowed her down, forcing her to spend more time on each vehicle. The delays gave the rotters a chance to gather around. Shifting to the left, she jumped onto a Hyundai that Duncan had passed over earlier, turned right, and hopped over a rotter corpse onto the hood of an Outback. Because of the brains and blood splattered on the hood, Ari slipped. Her legs went out from under her, and she smashed chest first onto the windshield.

Half a dozen rotters descended on her. Ari tried to get up, but four sets of hands grabbed at her legs, making it impossible to get her footing. She kicked and thrashed, reaching out for the roof rack, hoping to pull herself to safety. Her fingers clasped around it, and she pulled herself up. Suddenly, a pair of dead fingers grabbed her hand. Teeth dug into her knuckles, piercing the skin and muscles and grinding against the bone. Ari yanked her hand back, tearing away a chunk of flesh. Another set of hands grabbed her backpack, trying to rip its way through the material to get to her. The hands around her legs threatened to pull her off the hood.

Gunfire cut off Ari's screams. When she felt the hands release her legs, she kicked away. Another shot, and the rotter pulling on the backpack let go. Ari scrambled up onto the roof. One by one, the rotters attacking her were taken down by headshots. Josephine stood on the next car over. She popped out the empty magazine and, as she replaced it, smiled at her friend. The two women made their way forward in tandem, slowly but steadily.

* * *

Natalie and Amy found themselves at a disadvantage. The commotion the others made advancing along the line of traffic had drawn the rotters between the vehicles, blocking their path. The two women would jump to a vehicle, choose which direction they wanted to go, and then clear the way with their weapons before moving to the next. To do this, they had to expend ammunition, which in turn attracted more of the living dead. Within minutes, they fell behind the others and were in danger of being surrounded.

Natalie called out to Amy, "Follow me."

Making her way to the outer lane of vehicles, Natalie headed for an eighteen-wheeler. She made the jump to the bed of a pick-up truck in front of the rig and waited until Amy joined her. She shot the three rotters between them and the rig.

"Jump!" she ordered.

Amy did not hesitate. She leaped off the bed, covered the few feet between vehicles, and landed on the truck's left fender. Getting her footing, she scrambled up onto the hood. Natalie made the same jump. When she landed on the fender, her right foot slipped and she fell on her left hip. The fall gave the closest rotters a chance to grab hold of her leg. Natalie tried to kick away. When she rolled over, she saw three of the living dead trying to bite her or pull her into the horde. Natalie reached up and grabbed the side mirror mount as more rotters approached. From the hood, Amy fired three three-round bursts into the head of those rotters holding Natalie, and then grabbed Natalie's hand and lifted her up onto the hood seconds before another five of the living dead descended on the fender.

The two women scurried onto the roof of the truck and made the leap onto the semi-trailer. They raced to the end, hoping to make their escape. Instead, they had come upon a dead end. A Harley Davidson motorcycle sat directly behind the trailer and, to the left of the truck, was an SUV with luggage attached to the roof rack as well as a VW Beetle. They could not jump to any of these vehicles without seriously injuring themselves, which would be a death sentence since dozens of rotters already swarmed around the truck, with a hundred more closing in from all sides. Glancing back over her shoulder, the way they had come had been cut off.

"What now?" Amy asked.

"Shoot as many as we can with what little ammo we have, and then hope for the best."

* * *

Stephanie had made it only a thousand feet when enough rotters had fallen over the guardrail to block her path. More than a dozen closed in on either side, with too many more beyond that to allow her to escape even if she could push her way past these. Stephanie contemplated whether to die fighting or spare

356

herself and jump. From out of nowhere, a loudspeaker cut through the moaning of the living dead.

"Drop to the ground now."

Stephanie did as ordered. A second later, she heard a metallic whir similar to a blender being turned on, followed by a steady stream of gunfire that lasted five seconds. Something rained down on her back. When the shooting stopped, she lifted her head. Small chunks of rotter lay scattered on her and across the pedestrian walkway. Not a single living dead remained standing. Vehicles drove past her as well as a dozen soldiers rushing in her direction. Stephanie remained still, not wanting to appear to be a threat. The soldiers came up to her, most forming a circle around her. Their leader, a young Hispanic woman, asked, "Are you all right, ma'am?"

"I am now."

* * *

Ari and Josephine continued their forward advance when they heard the sound of motors followed by the roar of gunfire. A line of Bradley fighting vehicles moved past, chain guns mowing down a horde of rotters on the eastern pedestrian walkway. The women had no idea what to make of this until they saw Duncan jumping up and down on the hood, waving his arms. Three twelve-man squads broke away from the main group, one heading for Duncan and the other two for Ari and Josephine. The squads fought their way through the vehicles, eliminating any nearby rotters. When they reached Duncan and the Angels, they helped them off the vehicles and escorted them back to the Bradleys. The rear doors dropped open and a tall man wearing sergeant stripes ushered them onboard.

"You guys are safe now."

* * *

Natalie and Amy saw everything play out from the rear of the semi-trailer. Several of the Bradleys stopped to rescue Stephanie, Duncan, Ari, and Josephine, while three more headed for them. The chain guns mounted on the roof opened fire, sending thousands of rounds into the sides of the semi-trailer and the surrounding vehicles. Windows erupted; metal was punctured; rotters were shredded. The carnage lasted less than ten seconds. When the guns wound down, no rotters remained and the lower half of the semi-trailer looked like a sieve.

The lead Bradley pulled up alongside the eighteen-wheeler and stopped while two more continued ahead. The rear door came down and five soldiers ran out. Two of them crawled onto the Bradley. One by one, they helped Natalie and Amy off of the semi-trailer, where the other three then helped them onto the bridge. A middle-aged man wearing captain insignia exited the Bradley and strode up to them.

"Do you know where Lieutenant Pandelosi is?"

Natalie lowered her head. "She didn't make it."

"Damn," the captain muttered under his breath. "Which one of you has the Revenant Vaccine?"

"How do you know about that?"

"Pandelosi radioed us yesterday about your arrival at Offutt. Secretary Fogel is excited about the prospect of being able to take back the United States from these things."

"One of my girls is carrying a backpack with the vaccine," said Natalie. "You picked her up a few minutes ago."

"How many of you are there?"

"I'm not sure. There are the ones you just picked up, three more on the pedestrian walkway closer to shore, and the pilot, who's wounded. We left him back at the airstrip in Sausalito in a C-130."

"We didn't see the other three on the way in." The captain turned to one of his subordinates and pointed to the western walkway. "Sanchez, have one of the squads check out that portion of the bridge. We're looking for three more people. And radio the Beachhead that we have a wounded survivor back at the emergency airstrip who needs to be rescued."

"Yes, sir!" the soldier said and ran off to follow orders.

The captain turned back to Natalie. "Are you ready?"

"Who are you?"

"Sorry." He offered his hand. "I'm Captain Rogers. I'm in charge of the military unit protecting the Beachhead. We're here to get you to safety."

"How'd you know where to find us?" asked Amy.

"Alameda alerted us that you had arrived early and tracked your movements until you landed in Sausalito. We mobilized to come and get you. When you blew up half the bridge, we knew exactly where to find you." Rogers stepped aside and motioned toward the Bradley. "If you'll please get on board. We have a lot of revenants heading this way, and I need to get us out of here ASAP."

Natalie and Amy entered the Bradley. Rogers barked some orders to his men, and then climbed on himself and closed the rear hatch.

CHAPTER FIFTY-SIX

The drive back to the Beachhead was uneventful, especially after the last hour. Once near the southern end of the Golden Gate Bridge, the foot soldiers boarded the Bradleys. They joined up with five additional fighting vehicles deployed along the bridge's southern approaches that had been holding back rotters, and together the convoy made its way home. Natalie noticed that here, like on the bridge, lanes of traffic had been cleared of abandoned vehicles to allow for easy access. The trip lasted less than five minutes.

The Beachhead was actually the old San Francisco Port of Embarkation located inside Fort Mason, now known as the Fort Mason Center. The cement wall that surrounded the complex had been augmented by guard towers every fifty feet and strands of barbed wire erected along the top. Two rows of Jersey barriers ran parallel to the perimeter at fifty and one hundred-foot intervals, the former being stacked two barriers high. Various cars and small vehicles had been placed between the two barriers, creating a nearly impenetrable defense against rotters. M1 tanks blocked each of the three entrances through the walls. As the Bradleys neared, Rogers fired two flares into the air. The tanks pulled aside, allowing the convoy through, and then rolled back into position. The convoy entered the parking lot. When the rear doors opened, Natalie stepped out.

The complex itself didn't look very impressive. Four three-story barracks that had been converted into office space spread across the grounds. To the north, three piers extended into the Bay, each dominated by a warehouse. Two ferry boats, a barge, and several speedboats were tied alongside them. Another dozen Bradleys and a few Humvees were parked near the buildings.

Everyone wore camouflage uniforms and carried a weapon. This place appeared more like an armed camp than the *de facto* government-in-exile. Natalie felt her hopes fading away.

Rogers stepped up behind Natalie and cleared his throat to get her attention. "I'm sorry, ma'am, but I'm going to have to ask you and the other ladies in your unit to follow me."

"Where to?" Natalie felt her suspicions rising.

"All newcomers have to be placed into quarantine for forty-eight hours. That includes the military personnel who flew in with you. It's protocol, especially since one of your number has been bitten."

"Who was bitten?" Natalie asked.

Rogers hesitated, trying to remember the name. "Arianne?"

"You mean Ari?"

"Maybe that's it. She received a minor bite to the hand. She claims you've all been inoculated, but we still have to place you under quarantine."

"I understand."

"Thank you."

Natalie followed Rogers to the farthest of the three barracks. The rest of her Angels and the surviving military members were being escorted in the same direction, though none of them at gunpoint. In fact, Duncan seemed to be chatting amiably with his escort. Batchelder, Sandy, and Josephine were not among them

"Did you find the other three members of our group?"

"Not yet. Once we pick up the pilot in Sausalito, I'll send out a search party for them."

"Thanks," Natalie said. A moment of silence passed between them. "I have to admit, I'm a little disappointed."

"Because we couldn't find your people?"

"We were told Secretary Fogel had gathered a lot of people under him and was preparing to take back the country from the rotters. I don't mean to be rude, but this doesn't look like much."

"Ma'am, we call this the Beachhead because it's the part of the complex attached to the mainland. This is where we bring in survivors and quarantine them." Rogers pointed out into San

Francisco Bay. "Secretary Fogel and the main community have set themselves up there where they're safe."

Natalie followed his finger. The captain was pointing to Alcatraz.

* * *

It took five hours for Robson's team to wrap up things at the storage facility and return to base. While Dravko and Tibor finished releasing the prisoners chained to the perimeter defense, Robson had taken DeWitt back into the compound to kill off rotters and rescue survivors, including Caslow, whom they found cowering inside one of the units. In total, they had saved thirty-three people from the perimeter defense and five women from inside who had remained hidden throughout the battle, and helped them into the Ryder for the trip back to camp. They also had gathered up the bodies of their fallen companions, as well as those women killed inside the compound who had been innocent victims. The bodies of the gang members were left to rot amongst the corpses of the living dead. Some of the survivors had complained about having to ride with corpses. Robson had stopped their whining by reminding them that those people had died trying to save them. He would make certain the dead got a proper burial and memorial tomorrow.

Unfortunately, they had not found Windows. According to the women who had been rescued from inside the compound, she had been alive as of that evening, and some of the survivors from the Line had reported a young woman and little girl sneaking through the fence during the battle, so what the old man had told Robson about her having an escape plan must have been true. Roberta had spent an hour driving up and down Route 28 and some of the side roads searching for Windows, but never found her.

Wayans had suffered only a superficial wound. While Roberta had stitched him up, Simmons had cooked the survivors a hot meal. Not that he had much to offer—bacon and scrambled eggs. For the survivors, it was more than they had eaten in months. Robson stood by the door of the construction company garage watching them. When Simmons handed out the meals in paper bowls, some of the survivors grasped his hand and wouldn't let go, or cried at their good fortune. Most, however, silently devoured their meal.

Simmons made his way back to the garage door and stood by Robson. "You know, most of these people are so emaciated and sick, a third of them will probably be dead within a week."

"I know. At least they had a chance to regain their humanity before they die."

"Amen to that." An awkward silence passed between the two men. "Where do you plan to go from here?"

"I promised I'd only stay a day or two, and then we'd move on."

"That's not what I meant." Robson detected a tone of guilt in Simmons' voice. "I really do want to know. What's next?"

Good question. Too bad Robson had not thought it through more thoroughly before now.

Because of the trip to Site R to obtain the vaccine, he had ultimately lost most of his team, his camp back in Maine, and the Angels. He would probably never know whether or not Natalie and the girls were successful in delivering the vaccine to the government-in-exile, or if they were even still alive. In the grand scheme of things, that concern was minor. He had to provide for and protect thirty-eight invalids, and do it with a team that now numbered five people, with DeWitt and Roberta being the only ones he could truly rely on. He still questioned the vampires' loyalty, and Caslow would be only slightly more useful than the survivors.

Robson felt woefully unprepared for all this.

"So," prodded Simmons again. "What's next?"

Robson shrugged. "It's time to move on and start over."

* * *

Windows had stopped thirty minutes after leaving the construction site, and then just long enough to gather some food and water for Cindy and to arm herself with one of the AK-47s in the back. After that, she continued to drive north, staying to the back roads as much as possible, while Cindy slept in the front seat. Earlier, she had passed signs for Laconia and Lake Winnipesaukee. About three hours ago, she had to turn east because of the White Mountains looming in the distance. The last sign she remembered seeing was for Conway, and that was almost ninety minutes ago. As the sun burst over the horizon, she pulled over and consulted the maps she had found under the front seat. After staring at it for ten minutes, she still could not figure out her location. Placing the map on the dashboard, she drove on, planning to get her bearings the next time she came upon a road sign.

The sun crested the trees and poured through the windshield, falling across Cindy. The girl stirred. She yawned and stretched, and then opened her eyes. Upon seeing Windows beside her, she smiled.

"Good morning, honey. Did you sleep well?"

Cindy nodded and sat upright in her seat. "Where are we now?"

"I don't know."

"Where are we going?"

"I don't know."

"That's okay." Cindy looked over at Windows. "When we get there, will we finally be safe?"

"I hope so, honey." Windows reached out and gave Cindy's hand a gentle squeeze. "I really hope so."

Acknowledgements

I want to thank all my readers who have patiently waited for this sequel to *Rotter World*, and an apology for taking so long to get this into print. The delay was a combination of a series of life changes and business issues beyond my control. However, that is all in the past, and *Rotter Nation* has been released. I hope it is worth the wait.

A major debt of gratitude goes to Felicia A. Sullivan, my editor, who worked closely with me to tighten up the manuscript. Felicia is a consummate professional who did a superior job, and I value her expertise as well as the fact that she is also a fan. However, any errors in the final product are mine to own.

Zach McCain provided the cover art. He took my original concept and greatly improved on it. I love having this cover associated with my novel.

I am grateful to my readers—Alison, Tony, and Odyn York—for reviewing the first draft and providing their honest feedback. I rely on my Beta readers to point out my mistakes and plot flaws, and they did a fantastic job. I also want to give a special shout out to Steve Konkoly who provided a sanity check on my yacht-related scenes and made me sound like I wasn't a complete land lubber.

As always, a special thank you goes to my family, human and furry, who tolerated the long hours I spent with the living dead rather than with them. I cannot remember how many times I sat in front of my computer with a drooling snout resting on my leg and a pair of large brown eyes staring up at me begging for attention. To all of you, thank you for sharing me with my passion. I love you all.

About the Author

Scott M. Baker was born and raised in Everett, Massachusetts and spent twenty-three years in northern Virginia working for the Central Intelligence Agency. Scott is now retired and lives in Gainesville, Florida as a full-time writer along with his wife and fellow author Alison Beightol and his stepdaughter. He has written *Yeitso*, his homage to the giant monster movies of the 1950s that he loved watching as a kid; *The Vampire Hunters* trilogy, about humans fighting the undead in Washington D.C.; as well as *Rotter World*, which details the struggle between humans and vampires during a zombie apocalypse. Scott is currently working on the final book in the *Rotter World* saga and a series of young adult post-apocalyptic fiction.

Scott has also authored several short stories, including "Cruise of the Living Dead" (a zombie outbreak aboard a cruise ship), "Deck the Malls with Bowels of Holly" (an alcoholic mall Santa battles zombie reindeer), "Last Flight of the *Bismarck*" (steampunk zombies), "The Hunger" (cannibalism during a zombie apocalypse), "*Lebenden Toten* at the Gate" (Nazis versus zombies in Stalingrad), "From Space It Came" (a giant spider from space), and the novellas *Dead Water* and *Nazi Ghouls From Space*.

When not writing, Scott can usually be found doting on the two boxers and one cat that kindly allow him to live with them.

Please visit the author on his blog at http://scottmbakerauthor.blogspot.com/, or on Facebook (Scott M. Baker, Author), Twitter (@vampire_hunters), Goodreads (Scott_M_Baker), or Pinterest (Scott Baker, Horror Writer).

Praise for Other Books by Scott M. Baker

Rotter World

Eight months have passed since vampires released the Revenant Virus on mankind, nearly wiping out both species. For Mike Robson, the situation could be far worse. He has joined up with a small band of humans and the last coven of vampires who are riding out the zombie apocalypse in an old fort along the coast of southern Maine. The uneasy alliance between humans and vampires is strained with the arrival of the creator of the Revenant Virus. Compton claims to have a vaccine that will make them immune from the virus and allow mankind to take civilization back from the living dead. However, the vaccine is located in a secure underground facility five hundred miles away. To retrieve it, Robson leads a raiding party of humans and vampires down the East Coast, which has been devastated by the outbreak and overrun by zombies and rape gangs. Yet none of the horrors he deals with on the road can prepare him for what he will find in Pennsylvania. Once inside the underground facility, the Robson encounters the greatest threat his group has faced to date, not only from zombies but from betrayal within their own ranks.

"With *Rotter World*, Scott M. Baker pulls out all the stops in a zombie thriller that is brutal, violent and terrifying. Definitely not for the faint-hearted."
—*New York Times* bestseller Jonathan Maberry, author of *Patient Zero*

"Think there are no new or original zombie authors? Think again. Scott M. Baker provides an exciting voice and fresh outlook on the undead. Fun, compulsive reading."
—Brian Keene, author of *The Rising* and *City of the Dead*

"Scott M. Baker writes in the tradition of J.L. Bourne and Joe McKinney. Fans of thriller writers like Brad Thor will also find powerful, welcome similarities in *Rotter World*."
—Scott Kenemore, author of *Zen of Zombie*

"Scott M. Baker has managed to bring together the best of what I love about end of the world, vampire and zombie tales in one glorious story. If you think zombie and vampire stories are overdone and there is not anything new you can do with them, *Rotter World* proves that theory wrong."

—Peter Schwotzer of *Famous Monsters of Filmland*

Yeitso

Veteran detective Russell Andrews has seen the dangers of big-city life: rape, murder, gangs. It's not a place he wants to raise a teenage daughter on his own. After his divorce, he moves with her to serve as the sheriff of a sleepy New Mexican town. But the desert has dangers of its own—deadly secrets that eat men alive. Secrets growing in power. Andrews comes face-to-face with a thing out of myth, a force without a name in the modern world. The Navajo, though, call it Yeitso.

"Scott M. Baker builds tension and explores characters like a seasoned pro, all before offering them up as dinner for some of the creepiest crawlies you'll experience on this page. *Yeitso* is the perfect blend of small town quirk and pulpy monster madness that will leave you cringing and wanting more! "

—Ryan C. Thomas, author of *Hissers* and *Salticidae*

"*Yeitso* brought me back to those glorious Saturday afternoons of my youth watching Creature Double Feature. "

—Peter Schwotzer, Literary Mayhem

"It's giant killer beetles! How can you not love it?"

—Jeff Strand, author of *Mandibles*

The Vampire Hunters

As former Boston cops, Drake Matthews and Alison Monroe thought they had experienced it all... until they found themselves tracking down a serial killer who turned out to be one of the undead. Stopping him cost them their careers and almost their lives. Thanks to an influential and anonymous benefactor, Drake and Alison find a new job ridding the streets of Washington D.C. of the vampiric threat terrorizing the nation's capital. Only this time, Drake and Alison are not facing a single vampire but an entire nest led by Ion Zielenska, one of history's most evil and twisted masters. As the vampires indiscriminately prey on humans, seeing them as nothing more than food to satiate their hunger, they create a wave of violence that threatens to engulf the city. Orchestrating the carnage is Antoinette Varela, the mistress of the nest, who realizes that for the nest to survive the hunters must be eliminated. However, when her vendetta turns personal, the hunters find themselves in struggle they are not prepared for.

"Those that know me and follow my on-line work know that I am a vampire fanatic. By that I mean real vampires, the undead creatures that prey on humans for survival, not the glorified sissy boy vampires that keep getting shoved down our throats. If you've read Justin's Cronin's *The Passage* and Guillermo Del Toro and Chuck Hogan's *The Strain*, you will absolutely love *The Vampire Hunters*. "

— Pete Schwotzer of Famous Monster of Filmland

"Scott M. Baker's *The Vampire Hunters* is a gut-wrenching, fast-paced horror thriller that takes you from the back streets of Washington to the rat infested sewer systems below. You cheer for both the hunter and the hunted as the author rains battle scenes with stomach turning death and destruction around every corner."

— Fangoria

The Vampire Hunters: Vampyrnomicon

Within the vaults of the Smithsonian Institute lies the key to finding the *Vampyrnomicon*, the *Book of the Undead*, which contains the history and secrets of the vampires. According to legend, whoever possesses the book can establish a vampire nation on earth – or destroy the undead once and for all. With an opportunity to end the war against the undead so close, Drake Matthews is determined to find the book. But the vampires also want *The Vampyrnomicon*. When Master Chiang Shih and her coven of the most powerful and dangerous vampires arrive in Washington to claim the book as their own, the hunters find themselves facing their most dangerous enemy yet. With the stakes so high, so is the ferocity of the struggle.

"*Vampyrnomicon* continues where Book I leaves off and I have to say that Book II is even better than Book I. Mr. Baker has expanded the story line substantially with a group of new vampire masters that are lusciously evil and decadent, as all vampires should be. He also delves into the back history of the vampires with a series of flashbacks that greatly adds to the details of the story. *The Vampire Hunters* trilogy is a must read for all vampire lovers. Book II is full of great characters, action, blood, carnage and some of the most evil vampires this side of Brian Lumley's *Necroscope* series and I highly recommend it."

—Peter Schwotzer of Famous Monsters of Filmland

"*Vampyrnomicon* is as well written as the first book. It continues the story and begins to fill in the origins of the masters and their race of killers. The pace of the story is strong and there plenty of gore and blood splatter to go around."

—Colleen Wanglund of The Monster Librarian